# STONE-COLD HEART

A MYTHOS LEGACY NOVEL

# Also By Jami Gold

*Unintended Guardian (A Mythos Legacy Short Story)*
*Treasured Claim (A Mythos Legacy Novel, Book One)*
*Pure Sacrifice (A Mythos Legacy Novel, Book Two)*
*Ironclad Devotion (A Mythos Legacy Novel, Book Three)*

# STONE-COLD HEART

A MYTHOS LEGACY NOVEL

# JAMI GOLD

BLUE PHOENIX PRESS

PHOENIX, ARIZONA

Cover Design by Melinda VanLone of Book Cover Corner
Content Editing by Jessa Slade of Red Circle Ink
Line Editing by Erynn Newman of A Little Red Ink
Copy Editing by Julie Glover
Cultural Advising by Deb Osorio and A.V. Scott
Military Advising by Shannon Beadles Nemechek
Author Photo by Mark Oxley/Studio 16

Blue Phoenix Press
18337 E San Tan Boulevard, #9435
Queen Creek, Arizona 85142
Visit our website at bluephoenixpress.com

This is a work of fiction. Names, characters, places, and incidents are a product of the author's imagination or are used fictitiously. Any resemblance to actual events, locales, or persons, living or dead, is coincidental.

The author acknowledges the trademark status and trademark owners of various products or copyright material mentioned throughout this work of fiction, including the following: Monopoly, U.S. Army, Beretta, Google, Pollyanna, Terminator, Terminator 2: Judgment Day, and Disney's Beauty and the Beast (animated). The publication and use of these trademarks is not authorized, associated with, or sponsored by the trademark owners.

Ordering Information:
Quantity sales. Special discounts are available on quantity purchases by corporations, associations, and others. For details, contact the Publisher at the address or website above.

Stone-Cold Heart / Jami Gold. -- 1st ed.

Publisher's Cataloging-in-Publication Data
provided by Five Rainbows Cataloging Services

Names: Gold, Jami.
Title: Stone-cold heart : a mythos legacy novel / Jami Gold.
Description: Phoenix : Blue Phoenix Press, 2017. | Series: Mythos legacy, bk. 4.
Identifiers: LCCN 2017903708 | ISBN 978-1-942928-08-9 (pbk.) | ISBN 978-1-942928-07-2
    (Kindle ebook)
Subjects: LCSH: Gargoyles--Fiction. | Women heroes--Fiction. | Women veterans--Fiction. |
    Magic--Fiction. | Romance fiction. | ISAC: FICTION / Romance / Paranormal / General.
    | FICTION / Romance / Paranormal / Shifters. | FICTION / Romance / Fantasy. | |
    GSAFD: Love stories. | Occult fiction. | Fantasy fiction.
Classification: LCC PS3607.O436 S76 2017 (print) | LCC PS3607.O436 (ebook) | DDC 813/.6--
    dc23.

To join the author's mailing list and take advantage of
**pre-order-only sale prices** for new releases, visit
*jamigold.com/mail*

*For all those who fight for freedom,*
*including the pioneering women of the CST program —*
*Your bravery inspires us all...*

Readers:
Don't miss the Author's Note at the end of the book
for background information about the U.S. Army's
Cultural Support Team (CST) program.

# Chapter One

H EAT ROILED UP FROM THE SIDEWALK, AND RAQUEL LIFTED her head skyward to avoid the worst of the eye-searing wave. Apparently, autumn hadn't received the calendar's memo that warm fronts were banned for the rest of the year. Her gaze landed on the fifth floor windows of the apartment building that was to be her new home.

*Dump sweet dump.*

The cabbie tossed her duffel bags—less than gently—onto the pavement beside her. Luckily, she didn't own much, and most of it wasn't breakable.

Her now-former roommate didn't accept his treatment as quietly. "Hey, hey! That's her whole life in those things. A little respect."

Raquel ignored the ensuing argument and sidestepped Brianna's exuberant gesturing to give the guy his fare. The taxicab was a block away by the time Brianna wrapped up the last of her insults. Raquel righted the one bag with wheels and yanked up the handle.

Brianna eyed her. "Are you sure you're going to be okay on your own, Kell? What are you going to do when you don't have me around to defend you?"

Defend her? *Seriously?* Which of them had been in combat?

She didn't bother with a reply. Brianna simply was who she was. They might share a Puerto Rican heritage, but Brianna's boisterous take on the world was far closer to the fiery Latina stereotype than

Raquel's style would ever be.

She'd much rather stay dispassionate. Emotions were distractions—interfering with her situational awareness of dangers around her.

"I'll be fine. It's better this way. Trust me."

Brianna grabbed the suitcase, leaving the non-rolling duffel bags for Raquel. "I don't blame you, you know."

That was the trouble. Brianna treated her like an innocent bystander instead of the lethal killer she really was. PTSD wasn't a *Get Out of Jail Free* card for every unacceptable behavior, the way Brianna seemed to think it was.

"Paula was already sick of my nightmare-screaming every night, so the sleepwalking thing was the final nail."

In truth, sleepwalking was *her* final sign that she needed to live on her own before she hurt someone. What if she'd forgotten to take the magazine out of her weapon before tucking it under her pillow? An icy shiver shot up her spine. She refused to be responsible for more deaths just because she needed a metallic security blanket to sleep.

"Yeah..." Brianna slipped her oversized sunglasses off the top of her head and untangled its arms from her long, highlighted hair. "Maybe I wish Paula was the one moving out and not you." She put on her sunglasses and finally checked out the building in front of them. "This is the place, huh?"

Brianna's voice lifted on the last word, probably in an attempt to disguise her disappointed-teacher tone. Granted, the old midrise didn't look like much anymore. Back in the day, though, it must have been something.

Like many of the older buildings in the Upper West Side of New York City, carvings of leaves, flowers, and scrolls decorated the stone façade, but the years had not been kind. In addition to the usual fire escapes and air conditioning units cluttering the front, patches of mismatched bricks filled in damaged sections every few feet.

"Oh, a grotesque!"

Raquel leaned, scanning past the tree branches for what Brianna was focused on near the roof. "What's gross?"

"Not *gross*. A grotesque, a carved stone figure. There, where the center of the building steps back from the front, making that section one floor shorter than the rest. You can see its head just peeking over the wall on that lower section of the roof."

"Oh, you mean the gargoyle? Yeah, that's my new apartment to the right of it."

Raquel hefted a duffel bag strap over each shoulder and climbed the steps to the entry door. Brianna followed with the suitcase, her voice in teacher mode.

"Technically, it's a gargoyle only if it acts as a water spout."

"Huh." Raquel didn't bother faking enthusiasm for the subject and instead squared her shoulders, bracing for Brianna's reaction to the interior. A century ago, the building had been a swanky hotel, and the place still sported peeling vintage wallpaper and a tarnished chandelier, which hung precariously in the high-ceilinged lobby.

The squeak of suitcase wheels behind Brianna stopped. "This has *got* to be the biggest dump in all of the Upper West Side. And here I thought you were moving up in the world by leaving Bushwick. How did you find this place?"

"A search for the cheapest place I could find within walking distance of work."

Everyone had their priorities, and for Raquel, that meant avoiding the crowds of public transportation. Yet the cab fare for the alternative made the old neighborhood in Brooklyn a no-go for her current Upper West Side job. This central location would also be better if she ever got her act together and returned to college.

Someday she might not be as broken, right? A girl could dream anyway.

She steered them toward the stairs. Brianna side-eyed the ornate, open-cage elevator. "Let me guess, the elevator doesn't work?"

"Uh, no." Raquel held in a laugh. Even if the elevator *was* working, she wouldn't trust such an enclosed space. The open scrollwork of the elevator cage made it a fancy-looking trap, but a trap nonetheless. "But the apartment includes all utilities, even internet, and comes furnished."

"Yeah, with bedbugs."

Compared to her deployment at one of the most remote forward operating bases in Afghanistan, *any* bed was a luxury, so

Raquel wasn't going to complain about the possibility of a less-than-pristine mattress. "I'll deal."

By the third floor, Brianna was huffing and moaning at each step. "You go ahead. I'll catch up after I find my lungs."

Raquel didn't wait to see if Brianna would change her mind. She took the remaining stairs two at a time, relishing the ability of the scarred skin on her left leg to make the full stretch, and opened the door to her new apartment. Bright sunlight greeted her from the multiple windows of the studio unit, and she dropped her duffel bags, enjoying the silence.

Her own apartment. She felt almost hopeful for the first time in months. Years? This was a moment to be savored.

Financially, the no-roommate thing wouldn't help her all-too-empty wallet build up savings, but it would be nice to relax and not have to worry about what she might do to others during the night. The nightmares didn't need any assistance impeding her sleep.

After the moment passed, she went back to rescue Brianna from responsibility for the suitcase, and her former roommate followed her up the stairs. "Thanks, Kell. Not all of us can be über-tough Sarah Connor *Terminator* chicks."

Just the ones who had to be that way to live. Exercising to the point of exhaustion—pushing herself to be stronger, faster, better—was a healthier distraction from the memories than drowning herself in drugs or alcohol. Even that idiot of a counselor she used to see had said as much.

Brianna entered the apartment and whistled. "I think my dorm room was bigger than this."

A wall to the left of the door separated the small bathroom and closet from the main space and beyond that lay the alcove for the bed. Bedbugs or not, the queen-size mattress would be downright luxurious come bedtime. A mini-kitchenette filled the corner on their right, and a dresser sat along the back wall.

But the windows—the windows were what made the location great. As Brianna had noted, the center of the building inset at the fifth floor, so this unit was like a corner apartment, with two tall windows opening to the fire escape above the street and two more overlooking the roof of the lobby and common rooms. Despite its small size, it *felt* bright and airy, and that trait was virtually impossible to find at this price range.

"No kitchen? God, you're going to be eating those pre-packaged crap meals all the time now, aren't you?"

"Fridge, microwave, toaster oven. What more do you need?"

Brianna checked the view from each of the windows. "Well, you can't see the river from here, but you have this bonus square footage of the roof area." She opened the window facing the central roof and climbed out.

Raquel lunged to the window. "Wait, do you think that's safe? What if you fall through?"

"Kell, even though I weigh twice as much as you, that grotesque"—she pointed to the larger-than-human-sized stone sculpture in the middle of the roof—"weighs a *ton* more than I do. Trust me, if the roof can hold up his weight, you and I are fine."

Under her breath, Raquel grumbled, "You better not get me evicted before I even move in."

She followed Brianna out the window. The roof's surface was solid under her feet, and piles of cigarette butts in the inner corner where the inset met the rest of the building proved others had come out here and survived. It *would* be nice to have a place to stretch out and do her exercises without fear of smacking a wall or being stared at in a public gym.

A quick check of the surroundings reinforced her gut instinct. The building across the road was one story shorter, a sidewalk tree and a wall along the roof's edge mostly hid the location from street level, and the only other apartment overlooking the roof was the corner unit at the opposite end, but that resident had covered the windows with furniture.

For being in the middle of the city, the rooftop was surprisingly private and secure. The light color of the roofing surface reflected sunlight, and the elevation of several stories even caught a breeze, keeping the heat at bay.

"Wow, this thing is huge!" Brianna stood at the foot of the sculpture.

The gargoyle was taller than her former roomie, despite the fact that the creature was crouching. Horns protruded from the top of its head, and wings spread from its back, stretching about eight feet tall. Hopefully the beastly shape wouldn't star in her nightmares later. That was the last thing she needed.

The statue perched several feet back from the edge of the roof. She approached the monster and circled. Long, clawed toes gripped the edge of its low pedestal, and matching fingers curved around a shield held in front by its extended arms. Its face was frozen in a permanent snarl, displaying long canines, top and bottom. Yet other aspects of the creature were human looking, like its broad shoulders and six-pack abs.

Brianna peered over the shield, her head angled down toward the creature's abdomen. A person could fit in the space between the sculpture's arms, legs, torso, and shield.

Raquel snorted. "Are you checking if it's anatomically correct?"

"Ha. No." Brianna sat on a low section of the roof's street-side wall, which stepped up and down like battlements on a medieval castle's parapet walls, and touched the stone shield in the creature's hands. "I was checking for other marks because there's writing on the front of his shield." The social-studies-teacher aspect of her personality took over, and Brianna tilted back her sunglasses over her head and tugged out her cell phone. "I have to look this up. All I know is that it's not English."

"Okay, you do that. I'll go unpack."

Brianna didn't respond, and Raquel didn't expect her to. Good thing she hadn't planned on Brianna's help for her move. Technically, she hadn't even asked the woman to be here.

Back inside, she analyzed the space for the necessary reorganization. The bed was in a good protected location, not in a direct line from the door, but tucked into the alcove behind the bathroom and closet. The dresser was another story.

The window-mounted air-conditioning unit impeded one exit to the fire escape, and the dresser sat in front of the other. Not good. The more escape paths, the better for her sense of security.

She shoved the dresser over the threadbare carpet, rotating it into the corner and leaving the window Brianna had opened unobstructed. Three escape paths—the main door, the fire escape, and the roof. That would work.

Next step, securing her Beretta M9. New York City's strict handgun regulations meant she couldn't get anything more than a premises-only license, but having a weapon she'd trained with available in her apartment was better than nothing. Sleep was already impossible *before* the thought of facing a night without her security blanket under her pillow—unloaded though it was.

She opened her suitcase and unburied the separate cases for her handgun and ammunition. After unlocking the cases, she popped the loaded magazine into the M9's handle. Now, where to keep it during the day?

Enemies would check the drawers of the dresser or kitchenette cabinets and around the bed. She scanned the room, forcing her usual hyper-vigilant eye for threats to focus instead on concealment options. The curved opening in the bottom fascia board of the dresser? She knelt down and tested the space.

Her small hand fit easily, even with the pistol in her grasp, but most wouldn't be able to get their hand into the opening, which meant they wouldn't think to check that location. Perfect. She slid her Beretta behind where the dresser's wood fascia curved down to create a foot. Hidden and yet easily accessible, just what her paranoia required.

The priorities taken care of, she made quick work of unpacking her clothes and personal items. If it weren't for the dress clothes she needed for her job, her whole life really *could* fit into one duffel bag. Army habits stuck hard.

The walls were already a pincushion for nails remaining from previous tenants, so hanging her pictures was easy too. The Guerrero family picture taken at her brother's graduation from basic combat training was assigned to a hook by the door so she wouldn't have to constantly see her father's proud, beaming grin—the grin he hadn't bestowed upon her. The picture of her brother and her, both in uniform, taken a month before he'd died, earned the place of honor by her bed.

She pressed her fingertips to her lips and then to Eduardo's face. "Help me be worthy."

Her brother's faith in her—that she *was* good enough—had helped her survive childhood. Too bad his faith had been misplaced.

Finally, the picture of her special operations combat team claimed the spot between the front windows. Her guys would be able to keep an eye on the whole apartment from there.

Some uppity-ups would sniff that they weren't technically *her* guys or *her* team—just the special ops team she'd been attached to in her Cultural Support role—but they hadn't been there, serving side-by-side, taking enemy fire together. Heck, most of those *in* the U.S. Army didn't know her program had ever existed. To hell with official labels, she'd promised she'd never forget her guys, and she was going to keep that promise no matter what.

"Hey, Kell!" Brianna's call wafted through the open window.

Raquel climbed onto the roof again and joined Brianna at the gargoyle, prepared for another lecture. "What's up?"

"See these odd letters? The one that looks like a lower-case *B* with the tail of a *P*, and this *A* that's stuck to this *E*? That was the key I needed to translate these words. This shield says *Duty, Valor, Loyalty*."

"Sounds like a military motto."

"It does, doesn't it?" Brianna examined the pedestal at the creature's feet. "I don't think he's original to this structure. Most grotesques I've seen are right at the edge or on the side of a building, but he's set back from this wall. Weird, right?"

"If you say so."

"I wonder if he was taken from a military installation, like an old fort or training academy, but the people installing him for decoration here were limited in where the roof was strong enough to support him."

From a military installation? Raquel gave the statue another once over. Maybe its snarl could be seen as a challenge, daring its enemies to show themselves. She could relate. Enemies who showed themselves were much easier to fight than those that hid in the shadows or pretended to be allies.

She gave the stone sculpture a fist bump on its speckled gray knuckles at its shield. "You tell 'em, Gross-whatever-dude."

"So..." A glint of smugness lit up Brianna's eyes. "You're glad I looked that up?"

"Yeah." Her apartment already felt perfect before, but this tie to the military right outside her window made it seem like this was where she was meant to be. A fraction of tension released its hold on her chest. "I am. Thanks."

And if she slept better tonight with the knowledge that a military warrior figuratively stood watch outside her apartment, maybe the creature wasn't such a monster after all.

# Chapter Two

R AQUEL TOSSED ON THE BED IN HER NEW APARTMENT, BUT THE
security-blanket lump of her Beretta M9 under her pillow
settled her back toward sleep. The blackness behind her
eyelids turned into images she couldn't leave behind, and the scattered traffic noise through the open roof-side window merged with
her memories of the hustle and bustle foreshadowing a battle.

Some part of her dreaming mind recognized the nightmares had
started, but as always, she couldn't stop them, change them,
control them. Only suffer through...

Rips of Velcro sounded as the gathered special ops soldiers
adjusted their clothing and body armor in preparation for her
guys' night-raid mission. Crockett, the team's squad leader, caught
Raquel's eye.

"Rocky, you're in charge of the women and children. There
shouldn't be any out this late, but if you see them on the streets,
check if they have intel for us and get them into their homes or the
mosque, away from the target location. If the targets decide to run
rather than come out peacefully, be prepared to take fire and
protect your translator and any locals. Otherwise, remain in the
secured areas."

She nodded and triple-checked the M4 rifle strapped over her
shoulder and the M9 pistol at her thigh. So far, only a few dozen
women had completed the U.S. Army's highly selective Special

Operations Cultural Support Team training to attach female soldiers to special operations combat forces. The fact that she'd not only been selected for the program after a grueling week-plus assessment of physical, mental, and psychological testing but had also excelled throughout the later months of tactical and cultural training was her greatest pride.

Crockett's forehead tightened in a pattern she recognized as matching his deliberations, and given that he was still focused on her, she had a good guess of his internal debate.

She tucked her combat helmet with night-vision goggles under her arm and gave him a level stare. "You know how I feel about the risks to the team if you're undermanned because someone's babysitting me." She cleared her throat and added, "Sir." She'd fought hard to earn the respect of her guys, but it was his ass on the line with command if anything happened to her without a security detail assigned. "I promise I'll be careful."

Deep in the front lines of battle, CSTs were the only female soldiers qualified to serve alongside the army's special operations forces, and in that high-threat environment, the military's rule against women in combat was irrelevant. She relished the constant pressure—and opportunity—to prove herself. When she did her job well, her guys' missions were more secure.

Crockett's lips twitched so subtly only someone looking for a sign of his approval would see the fraction of a smile. Then he moved on to his next orders, letting that action speak as his decision.

"Ramirez, Lewis, take your men and make a path to the target. Cruz, you and I will lead the strike force. Let's have a nice, clean capture of these insurgents and then get the hell out." He gave her one last nod. "Stay safe, Rocky."

She kept her face serious despite an urge to do a fist pump in celebration. "I intend to, sir."

His confidence in her, despite his concern, filled her with hope that her father might have been wrong. Maybe she wasn't worthless.

Hell, if she wasn't as toxic to others as her father claimed, maybe someday she *could* try a relationship. Crockett, for example. His respect felt damn good, soaking deep into the fractures of her soul, and eventually it might be nice to see if he was interested in more.

As the group broke apart, Raquel grabbed Anosha, her translator, from the sidelines and explained the mission. Thank God Anosha had showed. This was the woman's first nighttime assignment, and a couple weeks' worth of intelligence gathering and gaining the locals' trust weren't enough for Raquel to overcome the language barrier.

Her minimal familiarity with Dari and Pashto was adequate for letting locals know she was a woman and not a threat—but not much more than that. Most CSTs worked in rotating two-person teams, but this remote long-term assignment left her on her own, other than her translator. She could do a lot of good out here with her ability to interact with the fifty percent of the population her guys weren't allowed to approach, especially if Anosha was at her side.

Her helmet's night-vision goggles illuminated the path ahead, a route she'd committed to memory during her dozen-plus daylight patrols. She took the back way through the village, closer to the compounds where the women and children spent their time.

Sixty feet ahead, a shadow peeked from a darkened doorway at the corner of the village's main intersection. Adrenaline electrified Raquel's limbs. An insurgent? Before she could aim her weapon as a precaution, the shadow stepped from the alcove, revealing a woman in a headscarf.

The initial rush of energy in Raquel's chest faded, and in its place, a sense of foreboding unfurled in her gut. Why would a woman be out—by herself—at night? Was she trying to deliver intel?

The woman spotted Raquel and Anosha and waved them closer. Whatever information she might have, they needed to get her off the street and into a protected location. Her guys would be making their way down the main streets any minute.

She whispered her thoughts to Anosha and spun, walking backward toward the woman, checking for hostile witnesses and other threats behind them. The block held no sign of others, but she couldn't shake the ominous feeling permeating the darkness. She turned forward again, but Anosha was no longer beside her.

Damn it. Anosha had jogged ahead, closer to the woman. Not a time to break regulations.

Anosha quietly called out a greeting in Pashto and Dari. The woman spread her arms, opening her long coat.

*Oh fuck!* A suicide vest.

Raquel yelled a warning, but it was too late. Light and sound invaded her brain, and a blast of heat seared her face. The explosion lifted her up and threw her backward. Blackness crushed her from all sides.

Had she been knocked unconscious? She tried to lift her head, but singeing pain exploded along her arm and leg. Fire. She was on fire.

She tucked toward her shoulder to smother the flames, but a strap across her other arm pinned her in place. Each second, the fire burned deeper. She yanked her arm free and rolled in the street. Dirt and building debris ground into raw skin.

The pain shredded her nerve endings, overwhelming every other thought in her mind. In the tornado of agony, a single command worked its way through the chaos. *Move.*

Her guys...

She collapsed onto her chest, and another eruption of pain ripped through her. Her guys would come running. *Warn them.* Suicide bomber. There could be another one.

Her left arm and leg screamed, refusing to cooperate. Pain. So much goddamn pain.

Anosha? Was Raquel calling for her? Her head was ringing too much to hear herself.

*Focus.* Warn her guys, and then check on Anosha.

She scanned the wreckage around her. M4 rifle? Buried. Radio? There.

She seized her equipment and broke radio silence. Although for all she knew, they'd been calling for her. She didn't bother with the usual radio protocols, as she couldn't hear a damn thing.

*Enemy combatant. Improvised explosive device. Do not approach. Repeat. Enemy combatant. Improvised explosive device. Do not approach.* At least, that's what she thought she said.

At their remote location, air support or an evacuation would be at least an hour away—if it came at all. Crockett could make that call, but either way, there was no point in reporting her coordinates for an evac yet. Not when she still had work to do.

She crawled, one-armed, along the back street. Rubble from the now-flattened wall beside her littered the street, and she dragged herself over the sharp chunks. If she was shredding her body with more injuries, she couldn't tell. Every sensation from her nerve endings insisted her left arm and leg were still on fire, despite what her eyes told her. Agony beyond that searing torture was irrelevant.

*Focus. Ignore the pain. Just focus.*

Anosha's body lay at the corner, thirty feet ahead. Even from here, Raquel could tell Anosha hadn't been so lucky—a ripped-open chest as evidence—but Raquel couldn't stop.

*No...* Not Anosha. Not Anosha.

Either the explosive force or rolling to put out the fire had knocked away Raquel's helmet and night-vision goggles. Without them, the blood and guts of Anosha's body spilled out in various shades of gray, illuminated only by moonlight.

*I'm so sorry, Anosha.* She should have been more aware and stopped her from approaching the woman. Too many of the locals in these remote villages were more than they pretended to be. She should have known.

A flash and concussive vibration caught her attention. Another explosion on the main street.

*No!* Damn it. She'd told them not to come.

She'd lost her radio again. She crawled around the corner, yelling at what she thought was the top of her voice. *Do not approach. Do not approach.*

Screw the protocols regulating that she was supposed to take cover and wait for support. It might never come. She needed to go to them. Show them she was safe.

But another flash lit. And another and another in a chain reaction of hidden enemy bombs. The village was a trap.

The explosions continued until she lost count. She never stopped yelling. Never stopped telling her guys to stay away. Stay safe.

Her body protested that she moved at all, much less how hard she pushed herself to go faster. Pain be damned. She *would* be strong.

Weakness wouldn't help her guys. They depended on her. She'd worked her ass off to earn their respect, to prove that her father was wrong. She *was* good enough, and she wouldn't let them down. She wouldn't fail them.

Failure would betray their trust. Failure would betray Crockett—betray them all.

She crawled as fast as she could, over obstacles and down hiding places. The terrain didn't match her memories anymore, but she continued crawling.

Her limbs grew cold. She was going into shock. Keep moving. Ignore the pain. Ignore the cold. Just move. Move. Move.

Her functional right hand encountered a large curved rock unlike anything in the village. A flash of speckled gray stone came to mind. Her instincts told her this was a place of safety, where she could wait until her guys found her. She crawled up and found an area protected by stone on all sides. This would be safe.

Pain from her limbs nudged her closer toward unconsciousness, and she curled into a ball in her protected place. It was okay if she blacked out. She could let that happen now.

She could sleep.

She was safe.

# Chapter Three

WARMTH CREPT THROUGH GARRETT'S CHEST AND SPREAD into his limbs. Tingles followed, racing along his nerves, stirring sensations in his body.

For the first time in countless years, he awoke from stone-death. The human female curled between his limbs explained why. She must have focused enough trust toward him to help him regain full consciousness.

About blasted time. Although these circumstances weren't the situation he wanted to encounter when he awoke.

Of all the things he'd seen during his stone-death, he *hadn't* seen the one thing he'd expected. None of his regiment had brought a human female he could use to awaken—or had even come by to check on him.

All those years in his vulnerable form, where his prison of stone could have shattered—ending his life. Years without word, without reports from the field, without conversations with his regiment. Years left alone. Abandoned.

A wave of chills followed the effects of the woman's warmth. No matter his inadequacies, loyalty should have taken precedence. The betrayal—if it was one—of his regiment was unforgivable.

His muscles and skin softened, the tugging sensation on his face indicating that his features were taking on their humanoid shape, and his neck loosened enough that he could twist his head and scan his surroundings. He caught sight of an open window on his left. Ah, the human female must live in that room.

Strange that females would live on their own in this era, but then again, he'd seen plenty of changes during his time of stone-death. He'd have to find a talkative boulder to catch up on all the news he'd missed and see where his regiment had spent their intervening years. Whether they wanted him back or not, he *was* their commander.

His limbs shortened to human proportions, and the shield in his hands reformed. The stone split in half and flowed like water up his arms, creating a shirt, trousers, and boots. His wings flapped and settled over his shoulders in the guise of a cloak. He stood from his pedestal and stretched. He'd been condemned to stone-death for far too long.

*Oh, to be awake again.* Despite the granite-like heaviness of his worries, he felt like roaring.

Just as quickly, the surging excitement in his chest faded. His wakefulness would last only until the next setting of the full moon unless he could convince this woman to share her soul with him—and unless he used trickery, that didn't seem likely.

While in his half-conscious state of stone-death, he'd seen her approach and touch him, but that potential interest was out-weighed by her earlier odd words. He needed to earn her trust, yet her behavior hadn't given him the impression that she cared about anything, much less a stranger.

Although... She *had* crawled out to be with him. Why? That seemed unusual behavior for any human, much less this one.

The woman stirred at his feet. He should probably return her to that room before she awakened. He had too much to do, too many answers to find, and too much to learn to spend time with a human's questions right now. Discovering more about how to persuade her could wait.

His knees stiffly protested at returning to his crouch, and he scooped the female into his arms. Her body was light and compact, yet almost as firm as his. He'd never known a female to work her-self into a state of readiness for battle as he did. That didn't bode well for her mind being malleable and compliant.

She moaned and snuggled against his chest. A soft warmth of

sensation coalesced in his core, and he held his breath.

Maybe she wouldn't be so difficult to convince after all.

He ducked into her room and spotted the bed in the corner. The squishy covering over the floor muffled the sound of his boots. The bed and the rest of the room were empty, the woman's companion nowhere to be seen.

Pity *that* woman hadn't been the one to wake him. She'd seemed easier to manipulate. But that opportunity was lost now. He had one chance to avoid returning to stone-death, and this woman in his arms was the key.

He laid the female on the bed and covered her with the sheet. She twitched, as though dreaming, and her hand slid under her pillow.

He rested his fingers on her forehead and ordered, "Sleep."

Even though he whispered, his deep, rumbling voice filled the small room. The human female settled, obedient.

The encouraging response calmed his worries. Even if he needed to resort to trickery, this one might not be too difficult at all.

He slipped out the window and breathed deep of the night air. The scent of nature drew him to the east. He took two quick strides and leaped off the low wall at the edge of the roof.

His form changed instantly, his cloak spreading into wings, his body and limbs growing into his natural state. But despite the mottled gray appearance of his skin in this form, his flesh and muscles remained supple, like stone that wasn't stone.

He extended his wings, grasping the air around him. After being imprisoned for so long, the rush of wind—the ability to stretch, to fly, to soar—was glorious.

Several more flaps lifted him higher over the buildings. By the Maker, how *huge* was this city? Unfathomably tall buildings appeared in every direction, and lights shone everywhere, crawling, moving, like ants in a hole. Honking and squealing noises resonated from every corner, and the unnatural odor of human technology fouled the air.

He sought to fly higher than the tallest buildings, searching for nature amidst the endless city. But the lights stretched as far as he could see, even spanning the nearby river to invade the other side.

Where was this blasted nature he'd smelled? He gave up on

using his eyes and followed his nose.

The scents led him to a dimly lit, less-developed area in the middle of the city. His senses searched for ancient boulders among the grass and trees. He finally detected a giant glacial artifact perched on a hill and landed beside the stone.

Along with his humanoid form, his clothes reappeared, and his cloak fluttered around his shoulders. He bowed to the venerable witness. "I am Garrett, supreme commander of the Earthen plane regiment of the gargoyle army from the Mythos plane. I have not walked these lands in many moons, and I beg your indulgence. May I join with you to learn what I have missed?"

STONE BROTHER UNKNOWN. NOW KNOWN. GREETINGS, GARRETT.

The boulder's acknowledgment grated on his mind. He'd forgotten about the abrasiveness of their communication style.

Ignoring the false sensation of pain from the mental conversation, he bowed again. "Thank you."

He placed his palms against the cool stone face and joined with the boulder's memories, playing back the centuries of change it had witnessed. His shoulders relaxed, and he drew a deep breath, even this limited contact soothing his loneliness. It had been too long since he'd last connected with any of his kind.

Yet as history passed, his hands curled into fists, and his knuckles scraped across the jagged surface. While the boulder had seen much, the information didn't answer his questions. Nowhere in its memories was an explanation for his regiment's abandonment.

The ancient witness spoke into his mind again. MISSING?

He'd never known stone to have a sense of inquisitiveness, but perhaps the fact that it had never met one of Garrett's kind before was reason enough.

"I need to know what happened to my regiment—why they did not come for me."

EARTH WITNESSES ALL. QUERY EARTH. PATIENCE.

Was it possible for this boulder to tap into the collective memory of the Earth itself? His muscles loosened, tension flowing of out him, and warmth filled the emptiness left behind. He wasn't alone in his quest. He *would* find and reconnect with his regiment.

"I thank you. I would be much obliged for whatever information you can gather."

A chorus of impressions abraded his senses, invading his mind with coarse testimony. He lurched back and shook his head. Blast! His hands instinctively went to his ears, as though blood dripped from them, despite the fact that stone didn't communicate through sound at all.

If he wanted answers, he'd have to endure the rasping sensation in his skull. He placed one fingertip on the cool surface of the stone and let the narrow contact drill into his mind. During his absence, the very foundation of the Earth had compared notes with mountains, cliffs, and beaches worldwide, and now the boulder was eager to share the report.

STONE BROTHERS NO LONGER WALK EARTH.

Shock resonated through his thoughts. *No longer walk?* Cold much deeper than the chill of the rock's face sank into his awareness. His regiment hadn't come for him because they'd ceased to exist on the Earthen plane.

He was alone.

All alone.

He staggered and fell onto his backside. His chest constricted so hard it nearly felt like stone again.

Alone? That was impossible.

His head dropped between his knees, and he struggled to draw breath. Ringing dug into his brain, although whether that was an aftereffect of the communication style or from barely constrained panic, he couldn't be sure. He sucked in air and tried to make sense of the impossible.

Gargoyles were immortal. Indestructible under normal circumstances here on Earth. They *couldn't* cease to exist.

Right. That *was* impossible. He drew a deep, calming breath, loosening the bands around his chest. His time in stone-death must have impaired his ability to keep his emotions clear. Perhaps it was a good thing his regiment *hadn't* witnessed that loss of his composure. He didn't need to encourage their doubts in his ability to lead.

Of course there was an answer. He simply didn't know what it was yet.

His regiment must have rejoined the rest of the legion in their homeland on the Mythos plane—without him. That was the only explanation that made sense.

But why would they do that? What about their mission, their duty?

The dozen-plus members of his regiment were responsible for protecting the portal to their homeland. They alone were all that stood to prevent extinction for the hundreds of gargoyles serving the faeries back home. Just because he didn't want to take on the risk of finding a mate or creating progeny on Earth didn't mean others felt the same. He served the *legion's* needs.

And what about his regiment's supposed *loyalty* to him? Yes, he lacked the abilities of a true supreme commander, but was that failure bad enough to earn him banishment and death? Each answer created more questions.

He scrambled to his feet and made a hasty bow. "Thank you for the information. I fear the news was not good, however. I must return to my homeland and discover the meaning of these mysteries."

*STONE PATH NO LONGER FLOWS.*

The screeching observation from the boulder froze him to the spot. No, no, no...

He bent over, lightheaded again, and his vision narrowed. His hands clutched his thighs, bracing himself—for even as he reached out with his senses, the horrible truth behind the boulder's statement sank deeper into his mind.

The portal to his homeland on the Mythos plane didn't press upon his awareness. The pathway between planes didn't exist. The portal had closed.

He collapsed to his knees, one realization after another crashing into his awareness. Without the flow of magic through the portal, his escape from stone-death wouldn't even last until the full moon.

A temporary trust-bond could keep him awake for this moon cycle, but the human female would first need to be *conscious* of her trust for that to take hold—and as the woman had come out to him in her sleep, she hadn't been conscious of anything. At the first rays of morning's light, he would once again be caught in an eternal prison of stone.

His eyes pinched closed, and he wrenched his hands through his hair. His breaths came hard and fast, his mind whirling to think of an escape.

But the bounds of his magic were clear. Gargoyles were invincible, indestructible—except for the ways they were vulnerable.

Without access to the soul of the human who woke him, his life of wakefulness on the Earthen plane was temporary—and he was doomed.

Blast! Whether the human female was easily commanded as he hoped or the hard-hearted fighter she appeared to be, a few hours weren't enough to persuade any human to share their soul with one who was soulless. No human would trust a strange being in their bedroom either, so he couldn't convince her to consciously make even the temporary trust-bond. Especially as she struck him as too much like himself to allow any vulnerability.

He wouldn't give up though. He couldn't.

After granting his thanks to the boulder, he leaped into the air and flew over the city again. Maybe the portal wasn't closed. Maybe he simply couldn't sense it when he was surrounded by all this human interference.

His chest loosened a fraction. Yes, that explanation made far more sense than sealing off the portal. That act wouldn't doom just him but would condemn all gargoyles at home to extinction as well. His regiment would never allow such a fate to befall his kind.

He rose higher and headed southeast, toward the largest darkened area he could see. Mist from the surrounding clouds coated his skin.

The salty tang on the wind revealed the darkened area as the ocean. Water wouldn't connect him to the magic of the Mythos plane as well as land, but the waves below were certainly better than the chaos of humanity.

He stretched his wings, drifting, and opened his senses to the world. The anchoring sensation of the portal still eluded him. His way home was truly gone.

His heartbeat grew almost as sluggish as when encased by stone-death, and the weight in his chest joined forces with gravity. How was he to survive? Was he doomed to spend eternity watching the world pass him by? Or should he let the sunlight overtake him right here, where he'd sink and spend his life in a watery grave? Maybe after eternity, the ground would reclaim him, and he'd finally be released from his rocky prison into death itself.

A cold splash touched his toes, his wings no longer keeping him aloft. The chill snapped him from his depression.

If he sank here, the chances of a human female ever finding him on the bottom of the ocean were non-existent. At least in the city, he'd have a chance.

He sped back to the roof he'd called home for far too long. The woman had come out to him once—maybe she would again. Next time, he'd have a plan.

The lightening sky chased his rushing wing-beats. The eastern horizon glowed orange by the time he landed on the rooftop. He crossed to her window so quickly his body had barely changed back to human form before he crawled through the opening.

She still lay in the same position as when he'd left her. His best chance now was to encourage her to wake him again. Consciously next time, so the trust-bond would be fully established to keep him awake—even during daylight hours—until the next moon cycle.

He placed his palm on her forehead. "My name is Garrett. Come to me. Trust me."

His joints stiffened. It was almost time. He needed to leave before dawn or else the surprise of finding him in her room would ruin any chance of convincing her to trust him. He'd done what he could to create the opportunity for another meeting between them.

He exited the window and stood on the pedestal. The human-made platform was irrelevant to any of his forms, but that location was where she'd expect to find him.

Pink rays streaked across the sky. His body instantly hardened into his stone-death form—his wings spreading, his legs crouching, his arms holding the motto of his regiment, his mouth screaming a battle cry.

All he could do now was hope.

# Chapter Four

ASIREN ECHOED THROUGH THE CANYON OF MID-RISE structures and screamed directly below. Raquel startled awake and sat up in bed, weapon in hand, muzzle pointed toward the open window and the source of the noise.

Before adrenaline even hit her system, she lowered the empty pistol. Others wouldn't understand how an unloaded gun could act as her security blanket, but she didn't trust anything else with a trigger-happy soldier suffering from PTSD sleepwalking and nightmares—otherwise known as *her*—during the night.

Sunlight slanted over the roof outside. She'd slept. She'd actually slept.

This apartment might be just what she needed.

She loaded the magazine into her M9's handle and slipped the weapon into its daytime hiding spot. Habit prompted her to create an agenda for the day.

Sunday—a whole day of nothing planned. A whole day of not having roommates distracting her from the demons haunting her memories. That change would *not* be so good.

Time to keep her mind occupied. She started with breakfast, which turned into a difficult proposition, as she had no food in her apartment other than a smashed granola bar at the bottom of her backpack. Brianna had taken her out for falafel at a place on the corner for dinner the previous night, but Raquel had neglected to stop at a market afterward.

*Good.* Grocery shopping, something she could put on her to-do list.

Before her usual efficient shower and moisturizing session for her scars, she decided to see how long she could stretch out her exercise routine. She smoothed her hair back into the tidy bun she'd perfected during her time in uniform and changed into a sports bra and yoga shorts. The outfit would never be one she wore in public, so it was a good thing she had no plans to go out where others would see her.

Scars scrolled over her left arm and leg, her skin uneven and discolored a light pink. But if the rooftop was as private as she hoped, no one would be around to stare.

Pity was the hardest reaction to deal with from others. She didn't deserve pity. She'd made it home when so many other soldiers hadn't.

She climbed out the window, scanned her surroundings for any new threats, and strode toward the statue. Maybe her night of good sleep was due to its presence acting as an additional security blanket for her mental state, and maybe it wasn't. Regardless, the urge to thank the creature sat on her tongue, and she poked at its elbow, waiting for the silly impulse to pass.

The rough stone under her fingertip reminded her of something, but she couldn't remember what. She squeezed the creature's arm, as though she could shove the odd thoughts away, and then stood in front of the statue. Only carved orbs marked where its eyes would be, but she gazed at them anyway.

The silly impulse hadn't passed.

"Okay, I'm only going to say this once. I got real sleep last night for the first time since I can remember, and if you had anything to do with that..." Her speech sounded more ridiculous by the minute. "Well, thank you, Garrett."

She spun and walked two steps before she realized what had come out of her mouth. Garrett? Where had *that* come from? She'd meant to call him Grotesque-dude or Beast or something like that, not an actual name.

The creature still looked as snarling as before, but her impression had definitely changed since Brianna had told her about its shield. Had it changed enough that her subconscious wanted to name the thing—like a giant pet rock?

The idea almost prompted a giggle. At least a pet rock was one friend she couldn't hurt. Hopefully naming the statue wasn't a bad sign for her mental state.

For the next three hours, she propelled herself through her usual exercises and added several new ones appropriate to the location. The rooftop area between her apartment and the opposite unit was long enough to run sprints. A metal support bar that ran diagonally across the rooftop's inside corner and connected the structure of her apartment to the rest of the building was perfect for chin-ups and pull-ups. And if she stood on her tiptoes on the creature's pedestal and wrapped her hands around its arm, she could do calf raises off the platform.

Pushing herself felt good, as though the memories were being flushed out through her pores. Even though she was exhausted, she didn't want to stop. What else could she do?

Her back muscles? Maybe she could figure out a way to do back extensions, stretching her body up from her hips.

The arms of the statue could work, one to elevate her hips and one to hold down her legs. Its arms seemed solid enough, each one bigger around than her waist, so her weight shouldn't be damaging. Disrespectful maybe, if she was supposed to treat the sculpture as art. But not damaging. Especially not if she took off her shoes.

Either because the gargoyle was right outside *her* window or because of the pet rock thing, she'd already started to think of it as hers.

She climbed inside the open space between its limbs and shield and wriggled her hips, facedown, onto one of its arms. From that position, she hooked the backs of her ankles under its other arm and successfully did hyperextensions, using her back muscles to lift her whole torso.

She added a twist to some of the lifts to engage her side abdominal muscles as well. On one twist, her peripheral vision landed on the statue, and she saw what this position would look like from an outside perspective—her ass right in front of the creature's face.

Good thing she didn't care about being ladylike, because a most indelicate snort erupted from her. "You enjoying the view there, Garrett? I'd say sorry for using you this way, but I'm really not sorry."

Forget a face-to-face meeting. Given that they'd now met ass-to-face, he deserved a real name, and Garrett seemed as appropriate as any other name that might pop into her head.

*Boom!* An explosion reverberated from the street.

Raquel dropped to a crouch in the center of the sculpture. Her chin scraped the creature's arm on the way down, and her heart thudded wildly in her chest. Damn it, she didn't have a weapon.

From her safe position, her eyes saw her location—the rooftop, the gargoyle, the city—not a remote Afghanistan village. And her brain belatedly recognized the sound of a semi-truck's rear door slamming closed. But her emotions didn't want to accept those facts.

Instead, overwhelming dread surrounded her, suffocating her, drowning her. Her limbs shook, and chills crawled up her arms, despite the late morning's rising temperature. She closed her eyes and curled into a ball. Acid rose up her throat, burning, and she clenched her jaw.

She wouldn't lose it. She wouldn't.

Images flashed in her mind of Anosha's gruesome death. Her torso ripped open, her body torn in half. Raquel shoved the thoughts away before other faces could become superimposed on the memory.

*Focus.* One. Two. Three...

She counted up to one hundred, and then started over again at one. She concentrated on the rough texture of the stone base under her bare feet. She noted the tickle on her chin from blood collecting at the scratch. She felt her nose flare with each determined inhalation.

By the time she got to her fifth set of hundred-counts, her breathing settled, and she opened her eyes. A drop of blood quivered off her chin and landed by her toes. She'd ridden out the flashback.

All the emotions she'd held in earlier burst out in a nervous laugh. "You didn't see that, okay, Garrett? And I'm sorry I bled on you."

Shadows moved, and the splash of blood on the pedestal glistened in the sunlight. What the—?

Her head snapped up, and then her jaw dropped open. Instead of a monstrous beast at her side, a very human-looking man stood in its place. A very *manly* man at that.

The elite-and-they-knew-it Spec Op soldiers she'd worked with couldn't compete with the worthy-of-the-devil-himself cocky expression on this guy's face. Dark eyebrows framed his light gray eyes. And as her jaw continued to hang open, those eyes glinted with a challenge.

Right on cue, a breeze teased his open shirt, reminding her of the covers of the romance novels Brianna loved. Especially when a wind gust played with his longer-than-army-regulation black hair.

This. Could. Not. Be. Happening.

She dropped her gaze and fought against a wave of dizziness. She'd lost it. She'd really lost it.

All this time of trying to keep herself together, to not let PTSD rule her life, yet she'd crumbled from a stupid slammed door. And here she'd thought she'd grounded herself so well during that flashback. But this hallucination was too real.

Her breaths came in short pants, and she twisted her knuckles into the stone platform at her feet. That pain was real. Hold onto that. She licked the abrasions on her hand. Sharp tang of blood, salty taste of sweat, gritty speckles of stone. That was real.

The shadow that now moved? The figure that stood beside her? That was *not* real.

# Chapter Five

GARRETT SCRUTINIZED THE FEMALE CRINGING ON HIS ROOFTOP pedestal, but he couldn't make sense of her actions. Then again, he hadn't been able to make sense of a single thing she'd done all morning.

At first he'd thought he'd have an easy victory when she'd talked to him right away. But whatever level of trust her declaration signified hadn't been enough to wake him, especially not during daylight hours.

After that, she'd insisted on punishing her body for hours, acting the role of a warrior determined to survive a battle. Or rather, survive *another* battle, if the scars engulfing her arm and leg were any indication.

He'd never seen a warrior sustain such injuries—and whatever must have caused them—and lived to tell the tale. Despite being human, a warrior like her—determined, strong, dedicated—would be a match for many of the soldiers he'd trained. If he was honest, she could probably teach him a thing or two about focus as well.

And then she'd draped herself over his arms in a skimpy outfit he wouldn't even call clothing. He hadn't known whether to wish for his wakefulness that second or be grateful he couldn't jeopardize her trust with a rash action.

The practicality of gargoyles needing human females to share their souls for survival on the Earthen plane didn't mean he was blind to other possibilities. Especially when faced with such a temptation as *this* female. From her chestnut brown hair and light hazel eyes to her surprising curves and toned limbs, she was enticement personified.

But what to make of her terror at that explosive sound? She'd ducked and turned to him for protection, which was what he'd needed to awaken. He'd been ready to enact his plan to win her over. And now...

Now she was hurting herself and hyperventilating. Should he stop her? He bent closer, trying to make out her whispering.

"You're not real. You're not real. You're not real."

He grunted. Her denial was *not* going to help him maintain her trust. He'd dealt with many humans thinking him a demon over the centuries—but never utter denial to the point of self-harm.

When she started grinding her fist into the stone again, he seized her wrist. "Stop."

Her head jerked up, and she met his eyes. "I heard you." She attempted to twist her arm in his grasp. "I *feel* you."

She yanked against him, but he didn't let her go. Instead, he gripped her other wrist as well. "You feel me because I *am* real."

"Ha! Now I'm talking to myself *and* the voices in my head." Her lips dipped into a delectable pout. "But does the ability to question all of this mean I'm not crazy?" She tugged against his grasp again. "It doesn't matter. I'm stronger than this. I refuse to let my mind believe in this—this *insanity*."

Her skin, which normally had a slight brown tinge similar to his human-form, became clammy and pale, and if anything, her breaths came more rapidly. Maybe she hadn't been drinking enough water during her exercises.

He picked her up—ignoring her protests—and carried her through the window for the second time that day. A washbasin sat in the other room, but he didn't spot a water pitcher beside it. The room didn't contain any chairs either, so he plopped her onto the bed. "Get yourself something to drink."

She thrashed at his arms. "I do *not* take orders from the voices in my head."

"Would you rather faint?"

She shoved away from him and twisted a handle on the

washbasin. Water flowed from the spout and filled a cup she'd grabbed off a shelf.

Ingenious. Obviously humans had been up to far more than the inventions he'd seen from his perch since he was last awake.

After she drained the cup, she glared at him. "Even though you're not real, you're still not allowed to see me shower."

And with that, she slammed the door of the little room in his face. A moment later, splashing, like a downpour of rain, sounded from behind the door.

While she was occupied, he made a thorough survey of her room to learn everything he could about her. Other than the images of her with people he assumed to be family and friends, there wasn't much to provide clues. During his search around her bed, his boot knocked a dark, hinged rectangle that opened like a book.

One side of the interior glowed, and colorful letters appeared: GOOGLE. Beside those letters was a phrase: MILITARY MOTTO DUTY VALOR LOYALTY. A list displayed below, none of which were an exact match to the phrase.

Why was *his* regiment's motto on this glowing box? He picked up the rectangle and noted buttons with letters on the other interior side. He pushed the button for *G* to see what would happen if he spelled out his name.

The *G* appeared next to the motto above. An instant printing press?

He touched the fresh letter, but no ink stained his fingers. With one finger brushing along the *G* above, he pressed more buttons below. More letters appeared, and still no ink coated his hand.

He quickly poked each button in turn, watching for the results above. The *Backspace* and *Enter* buttons were most enlightening, as the instructions PRESS ENTER TO SEARCH displayed, and the list changed when he complied.

A method to search human knowledge? How was such a thing possible? In this little book-like object?

He rotated the machine but could not determine its secrets. If it truly was a way to search human knowledge, however, this might be his opportunity to investigate his predicament. After a moment of trial and error, he entered his own searches for information.

Sometime later, he'd discovered that humans still didn't know anything about his kind. And that meant humans couldn't help him find where his regiment might have traveled or why they'd left.

Regardless, this seemed to be an important little device. Part of his mission, his duty, was to stay on top of human development so his kind would always know their best options and approaches for bonding to human females. Perhaps this machine could teach him what females expected in this era. He got as far as spelling out "how to get women" when the glowing rectangle offered suggestions ranging from "how to get women to chase you" to "how to get women in bed."

Yes, a very useful device indeed.

A knock rapped on the closed door next to her washroom. "Kell, you home? You didn't answer your phone this morning, and I wanted to make sure you hadn't been murdered in your new place already. Kell?"

The voice sounded like that of the female's companion. He replaced the machine and strode to the door. "She is showering." Was that the right terminology?

"Whoa. Open up. Who are you? What are you doing there?"

He found the latch and opened the door. The companion stood on the other side, and her eyes widened.

"Wow. Wait, I have the right apartment, right? This *is* Raquel's place, isn't it?"

"Raquel—who was with you yesterday." When the companion didn't look confused at his guess, he confirmed and indicated the other door. "Yes, she's in there."

"So, uh..." The companion squeezed by him and entered the room. "Are you like a neighbor or something?"

He closed the door and bent down in a low bow. "I am Garrett."

Her hand fluttered in front of her chest. "Look at you—all gentlemanly. I'm Brianna." Her gaze cut toward the washroom. "So, uh, no offense. But why are you hanging out here while she's in the shower?"

He doubted his real reason would improve his chances with Raquel. A falsehood seemed more appropriate.

"I was worried about her. She didn't seem well." He moved

toward the windows overlooking the street. Given this woman's interest in his stone-death form yesterday, he wanted her focus away from where she might notice the disappearance. "She may not have had enough to drink during her training this morning."

"Dehydrated, huh? Yeah, that sounds like my Kell. I told her yesterday that I didn't know how she was going to take care of herself without me around." She sat on the bed and flipped her hair over her shoulder. "Thanks for watching out for her."

That description of helplessness didn't sound like the female he'd seen. Imitating her casual stance, he leaned back onto the bottom of the window ledge. "Of course."

The downpour noise stopped from the other room.

Brianna wasn't subtle with her attention, scrutinizing him from head to toe. "Are you an actor?"

An *actor*? At the insult, he gave her a blank look, but figured the less he said, the better.

"That's a to-die-for accent you've got going for you, and your costume is really cool—with the cape and everything."

His forehead tightened. Yes, that was careless of him. He'd seen enough humans from his perch to know their style of dress had changed during the interim. Maybe later he could search on that glowing box near his feet for a more appropriate look.

The washroom door opened, and Raquel exited, her long hair dripping. Only a rectangle of fabric wrapped around her middle hid her flesh from his sight.

He straightened to his feet and held in a groan. This female seemed bound and determined to distract him from his plans, his mission—his everything.

Her gaze landed on him, and she stopped in front of the chest of drawers. Her mouth turned into that luscious-lipped pout again.

Brianna stood from the bed. "Hey, Kell. When you didn't answer your cell this morning, I decided to come by and check on you."

"Brianna?" Raquel twisted toward the main door. "I *know* I locked that. How did you get in?"

"Duh, Garrett here let me in."

Her brows slammed together. "Garrett."

"Yeah..." Brianna looked almost equally confused and gestured toward him. "Your hottie neighbor. Just how dehydrated did you get this morning?"

The situation was unraveling faster than he could predict, and he had no way of knowing if he would immediately return to stone-death if her mood shifted too much. Time to take control.

He bowed low and added a flourish with his cloak. "I apologize, Miss Raquel. I was so concerned for your well-being that I neglected to properly introduce myself. I am Garrett." He cleared his throat. "Your neighbor."

Brianna grinned and stuck her thumb up from her fist. "Whatever play you're in, you are *rocking* that part." She tilted her head and focused on Raquel. "So about that dehydration thing. You *have* to take care of yourself, Kell. Garrett here made it sound like you nearly fainted."

Raquel's eyes narrowed on him, and she tightened the fabric around her body, which only served to accentuate her curves. "I did *not* almost faint."

Now that she seemed to be reacting to him more normally, he settled back into his plan to keep her trust. "True. Your friend here is exaggerating what I actually said, but I believe it's because she means well. We were both concerned for your health." He approached and tilted her chin to examine that scratch and then gently took her scraped hand in his. "Especially as you *did* injure yourself."

He held her wide-eyed gaze and placed a kiss below each abraded knuckle. Her throat moved along with her swallow. His chest warmed—yes, he could do this.

Warrior though she may be, she was also a woman. And he knew how to persuade a woman to give him what he needed to survive.

# Chapter Six

RAQUEL STEPPED BACK AND YANKED HER HAND AWAY FROM Garrett's grasp. Long ago, her counselor had warned about the possibility of her combat-related PTSD causing secondary psychotic symptoms, like auditory and tactile hallucinations unrelated to her trauma. So the scene outside had been worrying enough—but the reality?

Unless she was hallucinating that Brianna was here too, Garrett was real. Alive. Not a monstrous statue, but a real man. A dangerously good-looking man. Standing in *her* apartment. Paying way more attention to her than a muscular, sexy, drool-inducing—oh God, shoot her now—hunk like him should be.

Or maybe Garrett really *was* a neighbor—because the hottest guy in New York City just happened to live in her dump of a building—and she'd simply hallucinated all the weirdness earlier?

*Right.* And she'd also just happened to leave her apartment door unlocked, which she'd *never* do.

So that meant...

She glanced out the window to her right. Nope. No gargoyle sitting on the pedestal.

The world had gone mad. Utterly, completely mad.

The next couple of hours kept her too occupied to dwell on the insanity question, as Brianna dragged her out to lunch. Raquel went along with the plan, mostly because she had no food in the apartment anyway. Brianna invited Garrett to tag along, and of course, he had no wallet, so Raquel had to pay for his meal.

Who was this whatever-he-was? If she could trust her instincts—which were very much under suspicion today—he was at least appreciative and apologetic for her picking up his tab.

As they waited in line at a Mexican restaurant, he bowed over her hand. "I promise you, Miss Raquel. I shall make it up to you."

His eyebrows quirked, as if teasing about the nature of his promise, but the ends of his cocky grin twitched with what could have been a touch of vulnerability. As he stared at her longer than necessary, she forced her attention away from him—and the unspoken needs hidden inside the intense depths of his gray eyes.

Nope, not thinking about him or his sexiness or how he elicited warmth in places she wouldn't admit to. Or, God, that delectably hot, vaguely British accent. She needed a clear head to analyze the situation and figure out who he was and why he was focusing on *her*.

The afternoon didn't present any opportunities to interrogate him, however, as Brianna seemed oblivious to his oddities, from his habit of picking up and examining everything from every angle to the way he'd shadowed Raquel's lead for what to order at the restaurant, right down to her taco configuration and side choices. Brianna even shrugged off the no-wallet thing by making excuses for his "costume" not having any pockets.

During their outing, others treated Garrett as real too. The server at the restaurant didn't blink at delivering food to him, and people on the sidewalk jostled their way past him, just like normal. If he wasn't real, the whole *world* was hallucinating.

Outside her apartment building, Raquel adjusted the two grocery bags she'd picked up at the market and towed Brianna aside. "Thanks for coming out to check on me, but I can take care of all this. You don't need to climb those stairs again."

Brianna eyed Garrett, who was reading a newspaper that had blown by. "Yeah, I bet you want to get to *know* your new neighbor. I get it." She winked. "Promise you'll call me later, okay?" She blew a kiss to Garrett. "Bye, Hot Stuff."

A minute later, Raquel was alone with Garrett. Time to take control and get to the bottom of his unexplainable appearance.

Jami Gold

She handed off one of her grocery bags. "Here. Make yourself useful."

"My pleasure." He gave her a grin filled with innuendo. "Use me as you wish."

She rolled her eyes and led him up to her apartment, refusing to think of how well his body could fulfill those fantasies.

What the hell? Where was her detached, unemotional attitude? Her brain had completely flipped out—that was the only explanation.

He trailed behind, and she had the feeling he was checking out her ass in her jeans all the way to the fifth floor. While she put her groceries away, she tried to organize her thoughts.

Okay, a gargoyle had come to life right outside her apartment. Weird. Now he was following her around and acting as if he thought she was the most desirable woman on the planet. Bizarre. And worst of all, her hormones—the same hormones she'd have sworn were non-existent yesterday—were *not* helping her keep a level head about this. And that was... Disconcerting.

Once all the groceries found their place, she whirled on him. "Okay, spill. What the hell is going on?"

He tilted his head and gave her a devilish smile. "Isn't it obvious?" He crowded her against the kitchenette's cabinets, and his voice dipped to a sinful baritone. "You brought me to life."

Tingles whispered over her skin at his proximity. She ignored them and directed her denial into a grimace. "Is this because I bled on you—or your little platform thingy?"

"No." He held her jaw and tilted her head back, shifting it from side to side, scrutinizing the scab on her chin. "That was merely an unfortunate accident for you." His thumb shifted and traced the corner of her mouth. "You, my little warrior, brought me to life with your trust that I would protect you."

She jerked her head out of his grasp. "I did no such thing."

She didn't trust anyone else to protect her. Not anymore. No one would ever be hurt on her account again.

A wince creased his eyes, and he drew in a sharp breath. If she didn't know any better, she'd guess him to be in pain. But she hadn't even touched him, much less elbowed him or anything else violent.

His lips twisted into a wry smile. "I hesitate to bring it up, as you *did* ask me to forget what I saw, but I do clearly remember the incident. Do you need me to remind you of what happened?"

She froze. Even in his statue form, he'd witnessed—and remembered—her freak-out at the slamming truck door.

Oh God. He'd seen her cowering and cringing. No wonder he thought he could be pushy with her now. Time to correct *that* assumption.

She braced herself and shoved him away. The slight opening allowed her to escape his crowding maneuver. "No, I remember just fine, thank you very much. But that had nothing to do with *you*. During an unexpected attack, it's usually best to take cover and analyze the situation. My training took over. That's all."

"Yes, you're obviously well-trained. A person of your stature shouldn't have been able to move me, yet you did."

His long stride brought him face-to-face with her again—this time against the bathroom wall. Her breath caught in her chest, not out of fear but something else she didn't want to examine too closely. Whatever it was, her apartment was too small for this crap.

"But you're changing the subject." His scrumptious grin curved his lips again, heating the air trapped in her lungs. "Because you're forgetting the part where you also came to me for protection last night."

"Last...?" The rest of her words fell from her open mouth and dribbled silently onto the floor.

No... A sinking feeling dragged her stomach down near her toes. He was lying. Wasn't he?

Unless he wasn't.

Her nightmares *had* been triggering sleepwalking episodes lately. Hell, the main reason she'd gotten her own place was to avoid hurting her roommates during one of those excursions. So it wasn't inconceivable that she'd walked out to him—the statue version—last night.

But then she'd awakened in her apartment. Had she returned to bed on her own?

Warmth prickled across her face. Or had he carried her back into bed? And if so, had something else happened between them?

She straightened and arranged her features into a placid expression. "I don't remember last night. You'll have to remind me of that one."

"Oh, I'll do more than remind you."

Before she knew what had happened, he'd scooped her into his arms. Just as quickly, she twisted away and elbowed his throat—not enough to cause serious injury, but enough that he should drop her. He didn't loosen his hold. Instead, he tightened his grip and stared down at her.

"Before you hurt yourself, I should point out that I'm not human, so most of your training won't be effective on me."

"Well, I *am* human, and it's rude to ignore my boundaries. Put me down."

"Do you want to hear the story or not?" A lilt of confusion colored his voice, as though he couldn't imagine how to answer her question without this step.

How could someone so pushy make himself sound reasonable? His damn-sexy accent made everything he said sound serious and important. It also helped his case that she was becoming hyperaware of everywhere their bodies touched and that he wasn't molesting her in this position, like she'd first assumed he'd do.

Instead, he'd simply swept her off her feet. Literally.

Good thing she wasn't the swoony type.

No matter what her hormones said.

# Chapter Seven

FROM HER BACK TO HER THIGHS, HEAT BLOOMED THROUGH Raquel's clothes from Garrett's firm hold of her. She needed to get his little show-and-tell over with. Now.

"Fine." She wedged her elbow between her side and his chest, creating as much space as possible between them despite the fact that he carried her. She crossed her arms. "I'm listening."

"Last night, you came out and curled at my feet. You were disturbed in your sleep and must have known I would be a safe place for you." He crossed to her bed. "I brought you inside and laid you here, ensuring you were comfortable and secure."

He gently settled her on the mattress and straightened, his face patient and innocent. But her training included far more than the physical aspects he'd witnessed. A year and a half deployment that often focused on gathering information from the women and children in the villages had given her a strong gut instinct for detecting when there was more to a story.

"And then?"

"And then I left." His smirk was half-teasing and half-invitation. "I prefer my bedmates to be conscious and enthusiastic."

In defiance of the thrill of awareness that zinged through her body every time they shared personal space, she stood from her bed and stepped closer, refusing to let him intimidate her. Or tempt her.

"You forgot to explain the part about whether your name is really Garrett, and if so, how did I know that?"

His smirk twitched. "Quite true. My name is indeed Garrett, the supreme commander of the Earthen plane regiment of the gargoyle army from the Mythos plane. And you knew my name because I told you—right before I left—when I thanked you for trusting me."

"Uh-huh. What was that title again?"

"Supreme commander of the Earthen plane regiment of the gargoyle army from the Mythos plane?"

"Yeah, that's the one. What the hell does all that mean?"

"Well…" He dropped his gaze and then met her eyes, as though deciding something. "You'll note that I didn't share that information with your friend. I'm sure she's a lovely person, but…" He took her hand and placed it over his heart. "*You're* the one I trust, because *you're* the one who trusts me. And I appreciate that more than you could ever understand, so I want to be honest with you." He stroked her cheek, and his voice dropped an octave again, resonating through her body. "We can trust each other enough for me to be honest with you, can't we?"

She stifled a startle, refusing to give him the upper hand. His was a loaded question if she'd ever heard one. But she *did* want to know and understand whatever-he-was, especially as he didn't seem inclined to disappear anytime soon.

A shiver built from his gentle brushes near her lips, traveling along her spine. "Sure."

His caresses had nothing to do with her decision. Not a thing.

"I am a gargoyle—"

She held up her hand. "You call yourself a gargoyle and not a"—What word had Brianna used? Not *gross*, but—"grotesque?"

He scowled. "Certainly not." One of his brows cocked high. "Do you consider me grotesque?"

Ha! She wasn't going to feed his ego, but she found it amusing that Brianna was wrong. At least when it came to what he called himself.

"Okay." She waved. "Carry on."

He enfolded her hands in his. Maybe to keep her from interrupting again.

"I am a gargoyle, a race of beings from the Mythos plane. The Mythos plane is the source of all Earthen myths, from unicorns to faeries. Sometimes, those of my kind spend time on the Earthen plane. While they are here, I am their supreme commander."

Logically, she knew she was supposed to be asking about whether *all* myths were based in reality, how the different planes worked, and how travel was possible. But her mind had already sped past those questions to the details that *didn't* make sense.

Maybe that fast-forwarding was a result of her Cultural Support Team training. The army hadn't trained the few women accepted into the elite CST program to question or change the Afghan culture. It hadn't been their place to overhaul the systems of an entire country that relegated women to the role of property. Instead, they were trained to simply deal with the situation as it existed. So now, rather than questioning Garrett on his reality, her mind latched onto the pieces that didn't fit.

"No, you said you were the supreme commander of the Earthen plane *regiment* of the gargoyle *army*. You're not the travel coordinator and tour guide for fellow gargoyles who come here to visit. You're military. Of an army. Here."

There must be thousands of gargoyles in New York City alone. Could they all come to life?

A tremor of fear swept through her. She shoved it away and wrapped the instinct to gather intel around her like a shield.

She leaned closer and adopted a teasingly confidential tone. "Are we talking about an invasion force?"

He gave her a bittersweet smile. "There are far too few of us to invade humanity—even if that was our mission. Which it is not."

Her instincts told her to believe him. Maybe the regret tingeing his words explained the hint of vulnerability she'd sensed earlier.

To make sure he wouldn't get defensive, she dialed her interrogation down another notch, rocking back and softening her voice. "But you're all military, right? Not tourists."

"Correct. We are all military, but in part, that is due to the fact that *all* gargoyles are military." A pensive expression flashed over his face. "Our entire culture, our ruling structure, our means of productivity, everything is part of the military because the military *is* our culture." He tilted his head with a shrug. "Our kind is technically a *legion*—not a *race*."

Understanding flowed through her and settled in the soles of her feet, grounding her to the floor. Their soldiers never had to adjust to civilian life because civilian life didn't exist. Given her trouble adjusting after her discharge and release from the hospital, she almost envied him.

"What do you do as part of this army here on Earth?"

"Our mission…" He paused and cleared his throat. "Our mission is to protect the portal between the Earthen plane and our homeland on the Mythos plane."

His answer sounded rehearsed, as though he'd had to force himself to give her the *official* answer. And she still didn't have enough information to understand him.

She went into the casual-social interrogation mode she'd perfected during her deployment. She sat on the mattress and crossed her legs, and he scanned the room, as though searching for a chair that didn't exist in the small space.

"Who do you have to protect the portal from?" She patted the space in front of her, using the invitation to distract him from the interrogation aspects of her questioning.

He joined her on the bed, where his cloak spread out without his adjustment. Was it alive, or somehow part of him? She added the detail to her mental notes.

"I don't know of any enemies who would want to destroy the portal. However, the portal is what allows us our freedom, so we must protect it—just as humans in a village would protect their drinking well. It sustains us."

"Sustains you? How so?"

"Unlike many of the other Mythos races, gargoyles cannot travel between the planes using our innate magic. We require a physical portal." A crease appeared between his brows for a microsecond. "Without the portal, we are trapped—and weakened."

Now she was getting somewhere. She rearranged her features into the innocently curious and eager expression that had served her so well in Afghanistan.

"Do gargoyles need to travel back and forth a lot?"

"We all must travel to the Earthen plane at least once."

"There are thousands of gargoyles just in New York City." She leaned forward, feigning simple interest. "That must be a busy portal."

He laughed. "No, my dear gem of a warrior, *real* gargoyles, those of my kind, are far more special and rare than a mere carving on a building. However, I do think it likely that human stone carvers got the idea for their sculptures by witnessing our existence."

Good to know that an invasion force wasn't hanging out on hundreds of buildings throughout the city.

"Well..." She gave him a smile that *would* feed his ego. "Brianna *did* say that she didn't think your statue was original to the building. So I suppose it was obvious that you were special."

He blinked hard and gave her a breath-stealing grin. Her pulse intensified and clogged her throat, preventing her from replacing the lost air. Maybe she'd laid it on a little thick, handing him too big of a victory. But while he was off-balance, she might be able to get answers on the next missing puzzle piece.

"Is your portal here? Is that why you were hanging around?"

"No, I was brought here years ago during my"—he seemed to fumble for the right word—"sleep."

Interesting. It hadn't been his choice to hang out on this rooftop. Put together with his claim that she'd "brought him to life," especially given her suspicion that he'd slept for *years*, he apparently didn't have the power to wake himself up.

He'd needed her to awaken, and if his attention now was any indication, he still needed her for something. The question was, what did he need? Would he return to his sleeping state without her? Or was it something else?

A rush of blood sped through her limbs. He *needed* her.

She rubbed the ribs over her heart and then dropped her hands, her fingers curling and straightening. He was vulnerable and needed her. Was this good or bad?

On the one hand, a sense of strength and competence she hadn't felt since before the attack expanded in her chest. But on the other, she didn't want anyone depending on her. Not after what had happened last time.

Yet what could she do? For all his arrogant swagger, he'd been, and might once again be, helpless and not in control. She wouldn't wish that feeling on anyone. If he was anything like the special operations guys she'd known, that helplessness likely *caused* his bravado.

"Okay, so now what? You're awake again. Shouldn't you be getting back to protecting that portal?"

His head angled down in a sexy charade of shyness, and he regarded her out of the corner of his eye. "I'm in no hurry to leave you, my beautiful warrior. I've let you ask all the questions so far, but now I want my turn."

Her body went rigid, and she openly goggled at him. A part of her knew that she should be analyzing the clues in his statement, like how he'd indirectly confirmed that he *still* needed her for something. That he *couldn't* leave her. But another part of her—a part that recognized that his words meant nothing but wanted to believe him anyway—couldn't ignore that he'd called her *beautiful.*

It wasn't that she had body issues about her scars—much worse things could have happened to her than being scarred for life—but they'd brought her nothing but the pitying kind of attention. *Beautiful* wasn't what would come to any man's mind upon seeing them. Yet this not-man had seen more of her scars—given the sports bra and boy-short-length yoga shorts she had on earlier, not to mention the towel she'd worn out of the shower—than any man since she'd left her doctor's care, and he'd called her beautiful.

No, this had nothing to do with her and everything to do with whatever he needed.

This stunning hunk of a not-man was trying to manipulate her in the most heartbreaking way possible. He saw her scars and fig-ured she was desperate for attention—that he could flatter her into meeting his needs.

Well, he'd picked the wrong woman. Not only was she smarter than that, but she also wasn't looking for a *friendship* with any-one, to get close to anyone, much less looking for a *relationship* with a man. Or a not-man for that matter either.

Her lips pressed together. "All right. Your turn."

Maybe letting him talk would be the best way to determine what he needed from her. Then she could plan her counter-move.

# Chapter Eight

GARRETT FORCED A CASUAL SMILE AND SCOOTED CLOSER TO Raquel on the bed. One minute he'd swear he was successfully manipulating her, and the next he feared she knew his situation better than he did.

He'd tried to keep his answers to her questions vague, but he still had the sense that she understood more than she let on. This warrior definitely wasn't to be underestimated.

"Tell me about yourself." He allowed a touch of vulnerability to alight on his face and softened his tone to draw her closer. "I know nothing of the modern world. Is it common for females to be warriors now?"

"No, it's not common—at least not in this country—for women to be soldiers. But it's not unusual either."

Not common. And yet his bad luck had drawn one of the few female warriors to his side.

"Tell me about this training you've had. What was your mission?"

A shadow crossed her face, and her mood changed in a flash, from evasive to angry. "I don't like talking about it."

Ah, he knew that perspective. She'd endured more than her share of horrors.

He sat beside her, inviting himself further onto the bed. Given his experience with the countless human females he'd needed to seduce over the centuries to stay awake, most would react to his advances with a mixture of nervousness and excitement. He detected neither in Raquel, but he didn't doubt that she was planning several ways to escape and would fight him if he transgressed her boundaries. She was a challenge like none he'd ever faced before.

He took her hand in his and intertwined their fingers. He'd never needed to rely on touch to this extent with other human females, but at least this one *was* pleasing to look at. More than pleasing in fact.

She was still a means to an end, but he could enjoy the view along the way. His thumb traced gentle circles, and he was careful not to disturb the skin near her scraped knuckles.

"I'm sorry. I didn't intend to bring up unpleasant memories."

"Unpleasant memories?" She yanked her hand back and whirled on him. "That makes it sound like I was upset about a thirty-five-mile hike while carrying my rucksack, or that I didn't get to take a shower often enough, or that I slept on bug-infested sand. Not that I saw—" She snapped her mouth closed.

Her chastisement cut deep. How had she come to that conclusion of his meaning? Her nightmares and reaction to the explosive sound were more than enough evidence that she'd survived real battle, and her scars proved it beyond a doubt.

He wrapped both of his hands around one of hers. She tensed in his grasp, her fingers tightening to curl into a fist. He kept his hold light but firm, determined to make her listen.

"Please forgive me. My word choice was meant to avoid causing you to think further of the atrocities you saw, not to disparage your experiences."

She scoffed. "If that's true, then you understand better than any of the others."

"Maybe I do." When her eyes narrowed on him, he pushed himself deeper into her circle of trust. "Remember that I am from a warrior culture and quite used to the ugliness of battles. I recognize a fellow warrior when I see one." He rested their joined hands against his chest. "There is no question that you *are* a true warrior. In truth, I'd just as soon have you fighting at my side as many of those I trained myself."

His pulse quickened, beating so hard he felt it in his throat. Where had that admission come from? But he couldn't take back the statement when it was the truth.

Her lips parted, emphasizing their lush fullness. He looked away before he could be tempted to ruin the trust he sensed building in the moment. "I'm sorry others have not seen your strength as I do."

He glanced up in time to see her swallow and bob her head in a small nod. "Thank you. Those I fought alongside respected me because I proved myself and earned it. We were in it together. One unit. One team."

Her gaze shifted toward the windows. Or perhaps to the picture hanging on the wall between the panes of glass.

"But ever since I came back, it's been one battle after another with those who don't understand. Like the bureaucrat doctors who didn't approve my PTSD claim and labeled me *uncooperative*—because I refused to let their tests break me even more. Whatever. I knew they couldn't comprehend the hell I experienced when they spouted official *policy*, stating that back when I served, female soldiers weren't allowed on the front lines of combat, so I couldn't *possibly* have gone through the trauma I claimed..."

Tremors shook her arms as her outburst continued. "...despite the fact that the army found loopholes around the policy, like *attaching* women to combat units instead of *assigning* them to the units directly. Or like when people think it's okay to ask if I saw anyone die. It's been one long, draining..."

The words of her rant faded, and he squeezed her hand. "Perhaps there is a reason fate led you to me. One who would understand."

A tickle deep in his gut fluttered at his words. He was losing track of the line between his manipulations and the truth. But if he got what he needed, maybe it didn't matter.

A weak smile curved her face. The expression wasn't as dazzling as the smile she'd given him earlier, but this one felt more sincere—genuine—which made it far more precious.

"What happens now? You said you're in no hurry to leave, but you have no money and no ID." She scanned his clothes. "And let's face it, you don't exactly fit in."

The fluttery feeling in his gut hardened, and a sour taste rose up the back of his throat. To provide answers to her questions, he'd have to move forward with his ploy, but he wasn't ready to take that step yet. *She* wasn't yet under his thrall enough to react the way he needed her to.

He had *one* chance to ask the favor that would strengthen their tenuous trust-bond into a more stable soul-bond. If he pushed and she reacted poorly, revoking the temporary trust-bond, the effect would be permanent. A revoked bond with a woman could never be regained. He'd instantly revert to stone-death—with no second chances.

A change of subject was in order.

"I'm not done with my turn yet." One of these times, the smile he'd perfected to charm human females might work on her.

She rolled her eyes. "All right. Shoot."

"Tell me about your life *now*. You said, 'ever since I came back,' which would seem to indicate that you are not an active soldier now, yet you are apparently not a wife or mother." He needed to understand her, what drove her, if he ever hoped to gain access to her soul. "What is your life?"

"Good question." Her tone was more like a quiet grumble than a straight answer. "For a while there, I thought I knew my purpose in life, but now that I can't handle it anymore, where does that leave me?"

He took that as a rhetorical question, but one that illuminated where *she* might be vulnerable. Perhaps he could persuade her to see her assistance to him as a new purpose for her life.

"I'm afraid I don't understand. Although I admit it might be my fault for being unfamiliar with modern language." Anything to keep her talking.

She shrugged. "I knew from the time I was little that I wanted to enlist in the army like my big brother."

She nodded toward the picture hanging on the wall beside her bed. In the image, she stood beside a slightly older man with the same eyes and smile as her, both wearing identical uniforms, right down to the lettering on the front label: GUERRERO.

"Enlisting was my way of dealing with the machismo in my family. Like an *if you can't beat 'em, join 'em* thing." A wry smile twisted her mouth. "I enlisted as a health care specialist, learning emergency medical treatment, so I'd be in the field and as close to the front lines as possible, and if I chose to leave the army later, I could study to be a civilian nurse. In other words, I had a *plan*."

He didn't recognize the words of several of her points, but he picked up enough to understand that she had drive and ambition to spare.

"My specialty gave me the opportunity to try out for an elite program. I could be in combat and on the front lines alongside the best-of-the-best special operations forces? Hell, yeah. Sign me up. The two proudest days of my life were when I was accepted into the program and when I graduated." Her mouth curved into a smile that was confident and fierce, and yet bittersweet at the same time. "All of us—all my CST program teammates—we kicked ass."

Her hand slipped from his grasp as she shifted on the bed. Without that connection to her, a sense of emptiness stole through him—not focused in his palm, but in his chest. He leaned back at the odd sensation. The feeling wasn't quite like the coldness that had threatened earlier when she'd denied trusting him, but it was similar in a way he couldn't put into words.

She crossed her arms, and her shoulders hunched. "But the things I experienced..." She shook her head. "I failed at everything I'd set out to prove. I lost everything I cared about, everything I'd fought for. And I'm too broken now to handle stressful situations, like helping out in war-torn areas or anything in the medical field."

She squeezed her arms tight and then sighed and released herself. "So now I'm working a random office job at a random lawyers' office, barely able to make ends meet, and feeling like I don't know what to do when I grow up." Her lips pinched, and she met his eyes. "And that's my sob story."

He'd lost track of blinking or breathing sometime during her answer, and his throat grew thick. She thought *herself* a failure? If she was a failure, what did that make him?

His apparent failure to earn the loyalty of any member of his regiment—not even from Kamen, his second in command and supposed best friend—had left him trapped in stone-death for countless years. Judging by the boulder's memories, perhaps two centuries or so. He'd failed so horribly that they'd *abandoned* him to an eternal prison, alone for the duration.

Worse, his entire mission—protecting the portal over the centuries—was nullified by the fact that it now lay sealed or destroyed. That failure meant the hundreds of gargoyles of his legion on Mythos—the whole population of his kind—were doomed to extinction, unable to reach Earth to create progeny.

If he ran a search for "failure" in the glowing rectangle on that device beside the bed, he wouldn't be surprised if his name appeared at the top of the list.

She cleared her throat and looked down. The interruption of his thoughts knocked him back a fraction.

"I am not familiar with the term 'sob story,' but I can guess." He stroked her cheek until she met his eyes. "I do hope you do not consider yourself a failure. You are able to try again." Unlike his inescapable situation.

Her gaze wavered, indicating she indeed saw herself as a failure.

He knew what he could say that would play his needs into her weaknesses, but he hesitated. His gut tightened, and his chest grew heavy with the weight of the manipulations he held inside. His fingers tensed along her jaw.

Was this guilt? Since when had he ever felt guilt for using human females? Never.

He should say it. His mouth opened, ready to enact his plan. Nothing.

For some reason, he didn't speak at all.

He closed his mouth. No, he didn't need to pressure her with lies. She was a warrior, she deserved his respect, and she was playing into his hands well enough that getting her to agree to help him with the soul-bond could wait.

After all, here it was daytime, and he was awake. This trust-bond, tenuous though it may be, should last until the next setting of the full moon as long as he remained at her side. The only thing that could doom him before the next moon cycle was if he pushed too hard, too fast, and she rejected him or his request, breaking the trust-bond and all magic potential between them.

He could be patient. He could wait.

Instead, he said the truth that would strengthen their bond. "You saved my life. You saved my life when my own soldiers failed me for years. *You* are not a failure."

"Yeah, I saved your life by being broken in mine." She shook her head. "Sorry, no offense, but I don't see that as a win."

He held in a growl. Or maybe it *wouldn't* strengthen their bond.

This woman was infuriatingly difficult to predict. Good thing he'd decided to hold off on his request until he could be sure of her answer. The stakes were too high to guess wrong.

She stood and fetched a drink of water, breaking the mood. Apparently, his turn to ask questions was over.

She leaned against the chest of drawers, keeping her distance. "Okay, this passive-aggressive thing of not telling me what you really want is starting to irritate me. I take it you're not planning on leaving any time soon?"

"No." He tried his most successful smile again, even though it seemed to have no effect on her. "I'm enjoying my time here with you too much."

"So you're thinking you're going to hang around overnight?"

His smile crumpled. Still no effect. Her direct questions veered too close to dangerous territory.

He rubbed at the back of his neck and stood, shaking out the tightness her attitude had provoked. Why were things so different with this female?

Perhaps he could distract her with a kiss. Yes, her luscious lips were far past due for that tactic.

He strode toward her, but she slid away before he reached her. He followed her, and she sidestepped his advance again. After three more failed attempts, their dance nearly reached comical proportions. Finally, he stopped and heaved a deep sigh.

Blast. He was going to have to give her a straight answer.

"Yes, it won't be a problem for me to stay tonight, will it?" He wasn't too proud to let a hint of his desperation show. "You know quite well that I am without a home."

Her eyes narrowed, and her jaw shifted. The floor seemed to suck him down, and he resigned himself to losing his life again that very second.

"Fine." Her glare said the situation was anything but *fine.* "For one night, I will allow you to sleep here—on my floor." She stepped closer and held up a finger for each of her points. "This is not an invitation to share my bed. This is not an invitation to try anything during the night. This is not an invitation to think you can push me around. This is me saying you're welcome to lie on that filthy carpet while the sun is down. That's it. Are we clear?"

A twitch started near his right eye. "Quite." He covered up his irritation with a gallant bow. "You have my word, my warrior maiden."

"Ugh." She threw up her hands and spun away.

Oh yes, they were getting along *splendidly.*

# Chapter Nine

THE REMAINDER OF THE AFTERNOON, GARRETT MANAGED NOT to upset Raquel, mostly by dropping any attempt to learn more about her. Instead, he requested only her permission to search on the glowing device in her apartment for a more appropriate outfit. According to her grumble, she went along with the idea because the better he fit in with the modern world, the less guilty she'd feel about "cutting him loose."

That idea wasn't comforting at all. If he couldn't remain at her side, the trust-bond would be broken. For prudency's sake, he'd need to establish the more stable soul-bond sooner than he'd like.

The Google showed him images of various men's outfits with coats. The variety was astounding—endless colors, shapes, and textures. Was there such a thing as *too* many choices? He sat back and rubbed his temple.

"How should I decide? I haven't any idea what style would be appropriate."

She leaned closer to the device she called a laptop. Her scent, feminine yet earthy, blasted through his logic and hooked into a primal part of his brain.

"Well..." She shrugged. "First you have to decide what you want people to think of you."

He'd forgotten what they were talking about, his mind instead whirling on what *she* thought of him. What was happening to him? How was she distracting him from his mission?

She'd apparently expected an answer because, at his silence, she pointed to an image, as though explaining to an idiot.

"Pick something like this if you want to be seen as a business executive." Her fingertip moved to another image. "This if you want to be pretentious." And another. "This if you want to be a slacker."

He ignored her tone. "Ah, these are like civilian uniforms. What if I want to be none of those things? Do they have a 'common' or 'normal'?"

"Really? I thought the pretentious one might fit you."

"If you believe that, I fear you have not caught me at my best."

That was an understatement. Stone-death had been a rarity in his life, much less one that went on for endless years, because he'd always had a plan and at least one backup plan. Perhaps some part of him had always suspected his regiment considered him inferior due to his missing command abilities and prepared accordingly. Yet this time he'd succumbed to stone-death because he *hadn't* been prepared, and now he was stuck in a situation where he was even less prepared.

Rather than confess any of that, he added, "As you said, it would be better if I fit in, so something more common would meet both of our needs."

She considered the pictures for a moment, her expression now more serious than deriding. "Maybe something like this?"

The outfit she pointed to consisted of a fitted black coat, a long-sleeved white shirt with gold buttons down the front, and blue trousers she called "jeans."

"This would make me fit in?" After her scorn, he wasn't sure whether to trust her advice.

"Yes, that would look put-together but not *too* put-together. Nice but not trying too hard."

"The abundance of choices in this era has made simple judgments entirely too difficult."

She laughed. "Tell me about it. Having to make decisions about everything *is* stressful. I much preferred wearing a uniform every day."

Her mood improved, she indulged his questions about the

materials, showing him different items from her wardrobe that had similar fabric. Of course, she didn't miss the chance to interrogate him about how his ability worked.

"You're going to change your clothes, just by thinking about it?"

"As I explained, gargoyles do not have external magic, like for traveling between planes, but the magic within our form allows us to do much."

A teasing sparkle lit up her eyes. "What about underwear? Or do you go commando?"

He suspected she wanted to mock him on the subject, so he said nothing and instead asked the Google for the explanation. The rough, thick fabric of her jeans still lay beside him. Definitely not commando.

Although... His clothes were literally a part of him, so he could make the inside of the jeans a different texture.

He eyed Raquel, who was on the bed reading a book but hadn't flipped a page in some time. The urge to return her tease tickled his thoughts. "I'll go commando."

Even though she didn't look up from her book, her eyebrows popped high on her forehead. He wasn't sure what the rules of their game were, but he'd consider that a success.

Once he had the details worked out, he stood and concentrated on the image he wished to copy. His clothes rippled over his skin and reformed into the chosen outfit. Raquel's gaze peeked above her book and met his for a second during the transformation. Maybe she wasn't as unaffected as she pretended.

He slipped her book from her hands and opened his arms. "Does this meet with your approval?"

She twirled her finger. "Spin."

He circled in place at the edge of her bed and waited for her verdict. She snatched her book from his grasp and buried her nose so deep into the pages he couldn't see her expression.

"Yeah, that'll work."

He tugged at the jeans around his crotch. Even though his clothes, by their very nature of being part of him, fit perfectly, the trousers still felt snug.

"Are you certain the jeans aren't too tight?"

She answered without glancing his way again, her voice breathier than usual. "I'm sure." Before he could bask in the idea that he *had* affected her, she dropped her book and nailed him in place with her stare. "If your clothes are a part of you, that means you can't take them off, right?"

"Are you asking me to demonstrate?" He didn't hold back his grin at the question.

She blinked hard and swallowed. "No." She picked up the book again and riffled through the pages. "Just scientific curiosity."

He pressed a fingertip on the edge of her book, forcing it down from her face. "I simply absorb them into my body temporarily, like so." He left his jeans, but made his shirt and coat disappear.

She gaped at his chest. "Oh. Okay."

Yes, he definitely had the ability to affect her. Now, how to use that power...

# Chapter Ten

URING GARRETT'S SEARCH FOR NEW CLOTHES ON RAQUEL'S laptop, the afternoon had worn into nighttime. Darkness enfolded the world outside, which gave him an idea for how to build on their connection.

Throughout his time on the Earthen plane, humans had too often assumed his winged, horned form to be that of a demon, so he'd always kept his gargoyle nature a secret, even from the human females he'd used to avoid stone-death. However, due to the circumstances of his first meeting with Raquel, secrecy wasn't an option, and now that she'd accepted he was real, she'd handled the truth far better than he'd expected.

How far would that acceptance go? She was eminently pragmatic and didn't seem frightened by the knowledge of what he really was. He was almost certain she would accept him in his gargoyle form, and if she did, that would surely strengthen their bond.

One way to find out.

He held out his hand and ignored the nervous tickle in his gut. "Come, let me show you the other side of who I am."

Creases formed at the corners of her eyes, but he waited for her curiosity to override whatever objections might be formulating in her mind. After a moment, she ignored his offered hand but followed him outside to the darkened rooftop, where he'd have the necessary room. A light breeze swept her long hair across her face, and he slid his finger along the strands.

"I have never purposely shown this form to a human. I am *trusting* you with the full knowledge of what I am. Do you wish to see it?" Unlike his manipulative words before, this time he spoke only the truth.

She closed her eyes for a moment and then nodded. "I'm ready."

For the first time in his very long life, he changed into his gargoyle form in front of a human. His shirt and jeans melded into his flesh, which turned a stone-like gray. His limbs lengthened and thickened, and his features changed, taking on his gargoyle form. The new coat reformed behind him as giant wings.

He rolled his shoulders back and blew out a deep breath. The nervous tickle had grown into full flutters. The sense of exposure—like being naked—had nothing to do with his lack of clothing in this form.

Her eyes widened, and she took a step back. "Wow."

From his taller vantage point, she appeared smaller than he'd become used to. He frowned at the thought of what he must look like from her perspective. "Do I frighten you? I will change back."

"No." She shook her head. "I just didn't know that you'd be as big as you are when a statue."

"I do *not* frighten you?" Maybe he'd guessed right about her reaction for once.

"No..." Proving her words, she moved closer and brushed along his arm.

His mouth grew dry, which was probably a good thing, as it prevented him from ruining the mood by pointing out that she was *touching* him. On purpose.

"It looks like stone, but it's not." Her gaze roamed over his body. "You're like a sculpture come to life. Your eyes are still there, which is good. Just a couple of gray bumps would be disconcerting. But the rest of you looks like your statue, except you're moving." Her gaze stopped at the top of his legs, and her lips squished into a smirk. "And you're still not anatomically correct."

He chuckled. "Do not think me deficient. In this form, the only way to maintain modesty is to hide my sexual organs inside. I can make them appear if I so desire."

Her chin popped up, as if she didn't want to be caught staring if he changed his mind. "Thanks for, uh, deciding to be modest."

"Gargoyles, even in this form, are not animals."

"No, but I can see why you wouldn't show humans this form. I think some of my relatives would be crossing themselves right now."

He dragged the meaning of the phrase from his memory. "Making the sign of the cross? Because they'd think me a demon."

"Or the devil himself." She shrugged and laughed. "Although, to be honest, I'm not entirely convinced you *aren't* him, but that has more to do with your behavior than your appearance."

He risked showing off his fangs with a grin. "If I were the devil, my behavior would be far worse."

"That's probably true." Her eyes twinkled in the low light. "Unless you're trying to trick me."

Not about that aspect, for he was most certainly *not* a demon.

She circled around him, stroking her fingers over his wings, as though the inhuman appearance of his skin broke through the barrier in her mind that kept her at a distance. Her fingertip caressed the folds of his wings, and he stifled a shudder. Had anyone ever touched him there before? No, and in fact, no one had ever touched him like this in this form at all.

He closed his eyes and willed himself to hold in a moan. Her erotic strokes—for that's what they felt like on his long-neglected skin—were exquisite.

"These feel so odd." Her voice dragged him out of her spell. "They're not feathery like birds' wings. They're more fleshy, like bats' wings. Do they work? Can you fly?"

Do they *work*? Her ridiculous question helped him shrug off his body's obsession with her touch. "What good would wings be if they didn't fly?"

"I don't know, ask a penguin." She stopped in front of him. "Could you take me flying?"

Tingles rushed from his limbs to his chest, and his pulse raced. She would *want* that? She would *trust* him enough to put her life in his arms?

He straightened, making himself even taller. "You want me to take you flying?"

Her eyes searched his. "Can you? I mean, I don't want to put you on the spot and make you uncomfortable or anything. It's okay if the answer is no."

She glanced down and shuffled her feet. "It's just that my brother died in a helicopter crash during a routine patrol..." She stiffened her posture, and her voice strengthened. "Flying a different way seems like it would be magical." She scrunched her eyelids and smiled, probably remembering that she was speaking to a *gargoyle*. "Like literally magical, I guess."

Given the background she'd shared about her brother, he suppressed his grin, but he couldn't stop the warmth heating through him. His heartbeat drummed so strongly the pressure seemed to strain his throat. He didn't know what his body's reactions to her meant, but he no longer cared.

"I'm sorry for the loss of your brother. And I would be honored to take you flying." He spread his arms, allowing her to approach him.

She didn't move.

She *did* realize that to take her flying, he'd have to embrace her, didn't she? He said nothing, letting her work out the logistics for herself.

Her hands curled into fists, and she tapped them against her thighs. He kept his arms wide, patient and silent.

He'd win this battle in her mind. He knew it. Either her curiosity, sense of adventure, or fearlessness would win out.

After a moment, she stepped closer, her arms outstretched but oddly stiff. "Okay, where should I hang on? I want to be able to see."

"Let's try this." He picked her up as he had before, one arm under her knees and the other behind her shoulders.

She squealed. "A little warning would be nice. It's bad enough when you do that and you're human-sized. You're a lot bigger—and taller—now."

"We're about to jump off this building, and you're worried about me being a couple of feet taller?"

She bit her lip and glanced toward the roof edge.

"Have you changed your mind?"

"No." She emphasized her words with a vehement headshake even as she continued looking toward the edge. Oh yes, she was quite the stubborn one.

"You can hang on to my neck if that will make you feel more secure, but I swear I will not let you fall."

She wound her arms around his neck. Despite the fact that he had no body hair in this form, the prickly sensation of his hairs rising crawled over his skin. Temperature couldn't affect him either, but that didn't stop a shiver from flashing up his spine. This might be his best idea yet.

He held her tighter and met her eyes. "Are you ready?"

She stiffened her arms, pressing her chest against his, and nodded.

He kept his gaze on her and leaped off the building. His wings unfurled and snapped open, and they rose above the rooftops.

As he'd jumped, her eyes had widened like a full moon, and her mouth dropped into an *O* shape. But as he expected from his warrior, she didn't scream or panic. Her expression lit up more than the city lights below, and she shuddered.

"Are you cold?" The wind at this height seemed inconsequential to him, given the warm night, but maybe she was more sensitive.

"No, just excited. This is better than I could have dreamed."

Sounds from the city below wafted up to them, and he flapped his wings to take her far above the buildings of her neighborhood. His gray coloring naturally hid him in the dark, but her green shirt and jeans might not blend as well into the darkened sky.

"Where should we go? Is there any place you'd like to see?"

She craned her neck and let go with one hand to point to a tall building far in the distance with lights illuminating its top. "There. The Empire State Building. Although you might not want to get too close. There are two observation levels near the top."

He started in the proper direction. "If we can't get too close, why do you wish to go there?"

The breeze fluttered her hair around his neck, tickling his skin. "I've always wanted to go to the observation deck, but the tickets are expensive."

"Ah, so you want the view without the expense. I think that can be arranged."

As they neared, his superior eyesight made out moving figures on an open floor around the perimeter near the top, as well as more people behind windows on a higher level. He flew directly over the building, where people wouldn't be likely to notice, and flapped in broad strokes to spin in a slow circle. Everywhere he looked, the lights of humanity spread out and covered the earth.

She gave a soft sigh. "Oh, it's beautiful. Don't you think?"

"It is..." He struggled a moment for the right phrase. "Very different from what I am used to. Is there an end to the lights, or does the city go on forever?"

"New York City is one of the biggest and most populated cities in the world, but it doesn't go on forever. In other places, you can go outside at night and not see a single light."

"That would be more like what I'm used to."

"From Mythos?"

"The Mythos plane doesn't have technology, so yes, that's true. But I haven't spent time there in eons because of my mission here. I was thinking more of when I was last active here on the Earthen plane. Humans have developed much in that time."

She shifted slightly in his arms toward his chest, and the soft curves of her breasts pressed against him. "It's been *that* long? How long were you a statue?"

Her focus on him and not the sights around them made him choose his words with care. Something about her attention felt dangerous, but he couldn't be sure why.

"I don't know for certain. I wasn't paying attention to the human calendar." He didn't go into the fact that gargoyles didn't count by human years at all, or that due to the closed portal, he had no sense of the time passage at home.

"How long do gargoyles live?"

As he expected, she was back into question mode, and not paying attention to anything but his answers once more. This query seemed harmless enough to answer, but he waited for the worse ones he knew would come. "Under normal circumstances, forever."

"Normal circumstances?"

"No attacks with magical components."

"Or maybe shattering as a statue."

His muscles tightened. Even though she'd used a joking tone, as if not believing that to be the case, he wasn't sure what she really thought.

However, their time in stone-death *was* magical imprisonment, and they *were*, therefore, vulnerable. But she didn't need to know that.

He misdirected her with a grin. "Wondering if you could have destroyed me when you had the chance?"

Her fingers absently brushed against his chest, as though she'd forgotten, once again, that the speckled-gray flesh of this form *was* his skin, and she chuckled. "No." Her mouth twisted into a grim expression. "I just wonder how you adapt to such a long life interrupted by sleep. How you move on when everyone you knew or cared about died and disappeared overnight."

His heart stuttered so brokenly that his limbs became numb. He'd never grown especially close to any humans, not even to the women he'd temporarily bonded with for survival, but her question put words to his feeling of being adrift much of the time—even before his stone-death. Especially when it came to trying to live up to his inherited role of supreme commander for his regiment.

And now that he'd been abandoned by them all, including Kamen—the one member of his regiment he'd *thought* he'd connected with—and the closed portal cut him off from his whole legion, the sensation had curled in the pit of his stomach like a disease, gnawing away at his sense of purpose.

He'd been so focused on persuading her to share her soul that he hadn't yet thought about what would come next. How he *would* move on—assuming he could.

"I'm sorry." She latched onto his gaze and opened her palm on his chest. "I didn't mean to bring up unpleasant memories. Forget I said anything."

Her echo of his earlier words cracked the tension in his muscles. Just as much as he understood this warrior, she understood him. She understood far more than was safe, and he was allowing himself to be distracted by her appealing form.

Human females were a means to an end, and that was it. Even this one who had somehow awoken far more than his body—if his reactions to her touch were any indication.

He tilted his head toward the horizon. "Have you had your fill of the view?"

They completed one more rotation for her to enjoy, and then he headed back to her building. As soon as they landed, she laid her hand on his cheek. "Thank you for sharing that with me."

He wasn't sure if she referred to the flight or to whatever hints of his vulnerabilities she'd seen. And he didn't ask.

Back in the room and in his human form, she seemed torn about how to treat him. For whatever reason, his human appearance seemed to intimidate her more than the huge gargoyle one. Why something inhuman would be more acceptable to her, he couldn't fathom, but he made a mental note to offer another flight the following night if he was feeling strong enough to resist her distracting charms.

He would enthrall her one way or another.

# Chapter Eleven

AFTER RAQUEL SWITCHED OFF THE LIGHTS AND FELL ASLEEP, Garrett flipped open the laptop, determined to learn anything and everything that would help him adjust to this time. As she'd pointed out, even if his long-term plan was to find and reopen the portal to return home, he'd have to "move on" in this world for an extended period. It was a good thing gargoyles didn't sleep.

Hours later, Raquel moaned in her sleep, and she thrashed against the bed covers. These must be the nightmares that had driven her out to him the previous night.

He scratched his chin, debating. She'd instructed him in no uncertain terms that he couldn't join her on the bed, but she hadn't said anything about not touching her while he remained on the floor.

While sitting on the carpet, he leaned against her bed and caressed her forehead. "Peace. You are safe."

Her moans stopped, and her body relaxed. If only his instructions worked half as well when she was awake.

He added, "Trust me when you are awake too. Grant me my favor." The command couldn't hurt.

In her sleep, she clutched his wrist and drew his arm to her chest. Soft breaths of air passed over his fingertips, and he didn't dare move. If she woke now, she was sure to accuse him of "trying something." It would be a long night.

The approaching dawn lightened the sky by the time she rolled over and released his arm. And by then, he'd formulated the beginnings of a plan.

Raquel had mentioned that the other soldiers of her team trusted her after she proved herself, so maybe she would trust him more if he accomplished something that would help her. Humans of this era depended on currency, and if he could acquire some for her, she might be more likely to trust him and let him stay with her.

Her threats to kick him out the upcoming night sent chills that started in his fingers and slithered up his arms. Forcing him to leave her side before they'd formed a soul-bond would result in stone-death for certain.

He shoved away the dark thoughts. Far better to finalize his plan. He'd fly to an uninhabited location the next night and ask if the ground could propel up to him the gems, minerals, or metals that humans valued.

He'd never heard of the ground being capable of such a thing, but before the previous night, he'd also never known rocks could be curious or communicate with each other. He'd never *needed* to know.

If the ground could help, it should be a simple matter of collecting and selling the items. With that currency, he might be able to convince Raquel to travel with him to the portal's stone circle. From there, he could investigate his regiment's abandonment of him, the portal, and the mission.

By some time tomorrow, he might even be self-sufficient and well on his way to supporting her. He simply needed her to hold off on her threat for one more day.

A screeching noise erupted from beside her bed, and he startled, knocking the laptop off his legs. Just as quickly, she sat up, wide-awake and alert.

He stood and searched for the source of the noise. "Stay there. I'll kill it for you." Whatever it was.

She leaned over and tugged a small rectangle and cord from the wall. "While I might temporarily enjoy you killing my alarm, don't you dare touch my cell phone."

Ah, he'd learned of those things during his research. He'd never imagined they'd sound like the dying hiss of a lamian, one of the serpent people.

"Why would you ever choose to wake up to such a violent noise?"

She laughed and stretched, and her shirt pulled taut over her breasts. "Most of the other choices are even worse."

He tore his gaze away from the view. She was far too distracting.

He needed to focus on his plan: provide currency and earn her trust, ask his favor and gain access to her soul, and then he'd have until the next full moon to search for answers in regards to the portal. If he could *keep* her trust, he'd have even longer. And once he had a bond to her soul, he'd be free to seek out another female willing to share with him in case Raquel changed her mind. Given the tenuous nature of his situation, that plan was almost impressive.

She wiggled garments out of the wardrobe area and headed to the washroom. "Don't get too comfortable. I'm not letting you stay here while I'm at work."

All the self-congratulating thoughts for his plan crashed into the bottom of his gut. His legs weakened, and he sank onto her bed. He was doomed.

She closed the door and started the shower, and his plans lay as scattered in his mind as the chaotic downpour splashing behind the door. She wasn't going to try to kick him out *tonight*. She was going to do it *today*. This morning.

If he couldn't talk her out of that threat, he would *have* to ask for the favor immediately. Thrall or no thrall. Trust or no trust.

Without the portal's flow of magic to sustain him, he needed a constant connection to the one who'd awakened him. Trust-bonds were too weak and fragile to survive a separation, especially during daylight hours. Stone-death would overtake him the second she forced him from her side, so he had no choice but to try to gain access to her soul for a deeper connection before she shattered their trust-bond with distance.

The sound of the shower stopped too soon for him to feel prepared for the confrontation. A moment later, she stepped out in an outfit that—based on the pictures on the laptop—seemed business-like. The previous day must have been a day off for her, but today she was heading to the office for work. Whatever that meant.

There was no time to waste. "I'd like to see your office. May I accompany you today?"

"Uh..." Her brows scrunched together. "*No.*" She slipped on a pair of shoes. "Not only would my boss not go for that, but I can't babysit you all day." Her arm swept around the room. "Look, I let you stay one night, but that's it. You need to move on. Go somewhere else."

Icy cold, far colder than he could actually feel, crept through the center of his legs, and he stiffened. He sucked in a breath through a tightened throat. "I can't do that."

She moved closer, challenge in her expression. "Why?"

"Please, trust me." His voice wavered from low to high, and he swallowed. Maybe he wouldn't turn to stone if she didn't banish him completely. "Let me at least stay here."

She crossed her arms. "Why?"

The ice spread through his chest. "Because I need you to trust me." His face scrunched tight, and he nearly begged. "Please."

"Tell me why." Her eyes blazed with far too much understanding. "Tell me what you *really* need from me."

The truth dug bitterly into his tongue. Every instinct told him not to reveal the depth of his vulnerability—not to divulge how much power she had over him—but he didn't have a choice.

"My life depends on you."

She recoiled, and the coldness in his core threatened his ability to speak. He'd always had time before to allow a bond to form naturally, so he'd never needed to explain—much less outright ask for—what he required. Never needed to acknowledge what the risks were to him if she refused. Never needed to disclose how a bond worked only *once.*

Once consciously formed, no kind of bond—the fragile trust-bond or the stronger soul-bond—could survive breakage. A *broken* bond remained eternally broken, never able to re-form.

He wanted to reach out to her, hold her, touch her—make her understand—but his arms no longer moved under his control. He'd lost.

If he didn't ask his favor, he was dead. If he did, and she rejected him as he expected, he was dead. But he couldn't *not* try.

"Please." He wished he could caress her cheeks one more time. He spoke the words of the favor that would invoke the magic for a deeper soul-bond. "I want you to share your life with me."

Her answer would either bind them together or condemn him to death. Forever.

Her eyes widened, and she retreated another foot. "I can't do that."

The icy cold of his body crystallized into stone, throwing him forward into his gargoyle form and his stone-death pose. His mouth hardened before he could say a word.

*Goodbye, my beautiful warrior.*

# Chapter Twelve

NO SOONER HAD THE WORDS EMERGED FROM RAQUEL'S LIPS than Garrett's skin turned stone gray, and his mouth twisted into a grimace. Then his pain transformed, his expression growing into an open-mouthed battle cry. A giant statue suddenly filled most of her apartment, silent except for a few creaks from the floorboards.

She jumped back from his invading size and glanced up. The tips of his wings were denting the ceiling. Just great. So much for her security deposit.

"You idiot." She slipped her laptop into her backpack. "What the hell kind of question was that? 'I want you to share your life with me.' Really? What is that even supposed to mean?" She nearly stamped her foot with the rush of adrenaline pounding through her limbs. "Stop pulling this crap and wake up. Don't think that I don't know you're acting this way just so I can't make you leave."

Her toes tapped on the carpet, ticking down the last of her patience. Nothing.

She checked her phone for the time. Ugh. She couldn't deal with this right now. She was only guessing at how long it would take her to walk to work, and she couldn't afford to lose her job for being late.

"You have thirty seconds to wake up and get the hell out of

here, or I swear I'll kick you."

Thirty seconds later, he was still as stony as ever.

No, forget kicking. He'd probably enjoy causing her pain.

She grabbed a knife—it was only a butter knife, but it was all she had—and stabbed his hard shoulder. Try ignoring *that.*

The blunt knife was only supposed to get his attention, not damage him—after all, his hard exterior wasn't vulnerable like skin anymore—but a few gritty bits of his shoulder tumbled away. A nick was left on the statue.

Her empty stomach hardened around nothingness, and the knife slipped from her grasp. She stepped back. Two steps. Three steps. Her gaze bounced between the small crater and his face, waiting for him to change.

But he didn't. He hadn't even flinched.

No, no, no. She *really* did not have time to deal with... This. Whatever *this* was.

"Fine. You can stay here until I get back from work." Because, really, what choice did she have? "But when I come home, we are having a serious discussion about you and your disrespect for my boundaries."

She hefted her backpack over her shoulder and locked the door behind her. Guess she'd find out whether the apartment manager here let himself into places when the residents weren't home. She'd hear about it if someone encountered *that* in her room.

As she maneuvered the sidewalks of the Upper West Side, her cell buzzed. Ugh. Brianna. Calling to check up on her, no doubt.

Normally, she'd let the call go to voice mail so she could avoid distractions that would affect her situational awareness while out in public, but who knew how Brianna would react if the call went unanswered. Maybe her old roomie would have the apartment manager let her into the apartment, and wouldn't *that* be fun to explain?

Raquel sidestepped a crowd at a bus stop and took the call. "Hey."

"Hey, yourself. You didn't call me last night."

"I was supposed to call you?"

"Yeah, remember? Telling me about your get-to-know-you session with the hottie."

Oh, yeah, that... "Um, it was fine."

"Fine?" Brianna snorted. "You gotta give me more than that. Did you guys go out last night?"

Raquel pinched her lips together, holding in her laugh. "Um, he took me to check out the view from the Empire State Building."

"Aww, sweet. So you're going to see him again?"

Yeah, she wouldn't have a choice about that, considering he was *still* in her apartment and not likely to leave while she was gone.

"Yes, but don't read anything into that." A grumbling edge rolled into her voice.

"Oh, methinks the lady doth protest too much. You like him, and that's freaking you out."

"*Like* is a strong word for someone I just tried to stab with a butter knife."

"Wait, you saw him this morning? Kell, did he stay over last night? I had no idea that's why you wanted your own place." Brianna's tone was half-teasing and half-serious.

And how typical of her to ignore the bit about the *stabbing*.

"It wasn't like *that* at all. Yes, he stayed, on the floor, because he was"—she flailed for an appropriate answer and almost hit an Indian guy in a business suit passing by—"borrowing my laptop, and I didn't want it to leave my sight."

"Uh-huh. 'Borrowing my laptop.' Is that what the Upper West Siders are calling it now?"

"Seriously, Bri. He's too much trouble, even if I *was* interested, which I'm not. And I gotta go—I'm almost at work. Talk to you later. Bye."

She clicked off the phone and sighed. Seriously. Too much trouble.

# Chapter Thirteen

AFTER A LONG DAY AT WORK, RAQUEL SLIPPED HER KEY INTO the lock at her apartment. Her eyelids pinched closed. Maybe he'd be gone.

The eight-foot-tall statue of a snarling gargoyle met her inside the door. Nope. Not gone.

On the other hand, the floor hadn't collapsed from the weight, so that was good. Three cheers for the quality of construction a century ago.

She ducked around Garrett's form, set her backpack on her bed, and slumped beside it. Okay, she had a giant sculpture taking up most of her apartment, and the only way to get rid of it was to wake him up again.

Her gaze landed on the notch in his shoulder. She thought she'd been joking about gargoyles being vulnerable when statues, but maybe she'd been right after all.

Had that injured him? Permanently?

A tiny voice chirped from the back of her mind. Maybe she could shatter him and dump the pieces out the window.

Her throat thickened, and a shudder rolled through her limbs. Shattering was not an option. She wouldn't be responsible for any more deaths, and that included the death of an arrogant, stubborn gargoyle.

Incredibly arrogant and stubborn.

And just plain stupid too.

What had he expected her to say? *Share her life?* Was that a bizarre Mythos-style marriage proposal? Because that? That was *not* going to happen.

She was too dangerous and broken to be allowed connections to others at all, and that edict went double for men. She'd learned her lesson when Eduardo and Crockett—the two guys in her life who had mistakenly thought her worthy and deserving—died.

Yeah, her brother's death hadn't been her fault, but her toxicity still infected others, endangering everyone around her. And actual relationships were out of the question. The risk was too great.

Even for an arrogant and stubborn gargoyle.

Ugh. Irritation buzzed through her veins, and she stood, unable to keep her emotions silently restrained anymore.

"You are *such* a man. I *knew* you needed something from me. I asked you, flat out, what it was, and you refused to tell me. I swear, you'd think men having to ask for help or directions or something is akin to open-heart surgery."

Her arms whirled with each word, gesturing and pointing and clenching, just as Brianna's arms moved when she was worked up about things. Great, she was turning into a fiery Latina after all.

"And it's all your fault, you—you idiot."

She crossed her arms, tucking her hands under her biceps, and settled for pacing in the narrow strip in front of the windows by the fire escape. "I refuse to feel sorry for you. You did this to yourself. You and your stupid macho allergy to admitting when you need help."

She crawled over her bed to reach his side and shook her finger in his face. "I've lived my whole life with that bullshit, and you know what? I spit in the face of machismo. My father couldn't make me conform, and neither can you. I refuse to play by those stupid little games. I refuse to be labeled as the good girl worthy to be a wife or the bad girl worthy to be used. You know why? Because I *won't* be used for any of those labels. I'm my own person. I have my own job, my own apartment, and my own life because I won't ever be dependent on a man who treats me like shit."

Memories choked her throat. Memories of her mamá as she

wasted away. Memories of her father's refusal to admit his wife had AIDS, much less let her get treatment—even as *he* got the treatment he needed—because then he'd have to admit what his macho infidelity-strewn lies had done to her.

Her voice dropped with her vow. "I won't ever let that happen to me." She jabbed her fingertip at her collarbone. "Because I know all that bullshit is a *lie*. I don't need to give up my power and control to a man who thinks it's his right to run the show." She waved her hand. "And don't pretend you're not like that. You thought you could push me around and make me do what you wanted just because you said so. And look where that got you. Stuck, and dependent on me to fix you. Well, you can fucking wait."

She stomped out to the hall and slammed her door closed. Air whistled through her teeth, and she held her breath a moment to get her heart rate under control.

Damn emotions. What happened to being dispassionate and calm?

She'd left her *own* apartment to make God-knew-what point—to a *statue*. What the hell?

While her outburst had felt good in the moment, she needed to reclaim her detachment. No distractions, no emotions, no chance to disappoint anyone.

Her pulse still beat erratically. Maybe a time-out while grabbing dinner would help.

Her mood had marginally improved when she returned to her apartment. The two beers she'd allowed herself to have with dinner might have had something to do with that. Her sarcasm hadn't faded though.

"Still here?" She leaned over his shield and stared him in his stony little eyes. "Oh, that's right. You're stuck here because you *need* me. You're dependent on me. You're powerless and helpless and can only *hope* that I'll get you out of this mess you got yourself into. In fact, you're completely..." She leaned closer and enunciated each syllable. "Im-po-tent."

She snorted and removed her shirt, exposing her bra to the statue that couldn't do a damn thing about it. "Sucks to be you."

She stripped off her dress pants too. Her bra and panties

weren't much more revealing than the exercise clothes he'd seen her in the previous morning, but stripping felt more risqué because her intentions were different. Now she was taunting him. Still, he didn't deserve to see more than that, so she slipped into the bathroom to finish changing into a T-shirt and shorts for bed.

As she scrubbed her face at the sink, she ran through the options for how to wake him up again. He'd implied that it had something to do with trust. What had he said? That she'd trusted he would protect her?

How was she supposed to summon a mystical amount of trust when she was epic levels of pissed at him? Besides, it wasn't as if she'd *consciously* trusted him before. Hell, she wasn't sure she *could* consciously trust anyone—even herself. So how was she supposed to do this?

She exited the bathroom and stared at him, tapping her thumb against her lips. Even though he wasn't on a pedestal—a good thing as far as her ceiling was concerned—he still had the open area between his limbs, torso, and shield. Maybe she should sleep there tonight so the unconscious trust of her nightmares could work.

She plucked her pillow off the bed and switched off the light. "Apparently, *I'm* going to spend the night on the filthy carpet tonight. However much you appreciate my efforts to fix *your* mistake, it's not enough to make up for this."

The night passed, and her nightmares came and went in her little ball on the floor. At the sound of her alarm the next morning, she jerked up and hit her head on his elbow—his *stony* elbow. Her plan hadn't worked. Damn it.

Under the spray of the shower, the truth hit her. Her stomach hardened so tightly nausea threatened.

Garrett might really be gone. Dead. And she'd once again been the cause.

She hadn't been good enough to save them before, and now she wasn't good enough again. It was her fault. It was always her fault.

Her father was right. She was a menace to the world and not good enough for anything.

She'd fought so hard to try to be good enough—to *earn* her guys' respect. For a while, she'd thought she'd succeeded in proving her father wrong.

Instead, she'd gotten them all killed. She'd betrayed them with her mistakes. Despite her military training to *save* people, those who were close to her—who depended on her—died.

Even her mamá had almost died at her birth.

Sobs choked her throat, and tears mixed with the water rivulets on her cheeks. Where had she gone wrong this time?

She'd tried distancing herself from others. Not allowing herself any friends, any relationships, anything. Even with Brianna, the woman was as close as she was only because she ignored Raquel's attempts to push her away. But her efforts to avoid others hadn't been enough.

What more could she do? Did she have to withdraw from the human race and become a hermit somewhere? Why did her brokenness have to doom others?

Tremors wracked her body, and she braced herself against the wall. The sobs escaped despite her pinched lips, her breath stuttering. Her runny nose made a mess of her face.

No, not again.

She lifted her head, stepped back from the spray, and cleaned the evidence of her moment of weakness. She had to fix this. Somehow.

Otherwise, how could she claim that she'd learned from her mistakes? How could she say that she'd never again be the cause of tragedy? How could her guys ever forgive her?

She *would* fix this.

With that determination firing her thoughts, she got ready and went to work, where she spent her lunch hour searching online for potential solutions. Anything that might provide clues for how to release him from whatever enchantment, curse, or magic held him hostage.

But possible answer after possible answer failed—from one day to the next. Every morning, he remained trapped in his stone prison, and each failure ate deeper into her pain and fractured her soul.

After a week, his overwhelming presence had become so normal that she almost forgot and stripped completely in front of him. Like he was nothing more than a piece of furniture to be ignored.

Like he *was* dead and gone.

Tears flowed harder than usual in the shower that morning. Always in the shower. Never where he would witness.

Was *he* still even in there? *Could* he awaken?

She scrubbed the doubt from her face. No, there was nothing to worry about. He'd survived like this for years before, so a week or two shouldn't be a big deal.

That's what she told herself. That's what she hoped.

A WEEK AND A HALF AFTER GARRETT'S IDIOTIC MISTAKE, RAQUEL arrived at her apartment after work and psyched herself up for Plan... What was she up to? Plan Q?

Whatever. Although it probably said something about her that she'd been willing to purposely inflict a flashback on herself last night before trying this approach.

She didn't need to be afraid though. What she was about to do didn't mean anything. It didn't indicate that she'd failed to learn from her mistakes about involving herself with others. This wasn't about her hormones and their reasons for wanting her to take this step last week. This wasn't about getting *close* to him.

This was to save someone's life. That was it. She'd do just about anything to save a life, right? Right.

Quite simply, this *had* to work because her research had reached a dead end. She'd exhausted all the theories to try and the options to investigate, closing the last browser tabs of possibilities at the start of her lunch hour. Without anything else to do, she'd left the office to eat in a little corner park in hopes of the fresh air giving her new ideas. No such luck.

Instead, she'd broken down in *public*. During her whispered I-don't-believe-in-God-but-I'm-desperate prayer of "Please, help me—I just want Garrett to wake up," a stray tear had landed on the large rock she'd claimed as her lunch spot.

Crying. In public. She'd reached level eleven on the Desperation Scale.

Only a firm grip on the solid boulder under her palms kept her emotionally balanced enough to return to work that afternoon. As though the tingles in her skin where she touched the abrasive surface reminded her of her strength. As though the stone could harden her desire with a mix of sheer willpower to awaken him. As though sitting on a boulder while making a simple wish would mystically grant her the power to reverse his curse.

Yep, she was desperate enough to grasp at delusional hope. After all, she *was* hoping for a miracle.

Or magic.

Yet even the old fairy tales had lacked answers for her, and if anything would wake someone from the Mythos plane, she'd thought those would have the inside scoop. But in the original versions, *Sleeping Beauty* ended with the prince raping and impregnating the princess while she slept, and the princess in *The Frog Prince* answered the frog's requests by throwing him against the wall. Not helpful.

Instead, she was left with only the modern versions of the stories, and those used a kiss to break an enchantment. If this didn't work, she was doomed.

Failure would be the final sign that she'd never get better. That she'd always be toxic. Unworthy. Alone.

So here she was—at her last option.

She kicked off her shoes, stepped into the open space in the middle of the statue, and glared at the stone orbs of its eyes. "You don't deserve this, but I refuse to have another death on my hands, so..."

She balanced a foot on each of his knees, braced herself with a hold on his shoulders, and kissed his snarling upper lip.

*Come on, Garrett, wake up. Wake up for me.*

Gritty texture ground at her lips, but she refused to give up. Her tongue licked the inside of his mouth for good measure, and then she returned to mashing her lips against the hard surface.

The stone softened and became warm.

# Chapter Fourteen

SHOCKS FAR MORE POWERFUL THAN THE USUAL TINGLES OF A stone-death awakening jolted a cold, dead heart into a violent thump. One thump turned into another and another, building into a steady beat. A beat of life. A beat of potential. A beat of awareness.

Garrett *felt*. He felt warmth and softness. He smelled Raquel's mesmerizing scent, right under his nose. Everything he thought he'd never have again.

He sucked in a deep breath, drinking in her aroma, afraid to open his eyes. By the Maker, she smelled incredible. She tasted even better, a spice of indomitable strength flavored with a savory hint of goodness and heart.

Able to move once more, his muscles responded to his thought, and he stood and picked her up before she slipped off his knees. He crushed her against his chest, wrapping her legs around his hips, and melded his lips with hers. Soft. So incredibly soft.

He wanted to devour her, worship her, be one with her. He'd never wanted a woman like this in all his life.

His mind spun at the implications, but he couldn't stop to think. Lightheaded, he stumbled forward until the backs of his hands at her hips met a wall, and he leaned into her. Dizziness was a minor complication compared to the raw need burning through him.

His fingers tangled in her shirt in his haste to find the bottom hem. There. Her back branded his palms, and he groaned, unable to hide the desire building within him. Good, so good.

She froze and shoved against his shoulders, breaking off the kiss. His eyes popped open.

Her wide-eyed gaze flickered through a dozen emotions at once, from joy and desire to confusion and anger, and several others he couldn't make out. A flush colored her face around her lush, well-kissed lips, and her breaths came just as fast as his. She licked those lips and swallowed, and her legs slipped off his hips.

His ribs tightened, and an ache centered in his chest, but he couldn't say why. Logic was beyond him, his thoughts looping and swirling like a chaotic flock of birds in flight.

"Put me down, please." Her voice was maddeningly calm compared to his rampaging emotions, but he withdrew his hands from her shirt and shifted back a half step so she could get her weight under her. The ache inside him grew, consuming pieces of him he didn't know existed.

She sidestepped and retreated to the window. Facing the glass, she straightened her spine and rolled her shoulders back. Her arms crossed, and she spun toward him, her expression unreadable.

"You're awake. For a while there, I was worried"—she cleared her throat—"worried that I might have to call an exterminator to clear out an infestation of a very large pest."

His thoughts scattered like grains of sand on a windy day, and no response came to mind. Memories leaked into the void. Memories from his time in stone-death, when she'd been—he believed the phrase was—pissed. Very, very pissed.

Yet other memories filled in the blanks. Memories of true worry lining her features. Memories of her sleeping at his feet every night, subjected to her nightmares without his help, waking stiff and sore every morning from the uncomfortable position. Memories of her purposely triggering remembered horrors and clutching his waist in terror, screaming and trembling.

"Thank you." His throat thick, his voice sounded rougher than usual.

"Yes, well, I'm glad that worked. I was getting sick of having to climb over you to get to the bathroom all the time."

An itch started at the back of his mind, spreading into a

realization he couldn't ignore. "That shouldn't have worked."

Her face tightened. "What do you mean, it shouldn't have worked?"

"The magic of gargoyles allows us to attempt a bond with a human female only once. When you..." He paused. How could he word it so he wouldn't risk her wrath again? "When you *rightly* rejected my inarticulate request, I should have been condemned until another human female granted me her trust, which of course, would never happen, as I would have been destroyed long before that opportunity presented itself."

Her gaze flicked to his shoulder.

He absorbed the left sleeve of his coat and shirt into his body and touched the new fingertip-sized scar on his skin. "Yes, I can be damaged—or killed—while in that form."

She mimicked his motion, pressing on the scars he knew lay under her left sleeve. "I'm sorry."

"Don't be. This is a small price to pay for your miracle."

For it *was* a miracle. No magic in his experience could explain how she'd awoken him. Was a deeper magic at work? Deeper than the magic of the faeries?

She fidgeted with the fabric of her sleeves and then shook herself, forcing a teasing expression. "Well, you *did* deserve that injury."

Apparently, his warrior was uncomfortable with praise. He matched her teasing mood to break her discomfort. "Quite likely true."

Unease prickled up his spine. His words had been free of manipulative intentions, expressing only a genuine eagerness to forgive her and strengthen their relationship instead.

Something in his attitude toward her had shifted, and it wasn't just about the kiss. Something that signaled he had no choice but to trust her. Something that worried him but demanded his deference.

"I am..." His words faded in a confused haze, and he paced to the window overlooking the roof and the pedestal where he'd been displayed for more years than he wanted to admit. All because he'd trusted those he considered friends.

All because he'd trusted.

His fist pressed on the window frame, and the urge to be truthful ripped through his chest. Why he felt the need to drop all pretenses and trickery with her, he couldn't say.

A shudder rippled through him. Which situation was more troubling? The sudden urge to be truthful, or the mystery of what had changed and why?

"I have never trusted a human before, not like this." The admission ground from deep in his throat. "This is difficult for me."

She sat on the edge of the dresser beside him, her arms still crossed. "Yeah, because all those pretty words about how I *had* to trust you because you trusted me were flat-out lies and manipulations."

"Not all." He inclined his head, once again letting the truth leak from a vulnerable place. "But some."

Her quiet grumble landed in the space between them with a thud. "I should have left you as a cold, hard slab of stone."

Before he could stop himself, his curiosity took hold of his mouth. "Why didn't you?"

Her head moved a fraction, but she seemed to stop herself from glancing at the picture on the wall next to her. That frame held the image of her with a group of men, all in uniform. Fellow soldiers, he'd guess, but what that indicated for her reasoning, he couldn't fathom.

Instead of answering, she sighed. "What was so difficult to tell me that you risked becoming Mr. Statue rather than giving me a straight answer?"

"At first, I attempted to avoid revealing how vulnerable I am without your help. As that plan neared failure, I changed strategies but ran out of time to explain the situation." A compulsion forced him to share the full truth. "Gargoyles are not meant to live on the Earthen plane. To remain *alive*, we must form a bond with a human female. As you were the one who woke me, I had no choice but to attempt to form that bond with you."

"So you going all statue wasn't about *me* but about your bond not working?" An odd lilt colored her tone, as though she hoped he'd agree with her.

"Not quite. As long as you allowed me in your life—trusted me, so to speak—I would have been fine until the next full moon." He shrugged. "I had plans to earn enough of your trust that you would form a stronger bond with me before the deadline, but that last morning broke the temporary reprieve from my..." There was no point in hiding the extent of his vulnerability. She already knew more than any human before. "Stone-death."

"Stone-death? It's more serious than just sleep, isn't it? You'd stay that way forever without someone to wake you."

The pedestal outside, his "home" for so long, drew his eye again. "Yes."

She followed his gaze and frowned. "With the risk of stone-death, it'd be more logical to stay on the Mythos plane. Why come here?"

"We can have children only by traveling to the Earthen plane. If we all rejected the risk, our legion would be as good as extinct." He shook his head, refusing to follow the thoughts toward his current situation. "Besides, it *shouldn't* have been so risky." That truth drove him to hammer the window frame with the side of his fist. "My regiment should have found a way to wake me long ago." His shoulders slumped, weighed down by the extent of his failures. "They should have done a great many things."

"What now? Are we back to that temporary reprieve thing? Or are we bonded enough that you're not risking stone-death anymore?"

He met her eyes, and an odd lurch in his chest flipped his stomach. His hand itched to reach out and touch her, embrace her, caress her. He clenched his fingers so hard his nails dug into his palms, and yet the urge didn't fade.

That wasn't good. Whatever that impulse signified, he didn't like the way it made him feel lightheaded and out of control.

Despite his inner turmoil, he found himself answering honestly. "I don't know. I shouldn't be awake at all."

She did something to him, something that reached into deeper magic than he had experience with, and if there was ever any doubt in his mind, there was none now: She was in control of his future.

And he was not happy about that. Not at all.

# Chapter Fifteen

R AQUEL CROSSED HER ARMS AGAIN—THE BETTER TO RESIST THE
temptation of the hunk in her apartment. Her emotions
were so scattered that some of them had fallen off the edge
of reality and were partying without her in fantasyland.

How could her body have reacted that way to his kiss?

Well, technically, she'd started it. But it became *his* kiss as soon
as he'd started kissing her in return. If he hadn't groaned and
reminded her that it wasn't all happening in her head, who knew
what would have happened. And what a mistake *that* would have
been.

Sure, he was crazy-sexy and the hottest thing she'd ever locked
lips with, but that didn't mean *more* was an option. That didn't
mean she could ignore her history and be A-okay with any aspect
of a relationship.

No, she'd just been happy that he was himself again. Really
happy.

Damn it. She broke eye contact and forced herself to focus on
the picture of her brother's army graduation by the door. Forced
herself to pick out her mamá's frail body in the shadow of her
father. Forced herself to remember one of the reasons she wouldn't
do the relationship thing—emotions made people vulnerable,
especially *relationship* emotions. Like how her mamá had
surrendered her power to her father.

The reminder of her other reason hung on the wall by her elbow. It wasn't safe for her to become close to anyone. Her father had been right to say she wasn't good enough, she wasn't worthy of happiness. Her guys had paid the price when she'd tried to prove him wrong. She wouldn't make that mistake again.

Yet if she didn't want to be responsible for sending Garrett back into stone-death, she had no choice but to let a *bond* develop. Whatever the hell that meant.

*Shit.* So much for keeping her distance.

"Okay, tell me about this bond thing. What does that mean? How is it *supposed* to work? What would I have to do to maintain it?"

If it involved marriage, she'd stab him again right now. And the butter knife had better go into his skin this time.

He groaned and rubbed his temple. Upon releasing his fist, his knuckles flushed from white to his normal human shade, a similar golden-sand tone as hers. At least he wasn't any happier about the situation.

"You're not going to like it." His tone was half-grumbling and half-apologizing.

He dropped his arm, as though resigned to his fate. His eyes settled on her, creases at the corners pleading for forgiveness. "To avoid stone-death while on the Earthen plane, gargoyles must bond with a human female's soul. Or to put it another way, they must find a woman willing to *share* her soul."

She rocked back on her heels. *Share her soul?* What the hell did that mean?

Most of her relatives would think him a demon for even stating the idea. And to be honest, if she allowed her leftover Catholic guilt to have a say, the idea *could* give her the willies.

Luckily, she'd gotten very good over the years at overruling that part of her. Some soldiers found God on the battlefront, and others lost God in the midst of the horrors. Given her issues with her extended family—as everyone but her brother shrugged off her father's behavior—she'd had a shaky relationship with her childhood religion even before her deployment, so her loss of faith had felt more like the natural end of the story than the result of trauma. But still—sharing a *soul*?

"Okay, let's get past the freak-out and talk specifics. Does the woman feel pain at this sharing?"

"No."

"Does she suffer in any way?"

"Not that I've ever detected."

"Wouldn't she tell you?"

"I've never spoken about it with any of them."

How could the topic not come up in conversation? Unless... "Does she even *know* she's sharing her soul with you?"

"Unlikely. I simply ask the woman to share her life with me, and as long as she says yes, the bond is formed."

Uh-huh. "But it's not marriage or anything?"

He shuddered. "Most definitely not. A bond typically lasts only a few months, and as I sense the bond weakening, perhaps due to the woman tiring of my presence, I find another one to form a bond with."

A part of her relaxed at the *no marriage* thing, but just as quickly, she flinched at his casual reference to finding a replacement. *Tiring of his presence?* More likely, they'd become frustrated by the lack of progress in what they thought was a relationship.

He'd used these women for their souls and then left them when convenient. He might claim they never suffered, but she'd bet he left some broken hearts over the years.

"You *do* know that 'sharing someone's life' often refers to marriage? Those women might have thought you were proposing." Hell, that's what *she'd* thought.

His jaw slackened, and his brows slammed together. "Oh." He looked away, and his gaze unfocused. "That might explain a few things."

"Seriously? You hadn't thought of that?"

"Apparently not." His mouth curled into a grimace. "But now that you've pointed it out, I feel like a fool for not seeing it earlier. I simply recited the words I was taught for how to invoke the magic, never thinking beyond that context."

She couldn't help her laugh. "You're probably the most-often-engaged-without-even-knowing-it man in the world. That has to be the most ridiculous 'guys are clueless' story I've ever heard."

Spots of ruddy color appeared on his face, tickling her mood. She'd forgotten how much fun it was to embarrass certain guys.

He scrutinized her, his eyes wide, and rubbed his chin. "You're not angry? Even though you know that my goal was—and is—to share your soul?"

Her chuckle burst out of her as a snort. "Listen, I don't know who to feel more sorry for, you or me."

She led him to the mattress, where she could sit more comfortably. This might take a while.

# Chapter Sixteen

BEFORE TWO WEEKS AGO, RAQUEL COULD NEVER HAVE imagined having a conversation with a gargoyle at all, much less a conversation about *souls*. When had her life gotten so insane?

She smoothed out the bland gray bed sheets in front of her. What she wouldn't give for her life to be as easily untwisted. Who'd have thought that breaking down—praying and crying that afternoon—would come back to haunt her with even more religious stuff? Maybe if she barged her way through the subject, unemotionally, she wouldn't lose her damn mind.

"Okay, when you were last alive, or not in stone-death or whatever, people were superstitious about things like demons and souls. Now, while most people like to think they have a soul, they don't necessarily think of it as something that can be stolen. At least I know *I* don't think of it that way." Her relatives might be another matter.

He rested his head in his palm, his expression almost adorable with his concern. "And you're not worried about sharing it? That sharing might somehow damage or weaken your soul?"

"Do *you* think what you do causes damage?"

"No, but I'd always assumed that was because I have no soul and therefore couldn't know."

He thought he had no soul? Another reason for her relatives to freak out. In contrast, she found herself more curious. "Do you *feel* different during this sharing?"

"I sense the bond, but nothing like how I think I'd feel if I truly had a soul."

Emptiness hollowed out his voice, resonating with her detached existence too well. If she'd ever had one, her soul had likely suffocated under the weight of the blood on her hands.

Her gaze drifted to the darkening sky outside. But if she translated the idea to his Mythos plane magic stuff, she could understand how an "anchor" to this world might make sense. Strange as it might be to others, *magic* was easier for her to think about than *souls*.

"I wonder if you're actually doing anything with these women's souls. Maybe your magic relies on something to tie you to the Earthen plane, and as long as that connection exists, you're golden." She tugged her hair back and released it, her limbs twitchy with nervous energy. "In my case, that's a good thing for you, because I seriously doubt I even *have* a soul to share."

"You are born. Of course you have a soul."

His matter-of-fact statement interrupted her thoughts, and she couldn't remember her next point. Then the implications of his words smacked her in the face.

"You weren't born?"

"No, like all gargoyles, I was created by the ancient faeries of the Flikea clan, those who command the earth, to act as their army in the faerie war against the dragons. I was formed of the spirit of the elemental earth of the Mythos plane and emerged from the ground, fully-grown."

Her head spun with the craziness of his claim. A week and a half ago, she'd shoved aside the details of what this Mythos plane idea meant, but these tidbits brought it back into bizarre neon-bright focus.

"Let me get this straight. Faeries are real." She waited for his nod. "And dragons are real." She paused again. "And they're at war on the Mythos plane."

"They *were*. Dragons can control metal, and certain kinds of metal can kill faeries, so the faeries created us as an army to force the dragons to leave."

"Where did the dragons go?"

"They live here on the Earthen plane now."

"Oh..."

Of course. How could she not *know* there were dragons living on Earth? How stupid of her.

She stood and claimed a beer from the fridge. Maybe this would start making sense with a little alcohol in her. If she hadn't already *seen* him change—multiple times—she'd think *he* was the one suffering from hallucinations.

"I hope you didn't want one." She lifted the bottle, clarifying her statement, and returned to the bed. "This is the last one, and I'm not sharing."

Rude, but she wasn't sure how mad she still was at him.

"I don't need to eat or drink."

"Oh. Good." And yet another weird thing to accept.

She crossed her legs on the mattress and started over. "You weren't kidding about that whole military culture thing. That's literally the reason for your existence."

For some reason, her stomach twisted at the thought. Even ignoring the born-versus-created issue, the situation reeked of servitude or slavery. Despite their differences, he was as sentient as she was, and he deserved the same rights.

"What did gargoyles get out of this deal?"

"We were granted the dragon's old homeland as our own, and the earth-clan faeries constructed the portal so that we might travel to the Earthen plane and find mates."

She choked on her beer. "Find mates?" She set down the bottle and wiped the splatters off her bed sheet. "I thought that's not what the soul-bond idea was about."

"It's not. The vast majority of my legion remains on Mythos, serving the faeries. While they don't need to worry about bonds and the risk of stone-death there, the threat of magical attacks surrounds them—as every being on the plane possesses magic—so we're not nearly as indestructible in our homeland as among humans here. Their priority has always been to travel here when they're ready to find a mate and create their progeny."

He grunted and rubbed the back of his neck. "My regiment was assigned here permanently to protect the portal for the others, to prevent our extinction simply by the lack of access to potential mates. Thus, we've needed to share a soul to stay here for our mission, regardless of the search for a mate."

That made sense, but spoke to a divide between those of his regiment and the gargoyles on the Mythos plane. In a way, those in the homeland were the civilians of his culture, able to live normal lives while his regiment enabled their survival. The scenario raised more questions about his ability to adapt, given that he'd been cut off from his culture for so long.

He leaned against the wall and stretched his long legs across the mattress. "To be honest, within my regiment, none of us have made finding a mate a priority because we can father only one child during our entire existence."

"Only one kid?"

"That was a limitation the earth-clan faeries placed on my whole legion with their magic. We must consciously decide to cause pregnancy, and we can make that choice only once." He frowned. "I know I should be grateful the faeries allowed us that much, but the longer I stay here, the more I question..." He shook his head. "Never mind."

Yeah, she had plenty of her own questions about these faeries and their motives. No need for them to worry about a gargoyle population beyond a controllable number with that magical limitation. She didn't put voice to her cynicism, but these faeries didn't sound like the good guys.

She stretched out her legs beside him. "If you all have the same one-kid limitation, why do you think your regiment developed different priorities from those in the homeland?"

"We've *had* to adapt. The dangers here are different, and no one in our homeland is familiar with the Earthen plane. That's made us more independent by necessity. Also, because we *are* here, we're in no rush to find a mate and return home. And we've seen..."

He swept his palm down his face and sighed with a heavy breath. "We've seen what happens if we make the wrong choice. The original supreme commander here on the Earthen plane, Alann, found a mate and fathered his child, but then his child died in service to the faeries."

Garrett's eyes unfocused for a moment, hinting at memories replaying in his head. "Alann was never the same after the loss of his son. He abandoned the mission, and I was promoted as the new supreme commander of the regiment. Ever since, our mission's focus has been to keep the portal open for the rest of the legion but avoid the risks of mates for ourselves."

Once again, she was struck by how his regiment had veered from the "civilian" culture of the rest of his legion. On some level, they knew better than the rest that they were never truly free of the faeries' control.

The sneakiest tyrannies were those that gave people options. The ability to choose, even between two horrible choices—such as the risk of extinction versus the risk of losing their single allotted child—created the illusion of free will. Either way, the portal symbolized their freedom from the limits of their existence, narrow as that definition of freedom might be.

"I understand." As the next question built in her mind, a quiver trembled in her stomach in anticipation of a mental flinch. She snagged her backpack and bent over it with the pretext of searching for her phone. "So if this whatever-kind-of-bond between us holds, you'll leave to return to your mission of protecting the portal?"

She twisted away and plugged in her phone for the night. Did she hope for a *yes* or a *no*? What did it mean if she wasn't sure? The fact that she was avoiding watching his expression during the question probably wasn't a good sign.

"No."

She whipped her head around. He wasn't doing any better at facing the *what next?* issue, his gaze fixed on his hands, which curled and uncurled into fists.

"What aren't you telling me?"

"Why do you ask?" He rolled off the bed and stood by the window overlooking the roof, staring. A sigh settled in the space between them. "I promise I'm not keeping anything from you. It simply doesn't concern you."

She locked her hands together and forced them to remain still on her lap. "You said you wouldn't be leaving. How does that not concern me?"

"No, I said I wouldn't be returning to my mission. That difference means it doesn't concern you."

She shot to her feet. "Now *you're* abandoning your mission?"

He stormed across to her and seized her biceps. His voice deepened to a commanding level. "*Trust me* when I say it doesn't concern you."

He fiercely dragged her lips up to his and kissed her, silencing her protests. She yanked back and threw a right hook. Her knuckles crunched into his temple hard enough to stun a human. He gazed at her, astonished but unharmed, and released her arms.

"I'm sorry. I don't..."

She wiped her mouth with the back of her hand. "Yeah, remember that conversation I said we needed to have about boundaries? Do *not* pull that shit with me."

"Of course. I don't know what—"

"I don't care for your excuses, and I don't care for your 'this doesn't concern you' crap. You're asking me to bond with you, so if you're the type to think you can get away with that kind of treatment of women or the type who would abandon his assignment, you'd better believe I have a right to know that about you."

"You're pissed again." He worded the statement like a scientific observation, and then he inspected his hands, as though they were the traitors behind his behavior. "I don't blame you."

He bent over and sank to the floor. He leaned against her mattress and hid his face in his palms.

"Trusting you... Anyone. It's difficult. I've never experienced anything like this before." Each word ripped from his throat like a confession.

The hard rod of her spine softened, and a tiny part of her wanted to forgive him. He *wasn't* human, and he'd last lived in a very different world. At least he acted like he could be trained.

Great. Her subconscious had gone from thinking him a pet rock to thinking him a pet dog. Who was being disrespectful now? Maybe if she forgave him, they'd be even.

"Yeah, don't let it happen again. The world you're in now expects *decent* guys to ensure the woman wants it before they do something like that."

"Good to know." He rubbed his temple. "Are they all likely to punch as hard as you?"

Before she could prevent it, heat bloomed in her cheeks. "Uh no. That's just me. Most wouldn't punch at all."

With her history, her tolerance for macho *I-own-you* stuff was non-existent. But he didn't know that, and his temple had paid the price.

She shoved her hands in her pockets. "In the army, soldiers typically call each other by their last names. But my unit took my first name and turned it into the nickname Rocky because my first instinct is to meet force with force." She shrugged and couldn't stop herself from offering, "Sorry."

"Luckily—for me anyway—I'm indestructible."

"Indestructible?" Maybe the butter knife *wouldn't* have a better chance against his human-looking skin.

"While we can feel pain in this form, stone-death is the only time we're truly vulnerable among non-magical humans."

"Good. I'd hate to have to add *hurting you* to my stuff-to-feel-guilty-about list."

"No. But this might explain why you are not yet mated."

The heat drained from her face and flooded the rest of her body. She kept her voice so level it sounded flat. "Not that it's any of your business, but I'm not *mated* by choice. If I wanted a relationship, I would have one."

He stood and held up his hands. "I worded that poorly. I have no doubt that you are a desirable woman." He winced. "As I've already so inappropriately demonstrated to you."

Her weight rolled back onto her heels. Was that kiss really about desire? For her? Not likely.

She lifted her chin, shoving the impossible from her mind. "Now that we have that settled, how about explaining why you'd abandon your mission? I get that you think it doesn't concern me, but I have a right to understand who I'm sharing this bond with. I don't know what kind of military organization gargoyles have, but where I'm from, that kind of behavior can land you in prison. So if you don't want me to jump to the worst conclusion, explain yourself."

He rubbed a finger over his lips. The gesture no doubt reflected his internal debate, but she couldn't help focusing on his mouth.

Did a part of her wish for him to kiss her for real?

She shook the question from her mind. Where were these thoughts coming from?

Finally, he inhaled deeply and nodded to the now-darkened window. "May I request that I tell you somewhere else? I suspect you will have questions, and I'd like to take you to where we can get answers."

Wow. He *could* be reasonable when he tried.

The thrill that ran through her limbs at the thought of another flight with him didn't hurt her mood either.

# Chapter Seventeen

G ARRETT TOOK RAQUEL'S *AFTER YOU* MOTION AT THE WINDOW
by the roof to mean that she agreed to his plan. Despite
her apparent eagerness, he couldn't decide if this was a
good idea or not.

Getting out of this tiny room, where he had no choice but to
inhale her scent with every breath, was definitely a good idea. He'd
already proven that keeping his distance with his emotions wound
so tightly was nigh impossible. But taking her to the Central Park
he'd identified on a map would require them getting close—very
close—again, and that part might be a bad idea. His mind was too
distracted by conflicting desires to force logic into the situation, but
he had to admit she had a point about deserving to know.

Out on the rooftop, he changed into his gargoyle form. She
accepted the change in stride, even though he hadn't warned her,
and simply looked up at him. "Where are we going?"

"A place called Central Park. Have you heard of it?"

She laughed. "*Everyone's* heard of Central Park. It's one of the
biggest city parks in the world, so it's kind of famous. Won't we
need to worry about people seeing you? It's dark but not *that* late."

"There is a treed area near our destination, and I will change
back as soon as we land." He opened his arms. "Are you ready?"

She took a step forward. "No offense, but let's see if I can hang
on a different way this time."

His warrior definitely did not like when she wasn't in control of her body. He couldn't say he blamed her, especially as that was more they had in common.

She stood on tiptoes and wrapped her arms around his neck. "Will you be able to hold me tightly enough in this position?"

She pressed her whole body against him, and he couldn't stop a grunt from escaping him. He turned the sound into a non-committal answer. "I think so."

He squeezed her until her breasts squished into his chest. She glanced up at him and smiled, as though this was an innocent pose and not a prelude to the intimate embrace he felt it was. "Now you can't drop me if you feel like it."

He wanted to protest that he would never do such a thing, but he didn't trust his voice. This position was worse. Much worse.

Luckily, they weren't going far tonight, and a few minutes later, he settled them safely among the trees near the boulder he'd communicated with the previous week. As she'd predicted, humans were still about, jogging and walking hand-in-hand, but the darkness covered his descent. He changed back into his human form and, while he led her to the large stone on the hill, explained the context she needed to understand.

"Because gargoyles emerged from the ground of the Mythos plane, we can communicate with rocks and earth here on the Earthen plane as well. Most times, that ability is an interesting curiosity and nothing more. However, when we're trying to gain an understanding of events that encompass decades, centuries, or more, we've found the placement of certain boulders makes them excellent witnesses to the passage of history."

She didn't question his ability—or his sanity. Her openness to taking most things in stride never ceased to amaze him.

He stopped in front of the boulder and bowed. "Greetings from Garrett, supreme commander of the Earthen plane regiment of the gargoyle army from the Mythos plane. May I once again ask for your indulgence?"

GREETINGS, GARRETT. The gravelly acknowledgment crackled in his mind. GREETINGS, AWAKENER.

He startled and gave the stone a second look. The Earth—or at least this boulder—paid attention to gargoyle magic enough to understand the need for a human female *and* knew who had awoken him? Not that Raquel could hear the welcome, but this witness was surprising at every turn.

"Yes, she's the one who woke me."

AWAKENER QUERIED. EARTH GRANTED.

Earth *granted*? What had it granted? Had it given something to her? The communication style of Earth and its aspects sometimes made following conversations difficult, but that issue wasn't what they were here for right now. That discussion would have to wait.

He returned his focus to Raquel and continued their conversation. "I came here the first night you woke me with your nightmares so I could catch up on what I'd missed."

A corner of her lips quirked. "And here I thought you'd stayed with me all night."

"I said no such thing, but perhaps that idea was wishful thinking on your part."

Before he could stop himself, he winked at her. A part of him recognized the danger of this game, balancing between building their bond and maintaining his distance to keep the last thread of control over his chaotic emotions. Hopefully, he knew what he was doing.

He closed his eyes and let the horror of that night redirect his concentration to his point. "In reviewing history through this witness, I attempted to discover the location of my regiment. As you are well aware, we are vulnerable in stone-death, and the *loyalty* aspect of our motto refers to our vow to help each other avoid that fate. Stone-death usually lasts no more than a few days or a week—not years, much less decades or centuries. So my first priority was to discover the cause of their disloyalty and abandonment."

Her penetrating gaze seemed to see directly into his deepest vulnerabilities. "But you discovered more than you expected, didn't you?"

"*That* is an understatement. Thanks to this witness, I learned that gargoyles have not walked the earth for many years, perhaps since around the time of my stone-death. My regiment hadn't come to my aid because they simply were not here. They'd abandoned me *and* their mission."

She crossed her arms and frowned at the boulder. "Their

mission? This is the mission to protect the portal?"

"Yes."

"What's the status of the portal now if no one's been watching over it?"

Truly, his first impressions of this warrior—that he would gladly welcome her as a member of his regiment—stood as one of his best judgments. She understood instantly the importance and risks of his situation.

His heartbeat quickened, pulsing in his throat, but he couldn't say if that was due to his admiration for her or to the upcoming dead end of his story.

"Sometime while I was in stone-death, the portal closed. I don't know if it's been destroyed or sealed. All I know is that I can no longer feel the magic of the Mythos plane through the opening."

Her jaw slackened, and she reached out to the boulder, as though struggling with her balance. No doubt she understood the implications of the news.

"You're trapped here? Alone?"

"So it would seem." He inhaled and gazed blankly over the darkened park. Scattered around the lawn were loners and lovers who lived their lives, short though they might be, and never had to face the eternity of failure as he did. "Everything that drove my existence, the mission to keep the portal open, is gone. I am adrift—with no purpose."

She stepped closer and touched his arm. "I'm so sorry."

"I was created to fulfill a purpose. Fight the dragons. After the war, I was given a new purpose. Protect the portal. Now I have nothing." He met her eyes, which glistened in the low light. "Without a purpose, I don't know who I am anymore. I am no one. I am nothing."

She wound her arms around his chest and squeezed. "That's not true."

A tangle of emotions twisted inside him at her embrace. Her recognition of his anguish unleashed a painful wave of sensations humans would probably label nausea. Yet her understanding also sent warming tingles through his limbs.

She *understood.* On some level, he wasn't completely alone.

# Chapter Eighteen

T EARS BURNED RAQUEL'S EYES, AND SHE BURIED HER FACE INTO Garrett's chest to hide the evidence. She forgave him. She forgave him for *everything*.

In the forty-eight hours or so that he'd been awake over the past two weeks, he'd been through hell and back. She'd had her own struggles with feeling adrift after her discharge, but his situation was even more devastating—and more permanent.

A tear dripped down her cheek, and she sniffed.

"Are you—?" He leaned back and examined her face. "Are you crying?"

"No." Stupidly, she chose that moment to wipe the tear tracks with the back of her hand, drawing his attention to them.

He hugged her tightly and nestled his jaw against the top of her head. "Oh, my sweet Raquel. I am honored by your understanding."

Hearing her name in his deep baritone tickled her insides, and she pulled away. "Is there anything that can be done?"

He took her cue and released her. Definitely trainable.

"Before, when I was searching your laptop that night, I came up with a rudimentary plan, but there's no guarantee of success."

"What kind of plan?"

"That I would search for precious metals or gems from the ground that could be exchanged for currency to travel to the portal's location and determine its fate. Perhaps by knowing what happened to the portal, I'll learn what caused my regiment to abandon me and their mission."

"Where *is* the portal?" She glanced around the park, taking the opportunity to check her surroundings for threats again. "Is it here in New York City?"

"No. I was moved as a statue onto that platform after my stone-death. I don't know what the location is called now, but in my memory, the portal was in Great Britain."

"It's still called that. But we're across the ocean from there. Could you fly that far?"

"For myself, yes. Given the uncertain nature of our bond, I hope to convince you to join me. However, that long of a flight wouldn't be comfortable for you, so we'd need an alternate form of travel."

She saw a thousand flaws in his plan. For one, land was always owned by *someone*, meaning he'd technically be stealing if he mined valuables from the ground. Second, if she decided to join him for some reason, they'd need to travel by airplane, and he couldn't pass security at an airport without a legitimate identity. And those obstacles didn't even count the other troubling details.

She kept her worries to herself for now. No need to depress him any more than he already was.

"Any idea what might have happened? Could a war on the Mythos plane have caused them to retreat and close the portal temporarily? Could they have died here before they could get to you?"

"The possibilities are endless. All I know from the witness"—he indicated the boulder beside them—"is that they no longer walk this plane." He nodded to a question she couldn't hear. "The witness confirmed that is the extent of the information any part of the Earth possesses."

"No longer walk... That could mean death *or* leaving the Earthen plane."

She regarded the boulder. It's not like the thing had legs though, so how limited was its knowledge?

"Would witnesses like this know about gargoyles that lived in a city? Sidewalks and streets are man-made. Or can it recognize gargoyles in stone-death? They wouldn't be *walking* either."

Garrett gaped at her, and his brows scrunched together. But he didn't say anything.

Ugh. Now she felt stupid for speaking up.

"Er, I was just thinking that you were up on a roof and not someplace a boulder would see, and during the same time you were out of commission, cities sprouted all over the world. So I was wondering if there could be other explanations. You know, if you might not be alone after all."

He clutched her biceps. "I—" He winced and cleared his throat. "I would kiss you if you would let me."

She exhaled her tension on a laugh. "I might let you. Just this once."

She stretched up to allow a quick peck. He cradled her jaw and deepened the kiss. His soft lips meshed with hers in a kiss that was as tender as the last one had been fierce. Warmth tingled outward from her core, and yet the hairs on her non-scarred skin lifted with a chill.

Her head swam, and she softened in his arms. She should stop this, right?

Too quickly, he pulled away, and she nearly whimpered. Luckily, he didn't see her sure-to-be-pathetic expression, as his gaze bounced to the boulder.

"Could she be right? Could the others still be here and simply in stone-death?" His shoulders settled, and he bowed. "I thank you."

"Well?"

"It's checking with the rest of the Earth." A tentative smile flickered over his mouth. "Even if this turns out to be nothing, thank you." He brushed his knuckles along her cheeks. "Thank you for understanding and trying to help. Although you may wish I had not come into your life, I shall be eternally grateful that you came into mine."

A wobbly feeling fluttered in her chest, as though her organs were swooning at his words. "You're welcome. I—" She wasn't sure what her mouth was going to say, but she swallowed the words anyway and stuck to a more reasonable response. "It's the least I can do to help a fellow soldier."

He winced and clapped his fingers over his ears. "One moment. Let me see if I can get them to stop shouting."

He placed a fingertip on the stone face. His eyes became unfocused and then closed.

A couple holding hands strode up the hill close by. She mentally surveyed the situation. They shouldn't look too unusual here. They could be just hanging out talking.

When the handholding women neared, Raquel started rambling quietly, enough that her soft patter of words would make their presence here seem more normal.

"I didn't get a chance to mention this to you earlier, but Brianna keeps asking if you and I are hanging out together. She wants to know if you want to come with me to her place—my old apartment—next weekend. I told her I didn't know. I mean, at the time, you were still, er, sleeping, so I brushed her off, but I figured I should let you know that the invitation existed. She mentioned something about doing a movie night, maybe with the *Terminator* movies. At least the first two. I don't know that I want to do an all-day marathon."

Technically, Brianna had been at bit more crass with her question, asking if Raquel and Garrett could stop boning each other long enough to visit, but she wasn't going to pass on *that* part of the message.

Sometime during her ramble, Garrett's eyes had opened, and they now focused on her with an amused curve of his eyebrows. She darted her gaze to the departing couple to explain, and he grinned.

"An invitation for both of us. That sounds entertaining. What do you think?"

She glanced again at the couple. Far enough. "I think you should tell me what you learned."

His mouth remained curved but hardened with a fervent edge. "They believe you may be correct. The expansion of human development may have created significant gaps in their ability to witness, especially if a gargoyle is in stone-death. They sifted through their collective knowledge and found no evidence of *my* existence during my time in that state, so it's likely that gargoyles in stone-death don't justify their notice—either due to the lack of witnesses at their location or to their lack of physical contact with the Earth." He nodded toward the boulder. "This witness has been most helpful to me, partly because my existence came as such a surprise."

A strained smile stretched her lips. She wanted to be happy for the news, but the idea could easily be a wild goose chase.

He straightened and dropped his hand off the rocky surface. "Do you have any other questions we should ask while we're here? If not, I'd like to start my search for other gargoyles in stone-death using your laptop—with your permission, of course."

"Not that I can think of." Between the information he'd shared and the kiss and her emotions, her brain was a mess.

He bowed to the giant stone. "I thank you again, honored ancient witness."

He lightly touched the small of her back and led her back to the cover of the trees. Was that gesture sweet, possessive, or pushy? She couldn't decide, but her legs didn't want to move faster to get away from his palm.

"Tell me about the invitation from Brianna. What is a movie night? Would that be like a date?"

She stopped and ignored the pressure of his hand. "No. Not a date." When he halted and regarded her questioningly, she scrutinized him. "What do you know about dates anyway?"

"I don't. That's why I'm asking." His gaze shifted away, suddenly focused on a tree trunk beside them. "One of my earlier searches mentioned the word in the context of a planned activity with someone, and that's all I know."

"Uh-huh. A random search brought that up? I don't think so." She playfully nudged him. "What were you searching for? How to get women to like you?"

He stiffened.

She laughed. "You were! This was part of your plan to manipulate me, wasn't it? So sorry to ruin your plan."

Read: not sorry at all. Amused, in fact.

"Let me save you the trouble. I don't date. So this evening, despite you asking me to join you for this activity, is not a date. And *if* we go to Brianna's—and you're seriously making me question the wisdom of that idea—that won't be a date either. I do not date. Ever. End of story."

Her imagination filled in the details of what her body *would* be willing to do, but there was no way she'd admit to any of that. She also wouldn't admit that just as his human form was sexy as hell, his gargoyle form was strangely appealing as well. Maybe it was because his gargoyle form reminded her of a hairless version of the Beast from the Disney movie, handsome in his own way. But she couldn't afford getting even more entangled with this Beast, so her lips could get over their pout right now.

"Let's get back. I have to go to sleep so I can function at work tomorrow."

They resumed their path to the trees. And his hand didn't rest on her back this time.

# Chapter Nineteen

GARRETT STARED AT THE LAPTOP SCREEN, MINDLESSLY CLICKING through endless images of gargoyles. Blast! Humans had appropriated his kind for countless uses. From TV shows and movies to lawn ornaments and Halloween decorations—whatever all those things were. When his search had come up with over a million results, he'd thought that was a misprint, but no such luck.

On the other end of the bed, Raquel's forehead had the usual furrows in the bit he could see over her book. Other than during her regular exercise routine out on the roof, those furrows had been in place for almost a week, probably for as long as he'd been searching fruitlessly.

He felt the need to assure her again. "I'm fine. I don't need to eat, drink, or sleep. I'm indestructible, remember?"

She lowered her book and gave him a smile that didn't reach her eyes. "I know. Maybe I'd just like my laptop back someday."

He startled. "I'm sorry. I hadn't thought of that. I don't even know what you use it for. Do you need it?"

"No." Her smile now spread into her eyes. "I'm just teasing you. I use it mostly for email and keeping up with military forums. Nothing I can't do on my phone if I was desperate."

"Thank you. Again. For everything." It seemed like *I'm sorry* and *thank you* were the only things he could offer her.

"Eh, for a roommate, you're not so bad. You don't eat my food, you don't need a bed, and you're quiet. I've had a lot worse, and even the biggest apartments don't make *that* situation any better."

"I'll take that as a compliment." He winked. "For a human, you're not too bad of a roommate either."

She stuck out her tongue and returned to her book. He watched her face for several more seconds, long enough to see that tongue worry over her lips and turn them into a delectable pout.

In truth, she was *too* perfect of a roommate. Independent, not one to talk too much unless he asked a question, and very much kept to herself. Although, what he wished was different—or how to make it happen—escaped him.

Several more pages of images scrolled by, the task of paging down automatic by now. He refused to give up. If some of his regiment were stuck in stone-death, he had to know. He might be lacking a true supreme commander's abilities to sense and connect with his regiment across the globe, but he wouldn't abandon them to obscurity.

A flush of energy seized his arm. Had he seen—?

He held his breath and backed up a page. There, a gargoyle holding a shield just like his. Just. Like. His.

"Raquel..." His voice was strained.

He didn't want to look up from the screen, but the mattress beside him shifted at her approach. Her soft gasp proved she saw the same thing he did.

"Do you know who that is?"

"This picture is too small and dark to make out the features."

"Here." She opened her hands for the laptop.

He set it in her grasp, never taking his eyes off the monitor, and resisted the urge to remind her to be careful. He had to trust that she knew what she was doing.

Still, he swallowed a "wait" when the buttons she pressed cleared the screen. Instead of protesting, he paid attention to her movements over the keyboard and touchpad. Ah, she'd saved the image outside of the search function.

She returned the laptop to his waiting hands. "I've opened the picture in an image editing program. We can try lightening the picture or zooming in with this menu."

"Ingenious."

At least the constant need to adapt to the human world meant he was a quick study. He adjusted the brightness and enlarged the gargoyle's features.

The face of the gargoyle in the image became clear, and he straightened, his heart racing in his chest. "Kamen."

"You know him?"

"If any member of my legion could be compared to the human equivalent of a brother, it would be him." Garrett wiped a palm over his mouth, hardly daring to believe. His best friend *hadn't* betrayed him. A great invisible weight lifted off his body so quickly he laughed at the sense of lightness. "You were right. By the Maker, you were right."

Raquel squeezed his forearm. "I'm so glad."

"How can we get more information about where he is?" He offered the laptop again.

She took the device and clicked on the picture in the search page. "Oh! He's here in New York. This page is for a walking tour of gargoyles in the city." Her face drooped into a frown.

"What's wrong?"

Another one of those superficial smiles formed on her lips. "Nothing's wrong."

"Raquel..."

She sighed. "It's just—" She shoved her hair behind her ear and shifted on the bed to focus on him. "I don't believe in coincidences. Things that look out of place are telling us something. I mean, why is he in the same city—across the ocean from the portal—that you are? Yeah, New York City has a lot of gargoyles on its buildings, but other places do too."

"Perhaps he was searching for me when he was caught by stone-death."

"Maybe." She set the laptop on the corner of the mattress and stood from the bed, fidgeting. "But stone-death started for you closer to the portal, right?"

"Correct. My regiment took turns watching the portal as the remainder traveled within a few hours' range to find human females with whom we could create bonds. I'd established a bond with a woman in France and was on my way back to the portal when I succumbed to stone-death—I know not why."

He paused. Now that he thought about it, he truly did *not* know why, as the moon cycle had not yet reset. Could the portal have been damaged while he was in France, making his stone-death immediate upon the bond severing? Perhaps that clue would help his investigation.

He continued his explanation. "As a statue, I was moved several times by humans and eventually brought here." He stood beside her and held her hands before she could twist her fingers any more. "What are you trying to say?"

"You were in stone-death long before you were brought here, and if the rest of your regiment didn't last much longer, explaining why they never had time to rescue you, Kamen couldn't have been looking for you *here* before he succumbed—because you wouldn't have been here yet. So doesn't it seem suspicious that you were both brought here after the fact?"

"Or maybe most gargoyles *are* attached to buildings, so our statues—which *can* be relocated—might be interesting trophies for humans."

Her shoulders relaxed, and she smiled for real. "You're right. You might not know this about me yet, but I can be a bit paranoid."

Her casual reference to what he'd always heard was a serious mental delusion shook him, and the urge to correct her burst from his mouth. "You are not mentally ill."

"Aren't I? It sure feels to me like I'm broken, and that pisses me off." She shook her head, dismissing the subject. "I just meant that I'm easily over-suspicious."

"That's a common quality among good soldiers."

Her smile broadened into a grin, and she laughed and bumped against his arm. "You say the nicest things." She nodded toward the laptop on the bed. "Okay, so how do we help him?"

*We...* He hadn't thought to the next step yet, but her willingness to stick by him left his mouth dry.

"I—" His voice cracked with emotion, and he cleared his throat. "I'm not sure yet. Usually to help a gargoyle escape stone-death, we'd do something..." He swallowed. "Something that I think would be frowned upon in this day and age."

She rolled her eyes. "I can imagine. You need a woman willing to trust a stone sculpture. That would probably take lots of alcohol and manipulation."

He didn't deny her guess, especially as it wasn't that far off.

"Could I do it? Can a woman be bonded to two gargoyles at the same time?"

The fluttery feelings in his stomach hardened. Logically, he knew—recognized—that she was only trying to be helpful. But his breaths strangled in his windpipe at the casual way she mentioned bonding to another gargoyle. It shouldn't hurt when she was simply offering her help, but there it was.

Betrayal? Was that what this was?

Yet he didn't revert to stone-death, so she didn't really mean her words. She wasn't really changing her intentions. She wasn't really disloyal.

At least not yet.

Every woman reached that point eventually. Every woman's intentions would waver from their bond at some point. After all, that's how he'd been trapped in stone-death.

The woman in France must have betrayed their bond soon after he'd left to return to the portal. Perhaps a flirtation with someone in her village or a longing glance at a passing stranger—he never knew the details of how their intentions changed. All he knew was that her betrayal had happened so quickly that he hadn't yet established a replacement bond with another woman.

The story was the same every time he'd slipped into stone-death. Betrayal was unavoidable due to the nature of the bond.

He'd accepted that fact centuries ago. So why did the thought of Raquel's inevitable betrayal hurt deeper?

Perhaps it was because he sensed a kindred spirit and wanted her to be different from the rest. Perhaps he wanted her loyalty to him as a fellow soldier. Or perhaps it was something else he couldn't yet fathom.

He crossed his arms and let the hardness in his stomach infuse the other organs in his chest. "No. If a woman changes the focus of her intentions—changes allegiance, so to speak—even through an attraction to a human male, the gargoyle of her current bond is condemned to stone-death."

His gaze sought the window, where the eruption of human development outside proved how much the world had changed. "In the days when the portal was open, we'd have until the setting of the next full moon to find a replacement, as the magic flowing from the Mythos plane through the open portal could sustain us for a while. But now that the portal is closed, the condemnation is immediate."

As his last bond had proven, it had always been difficult to establish a replacement bond before a betrayal. A bond required time and attention to ensure the woman's focus didn't wander, so it eroded more quickly if a gargoyle directed some of his attention toward the next bond.

But at least back then he'd had some time to establish the replacement bond *after* the fact, depending on the timing of the moon cycle. In today's world, the lack of a grace period required setting up a replacement bond *before* a betrayal, and with society as it was now, that would be a difficult task. No, an *impossible* task.

Even if he managed it once, simply due to Raquel's understanding, what about the next time? And the time after that? He wouldn't get this lucky with a woman like her again.

Weight, like that of impending doom, squeezed him from all sides. He collapsed onto the edge of the bed and held his head in his hands.

Long-term, the only solution was to restore the portal. Restore the portal, and he and Kamen and every other member of his regiment trapped here would at least have the grace period once again.

He searched the light-outlined horizon through the window, desperate to see hope in the distance. But his determination to do right by his regiment didn't change the truth that could no longer be ignored.

He was a fool to think he'd be able to single-handedly solve the mystery of the portal and rescue his regiment. *Supreme commander* was merely an assignment he'd been granted by his legion back home after Alann abandoned the mission. He'd never inherited the magical abilities needed to do the job.

If he weren't a pretender to the position, he'd have *known* Kamen was still on the Earthen plane. As supreme commander, he was *supposed* to know—to feel—his entire regiment's location, status, and health at all times, to assist in the case of stone-death. His bonds weren't supposed to require trust either, to increase his own chances of avoiding stone-death.

Instead, he was nothing but a poor substitute for a deserter. His inadequacies were far more dangerous than a mere inconvenience, and he was paying for his failings now.

Besides, he hadn't been on duty during whatever calamity occurred to the portal, so if anything, he was the least qualified of his regiment to lead the inquiry. Yet even if he allowed Kamen, who *had* been at the portal, to take his place, the answers might still be elusive.

The quest for a solution might require a succession of his regiment to awaken—relying on a willing human female to bond to them one at a time if necessary—until one knew enough about the portal's damage to fix it. The best commander to mend the portal and help his regiment was someone who could oversee and coordinate information from each awakening to understand the full picture.

Raquel sat beside him and rested a palm on his shoulder. "I'm sorry. I wish I could help."

He stiffened. The answer coalesced in front of him. He almost wished he hadn't seen it—a way his mission could be fulfilled...

By relinquishing her.

# Chapter Twenty

ON THE BED, RAQUEL PIVOTED TOWARD GARRETT AND analyzed the dozens of emotions flickering over his face. What she wouldn't give to know what was going through his head.

In many ways, he reminded her of the soldiers she knew. Did that mean his mental process worked the same? Were his thoughts the same *leave no man behind* loyalty she'd feel in his place?

He took her hand off his shoulder and nuzzled her knuckles against his cheeks. His eyes pierced into hers, searching.

"You are willing to help me with my mission?"

"Uh, that depends on what mission you're talking about. The portal's closed, right?"

"I'm referring to the mission I spoke of in the park last week—discovering what happened to my regiment and the portal. If the rest of them are caught in stone-death, as Kamen is, the answers to what happened to the portal and what can be done to fix it are likely locked away with them. Uncovering that knowledge is the current mission—so the portal can be reopened, and all can be rescued. "

His jaw shifted, and his gaze darted away for a second. "I fear I judged them too harshly—that they did *not* abandon or betray me, but were caught in bad circumstances the same way I was."

He slid off the bed and knelt in front of her, clasping her hand between both of his.

"If that's true, I *must* show my loyalty to them by helping them, even if it requires a sacrifice. I *must* act as supreme commander and do what is best for them."

She threaded the fingers of her other hand into his hair. He was such an odd mixture of indestructible strength and heartbreaking vulnerability.

"I understand." Loyalty was everything.

He pressed her knuckles to his lips. "So are you willing to help me help *them*? To accept the responsibility of discovering the answer of the portal so that *all* might be awoken? To rescue them from their death?"

Her breath caught, and her pulse thudded in her ears. The picture of her guys on the wall drew her eye. These were *Garrett's* guys, and he wanted to *save* them. More than that, he was offering her the opportunity to help.

The answer rose up her throat so fast the words nearly tangled on the way. "Y–yes, of course I'll help you save them."

His eyes closed, and he sucked in air on a giant sigh. "Thank you. Your loyalty to me is more than I could have ever hoped."

"But how can I help? I thought you said I wouldn't be able to bring another gargoyle out of stone-death."

"You *can* bring Kamen out of stone-death." He seized her gaze. His stare was deep enough that if she had a soul, he'd see it. "By betraying me."

*Betrayal?* She yanked back as though electrically shocked. Jostled, her laptop slid off the edge of the mattress.

*Bang!*

She recoiled, drawing her legs in tight and taking cover. Shit! An explosion? How close?

The bang ricocheted in her head, opening a swirling vortex of memories of her failure. Of her betrayal.

Betrayal went against every fiber of her being. Yet through her mistakes, she'd betrayed her team and condemned them to death. She rocked forward, her spine curving, protecting.

Darkness invaded from all sides. Infecting her senses. Wiping out her surroundings. Her hold on reality.

Her arm... Her arm was on fire.

She scrambled backward, but there was no pain. No sensations at all. Her instincts to put out the flames faded, and instead she stared, transfixed and horrified.

Pieces of flesh burned off her arm and fell onto the ground. A few ash-thin slivers drifted onto the hair of her translator, Anosha, who lay with wide-open eyes, accusing, witnessing her failure.

Anosha waved to her entrails littering the dirt. "You did this. You failed and killed me."

A surge of pain ripped through Raquel's chest, bringing sensations back in an explosive blaze. The space inside her ribs felt empty of anything but agony, just like Anosha's.

Shame dragged her head toward the ground. "I know. I know. I'm sorry. I never meant to get you killed."

"But you did." A deep voice resonated from the empty ribcage, and Raquel looked up to see Lewis's face on the body. "You did get me killed. You got us all killed."

"I know." She sobbed. If she'd been smarter about the suicide bomber, less ambiguous in her instructions to Anosha, quicker to warn her guys, clearer with her radio message, or stronger, or faster, or louder... If she'd been *better*. "I'm sorry. I'm so sorry."

"I had a family." Ramirez now denounced her from the ripped-open body, where the bloodstain spread across the ground. "I had a wife and daughter. Why did you let me die?"

"I failed. I wasn't good enough." She clawed at her face, as though she could dig past the ugly truth and find a happier ending hiding under the surface. "I should have known that woman was a suicide bomber. I should have known the insurgents were planning something. I should have asked better questions during my time with the villagers to know, to gather that intel. I should have held on to my radio while crawling. I should have stopped you from coming to my aid."

"But you didn't. You didn't keep your promise to me." Crockett's indictment sliced deepest of all, and she doubled over. Dry heaves wracked her stomach with each charge. "You betrayed me. You betrayed us all with your failure."

"I know. I failed at everything." If only her nails were longer, she might be able to tear the weaknesses from her body. "I never should have believed I was a real soldier who could measure up. I never should have let you respect me. I never should have let you care about me."

Stings from her chest gave her hope that she might be able to dig deep enough, cut her betrayal out of her heart.

"If you didn't care"—she sucked in a breath and let the horrifying truth burn up her throat— "you wouldn't have come. You would have stayed away. You would have lived." Tears choked the rest of her words.

She should have been the one to die. She'd been at the front of the ambush, and yet she'd survived. She'd survived them all.

Her warnings hadn't been clear enough. Her shouts hadn't been loud enough. Her crawling to get to them—to show them she didn't need rescuing—hadn't been fast enough.

And instead of staying away, they'd tried to save her. Trapped in narrow streets riddled with newly planted mines, they hadn't stood a chance. One mine had knocked them back into others, in an explosive parody of a dominoes game. The ambush had caught them all.

All but one.

She'd survived. And her ongoing weakness only proved that she didn't deserve to live.

She'd been too weak then, and she was too weak now. Falling apart in civilian life. Letting PTSD take hold. Never good enough to deserve her guys. Never good enough...

Her heart and lungs and stomach twisted so hard that screams clawed up her throat, digging, shredding. She didn't want to live. She didn't want to survive. Not when so many others who were more worthy hadn't come back.

"Rocky, listen to me." She recognized the deep voice but couldn't place it, not here in her tortured memories. What stuck out most was that the voice had called her Rocky and was commanding like Crockett's.

Strong hands gripped her head and forced her to look up. The gray eyes that met hers seemed familiar too, but what she recognized most is that they were intense like Crockett's.

"I'm sorry, Crockett. I'm so sorry. You depended on me, the whole team depended on me, and I betrayed you by not being good enough. I didn't measure up. I didn't—"

"Rocky, I'm ordering you to listen."

Her mouth snapped shut.

"Rocky, I forgive you."

"No!" She fought, trying to tear the hands away from the sides of her head. "I don't want forgiveness. I don't deserve forgiveness."

"You do deserve it." He ignored her struggles and kept her focus on him. "You *are* good enough."

"No, everyone died because of me." The truth choked her, sobs breaking her voice. "Because I couldn't prevent it. Because I couldn't keep you away, where it was safe. Because I didn't know there were villagers willing to betray us. I should have known."

"Rocky, listen to me. We *all* should have known. We're a team. That means you alone cannot be responsible."

She stopped fighting. "And I should have died with my team. I shouldn't have lived."

"Rocky..." He stroked her dampened hair back from her temples. "I forgive you for being alive."

"No..." She felt around his grasp, but his hands blocked access to sticking her fingertips in her ears. "That's not possible. How can you not hate me?"

"Because you haven't forgotten any of us. Your loyalty still stands as strong as ever. By honoring us, you honor yourself."

Something about Crockett's words felt off, as though they weren't the words he'd choose, but her brain was in no shape to figure out why. Not when the ugliness of the truth demanded to be heard.

"It's not enough. Nothing I do is ever enough."

"Rocky, listen to me. You did your best. That *is* enough. That's all any of us can do."

She clutched his shirt, desperate to make him understand. "I wanted to be better. I wanted to do more."

"We all want that, but that's no reason to blame yourself for something beyond your control."

"But if you didn't care about me, you wouldn't have tried to save me. You wouldn't have died."

"Good soldiers always care about each other. That's what loyalty means. We watch out for each other. That's not your fault."

Her muscles had loosened from their cramped positions, and

now she tugged him to lie beside her. She buried her face in his chest. "I wanted better for you, Crockett. I wanted better for them all. I wanted Anosha to gain confidence. I wanted Ramirez to get home to his wife and kid. I wanted Lewis to be able to stand up to his dad when he got home."

He hugged her tight and ran his fingers over her hair. "I know, Rocky. I know. But we all want better for you too. Blaming yourself for this is no way to live."

She shoved against the warmth settling around her heart. She didn't want to forgive herself. She didn't want to move on. But each stroke of his hand lulled her closer to peace.

Time had no meaning here, but after a long period, her sobs settled into calm breaths.

"Crockett?"

He made a non-committal grunt.

"Did you ever think about me *that* way? Like, that after our deployment, you'd want to try a relationship with me?"

He stiffened and didn't answer. She was sorry for bringing up the thing he couldn't have. After a moment, he offered, "I'd expect almost any man would think about you that way."

"You included?"

He kissed the top of her head. "You make me think about you in ways I've never thought about any woman."

"I'm sorry for that too then. I always suspected you might wish for that, and I pushed you away because I needed to be respected more than I wanted a relationship. I wanted to be seen as a soldier first. Not as a woman. If I'd known..."

She swallowed, the confession like ripping off the last bandage. "I'm sorry for pushing you away. It wasn't you. That desperate need for respect, for someone to think me *good enough*, that's just how I was." She sighed, letting the truth take hold of her voice. "How I still am."

"I understand." His caresses paused for a second and then resumed. "Is that why you don't *date*?"

The way he emphasized the word *date* reminded her of someone other than Crockett, but the image she was searching for slipped from her thoughts, flowing like her tears.

"Yes, but it's more complicated than that. My whole life, my father told me that I didn't deserve happiness. That I'd destroy the lives of anyone who got too close to me. Complications from my birth that almost killed my mamá, my brother's death, everything that happened to you and the team. All of it proved him right. It's just easier not to let anyone close."

"Your father lied to you." The stone-cold hardness in his voice left no room for doubt. "You deserve happiness more than most. Besides, a good soldier knows when to take risks too."

"Maybe..." A leftover shudder from her crying fit trembled through her body.

"Shh." He squeezed her and kissed the top of her head again. "Rest now. I'll keep you safe."

Now that he mentioned it, exhaustion overcame her. The emotional breakdown had drained every bit of her energy.

"You'll protect me?"

"Always, my beautiful warrior. Always."

Those definitely weren't the words of Crockett, but sleep stole through her mind before she could make sense of them. Her nightmares stayed away, banished for the night while she slept in the arms of forgiveness.

# Chapter Twenty-One

WITH A GENTLE TOUCH, GARRETT HELD RAQUEL IN HIS arms and stroked her tear-streaked hair. Many soldiers fought the demons of memories and guilt, and he'd witnessed the effects several times, both in humans and in gargoyles. He'd thought no one's inner nightmares could affect him like those of his former commander, Alann, who had followed the haunting loss of his dead son into a darkness so deep Garrett hadn't been able to reach him.

He'd been wrong. None had ever ripped out his heart like Raquel's suffering.

Every torturous image, sound, emotion, and thought she'd experienced was *his* fault. Like for him, loyalty was everything to her, and asking her to betray him had triggered her buried self-hatred. He'd *caused* her pain.

When she'd first started seeing things that weren't there, he'd thought calling her name or seizing her wrists would have been enough. But she'd fought him so much the bedcovers were now in a heap at the end of the mattress.

If he hadn't remembered the nickname she'd told him about from her military days, he might not have been able to get through to her. As it was, his care to ensure he didn't break her bones meant he hadn't been able to stop her before she'd clawed ragged scratches into her face and chest. He never wanted to be responsible for hurting her again.

Perhaps he'd misjudged her. She didn't seem *capable* of betraying anyone. Did that mean that as long as he respected their bond, she would too? That, unlike the others, she wouldn't betray him in a matter of weeks or months? That he was not, in fact, doomed?

If so, the gift she gave him was invaluable. He couldn't risk their bond again.

Days ago, resentment had colored his responses to her because he hated the thought of needing to be dependent on *anyone*. But in truth, his life had always been that way. It was the nature of his kind's survival on the Earthen plane, and it was unfair to take his anger at that situation out on her. She'd treated him honorably, and he should do the same.

If he *had* to be dependent on anyone, she was a far better person to be beholden to than any other human he'd encountered. And if he had the opportunity to extend his time with her by treating her well, it was in his best interest to do so.

Tension released from his jaw, and his frustration flowed away with the surrender to his fate. Yes, he needed to bond to a human, but he might actually find enjoyment in bonding to *this* human. Any work to strengthen their bond might not feel like work at all.

He would find another way to help Kamen and the rest of his regiment. Just as much as they deserved Garrett's loyalty, she deserved his loyalty too. Perhaps even more so, as she'd not been created with the instinct to remain by his side, but instead had freely chosen to do so.

Another quiver and a stray hiccup shook her body. He slid his fingers between his chest and her forehead. "Peace."

She snuggled deeper in his arms and settled. Her trust honored him like nothing else, and his throat grew thick. If only he could solve all their problems as easily.

What was he to do to wake up Kamen now? Even if he managed to find a suitable human female, the methods his kind used to trick a woman into awakening a gargoyle from stone-death would betray Raquel's trust in him. She expected him to be a "decent guy," and he had far too much damage to repair with her already. He wouldn't take on the risk of further betrayal unless absolutely necessary.

On some level, she needed to be his top priority. If he lost her, he'd have no chance to attempt any other step of his plan.

He breathed deep, accepting his limitations, and nuzzled his lips into her hair. Yes, Kamen and the others had been in their stone-death state for decades at least, and they could wait a bit longer while he came up with a plan that would meet with her approval. Far better to ensure his bond with Raquel was strong and enduring.

Hours later, she stirred and blinked, confusion creasing her eyes. Filtered early morning sunlight illuminated the room, and he examined her injuries the best he could without moving. Surprisingly, the scratches on her face and neck had mostly healed, already just light pink lines. The biggest physical sign of her ordeal was her lashes clumped together with the grit of tears and sleep.

He loosened his hold, but wasn't going to let go until he knew the state of her mind. "Shh. It's all right. You're safe."

Her gaze darted around, trying to make sense of the situation no doubt. He wasn't sure what she remembered—or more importantly, what she *wanted* to remember—so he remained silent, other than his calming words, and let her work out the details the best she could on her own first.

Her mouth pulled down at the corners. "I had a really bad flashback last night, didn't I?"

Flashback? That must be the term for reliving past memories. "Yes. I'm sorry."

She looked near tears again. "That's the worst I've ever had—full-on hallucinations like something out of a horror movie. Secondary psychotic symptoms, just like the counselor warned might happen if my PTSD got worse." Her lips quivered. "I don't want to get worse."

He didn't think his heart could have sunk any deeper into the morass of guilt weighing down his chest, but it did. "I'm so sorry." He stroked her hair the same as he'd been doing for hours. "I didn't mean to cause that reaction. I never should have put you into that situation."

Pink spread across her cheeks. "I called you Crockett."

"And I called you Rocky." With his thumb, he brushed the tip of her lip, which was still trembling. "Don't feel embarrassed or ashamed. I understand."

He understood her far better than he'd ever thought he'd understand a human. An odd feeling suffused his chest, like a subtle shift in how he perceived the situation. The feeling wasn't uncomfortable by any means, but his instincts wanted to rip it away regardless.

Perhaps making light of the moment would loosen the tension and calm his instincts. "I'd call you Queen and let you call me a pompous buffoon if it'd help."

She laughed with a high-pitched, nervous giggle. "I don't think that will be necessary."

"All right, but let me know if you change your mind."

Her muscles relaxed within the hold of his arms. "You stayed with me all night."

"Of course." He caught her gaze, and the feeling in his chest strengthened again. "I promised to keep you safe. Always."

Her expression softened. "Thank you."

The vulnerable look in her eyes triggered the urge to enact habits centuries deep. He could so easily manipulate her in this moment, as he had with countless women throughout the years.

A part of him wanted to take advantage of her weakness, but another part—a stronger part—refused to condone that path. Besides, she'd seen through his other manipulation attempts, so trying to best her in that regard would only endanger their bond. Not to mention that he'd exposed so many vulnerabilities around her that he'd started questioning whether he even *could* lie to her anymore. No doubt, it was better to strengthen their bond without manipulation.

Instead of dwelling on the consequences of that decision, he changed the subject to state a truth that needed saying. "I'm sorry for your loss." His thumb drew circles on her cheek. "That's not a request to talk about it with me, but I want you to know that I'm sorry for everything you've endured."

Her eyes closed, and she nodded. "Thank you." Her front teeth worried at her bottom lip. "Did you mean what you said—about me deserving forgiveness?"

He tipped up her chin. "Every word." He paused, organizing his thoughts, and stroked her cheek. "We don't have to talk about it unless you want, but from what I gathered, these villagers were supposed to be allies of a sort, and they betrayed you and your team. You're not to blame for that. They are the only ones responsible for their actions. As I said last night, blaming yourself for things beyond your control is no way to live."

"I just wish..."

He trailed his fingers over her hair again, as that seemed to soothe her, and let her work out her words.

"I wish things were different."

"I understand." He tightened their embrace. "For your sake, I wish that too."

"Do you?" She leaned back and regarded him, her mouth teasing him with a curve. "If I weren't so broken, you'd still be in stone-death."

He grinned. "I can still wish you didn't have to suffer."

Her smile faded. "Maybe if I were stronger—better—this wouldn't bother me as much. Maybe the fact that I'm so broken proves how unworthy I am of being a soldier."

"No." He pressed a finger to her lips. "Never think that. Hell can break even the best of us."

His reaction when he first learned of his regiment's disappearance and the closed portal flashed in his memory. A confession probably wouldn't improve her impression of him, but she deserved to know she wasn't alone.

"My first night in this century, after the boulder delivered its news, I broke as well. No one—human or gargoyle—is meant to sustain emotional or mental pain without damage." He glanced away but forced himself to meet her gaze again. "I thought about giving up. But I didn't. Just like you didn't give up. *That's* what makes you strong."

Her fingers inched up from his chest and rested on his jaw. "I'm sorry I wasn't there to help you through that, and I'm glad you didn't give up."

Oh, his sweet Raquel. The pressure in his chest expanded outward until a lump formed in his throat. How could she be focused on him while he was trying to console her? He didn't deserve her concern.

"Just as I'm glad you didn't give up." His voice was thick. He nodded toward her shoulder. "If you sustained your scars in that battle, you obviously fought hard to survive."

She shook her head. "Not for my sake. The suicide bomber's explosion instantly killed my translator, knocked me unconscious, ruptured my eardrums—rendering me deaf for two months—and burned my exposed skin. Our unit was so remote we hadn't received our flame-resistant uniforms yet, and the fire burned through my clothes, giving me second and third degree burns where the fabric held the flames against my skin. But all I could think about was getting my guys to save themselves."

He didn't speak for fear that she'd take it as a request for her to continue. If she wanted to talk, he wanted to be there for her, supportive, but he didn't want to pressure her in any way. He couldn't risk losing her willingness to respond to him, not like what had happened to Alann.

"They were caught in an ambush. Enemy ordinances—explosives—had been hidden along their path in a daisy-chain. I later learned that I managed to crawl toward them one-armed for half a block, trying to prevent them from coming closer, but I eventually passed out from shock and blood loss. By the time the rescue team arrived the next day, the insurgents in the village had left me for dead. The doctors kept me in a medically induced coma for weeks while they started the skin graft treatment. My crawling over rocks and dirt left my arm and leg so dirty and infected they had to do multiple rounds of grafting. I was lucky they didn't amputate."

His mouth had dropped open. However strong he'd thought she was before, he was wrong. He'd wildly underestimated her.

"Even in the hospital, I fought to survive because I wanted to get back to my guys. I wanted to show them I was okay. So they wouldn't worry." Her face scrunched up, and her eyes glistened. "Because of my temporary deafness, it was easy for the medical team to keep the truth from me—that I was the only survivor." Her jaw hardened, and she swallowed. "When I finally learned what had happened, all I could think was that I wanted to be dead."

He held her tight. "There's no shame in that."

"So when you asked me to help you save your regiment..." Her voice faltered, and he knew what she couldn't say. A part of her wanted to save his regiment as a surrogate rescue for what she hadn't been able to do for her team, but she couldn't betray him, even for that. Not without losing herself in the process.

"I'm sorry. I never should have asked that of you. I'll figure out another way to help them. Don't think of it for another second."

Her lips pinched together. "Are you sure?"

"Positive." His voice strengthened with his determination, and he gave her a smile. "I hope you won't think poorly of me if I've decided that I value our bond too much to even *want* you to do that anymore. The loyalty I feel toward you is as strong as the loyalty I feel toward them. I cannot prioritize their needs over yours."

She trembled in his arms. "Thank you for understanding."

"Truly. You honor me with *your* loyalty." Whether his motivation to speak honestly had more to do with the bond he needed from her or from his acknowledgment of what she deserved, he didn't know. Did it matter? "Part of my mission now is honoring your trust. I intend to never lose our bond through any action or inaction on my part."

She stiffened. A flicker of fear and denial alighted on her face, but only a wry smile settled down to stay. "No backup women for you?"

A knot of tension he hadn't been aware of between his shoulders now loosened. Her first response had been to ensure that she understood his level of loyalty to her and not to protest that she didn't want him around indefinitely. That fact gave him hope that he might not be far off in his judgment of her and the potential longevity of their bond.

"Never. You deserve better. You deserve *my* loyalty."

Her smile broadened into a grin, and she opened her mouth, appearing about to speak. The alarm from her phone interrupted the moment.

"Crap!" She shot out of his arms and sat up. "I have to get ready for work." She bent down and gave him a kiss on his cheek. "Thank you for everything."

Then she was gone, headed for the shower. So much for their moment.

He shoved away the disappointment of a lost opportunity to build on their connection. He planned to have many more opportunities in the future.

Instead, his focus needed to be on what he *could* accomplish today. He'd let his mind work on the puzzle of awakening Kamen while he strove to move forward in other aspects of his mission. Perhaps something to do with checking on the status of the portal. Or even learning more about how to adjust to this time and Raquel's world.

He was back on the laptop when she came out of the shower.

She detoured from her usual straight path to the door and stopped to touch his arm. "Hey, real quick before I leave. I'm thinking of telling Brianna that we'll be there tomorrow for her movie marathon thing. Is that all right with you?"

"Of course." He fought to keep a straight expression. "I'd love to go to a planned event with you for a not-date."

Somehow, she managed to narrow and roll her eyes at the same time. "Ha. Just for that, I *won't* thank you again."

After the door closed behind her, he let his grin stretch his mouth. He didn't need her thanks. The fact that she'd volunteered to go out in public with him on a *not-date* was thanks enough.

In fact, it might even be better.

# Chapter Twenty-Two

R AQUEL CLOSED HER APARTMENT DOOR BEHIND HER AND dumped her backpack on the kitchenette's counter. No one greeted her. How could such a tiny room feel empty enough to seem big?

"Garrett?" No answer.

While she was at work, he'd made the bed and left a note on top of the mattress. Beautiful flowing handwriting decorated the paper.

*My Dearest Raquel,*

*I am hoping to return before you arrive, but if I succeed in my quest to procure a surprise for you, I might be late. Do not worry for me.*

*Yours Always,*
*Garrett*

*Do not worry for me?* Of course, now that he told her not to worry, that's all she could think about. He'd left to wander New York City in daytime by himself? What was he thinking? A surprise for her? He was entirely too...

She sank onto the bed, clutching the note, and her hand shook. Their conversation this morning replayed in her mind. All his talk about honoring her and protecting their bond "for always" had sounded nice in the moment, but she hadn't thought he was serious. Or at least not *seriously* serious.

The tangible evidence now in her hands stirred her doubts. Between the formal handwriting and language and words like *dearest* and *yours always*, maybe he really meant it. Maybe he meant to change his attitude toward commitment.

She dropped the note and clenched the edge of the bed. Air hissed through her teeth with her quick breaths. Commitment? That wasn't what she wanted. That wasn't her goal. Was it?

No, absolutely not.

Her screwed-up flashback episode with Garrett in the place of Crockett might have succeeded in a bizarre way at starting the process of forgiving herself, but that didn't mean she was magically healed and ready to move forward all Pollyanna-ish. The studies she'd seen on psychomotor therapy—with PTSD sufferers purposely reliving their experiences with a surrogate in the role of the source of their trauma—didn't convince her that any effects would be long-lasting. It'd be premature to declare herself suddenly ready for a relationship. She didn't believe in magic wands.

A tiny voice in the back of her head reminded her that three weeks ago, she wouldn't have believed in magical shapeshifting gargoyles either. Yeah, whatever. Not relevant.

Besides, for all she knew, his attention and those words were his latest attempt to manipulate her. *That* was far more likely than anything else.

Clicks sounded as someone fumbled with the locked doorknob. Garrett's voice resonated through the door. "Raquel?"

She snorted at the thought of being taken in by his manipulation and opened the door. He entered and burst into a grin when his eyes met hers.

Tension melted from her shoulders. She might not believe his motives, but she could still be glad he'd made it back safely.

"I'm glad you're home." His smile turned charmingly embarrassed. "After I left, I realized I didn't have a way to get back inside without breaking the lock."

"I'm glad it didn't come to that. I can't afford the repair."

His smile deepened, and he slid a duffel bag—one of hers by the looks of it—off his shoulder. As he set the bag down, the contents shifted and sounded accompanying *clinks*. His gaze snapped to the bag, and a wince flickered over his face. He strode toward her and picked the note off the floor.

"I hope you saw this right away and didn't worry."

"Yeah, about that. I'm paranoid, remember?" She returned to the bed and sat down to prevent herself from agitatedly pacing around the room. "Telling me not to worry doesn't work."

"Hmm, I didn't take that into consideration. At least I hope I didn't make you wait too long."

"I got home just a few minutes ago." She eyed the bag. "Are you going to tell me what you were up to, or am I supposed to guess?"

"Is something wrong? You seem tense." His gaze turned scrutinizing. "Did I upset you by leaving? Or by coming back?"

"Well, I was worried about you, just because this *is* New York City, which can be overwhelming to anyone, much less someone who spent the last couple of centuries asleep. But I'm not upset—not at you anyway."

"That is *not* reassuring." He sat beside her and held her hand. "Why are you upset at yourself?"

"I didn't say I was upset at myself." At his arched brow, she admitted, "Yeah, okay, that's what I meant."

She debated whether to be honest with him. He already knew her better than anyone else, but was that knowledge only making him better at manipulating her? On the other hand, if she put him on notice that she knew about his manipulations, maybe he'd stop, and she wouldn't have to question herself.

She withdrew from his grasp and pivoted toward him—the better to watch his expression. "I'm upset with myself because I almost believed all your words and actions meant something, rather than being the latest round of manipulation, and I almost believed you were serious about committing long term to whatever our bond is. I hadn't realized I was so..." Only one word fit. "Gullible."

His face furrowed, etched in pain, and he scrubbed a palm over his mouth. "I suppose I deserve that." He sighed. "I can't ask you to believe me when I say that I *am* committed—for the long term—because I haven't earned that level of trust, and I have to accept that it might take months or years for you to see the truth in my words. But I swear I speak the truth—I swear on the soul of my future child."

Blood drained from her face and body, stopping only when the flow reached the floor. Thank God she was already sitting, or her legs would have collapsed. Given what she understood of gargoyles' beliefs about souls and their inability to have more than one child, he'd sworn on the most powerful concept he could imagine.

He reached toward her and then pulled back, apparently deciding not to push her. "*You* are my priority, not just for now, but for my intended future. Yes, I'm still concerned about my regiment and the portal because those are my duty, but *you*—the bond we share—are my priority." An earnest sparkle shone from his eyes. "Ask me any question you wish, and I promise to answer honestly. No manipulation."

The idea that he might be speaking the truth swirled her thoughts. She wasn't ready for that possibility, and she wasn't sure how she felt about any aspect of the issue. Either he was once more very convincingly lying to her, manipulating her, or he meant that he *was* committed to her. Not just for a temporary bond, but for the foreseeable future.

Definitely not ready to dive into that uncertainty or the consequences of either situation.

She started and stopped several replies. Finally, she answered with the only fact she knew.

"I need some time to think about this. Let's pause this conversation and hold the questioning for later."

He gave a somber nod. "Understood."

"Although..." A tiny smile slid over her mouth. "You *can* tell me what's in the bag."

His grin reappeared. "Your wish is my command."

# Chapter Twenty-Three

CURIOSITY DREW RAQUEL CLOSER TO THE DUFFEL BAG GARRETT hauled up onto the mattress. As he set the bag down, the contents once again clinked.

His eyes lit up like a soldier inspecting a new kick-ass weapon. "Do you remember how I told you my plan to collect precious metals and gems while we were in the park?"

"Oh no." Her gaze shot to the bag. "Please tell me you didn't steal what's in there. There are laws about mining rights for people who own the land. You can't just take things you've dug from the ground."

He frowned, and his brows tightened. "*I* didn't have anything to do with this, and they weren't *dug* from the ground."

"I don't understand."

"The boulder. The one who's been so helpful to me. It overheard our conversation when I told you of my plans and has spent the past week directing the Earth to flow these toward it in the park."

"Wait, let me get this straight." Her arms itched to move, and she yanked her hair back and spun it into a bun. The motion wasn't like wringing anyone's neck, but it was the best she could do. "The boulder in Central Park listened to our conversation, understood what you meant to do, and took it upon itself to send shiny stuff its way. And then the *Earth*—which can't *move*—managed to transport what's in this bag from wherever to here."

"Yes, the boulder was so pleased to be able to help. It had the Earth hail me when they had this ready, and even though the ground here is buried beneath the building, I was still able to hear the Earth's call well enough to come to their signal."

"Oh my God, I don't believe this." She held her forehead in her hands, rubbing at her temples. "You *literally* have a pet rock."

She tugged her hair out of her bun and then twisted it back up again for lack of anything else to do.

"Okay." She sighed. "But who did they steal these from?"

"Let's ask them." He grinned, unconcerned with the legal issues, and unzipped the duffel bag.

Within reach of her hand, several gold-infused mineral ores as large as her head mixed with gold nuggets in leaf-like and crystalline structures. At his end of the bag, striations lined yet another gold formation shaped like driftwood, and several clear and colored stones the size of marbles tumbled along the bottom.

This was worse than she thought. The pile had to be worth more than she made in ten years. Maybe a lifetime. Maybe ten lifetimes.

He brushed his fingers over the contents, listening to whatever he heard in his head. After a minute, he met her gaze and flashed his cocky smile. Had she missed that version of his smile? Her stomach flipped over at the refresher.

"You'll be happy to know that these came from deeper in the Earth than any human has ever reached."

"Okay. That's *less* bad, I guess." She shrugged, helpless to figure out the legality of the situation when the proper owner would never miss them. "How did they get here?" She held up her open palm. "So help me, if you tell me they grew little arms and legs and crawled through the earth, I'm checking myself into a mental hospital."

He chuckled. "No arms or legs." He tilted his head, listening again. "Are you familiar with the term *quantum physics*?"

"Uh, only enough to know that it doesn't make any sense. Something about a cat being both alive and dead at the same time until you check on it?"

He stared at her like she'd grown a second head.

"Er, I could be wrong."

"I fail to see what a confused cat has to do with the movement of particle waves passing through one another."

Her mouth dropped open—the term *agog* probably applied. "*You* understand quantum physics?"

Amusement lit his features. "Not at all, other than what they told me."

Well, sure... If she was willing to accept that a *boulder* overheard their conversation and communicated across the planet, why the hell shouldn't she accept that chunks of minerals and ores could change observable reality at will by applying quantum physics?

She threw up her hands. "I give up. The world no longer makes sense to me, and if I try to make it make sense, I'm going to lose what's left of my sanity."

"I've felt that way since I awoke." Despite his understanding words, his lips twitched, fighting what looked to be an amused curve.

She sighed so loudly the sound was halfway to a groan. Maybe if she squinted, she could see a point where advanced science became little different from magic, and thus the reverse could apply as well. The collection in the bag drew her attention again.

"What are you going to do with your windfall?"

He shoved the bag toward her. "Give it to you."

*What?* She waved her hands in front of her. "Oh no. I don't want it. Do you have any idea how much all that is worth?"

"No. Gold is so common on the Mythos plane its value is negligible, and I don't know how its scarcity here affects the value."

"I don't know either. I'd guess somewhere between a butt-ton and a metric butt-ton."

His brows drew together. "I'm not familiar with those units of measurement."

She couldn't help but laugh. The whole situation was beyond ridiculous. "That's because I made them up. It's Raquel-speak for *I have no idea, but it's a big number—maybe even an insanely big number.*"

"Ah. And why would that answer affect whether you wanted these?"

"I don't know." She gazed up at the ceiling, but no signs from above displayed to help her know how to proceed. "I've never had money, so to be faced with this crazy pile of valuables is a little overwhelming. Some people win a lot of money in a lottery and later say it destroyed their life because it was too much all at once.

I don't want that to happen to me."

"So my *pet rock* was overly eager to help?"

Between his teasing expression and his lilting tone of voice, she burst out in a full-blown guffaw. "Yeah, that's about it."

He selected the largest of the clear crystals and rolled the marble-sized rock onto her palm. "This one is for you—a diamond—and I'll keep the rest until you're ready for it."

A diamond? Brianna would be swooning if she knew Garrett had given her a diamond at all, much less this mondo-humongous one.

Under different circumstances, she probably wouldn't accept this gem from him either, but compared to the heap of treasure still in the bag, this one stone didn't seem so bad, especially as raw diamonds weren't much to look at. Maybe it would turn out to be industrial quality and worth only as much as she needed to repair his statue's dents in the ceiling.

Just because these rocks understood how to manipulate quantum physics didn't mean they understood the jewelry market. She could hope.

Thankfully, the rest of the evening passed uneventfully, especially once Garrett stashed the bag out of her sight. Others would probably think her insane, but what else was new?

The past twenty-four hours had pushed her ability to think logically to the breaking point, and she didn't like feeling that off-kilter. From the flashback episode to Garrett's proclamations of commitment, she couldn't handle his insane gift on top of the confused emotions already swirling in her head. Better to shove everything under the bed—literally—and forget all the doubts, fears, and debates for as long as possible.

But as bedtime approached, her jitters increased, her mind buzzing and muscles twitching like she'd downed a triple espresso. The shakes were so bad she didn't feel safe keeping her M9 under her pillow for the night, no matter how empty it was. And that was bad news all the way around.

When she emerged from the bathroom, ready to switch off the light, Garrett glanced up from his search for someone who could handle the raw diamond. Better that he was dealing with the thing than her. She'd probably dump it in a drawer somewhere and ignore it.

He eyed her with a furrowed brow. "What's wrong?"

To his credit, his tone wasn't frustrated or impatient—just concerned. Which, truth be told, she felt too.

"I'm not sure. I think the last day and night have used up all my coping ability, and another episode is lurking."

"Another flashback?"

She tugged at the hem of the T-shirt she'd put on for the night and nodded. He closed the laptop and approached her, arms outstretched. She hesitated only a second before stepping into his embrace.

This was probably sending him mixed messages all the way to the Mythos plane and back, but the way her muscles relaxed in his arms made the worry beside the point. "I'm sorry. I don't mean to be—I don't *want* to be—so broken, but..."

"Shh. Think nothing of it." He leaned and flicked off the light and then led her to the bed. "If you wish, I'll stay with you all night again. I'll keep you safe, and you won't have any nightmares."

"And you'll just..." She fought against the serenity settling in her chest by grasping at a last flicker of cynicism. "*Hold* me?"

He chuckled. "I promise not to try anything."

Was taking him up on his offer an admission of weakness? On the other hand, she'd managed to sleep after her episode last night while in his arms, *without* her security blanket under her pillow. Maybe he was another kind of security blanket.

And *that* thought was messed up in its own way, but she couldn't deny how safe he made her feel. She didn't want to trust him—she didn't want to trust anyone. Nevertheless, her emotions seemed to have different ideas. If he was putting on a manipulative act, it was damn convincing.

They lay down together, and he tucked her inside the protective wall of his body and limbs. Her breathing settled, and her jitters faded, banished by his soothing whispers and gentle strokes of her hair. Each motion loosened her muscles, and she burrowed deeper into his embrace. Drowsiness soon followed.

The last conscious thought passing through her mind was that maybe it wasn't such a bad thing if he was committed to her. She couldn't deny that a Garrett-shaped security blanket was quite nice.

# Chapter Twenty-Four

THE WORLD OUTSIDE THE TAXICAB'S WINDOW HELD GARRETT'S attention, but he stroked his thumb over the back of Raquel's hand. He wasn't sure which of them he was trying harder to keep calm with the motion.

It was odd enough to watch the surroundings zoom by when he was so close to the earth. More disconcerting, though, were the details beyond the glass.

However big the city had looked from the air, the ground-level view was more shocking. Endless roads and buildings emphasized how many places stone-death-affected members of his regiment could be hiding beyond Earthen witnesses.

They'd already crossed the bridge to Brooklyn—after Raquel had argued with the driver on his plan to take the tunnel she'd deemed a security risk—and now they meandered through streets that seemed so similar to each other he'd have guessed they were going in circles if his sense of direction weren't flawless. Brick building stuck to brick building in long blocks interrupted only by intersections of roads.

Beside him, Raquel was quiet, just as she'd been since the previous night. Hopefully her pensive mood wasn't about this not-date. He resolved to keep his attitude understated so as not to add stress to her thoughts.

The more he accepted how they could help each other, the

more his thoughts turned from simply keeping her safe to also keeping her happy. The happier she was with him, the stronger their bond would be.

Finally, the taxi stopped at a line of three-story buildings like countless others they'd passed. He and Raquel exited the cab, and she paid the fare. During the upcoming week, he'd have to follow through on the sale of the diamond so she wasn't struggling for money, and he wasn't dependent on her income. Perhaps he'd even be able to take her out for another not-date.

Raquel led him up to the front door of the building. Colored paint scribbles decorated the bricks of the next door over. She shook her head at the marks.

"Sheesh. They *still* haven't cleaned up that graffiti? I reported that before I moved out."

Inside, a narrow staircase brought them to the second story, and Raquel knocked on the door at the end of the hall. A squeal accosted him as soon as Brianna opened the door.

"Yay! You actually made it. Paula was sure you were going to bail."

He followed Raquel inside. The living area was bigger than her whole apartment, and the construction was obviously updated, but unlike her apartment, only one window at the end of the adjacent skinny kitchen allowed in any natural light. The bright-white walls and high-gloss wood floor were all that prevented the space from being oppressively dark. The differences between the two apartments illustrated her priorities, emphasizing how little she cared for the superficial appearance of her surroundings.

Unfamiliar spices scented the air from what he'd guess was some type of meat cooking in the kitchen. As he didn't require sustenance, he'd paid only passing attention to the different foods humans ate.

Raquel sniffed deeply, and her lips rolled into a pursed frown. "Don't tell me you're making roast pork. Going a little overboard, aren't you?"

"Yeah, hi to you too." Brianna's tone sounded more teasing than upset. "I have to make sure you're getting some real food in you. Besides..." She gave him a wink. "I figured Garrett deserved an introduction to our culture. Or at least our food, with a little roast pork and *mofongo*, and I knew *you* weren't going to cook for him."

"Food is food." Raquel shrugged. "Especially as we're not first generation or anything. We're closer to *Nuyorican* than Puerto Rican."

Brianna wagged her finger in a gesture that involved her whole arm. "Don't you use that word to describe *me*." Despite the biting words, their argument seemed to be a long-running joke between them rather than anything serious. "Being a Puerto Rican living in New York doesn't automatically make me a *Nuyorican*. *I* still speak Spanish and dream of visiting the island, unlike *some* people I know."

"Yeah, whatever. Sorry for not *celebrating* the culture my father used as an excuse for his bullshit."

Brianna's face fell. Apparently Raquel had diverged from the pattern of their usual banter.

"What's wrong, Kell?" The brashness had abandoned Brianna's voice, and she moved closer. "Did that asshole call you or something? You know that wasn't what I meant when—"

"Yeah, I know." Raquel backed away, her gaze searching down the hall toward a couple of half-closed doors. "Is Paula here?"

"Nope." Brianna's expression recovered at the change of subject, and she rolled her eyes. "She and our new roomie are like this." She twisted her index and middle fingers together. "They're doing a whole girly shopping thing."

A tiny smile crept over Raquel's face for the first time that day. "I'm surprised you're not with them."

"*A*, I'd already made plans with you, and I *knew* you'd show."

"Uh-huh, that's why you sounded so surprised when you opened the door. And *B*?"

Brianna pouted. "I wasn't invited."

"Oh, sorry." Raquel touched Brianna's arm. "At least you found a new roommate right away."

"True." Brianna's gaze alighted on Garrett, and she grinned and opened her arms. "Hey there, Hot Stuff. What does a girl have to do to get a hug *hello*?"

Was it acceptable for him to hug other women? The social mores of the era still escaped him. He sneaked a glance at Raquel.

One tip of her lips quirked up, so he took that to mean the act wouldn't be forbidden.

He gave Brianna a quick hug and stepped back. "It's good to see you again. Thank you for inviting me."

"Yeah, with Kell's refusal to give me a straight answer, I wasn't sure if you two were ever managing to leave your apartment building. Not that I'm complaining—she's needed some good action for a while."

"Bri!" Raquel's face flushed crimson.

"Hey, it's the truth."

"But we aren't—you know—sleeping together."

He didn't sleep at all, so of course they weren't sleeping *together*, but he got the feeling that wasn't what either of them were referring to. Especially as the color in Raquel's cheeks had deepened more than he'd ever seen on her tan skin.

"I mean, we are *sleeping* together, but we aren't"—she winced—"having sex." Her hands went to her hips. "Not that this is any of your business."

Brianna scrutinized them both. "You're sleeping together but not having sex." She waited a beat, as though searching for a sign of deception from either of them, and then shook her head. "In that case, you're doing it wrong."

He wanted to protest what he could only assume were insults to Raquel, but once again, he had the feeling anything he said would only worsen the situation.

Raquel straightened, and her gaze focused only on Brianna. "Garrett, did you want to stay here? Or are you leaving with me?"

Before he could figure out the conflicting messages of the question, Brianna raised her open palms. "Okay, sorry, sorry. I'll butt out. I just figured that with a guy as good-looking as him, there'd be some screwing going on, and I could at least get a vicarious thrill." She spun toward him and grinned. "Garrett, you're a true gentleman. Do you have a brother?"

Raquel elbowed her aside and headed to a low cabinet. "Are we doing this movie marathon thing or not? If so, we should get started. It'll be harder for us to get a cab back if we leave too late."

Behind her back, Brianna muttered, "Party pooper." She hooked his arm. "Come help me with the popcorn and drinks."

He shot a glance to Raquel, who seemed to be digging through a pile of book-shaped packages, and followed Brianna to the fridge. She piled three bottles into his arms.

"Beer's okay with you, right?" After his nod, she checked on Raquel. "Is she doing okay? I worried about her being on her own, and she's seeming really edgy today."

Would telling her the truth break a confidence with Raquel? Although the women *had* been roommates, so he assumed Brianna already must know some details. "You're aware that she occasionally has flashbacks?"

"Yeah..." She punched in a number on the microwave for a bag she'd placed inside, and her mouth turned down. "Did she have one this morning?"

"Two nights ago, but she said it was the worst one she'd ever had."

Brianna's shoulders fell. "Aww, now I feel bad for razzing her."

"That's why I've been staying with her at night, to help her sleep."

"Wow, you're a real class act. I'm glad she has you." Her eyes narrowed. "She does, right? You're not going to take off on her just as she starts opening up to you, right?"

"I won't ever abandon her. She is..." He searched for an appropriate word and failed. "Exceedingly special."

"Yeah, she is." She fetched a large bowl from a cabinet. "Tell me about yourself. What do you do? Do you have a day job in addition to the acting thing?"

Considering that he wasn't an actor to begin with, he wasn't sure there was a safe answer to that question. "I'm currently researching the diamond trade, buyers and cutters."

"Oh, very cool." She leaned closer, spied Raquel's distraction, and whispered like a conspirator. "Not that I'm butting in, but that sounds like the perfect job for a person who might give a special someone an engagement ring in the future." She shrugged innocently. "Just saying."

An engagement ring? Based on Raquel's assertion that he was the "most engaged man without knowing it," he had a vague guess of the meaning of the term but wasn't sure. Did that mean he should he confirm or deny Brianna's observation?

He arched a brow and settled for a vague answer. "Indeed."

A minute later, Brianna stopped the microwave and opened the bag of popcorn. Raquel had curled deep into one end of the couch, her body language screaming for others to leave her alone. He let her select one of the beer bottles, and then she patted the cushion beside her before he needed to debate where he should sit.

He settled onto the cushion she indicated, and Brianna plopped onto the couch on his other side. Ah, Raquel wanted him to act as a barrier between her and Brianna. That was far from his earlier assumption that *he'd* need help to navigate this day.

Raquel held out a hand-sized rectangle. "Here's the remote. The first *Terminator* is already in and ready to go."

He passed the object to Brianna, as he certainly didn't know what to do with the thing. Brianna claimed the remote and her beer from his grasp. She then set the bowl of popcorn on his lap. Apparently, being in the middle also made him the designated table.

Brianna pressed a button on the remote, and music of a sort blared from either side of a large screen that displayed images. Startled, he flinched at the noise, and his gaze sought Raquel.

She didn't turn toward him, but her mouth curved up, and she gave him reassuring touch on his thigh. Her whisper barely reached his ears. "That's a TV, and we're going to watch a movie on it. Like a recorded play."

She uncurled herself from the corner, moving closer to him. At that positive sign, he intertwined his fingers with hers, holding her hand as he'd done in the taxi earlier. On his other side, Brianna eyed the scene with a raised brow and a smirk.

He ignored her. This wasn't about playing into hers or anyone else's expectations. He'd meant it when he said that Raquel was his priority now. He wouldn't do anything to hurt her or push her, and he was going to be there for her the way she needed.

Brianna might think he should be having sex with Raquel, but it wasn't her call to make. Luckily, the immortality and stone-death aspects of their lives made gargoyles patient. Extremely patient. Otherwise, sharing a bed the way they had the past two nights would have been torturous.

Or truthfully, even more torturous.

Raquel had gotten over her aversion to touching him in his human form, but he wasn't sure how much of a good thing that was. Just like how she didn't seem to think of his gargoyle-form exterior as skin, she didn't seem to realize that his clothes were part of him as well.

She thought nothing of snuggling right up against his groin. Thought nothing of the fact that he had full sensations through his clothes. And thought nothing of the fact that he could absorb his clothes into his body in an instant.

To be honest, he tried not to think of that fact as well. He usually failed.

# Chapter Twenty-Five

 WINCE CREASED RAQUEL'S FACE BEFORE SHE COULD PREVENT it, but she tried not to let her whole body cringe too obviously on the couch next to Garrett. Really? How could she have forgotten about the sex scene near the end of the movie?

Not what she needed to think about, or needed Brianna to think about. Or for that matter, it wasn't what she needed *him* thinking about.

When they took a break between movies for Brianna's roast pork and *mofongo*, Raquel spun toward Garrett. Brianna was in the kitchen getting the fryer prepared for the *mofongo*'s plantains, so it was safe to talk openly with him. "There you go. Your first movie, an oldie but goodie. What did you think?"

"Watching a story about time travel and the future, when I feel like *I've* traveled through time and have no idea what's real and possible or not, is enough to give me a headache."

She chuckled. "Yeah, I didn't think about that."

"In many ways, I related to the Reese character though."

"Oh?" *Please don't mention the sex scene. Please don't mention the sex scene.*

"He has to adjust to a different time period and is willing to do anything for his mission to keep her safe." He dipped his head and gave her *that* look. The one where he peered up at her from the corners of his eyes. Like shy, vulnerable hope and sexy seduction all in one.

She kept her face a mask. It wouldn't do to have him learn that she could eat him up when he made that expression. Yeah, Eat. Him. Up.

Brianna returned from the kitchen and caught the end of their conversation. "You haven't seen these movies before? Kell likes them because Sarah Connor goes all kick-ass in the next one. I tease her about *being* Sarah Connor when she's doing her stiff, never-trust-anyone thing."

He stroked her hair, and she barely resisted closing her eyes in bliss. He gave her a full-on grin. "In that case, I'm honored that she's chosen to trust me as much as she has."

"Seriously." Brianna took their empty beer bottles. "I've never known her to—"

Raquel glared at her, daring her to step over the line again.

Brianna cleared her throat. "Well, you're good for her." She pointed one of the bottles in her direction. "And I'm just saying that because I care about you, Kell."

Raquel stifled a groan. She should have known this outing was a mistake. *Note to self: Never let these two hang out in the same room again.*

Grasping at an attempt to control the conversation, she followed Brianna into the kitchen, and Garrett tagged close behind. Brianna dumped the empties into a recycling bin and pointed everyone toward assignments to finish preparing their meal.

While they worked together on the *mofongo*, Raquel encouraged Brianna to ramble about everyone from the neighborhood. Brianna took the opportunity to catch her up on all the gossip of the past few weeks. Raquel couldn't say who most of the people Brianna mentioned were. That probably said something about Raquel that the people from the old neighborhood were unknowns to her.

But the distraction was great for ensuring the focus wasn't on her anymore. And especially good for making sure the focus wasn't on her and Garrett together.

As Brianna fried each batch of plantain slices, Raquel mashed the previous batch. The cramped kitchen made it difficult for all three of them to work side-by-side, especially as Brianna added the requisite rice and beans to the mix to make it a real Puerto Rican meal. Raquel gripped the mashing bowl in her left hand to keep it from sliding across the counter.

She leaned, shuffling her legs out of the way of the oven for Brianna to remove a pan. A clunk sounded to her left as Brianna set something down next to her, but her concentration remained on the slippery bowl in her grasp and keeping it from skating across the countertop.

A minute later, sharp, burning pain cut through the back of her left forearm. She yanked her arm back, nearly sending the bowl to the floor. "*Yeow!*"

An ugly blistered line marked the scar tissue on her forearm. She stared at the mark, unmoving, and blackness crept in from the edges of her vision. Burned. She was burned.

A strong hand gripped hers and twisted her toward him. "You're safe." Another hand clamped onto her ear and jaw, holding her in place. "Rocky, listen to me. You're safe."

Her heartbeat slowed, and the edges of her vision returned. Garrett. Garrett was with her. She was safe.

Brianna fluttered by her elbow. "Are you okay? What happened?"

Raquel glanced at the counter. The pan of roast pork—fresh from the oven—lay beside her mashing bowl. Despite her grasp, the bowl must have glided alongside the pan without her noticing.

Scar tissue was unpredictable like that. Sometimes her skin was overly sensitive at the grafts, and other times the tissue was completely numb, registering sensation only when the deeper remnants of her dermis caught up with the pain or pressure.

In this case, the red mark on her forearm had already faded to a faint pink line. Weird. Her near-flashback must have made her see things that weren't there—she'd have sworn the burn had been worse than that. It sure had *hurt* worse than that.

Definitely a sign her scar tissue was in one of its overly sensitive moods. No way could a blistering burn have disappeared already. She should know—she was an expert.

"Rocky?" Garrett's deep tone of concern drew her closer to normalcy.

She took a deep breath. "Yeah, I'm okay. Just a little sensitive to burns." She lifted her gaze to Garrett. "Thanks."

He nodded, accepting her judgment of her mental stability, and inspected the skin on her arm. His brows knit tight and then notched high on his forehead. "Odd. I'm glad you weren't hurt worse."

"Yeah, me too." She gave Brianna a teasing smile. "See? Real food is dangerous."

"Ha ha. You're not escaping that easily." Brianna shooed Raquel to the table. "We're almost ready, so get out of my way before you find a better excuse for the next time."

Raquel wandered to the table against the opposite wall and rubbed at the faint line. The burn didn't even hurt. Lucky break.

A few minutes later, Brianna brought the dishes to the table, and Garrett followed with plates and silverware. Raquel took her first bite of *mofongo* and nearly moaned. The mix of fried plantains, crunchy bacon-like pork skin, and garlic and oil was a special treat she didn't get to enjoy nearly often enough. She'd never admit it to Brianna, but she missed the flavors of her mamá's kitchen.

Brianna eyed her with a smug expression anyway. Luckily, her excitement to resume her updates on everyone and everything kept her from noticing that Garrett ate only a few bites of their meal. Considering that he didn't *need* to eat at all, he probably just wanted a taste or to avoid standing out for not eating anything. But he and Raquel certainly made an odd pairing. She was half his size yet could eat most of a roast pork due to her exercise regimen, and he was this big guy who ate only a few bites.

He caught her smiling over that thought, and with the improvement to her mood, she settled more comfortably next to him for the second movie. This one *definitely* didn't have any sex scenes. She'd watched this one—with the kick-ass version of Sarah Connor—more times than she could count on all her fingers and toes.

Brianna wasn't far off with her analysis of Raquel's identification with the character. *Uh, let's see.* A little bit crazy and a lot bit paranoid—but for a good reason. Check. Determined to be prepared for the next time she could affect the future, complete with insane exercise habits. Check. Hurt in the past and unable to connect with people anymore? Check.

But Sarah Connor was also tough, strong, and willing to die for those who mattered. What wasn't there to like? If only Raquel had been able to prove that she was good enough during her deployment, they could have been twins.

By the time they got to the scene where the Terminator asked the kid why people cry, Garrett's nods and chuckles made it obvious he identified with the good-guy Terminator character in this movie. Like the Terminator, he was an outsider in the human world but had to adapt and fit in to fulfill his mission.

As Sarah Connor's voice-over played in the next minute, tingles crept over Raquel's skin, and she sat back and clutched the couch cushion, dizzy. On the screen, just as Sarah realized that the Terminator was the perfect father-figure companion for her son, because the android would never leave him, never hurt him, and would die to protect him, Raquel couldn't help seeing the parallel in her life.

If Garrett was serious about never leaving her, never breaking their bond, he *was* like the Terminator. Garrett would do anything to protect her, anything to keep her safe. For always, just like he'd said.

The better he did his job of watching over her, the stronger their bond would be, protecting them both. And like the Terminator, as long as their bond held for him to avoid stone-death, he was indestructible. He couldn't die.

He. Couldn't. Die.

The tingles multiplied until her skin almost stung, and adrenaline rushed through her limbs. She wanted to jump up and shout her epiphany to the world. Here was someone she didn't *have* to keep her distance from out of fear of hurting him. He *was* her perfect companion.

If he betrayed her, he'd break their bond and only hurt himself. If he failed to protect her, he was only endangering himself. Hell, if he failed to keep her happy by using some macho crap to try to overpower her, he was risking their bond and his indestructibility.

Those were some pretty strong reasons to trust his "for always." Almost as strong as Sarah's reasons for trusting the Terminator's robotic programming.

Although... She watched Garrett in her peripheral vision—the tension, the sadness, and the horror of the movie reflected in his expression. He'd been created as a mercenary-slave for faeries, and now he had to conform to his kind's limitations to stay alive. Where was *his* freedom? *His* happiness?

He glanced over and saw her staring at him. He ran his fingers through her hair and stopped at the nape of her neck, stroking, massaging, caressing. Her face melted into a smile, and his grin conveyed only joy at sharing this moment with her.

Maybe this was how she could help him find the happiness and freedom he deserved—by making sure she honored him and his sacrifices for the bond.

If she did her part to keep him happy, he'd have no reason to even think about the need for "backup women" to avoid stone-death. If she met him halfway, he'd be there for her, waiting. She knew that. Knew that he'd happily jump into a relationship with her.

Could she do it? Could she open herself to the emotions of a relationship?

Brianna seemed to think Raquel was afraid of all relationships. That she never *wanted* to get close to others. But was that the cause or just a symptom?

In her head, it felt like a symptom. Her thoughts were always how she didn't want to get close to others *because* she had reasons. Reasons like the fear that if she started a relationship, the guy would turn out like her father. Or the fear that if she let others close, she wasn't strong enough—good enough—to keep them safe.

So if she was just afraid of losing her independence to a guy and of being responsible for hurting others, maybe she *could* have a relationship with Garrett. He was the one being she knew *had* to respect her wishes—the one being she could never hurt unless she betrayed him. And betrayal was something she would die to prevent with *anyone*, much less him.

She could. She could do this. A part of her *wanted* to do this.

A soft whimper escaped her, and she let that part of her eager to move forward steer her body to lean against him. He wrapped his arm around her shoulder and tucked her close.

This felt right. This felt easy. This felt safe.

# Chapter Twenty-Six

B Y THE TIME GARRETT OVERHEARD RAQUEL RESPOND TO Brianna's teasing—another suggestive comment if he caught the meaning properly—with humor rather than irritation, he knew something about his warrior's mood had shifted, but he couldn't figure out the specifics. She'd let him embrace her through the second movie and then for the cab ride home. Back at her apartment, she'd released his hand only when it was time to change for bed. Hopefully that meant she'd recovered from her flashback trauma.

When she emerged from the bathroom in her nightshirt, she greeted him with a smile that nearly made his heart stop. The look was enticing enough that he debated whether or not he should hope she wanted him to keep her company in bed tonight. If she did, that would be torture. Sweet, sweet torture.

She crossed her arms and then quickly uncrossed them. "Hey."

"Hey." He matched her casual tone. "Thanks for including me today."

"Yeah, it was fun." She nibbled her lip. "I kind of don't want the day to be over yet." She linked her fingers together and fidgeted. "Would you be willing to take me flying again? We haven't gone for over a week, and I've been in the mood ever since I realized— too late—that we should have flown home tonight and saved the cab fare."

"Of course." He eyed her outfit of an over-sized T-shirt that hung down so long he couldn't even see the shorts she wore at night. "It's too bad you changed for bed. Now you'll have to get dressed again."

"Nah. This will be fine. It's a super-warm night, and..." She gave him a wink. "No one is supposed to see us anyway, so we shouldn't have any witnesses, right?"

"True." He let her lead the way to the roof, and he changed to his gargoyle form.

Even though she hadn't seen him this way for a while, she didn't flinch at his change. Her total acceptance was something he still couldn't understand.

"What do you see when I'm in this form?"

She stared up at him, confusion creasing her forehead. "What do you mean? Do humans see you differently from how you really look?"

"No, but it doesn't seem like this appearance bothers you, so I'm curious as to why you don't see me as a monster."

"You're not a monster. Not in any of your forms."

"I don't think other humans would agree." In fact, he knew from experience that wasn't the case.

"That's probably true." She leaned against the roof wall and gazed out into the night. "When I was little, I loved the *Beauty and the Beast* movie. It's about a prince who was cursed to look like a beast until a woman could love him regardless. Then the curse would be broken, and he'd be human again."

"Was there a happy ending to this movie?" Both movies he'd seen in his life had sad endings as far as he was concerned, but perhaps that was the nature of movies.

"Yes, but I always thought the Beast was better looking—and definitely more interesting—than the prince. And I didn't like the implication that he wasn't good enough for her as a beast and that he needed to change his physical form."

His pulse thudded loudly in his ears, deep and slow. Did she see him as the Beast?

She turned back to him and shrugged. "The funny thing is that others know the prince was pretty bland too. All the marketing—toys, posters, and so forth—always show the character in his beast form. People love the movie because of the *Beast*, not because of the prince, even though they might not admit it." Her lips curved, and he'd swear her eyes twinkled despite the darkness around them. "You remind me of the Beast."

Before he could swallow his heart back down into his chest and ask for more details, she straightened away from the wall and threw her arms around his neck. "I'm ready if you are."

Her body pressed against his, and her warmth sank into his heart. Without her bra on, her breasts squished into him even more than usual. She smiled up at him, eager and oh-so-tempting.

They were supposed to fly in this position again? His legendary gargoyle patience would be stretched to the limit tonight.

The Maker only knew what his voice would sound like if he tried to speak right now. Instead, he wordlessly held her and took off into the darkness. He flew straight up and away from the lights.

She rested her head on him and made a pleased moan that vibrated his collarbone under her cheek. "It's a beautiful night."

He gazed down, and his throat tightened at the sight before him. Her hair streamed around her face, flittering in the breeze, framing the most tempting woman in the world. "Yes, beautiful."

After a moment, she surveyed their surroundings. He'd taken them far above one of the rivers, where there'd be no chance of people spying them from below. The chaos of the city streets faded into background noise.

"Was there someplace you wanted to go tonight?"

"No, this is perfect." She stretched her fingers, stroking the back of his neck, and his skin tightened under her touch. "Is it work to carry me? Or is flying easy to do?"

"My wings are strong enough to carry at least three of *me*. Trust me, the flying part is easy." It was resisting her that was hard.

"Easy, huh? So even if I distracted you, we wouldn't fall, and you wouldn't drop me?"

He laughed. "We wouldn't fall. I don't have to think about flying any more than either of us have to think about making our hearts beat." He considered her, trying to determine the root of her question. "Holding on to you isn't quite as automatic, but I have excellent reasons for making sure I don't drop you. And even if I did, I'd swoop down and catch you before you fell more than twenty feet."

"That's good to know."

Her fingers trailed over his shoulder. If he had hair in this form, it would be standing on end. Her fingers curved forward and stroked his neck. His head fell back. Her forgetfulness of the fact that his grey-speckled exterior in this form *was* his skin was killing him. Killing him dead.

She rubbed her cheek against his chest, and then, so softly that he wasn't positive it had really happened, she kissed him along his collarbone. A second later, another kiss followed a couple of inches up. And then third kiss on the underside of his jaw. He couldn't doubt any longer.

"Raquel..." His voice came out breathy and husky.

"Yes, Garrett?" Her tone was innocent and teasing at once.

"If you do things like that, I cannot promise that my patience will hold."

Another nibble tickled under his ear. "Patience for what?"

"Patience for you to want the same thing I do."

"How do you know I don't already?"

He groaned loud enough that he wondered how far sound would travel from up here. "Then we should go back to your apartment. You cannot possibly want me in this form."

She pressed a fingertip to his lips, utterly undaunted by his large canine teeth. "*This form?* You're not a monster or an animal."

"What about my wings and horns?"

"What about them? Do my scars keep you from wanting me?"

"No, of course not. But it's not the same."

"Isn't it? My scars are part of who I am, and this form is part of who you are. I accept you as you are—in all your forms."

Dizziness swirled his head, and he scrutinized her, searching for any indication that she didn't mean *exactly* what she'd said. But he perceived only the stare of someone who saw who he was on the inside. Someone who, in just a few weeks, had somehow gotten to know him better than anyone else in his lifetime.

The dam holding his emotions in check broke, but he still didn't want to kiss her in this form. He settled for caressing her back, his fingertips spread backward slightly so there'd be no chance of accidentally scratching her with his claws.

He couldn't find the words for more than a whispered murmur. "Raquel…"

"No dropping me allowed, remember? Lift me up so I can wrap my legs around your hips and be more secure."

She interlocked her fingers behind his neck so he could adjust his hold on her without worry. His hands slipped down past her bottom, and he gingerly drew her bare thighs up and out. He slid his palms back up to her bottom to create a seat for holding her.

But his hands didn't encounter the fabric of her shorts. His hands didn't encounter the fabric of her underclothes either.

She'd gone commando under that long T-shirt.

His wings faltered a half-second, and his gaze snapped to hers. Even as he was trying to process the fact that her bottom half was *naked* and pressed against him, heat from her core bloomed over his pelvis.

His skin tightened, and his heartbeat threatened to pound through his ribcage. A feverish shiver jolted him from his shock.

"Raquel, no, you can't want this. Not like this."

"And I say I do—at least once. Just so you'll always know that I accept you. All of you. You deserve that. You deserve to be happy for who you are. You deserve to feel free to be yourself around me. No manipulation needed."

His breath quickened, and a pang ached in his chest. She understood him better than he understood himself.

"What about what you want? What about what *you* deserve?"

"Give me you—all of you—so our bond will be as strong as possible, and then I can let myself care without worry about anything bad happening to you. *That's* what I want. To know that you'll always be safe and that I don't have to hold back out of fear of losing anyone again."

His lovely warrior had surprised him yet again. He nuzzled his jaw over the top of her head.

"I promise. You never have to worry about me." He risked kissing her hair, careful of his fangs. "This. This connection between us will protect me, so I can protect you."

She unlocked her fingers and held either side of his neck. Her grasp forced him to meet her eyes. Wide-open awareness shone in her expression, her actions determined and deliberate.

The flaps of his wings keeping them aloft sounded out each long second as her fingertips nudged him closer, bending his face down to hers. Still, he didn't stretch to kiss her. Any moment she might change her mind and be horrified by his grotesque appearance.

She rubbed her lips against his and whispered, "Don't hold back from me."

Easy for her to say. He'd never kissed in this form, much less any of the other activities she seemed to have in mind. This form was for flying and killing. His teeth, claws, and horns were strong enough to tear into dragon scales. He couldn't risk hurting her by losing control.

So she took control *from* him, sucking his lower lip into her mouth. Her tongue stroked his lip, and he moaned.

His cock ached, begging to be released. He ignored it. This had to be her lead.

She turned her attention to his upper lip and ran her tongue lightly over his teeth, exploring, learning. Her fingers dug harder, demanding, and she dove deeper, brushing the inside of his mouth.

He let his tongue caress and swirl around hers. She flicked the tip of her tongue, as though beckoning him closer, inviting him inside her. Slowly, he eased his way into her mouth, ensuring his fangs weren't endangering her.

Her taste was so warm and welcoming he'd never felt more accepted in his life. She was everything he hadn't known he wanted. Strong, fierce, and most importantly, *his*.

His fingers tensed, itching to ravish her. He settled for kneading her bottom.

She squeezed her legs around his hips and rocked up and down his pelvis. Her meaning couldn't be clearer.

He leaned away. Each wing flap fluttered the hair around her face, revealing her expression, and he searched for any sign of uncertainty. "Are you sure?"

"Do I need to reach down there and put it in myself, or will you trust me when I say yes?" She tilted her hips, nudging him. "I'm saying, yes. I'm sure."

It no longer mattered that he had no soul. He'd found his heaven in her arms.

# Chapter Twenty-Seven

E VER SINCE HER EPIPHANY, RAQUEL COULDN'T FOCUS ON anything other than reaching this point with Garrett. Every desire, every hope, every wish that she'd held back and buried the past several years coalesced into embracing this situation right now.

Logically, she understood his hesitation, but being with him made *her* feel invincible. The possibility of falling from this great height didn't even faze her. Hell, the cool breeze on her bare ass and the star-point lights of the city below added to her excitement. She trusted him, and that's what this setup was about—proving that they trusted each other implicitly and completely.

Nicks and scratches would be a small price to pay for that proof. She needed him to trust her with every fiber of his being, trust that she would always understand, always accept—without lies or manipulation. Their bond needed that level of connection to be as indestructible as he was.

He shivered and hid his face next to her ear. She recognized the sign as another delaying tactic.

"Are you worried about me having a disease or something? I figured you'd be invulnerable to diseases, but I promise I'm clean. Or maybe you're worried about preventing pregnancy?"

She kept her tone light, as she knew darn well those concerns had never occurred to him. Especially because the *one kid*

# Jami Gold

limitation on gargoyles meant pregnancy required a conscious decision. But maybe the tease would get him to reveal what *was* bothering him.

"No..." The warm breath of his sigh tickled the side of her neck. "I want to tell you something I've never explained to anyone. Honestly, I've never *needed* to explain it because I've never been in this situation before."

She matched his serious mood and kissed his cheek. "I'm listening."

"You know how I can change some aspects of my external appearance, such as changing my clothes when I look human or hiding my 'anatomical correctness' when I'm in this form?"

"Yes."

"That means when I'm in this form, I can also change the size of my..." He paused and shook his head. "I'm not sure what terms are acceptable in this era."

"Guys have a million words for it. Let's go with *cock*." She held in a giggle at their matter-of-fact conversation and tried not to think about the even-sillier names guys used. "And that makes sense. In this form, you're able to absorb it into your body completely, so you must have a lot of control over its size and shape."

His breath wasn't brushing her ear, as though he was holding it, waiting for her verdict on his "confession."

She trailed a line of kisses toward his mouth. "I hope you're not embarrassed by being different in that way. As far as I'm concerned, you're telling me that you can make yourself the perfect size for me. Now that I know, I might not want this to be a one-time experiment."

Warmth floated over her neck again, and he squeezed her ass. "*You* are what's perfect."

"I don't know." She lightly bit his shoulder, giving him the message that gentleness wasn't required. "I think I'm starting to get impatient."

Emptiness ached inside her, and she tilted her hips toward him again.

He groaned and rested his forehead on hers. "Stop me if anything hurts or if it's too big."

Pressure nudged her below, and she closed her eyes,

determined not to pull away and be distant but to feel *everything.* His length grew and slipped inside her, spreading her, filling her.

She shuddered. "Oh God, that feels good."

At that encouragement, he gave her more, stretching her walls. "Is that too much?"

"No, no, not at all." Between her anticipation and the exquisite satisfaction of her empty craving being fulfilled, she felt near orgasm already, and she panted through her words. "God, I could become an addict."

He remained still, letting her lead. Every couple of seconds, she squeezed him, just to hear his sexy-ass *mmphh* groan.

Finally, she wriggled and angled her hips to kick them into the next gear. She was so close to coming that her walls were tightening all on their own.

He pressed on her ass, slowly lifting and sliding her along his length. The delicious friction sent her right to the edge, and her head fell back to meet the dark sky above. She sucked in quick gasps that ended on a quiet squeal. One part of her wanted to beg him to go faster, but another part of her wanted the torture, wanted the tease, wanted this to last forever.

Just as slowly, gravity drew her away from him, and he repeated the leisurely, so-fucking-good process. Her toes were already curling. She resisted for only five strokes.

"Faster. Harder. Now."

He seemed just as eager and yanked her close, sending shocks through her nerves. His claws dug into her ass cheeks, pumping her up and down. The electric sensations built immediately, and her body overloaded, her orgasm clenching through her muscles. A strangled scream escaped her, and she buried her face into his neck.

He kept thrusting them together, and her right arm tightened around the back of his neck, anchoring her. Waves of ecstasy rolled through her, over and over. She'd never known an orgasm to keep going, but she definitely wasn't complaining. Her walls squeezed him as hard as her legs clamped around his hips.

With her free hand, she stroked his head, his lips, his horns in a crazy-desperate need to connect with every inch of him. None of his differences mattered. They were one.

Her orgasm continued, shattering harder and climbing in intensity until only his grasp, clutching her tightly, kept her from falling. A second later, he followed with his bliss, his intense pulses swelling inside her. He yelled a snarling growl that filled the empty sky.

For many moments, their breaths mingled on his chest, and his heartbeat thumped under her cheek. She'd bet their bond was strong now.

"Oh God, that was..." She shuddered with an after-quake. "Amazing."

His chin tickled her forehead with his nod. "Perfect."

His voice sounded as shaky as she felt. Her muscles quivering, she was limp in his arms. Her legs no longer wanted to keep their grip, and her ankles unhooked.

"I'm slipping."

"Grab my neck."

She did as he instructed, and he swung one arm under her knees and slid the other behind her shoulders so he was carrying her securely once more. She relaxed against him. "Thank you. For everything."

"No, thank *you*."

His eyes glistened, and she wiped a drop from his cheek. "Are you okay?"

"I don't know." His fingers at her back twirled in her hair. "I think I want to take you home and kiss you and hold you and caress you all over."

She nearly purred. "I don't think I'd mind that a bit."

He swooped toward her apartment, taking her up on her offer immediately. Her stomach dropped like from a rollercoaster. With his speed, it seemed like only a minute later he carried her in through the window and laid her on the mattress.

She thought he'd ravish her right away, but he stood at the end of the bed. Clothed, of all things. He dipped his head and gave her *that* look—her favorite sexy grin.

"Are you disappointed I'm not the Beast anymore? Do I also make a bland prince?"

"Definitely not and hell no. And if you don't believe me, I'll happily throw myself at you again."

"Mmm..." He knelt, straddling her calves, and trailed his hands up her thighs. "You sound quite convincing, but are you sure you could throw yourself anywhere? After all, I had to carry you home."

She sat up and slipped her fingers under his collar. "Are you daring me? You've seen my workouts. I recover quickly."

"Good point." He inched his hand under her shirt, slipping it up from her waist. "But maybe I want a turn to throw myself at you."

His thumb strummed her nipple, igniting a new round of shocks through her limbs. She gasped and dropped to the mattress.

"Oh. Okay." Yeah, she was easy. At least as far as he was concerned.

He removed her shirt and scanned her naked body so intently she felt more exposed than when she'd had her ass hanging out, mooning all of the Big Apple. Her shoulders hunched, instinctively curling inward for protection.

"No." He pushed her to the bed, laying her out for his inspection. "How can you even think of hiding yourself from me after what we shared? You have nothing to be ashamed of. You're beautiful."

"You don't have to say that. I mean, I know you're stuck with me because I'm the one who woke you, but I don't expect you to—"

He kissed her silent, his lips meshing and tangling with hers, his tongue caressing her with such skill she couldn't wait for him to use it on the rest of her body. She threaded her fingers into his hair and wanted to inhale him. They both moaned, and the vibration alone made her toes curl again.

Too soon, he leaned away and frowned at her. "Never think that."

Think what? He'd kissed her senseless, and she'd forgotten what they'd been talking about.

"I am *not* 'stuck with you.' Call it fate, call it luck, call it a blessing from the Maker herself, but *you* are the perfect woman to have woken me because you are perfect for me. And now I've made the *choice* to do everything to make our bond work long-term because there's no one else I'd rather have at my side for my lifetime."

He stroked her lips and gazed into her eyes. "This is love, not an obstacle."

Her breath stopped, her heart stopped, hell, for all she knew, the world stopped.

He'd said the *L*-word. What did that mean? What did she *wish* it meant?

She didn't have answers for either of those questions. A part of her recoiled from the idea of what he *might* mean. There was trust, which was logical and a conscious choice, and there was love, which was illogical and emotional.

They didn't have to go together, right? Just because she trusted him, had amazing sex with him, and cared about him didn't mean love belonged in the picture. It didn't mean she had to open her heart completely, did it?

*Idiot.* Even if she didn't *love*-love him yet, it was only a matter of time. Did she really think she could spend her life intimately bonded to him—this gorgeous hunk of a great and caring guy—and *not* fall in love with him? Ever?

She caressed his cheek. No, she would have to be stupid to believe that. Falling in love with him would be as easy as breathing.

She gave him a smile—and took a breath.

# Chapter Twenty-Eight

TENSION FROZE HIM IN PLACE, AND GARRETT HID HIS PANIC from his face. Under him on the mattress, Rachel had stiffened at his use of the word *love*. To be honest, he wasn't sure where that declaration had come from either.

He was just a soulless gargoyle. Did he—could he—really know what love was? Was that what he felt with her? The insatiable need to be with her, the compelling determination to do right by her, the overwhelming awe at his luck in encountering this amazing woman—was that love?

Or perhaps it didn't matter.

She gave him a relaxed smile, and his body released its tension at the same time her muscles loosened under his palms. He didn't know if she felt the same way he did, but if she wasn't worried about the questions and implications, he wouldn't let them undermine his enjoyment of this moment.

He maintained eye contact and dipped his head to her breast. Her eyes widened, and he extended his tongue slow enough to see her pupils dilate in anticipation. Finally, he circled around her nipple, which hardened to a point. He flicked the tip and then dove in, sucking deep.

She moaned and shuddered, and her head dropped back to the bed. After he'd sufficiently laved that breast, he shifted to the other one. Her flesh tasted of the salty exertions from their earlier activities.

This woman pretended to be hard and unemotional, like the Sarah Connor character as Brianna had teased, and yet he'd made her needy enough to—in her words—throw herself at him. That accomplishment was something to cherish. Even now, her hands slipped through his hair, holding him to her breast, showing that she wanted him.

Over the centuries, he'd never connected with other women enough to risk being truthful. He'd used them for survival, and at the same time, he'd let them use *him* for their own superficial reasons—a distraction, an ego boost, and given what he'd since learned of the history of human society, some had probably wished for a pregnancy to force marriage.

He'd never put in the effort to know any of them beyond what was needed for the bond, and he'd never let them know him well enough to truly care about him. Raquel was different.

She'd not only figured out far more about him than he'd shared—getting to know him better than he knew himself—but she also wanted him for *him*. Her insistence on following through on her intentions during the flight had made that unquestioningly clear.

More than that, over the past week, she'd understood his situation and needs in a way that had sped up his slow evolution since being on the Earthen plane, like a mountain's gradual erosion suddenly shifting with an earthquake. He'd *changed*, thanks to her. Now, somehow—even if gargoyles were incapable of carrying on a loving relationship—there was no doubt how he felt about her.

Her hands moved down to his chest, and she clenched the front of his shirt. "Okay, let's talk about these clothes. They're part of you, right?"

He chuckled against her breast and lifted his head. "I was wondering when you'd figure that out."

She mouthed *figure that out* and drew her head back. "You're telling me that you feel all of this"—her fingers whispered over his shirt—"just as well as you would on your skin?"

"Yes." He breathed a happy sigh at her caresses.

Her brows arched. "Well, that certainly puts a different slant onto the fact that you lay next to me while I slept. You may as well have been naked."

He couldn't stifle his laugh. "It did make for a couple of interesting nights."

She play-swatted his shoulder. "Oh, so naughty." She fingered one of the buttons. "Now, do I get to have any fun stripping these off of you, or does that work out to something gross and I should simply tell you to get naked so I can ogle you?"

"I can accommodate either request. Which would you like?"

She sat up and rolled them together, ending with her on top. "Oh, I'm going to enjoy the show."

She straddled his thighs and unbuttoned his shirt. Her fingers explored both the sensitivity of his clothes and bare skin along the way. After the tenth time she'd made him suck in a hiss, she lightly scraped her nails over his chest.

"I think you're wrong. I think you have more nerve or whatever endings in your actual skin than in however-your-clothes-work."

"I think you're right." He panted in time with her circling hands. "With all this experimenting, you're the expert."

"Mmm." She trapped his wrists and pinned him to the mattress. "I like the sound of that."

Proving her expertise, she kissed, licked, and nibbled him in areas he didn't know he had extra sensitivity. Far from his original resentment of his dependence on her, he'd happily follow her lead in every respect now.

As she worked her way from his chest to his lips, she wriggled her straddle to encompass his hips. She rocked against him, deliberately teasing him on his sensitive-enough jeans, and moaned against his mouth.

Their kiss was luscious and full and passionate and everything he couldn't do to her when concerned about his fangs. Dipping and swirling, sucking and thrusting, they made love to each other's mouths. His cock begged him to let it poke through the façade of his clothes, but he resisted, waiting for her to be ready.

Hopefully, that would be soon.

Without warning, she knelt off him, her breaths loud and quick. "Okay, next. Stand up by the bed."

He held in a groan but followed her directions. She sat on the edge of the bed in front of him and ran her palms up and down his thighs.

"Show me how you'd deal with your shirt if you didn't want anyone to know."

He separated his arm from the left sleeve and tugged the fabric-like material off his body. Then he slid the other sleeve down his right arm and held the wad in a ball. With a flick of his wrist, the shirt disappeared, absorbed into his body, but to anyone else, the motion would have looked like he'd flung it onto the floor.

"You're good." She grinned and winked. "But you knew that already."

She nudged him forward. Just as he'd done with his approach to her breasts, she seized his gaze and slowly leaned forward. Her tongue extended, and she licked the front of his jeans.

Shocks crackled through his limbs, and he shuddered, knees weak. A rumbling groan stole from his throat, and he fell forward over her. He caught himself before squishing her and savagely beat down the urges pounding through his body.

"Why are you trying to kill me?"

"You're right." She nudged him to kneel above her and then squirmed backward, getting her legs onto the bed. "Ditch the jeans. In me. Now."

In one motion, he scooted forward, absorbed the last of his clothes, and plunged into her. Her yell echoed his, and her grab of his ass proved that hers was a happy scream.

"Does that mean you like me in this form too?"

"Oh God, yes." She squeezed him below, and her fingers urged him faster. "So fucking good." She panted in time with his thrusts. "I hope to God... That you're serious... About this forever thing... Because no one else... Will ever... Ever... Ever... Get to have you."

His chest ached, bursting with happiness over her declaration. By the Maker, she was perfect, fierce even in her lovemaking.

"I'm yours." He stole a kiss between thrusts. "For as long as you'll have me."

"Forever work for you?"

"Forever it is."

Her muscles clenched, and she screamed. Her expression trans-formed into the sexiest scene of ecstasy imaginable. She dug her fingers into his ass, and he pumped deeper and expended himself inside her.

This was home. This was where he was meant to be. Forever.

After their breathing settled, he lay down beside her and tucked her closer. No other woman would ever measure up to her. That truth was clear. So what did that mean for his future?

His heartbeat pounded out the answer, pulsing loud in his ear, forming a plan that brought meaning to his life. That gave his life a purpose again.

The ache in his chest sharpened, as the thought of potentially losing her in the unknown future battled with the risk of her rejection in the here and now. But if anything happened to her, he'd want to die regardless of enacting his plan or not. This was the only step that made sense. Given everything they'd been through and shared, they were already more than halfway there.

He hoped with all his heart she meant her words. Because he intended to make her his *mate*.

# Chapter Twenty-Nine

TWO MORNINGS LATER, THE ALARM STARTLED GARRETT, AND he jumped out of bed, ready to kill the threat to Raquel. She rolled over, eying him from the edge of the mattress, and switched off the blasted sound.

"Good morning, sexy."

"Today is Monday?" He'd enjoyed the past weekend with her so much he'd forgotten they couldn't spend the rest of their lives making love.

"'Fraid so." She stood and caressed his chest. "But the sight of you standing there naked is enough to make me want to forget that."

He embraced her and enjoyed the feel of her body against his. "I could say the same."

"Unfortunately, I can't afford to lose my job." She pulled away and stepped toward the shower.

"You can, however." He slanted his gaze toward the bag under the bed.

She shook her head and answered before entering the bathroom. "I'm not ready to think about that yet. Honestly, I think you should keep it all."

"I'd simply spend the money on you."

From the bathroom, she poked her head out through the doorway. "This might sound weird, but I'd rather you keep it and spend some on me than give it all to me outright."

Then she closed the door and started the water running for her shower.

She'd rather he gave her gifts? He supposed they'd feel more personal, so perhaps her attitude wasn't as incomprehensible as it seemed. Gifts could certainly be arranged, if he knew more about what she'd like.

Her cell phone temptingly glowed from the floor. Now was his chance to call in reinforcements for help.

He picked up her phone and dialed Brianna's saved number. Her groggy voice sounded over the speaker. "Hey, Kell. What's up?"

"This is Garrett. I'm sorry. I hope I didn't wake you."

"Yeah, but I'll forgive you, handsome. What's wrong? Is Raquel okay?"

"Yes, she's in the shower. I called to ask you a favor. Would you be willing to help me pick out gifts for her?"

Brianna squealed loud enough that he had to hold the phone away from his ear. "Is this a diamond ring kind of gift?"

"Yes." Starting with the stone he'd already given Raquel—and that she'd already ignored—made the most sense.

"And she doesn't know, right? That's why you called while she was in the shower, right?"

"Correct." Surprises *were* the nature of most gifts.

"Perfect! I know a guy. He can take care of everything for you. Today's a school holiday, and I was planning on sleeping in, but since you've already busted that plan to hell, can you meet me at his place at ten o'clock?" She rattled off an address.

"Yes, I can meet you there." Hopefully Google would know where the place was.

"Awesome. I'm so excited I can't even tell you. Little Kell, getting engaged! See you there."

The phone connection clicked off, and he stared at the screen. Why did he get the feeling that he'd lost control of the situation?

He listened for the shower. Water still poured from the sprayer, so he started up Raquel's laptop. Brianna's comment had reminded him to look up the meaning of the term *engagement ring* before he made a fool of himself by guessing.

Five minutes later, he had his answer and a revision to his plan just as Raquel opened the door from the bathroom. Engagement rings were symbolic of the human version of proclaiming a mate, so Brianna's assumption would work perfectly. He shut the laptop before Raquel could spy the information on the screen.

She braced herself on the kitchenette counter and slipped on her shoes. "What are you planning today? I hope no more accepting valuables from strange rocks."

"No, I have enough work ahead of me to sell what I already have."

"Good." She straightened. "Oh, that reminds me." She opened a drawer in the kitchenette and selected a small item. "As long as you promise to behave, I suppose I should give you this."

He flipped over the object she'd placed in his palm and took a guess. "A key to your apartment?"

Her face tightened into a grimace, and she fluttered her hands, her words coming out in a scattered rush to match. "I'm sorry. Is that too sudden? I just figured—"

"Shh, it's okay." He enfolded her fingers in his and stroked her skin. "Slow down."

"Sorry." She settled under the weight of a deep inhalation. "In modern culture, it's usually a big step in a relationship to share a key and live together, but this doesn't *have* to mean anything special like that. We could say it's just for convenience if you don't want—"

He shushed her with a kiss and barely resisted the urge to remove her clothes. "Thank you. It's perfect. I'm honored that you've welcomed me into your life."

She gave him a liquid smile, reluctance to leave him for work evident in the creases around her eyes. Her heated gaze scanned him thoroughly, and she slowly retreated from his grasp.

"Oh, if you head out, you should change your clothes a little bit every day. Colors, buttons, seams, or something, so people don't think you're wearing the same dirty clothes day after day."

He *had* noticed that extreme cleanliness was an expectation now—maybe due to the convenience of faucets and running water. "Thank you for the advice."

She touched her fingers to her lips and blew him a kiss. The door closed behind her, and he returned to his research on the laptop.

Time to make their bond real in every way possible.

# Chapter Thirty

A COUPLE OF HOURS LATER, GARRETT HAD MANAGED TO survive the crowded streets and crazy drivers to stand outside the designated address and wait for Brianna. She showed up a few minutes later and insisted on a hug.

"Okay, let me do the talking at first. He knows me."

"I'd greatly appreciate that, as I'll admit that I have no idea what I'm doing."

"A guy admitting he doesn't know something?" She lightly pinched his cheek. "You're adorable."

Inside the shop, Brianna exchanged words in a staccato-fast variation of Spanish he couldn't follow with an older man who had the same light shade of skin as Brianna. The man approached and held out his hand, introducing himself as Howard.

"I understand we have a special ring to design. What budget do you have in mind?"

"That depends." He slipped the raw diamond he'd given to Raquel from his pocket and set it on the glass case. "What can you tell me about the value of this?"

Brianna's jaw dropped, and she backhanded his arm. "Holy crap, Garrett. Is that a raw diamond? Where did you get it?"

Luckily, he'd anticipated the question. "I recently inherited several gemstones and gold nuggets."

Howard frowned. "I take it you don't have paperwork for this?"

"No, but it's been in the family for eons." The Earth *was* a distant cousin—of a sort.

Howard gave an apologetic shrug to Brianna. "I don't know that I can help. Its octahedral shape and these smooth faces tell me that it's probably a cuttable stone, but this needs to be cut and appraised before I can do anything with it."

"But you know a guy, right, Howard?" She exaggeratedly fluttered her eyelashes and flashed a smile. "Please?"

He sighed and shook his head, a laugh on his lips. "Yeah, I know a guy. Best in the business and not quite fully retired yet. Give me a minute, and let me see if I can convince him to leave the recliner long enough to join us."

An hour later, the diamond cutter set down his tools, his eyes alight, and his age-thinned voice pitched high. "This is a rare find. Colorless, internally flawless. By the time I cut and polished this, you'd have at least two twelve-carat stones. Maybe bigger."

Howard whistled and rubbed his mouth, as though mopping up drool. "You think it's legit, Martin?"

"I'd have heard if a stone of this size and quality was stolen, and if it's been in this country with his family for generations, he wouldn't have a certificate. The KPC process has been around for only a little over a decade. There's no reason not to believe his story."

Garrett had no idea what any of those details meant. He leaned toward Brianna. "Would one of those stones work on a ring for her?"

"A twelve-carat diamond? Hell no! Do you have any idea how huge that is?"

He glanced at Howard for guidance, who shrugged. "I don't have anything that size in here right now. But Brianna's right, that's too big. A stone that size would be the width of her finger. Unless she likes flashy rings, she'd probably hate it."

"She'd hate it." Garrett sighed. "This stone has meaning to us, so I was hoping to use it for her ring. Now I'm not sure how to proceed."

Martin picked up the stone for another look in his gnarled hands. "I've cut thousands upon thousands of diamonds, and we usually want to get the largest gems out of a stone as possible, so I rarely make this recommendation. But if it means that much to you, with this one's flawlessness, I could try to cut a one- to two-carat diamond from the pyramid tip on this side. I should still be able to get an eight- to ten-carat diamond out of the rest of this end, leaving the other pyramid for the full-size large diamond."

Brianna clapped. "Somewhere between one and two carats would be perfect. Spectacular without being too flashy."

"It'd be more cutting work though, so I'd have to charge more for the job."

Garrett's shoulders tensed. This process was proving more complicated than he'd anticipated.

Howard wiped his mouth again and met Garrett's eyes. "Would you be willing to sell the larger stones to me? They'd be the prize of the store."

Garrett exhaled and nodded to Brianna. "I find myself stone-rich and cash-poor. What do you think would be fair?"

Martin, Brianna, and Howard all haggled around him, debating how to value the unknown size of the finished cut gemstones. In the end, Brianna negotiated a deal for Howard to pay Garrett a fair price for the stones at the small end of the possible range, while Howard and Martin would split the profit for any size the gems turned out above that minimum. With that arrangement, Garrett didn't have to worry about any of the costs, as the other men were happy to join the partnership.

Howard teased the old man. "I suppose that agreement will serve as an incentive for you to do your best work."

"Never better." Martin grinned so wide several gold caps gleamed on his back teeth.

Brianna tugged Garrett's shoulder and whispered in his ear. "You said you had more where this came from?" At his nod, she cleared her throat and addressed the other men. "Obviously, we'll be getting an independent appraisal of the finished ring to ensure the cut quality of his stone. Assuming all goes well, he'd be happy to consider this an ongoing arrangement for his future projects."

They both looked agog at him, and Howard held up a hand. "You have more like this?"

"This is the biggest, but the others are close to the same size."

"How many?"

Garrett shrugged. "Around a dozen."

Howard scrubbed his cheeks. "Martin, you weren't planning on retiring quite yet, were you?"

"I still have another year or two in these old eyes and hands."

"Good." Howard extended his arm. "Now, son, let's see what kind of setting your girl would like. You name it, and we'll make it happen."

With Brianna's help, he decided on a halo and diamond-encrusted setting, which Brianna said Raquel would like because the stone wouldn't stick out to catch on things. The setting also included his-and-hers matching wedding bands. Although he knew nothing about rings or the engagement and marriage process, Brianna proved herself beyond useful, and even he could see the beauty in the rings she pointed out to him.

He took advantage of her giddy mood to enlist her help in establishing a bank account to receive the proceeds of the sale, and she was happy to—as she called it—go shopping for life stuff with him. She didn't even question why he needed help getting an identification card, hinting that as a teacher, she came across immigrant families with all kinds of stories. Luckily, she "knew a guy" who was able to set him up with what he needed.

By the end of the day, she'd helped him procure legal identification as "Garrett Mason," which he figured was an appropriate surname, a way to access his money, a cell phone with her and Raquel's numbers already programmed in, and a promise to help him with the jewelry appraisal when the cut stones and rings were ready in a couple of weeks.

On the sidewalk outside the cell phone store, he attempted to express his appreciation. "Thank you for your help today. You are an invaluable friend."

"Aww..." She nudged her elbow against his. "I'm happy to help. It's not every day a girl like me gets to negotiate multi-million-dollar deals."

"I don't wish to take advantage of you, however. If it would not offend, I insist upon paying you for your help." He grinned. "Consider it a 'you know a guy' bounty for your expertise."

"Well, aren't you the sweetest?" She hooked his arm and gave him a wry smile. "I know as a friend I'm supposed to say that's not necessary—and it's not—but I could definitely use the money."

"Would a one-percent fee be sufficient? Or should it be more? I wish to be fair."

Her face paled, and she covered her mouth. He'd never seen her so silent—or so still. Usually her arms whirled in every direction with her emotions.

Finally, she spoke, "One percent? Of the proceeds from the sale?"

"I'm sorry, I didn't mean to offend you. Would five percent be more acceptable?"

"No, Garrett, that's crazy talk! One percent is fine. More than enough, in fact. That'll cover rent for a year. God, that's insane to think about, right?" She flung her hands through the air, as if trying to draw a diagram. "Two days ago, you were hanging out on my couch, watching old movies, and now you're super rich and have more where that came from." She yanked on his biceps. "Does Raquel know?"

He sighed and crossed his arms. How to explain *that* situation?

"She knows I've inherited these items, but neither of us knew their value. She suspected it would be somewhere between a butt-ton and a metric butt-ton."

Brianna giggled. "I think it's closer to a metric butt-ton."

A frown crossed his face. "I'm not sure she'll be happy about that. She seems uncomfortable with the issue of money."

"Yeah, I don't know the whole story because she doesn't talk about it. But my brother served with Eduardo, her brother—that's how we met—before he died in that helicopter crash, and my brother got the impression that their dad used money to control their mom and the whole family. So I can see why she'd be uncomfortable with a guy having a lot more money than she does."

"But I tried giving it all to her, and she wouldn't take it."

Brianna blinked and waved her hands in front of her. "Wait, you mean, give *everything* to her? Not just that stone but *all* of them?"

"Yes. Everything I'd received." When Brianna's jaw dropped into a horrified expression, his arms fell to his sides. "That was the wrong thing to do?"

"Holy crap, Garrett! You can't go around giving people that

much stuff. Money makes people weird. You saw how those two"—she gestured back toward the section of the city where the store was located—"reacted. Hell, you saw how *I* reacted. And for all of us, that was a reaction to a fraction of the money." She sighed, as though resetting herself. "It's not that you did anything *wrong*, but yeah, you freaked her out. At least with me, I feel like I did *something* to earn the money, but it would feel really weird to be *given* a lot of money for no reason."

Understanding clicked in his mind. Raquel had emphasized how she'd *earned* her team's respect. For some reason, she seemed to think she didn't deserve things unless she'd earned them, so of course giving her the equivalent of millions of dollars for what must have seemed like no reason would be cause for a "freak-out." Not to mention that she knew his original plan had been—for all intents and purposes—to *buy* her cooperation for his mission, so a part of her might still be concerned about his motives, especially given her history with her father.

He'd have to find a way to ensure she felt she deserved his gifts. The balance between cherishing someone, respecting someone, and making sure they respected themselves and felt respected was trickier than he'd thought.

"Thank you. That makes sense and helps me know how to present my gifts to her."

Brianna's brows arched, and she patted his arm. "You know, you're kind of odd, but you're also a really good guy. Are you sure you don't have a brother?"

Adrenaline rushed through his body and buzzed in his head. Now that he'd nearly secured his mate-bond with Raquel, it was time to turn his attention to Kamen and the rest of his regiment. Would Brianna's acceptance of his oddities stretch far enough? He didn't want to risk Raquel and Brianna's friendship, and thus his bond to Raquel, by sharing his secret without approval, but this might be the answer he needed.

"Maybe. I'd want to speak to Raquel about the possibility first."

"Oh, you *tease*! Can't you at least give me a hint?"

He probably shouldn't have said anything yet, given how expectantly she now looked at him. "Well, I don't technically have a brother, but I have a friend who's like a brother."

"Yes!" Brianna pumped her fist. "Sign me up."

He *definitely* shouldn't have said anything yet. Nevertheless, her enthusiasm was contagious. "Even if he's odd like I am?"

"Pshaw. If he's half as good-looking as you are and just as adorably sweet, I can forgive a lot of oddness."

"Let me check with Raquel to see if she thinks you'd be a good match. I'll let you know."

"You'd better. You have my number now, so no excuses." She tapped her phone with her reminder, and then she swore at the display. "Crap. I gotta go." She kissed him on the cheek. "Let me know when you hear from Howard that the ring is ready, and I'll go with you to pick it up."

She hailed a taxi and was gone practically before he had a chance to wave goodbye. The woman was a whirlwind, but a helpful whirlwind. Thanks to her, he might have both secured a mate and found a way to awaken Kamen.

Quite a productive day.

# Chapter Thirty-One

*Somewhere in the North Sea...*

THE LAST GLOW OF SUNLIGHT FADED FROM THE SLIT UNDER THE door. Jaida's cell grew darker, colder. Another day had passed. Still a prisoner. Still wishing she were dead.

She crawled to the far wall, dragging her chains behind her. The metal loops clanged and scraped against the stainless steel floor. In the darkness, her fingertips searched the wall panel for the scratches indicating where she'd left off her daily marks. There. Exactly where she remembered making the last one.

The rock in her other hand grew warm, absorbing her magic. The small shard was the one piece of comfort she'd managed to hang onto over the years, even as *he* had moved her from cell to cell. The one thing that reminded her of home, of freedom.

The fragment of flint wasn't like the rest of her cell, a prison of stainless steel at the floor, walls, ceiling, cuffs, and chains. Stainless steel wasn't pure enough to burn and kill a faerie of the earth clan, but she also couldn't manipulate her way out of the cage, like she'd have been able to do with a stone dungeon. Instead, the metal kept her trapped indefinitely—and forever on the edge of exhaustion.

At her mental command, the flint shard levitated and began the slow process of etching the stainless steel wall panel. Why she kept up this habit after so long, she couldn't say. Each move to a new location meant she'd had to leave the previous record behind, but it didn't matter when she remembered every detail with utter clarity.

Every detail of the night the monsters had come to the home she'd shared with her mother—their beady eyes shining in the torchlight, their unfamiliar sounds as they captured her, their heartless slaughter of her mother. Every detail of the open-mouthed horror on her mother's face, the screams they both made, the cold touch of the monsters' skin. Every detail of the two decades since that night, ever since the monsters had left her with *him*.

Over the years, he'd used every method of torture imaginable to attempt to force her to use her magic. Luckily, he didn't know her real name—with her mother dead, no one did—so he couldn't control her, and torture didn't work on her clan.

All faeries of the earth clan possessed a flawless memory, and that meant grudges against those who had wronged them were a way of life. Grudges were never forgotten, never forgiven, and never ignored. Giving in to *him*, the creature who had destroyed her family, destroyed her life, wasn't possible.

Someone like *him*, one who had worked closely with her clan for centuries, should have known that truth. Maybe he'd thought abducting a child would make a difference, but her clan's perfect recall went all the way back to the womb. Just as the earthen spirit of the land remembered everything, so did she.

Jaida called the rock to her palm and brushed her fingertip over the metal panel, checking the depth of today's scratch mark. One more day of her life stolen from her.

The metal under her legs already felt cool. Time to retreat to her nest of blankets in a desperate attempt to stay warm. This latest location he'd dragged her to—wherever that was on the Earthen plane—cooled off faster at night than some of the other places. She wrapped the threadbare blankets around her long shift dress and bunched up the material under her to create a barrier from the cold metal as much as possible.

Sometimes, when she was lucky and hadn't been drained of too much energy during the day, she could relax enough at night to stretch out her senses and feel the presence of the earth nearby. In one location, a stone foundation had been tantalizingly close under the steel at her feet, but usually she sensed the earth only far below the building itself.

Whether the frustration of failure was worth it, she couldn't decide. However, after those rare times she could make contact, a wave of freedom would envelop her, the entire Earthen plane open to her perception of the Earth itself.

She settled into her fabric nest and imagined leaving her body in search of the Earth. *His* presence darkened her awareness like a lava flow across a landscape, but she ignored him. The years had proven that he couldn't detect when she reached out like this.

For the first time in months, luck was with her tonight. The comforting embrace of the ground below welcomed her, and she dove into the sensation, relishing the contact with something that felt like her home on Mythos.

But the Earth was in no mood to relax—change had shattered its calm presence.

She listened for the flow of magic to determine the source of change. Through mountains and valleys, under oceans' great surfaces, and across endless fields, she listened for what would make the unvarying Earth interested in change.

Her eyes popped open, and she sat up. A gargoyle? Another one?

A shiver overwhelmed her body, half from the cold and half from the new threat. Gargoyles were supposed to be on the Mythos plane, serving the faeries. Had they *all* decided to betray her kind? Was their disloyalty how the monsters had gotten to her and her mother?

But even if that was the case, what was this gargoyle doing *here*—on the Earthen plane? Only one answer made sense. *He* must be attempting to gather reinforcements against her.

Well, she'd let him know what she thought of *that* idea. Nothing would change her mind. Not him, and not this new gargoyle working with him. Not even if he had a hundred gargoyles on his side.

Nothing would make her open the portal.

# Chapter Thirty-Two

WITH A TWIST OF HER KEY, RAQUEL OPENED HER APARTMENT door and met the grinning face of Garrett. His expression set off her suspicions. He'd been up to something. She set her backpack down on the counter.

"Hey. How was your day?"

He stalked forward and slanted his lips over hers. Her first instinct was to pull back and hit him—just out of habit—but she gave herself over to the heady feeling of his desire. He pressed her against the closed door and held her jaw, worshiping her mouth.

"I hope this is allowed, because I missed you." His voice was deep and nearly growling. "I've been thinking of you all day."

She smiled against his lips. "Thinking of me how?"

"It doesn't matter. As long as you're with me."

Words like that could make a woman melt. She twined her arms around his neck to stay upright and hopped, hooking her legs around his hips. He pressed into her, and she gasped, her head falling back. His lips tickled her jaw, trailing kisses, and he sucked, unleashing tingles under her ear.

A minute later, he had her naked and pinned against the door, her arms overhead. He rubbed their bodies together, teasing her. She angled her hips, trying to make him slip inside, but he tilted out of reach.

A teasing lilt colored his voice. "Does that mean you want me now?"

Her words came out on panted breaths. "That would assume I ever stopped wanting you."

"Mmm, I know the feeling." He gave in and filled her needs—in every possible way.

She would never get tired of this feeling. "Oh God." She squeezed her legs around him. "You're enough to make a girl happy about going to work if this is what she comes home to."

Slowly, luxuriously, as though they had their whole lives ahead of them to enjoy this, he pumped into her. The door thumped inside its frame with every thrust. Good thing she didn't care about what the neighbors thought.

At one point, her cell phone buzzed from inside her backpack, but she didn't care about that either. Probably just Brianna looking for something to tease her about, and Raquel would rather keep this secret to herself a bit longer. Secrets could be tantalizing, and this one was delectable.

Over the weekend, Garrett had learned all her most sensitive spots, and now he released her arms to stimulate every one of them with his talented fingers. Her excitement building, she muffled a scream against his shoulder.

Okay, maybe she cared about the neighbors a little bit.

After another minute of delicious sensations, he sped up his thrusts, and she immediately pitched over the edge, the easy response of the sex-crazed woman he'd turned her into. Colors spun at the edge of her vision, and her muscles clenched him desperately. So good, so good.

Pleasure ricocheted off ecstasy, and she no longer felt connected to her body. Every nerve ending spoke only of rapture that couldn't be contained. She bit into his shoulder to hold in her yell. He came a few seconds later with the sexiest growl on the planet vibrating their chests together. Their hearts pounded in unison.

Before she started slipping, he held her against him and brought them to the bed, where they could disentangle at their leisure. He stroked her lips and grinned. "I'm sorry. Should I have gotten permission to kiss you first?"

"Well, I *did* think about hitting you, but going along with your plan was a *much* better idea."

"Then considering I didn't have a plan beyond wanting to get close to you, that went surprisingly well."

"Shh." She giggled and pressed his mouth closed. "You're supposed to make me think you had such an extravagant plan that there was no point in trying to resist you."

"I can't resist you, so it would be fair if you were stuck in the same situation."

She snuggled against him and sighed dramatically. "I guess."

Was it illegal to feel this happy? Her gaze landed on the picture of her guys. Pain tightened the back of her throat, but even that guilt couldn't break her happy mood. Was she a bad person for allowing herself to move on when they couldn't?

Garrett's thumb traced the corner of her eye. "What's wrong?"

She nodded to the picture by the windows. "A pang of survivor guilt. Sorry. You're probably sick of hearing about it."

"Never. If it matters to you, it matters to me." His jaw shifted with his thoughts. "But I also think they'd want you to be happy. You being miserable won't make things better for them."

She flinched.

He hugged her. "I'm sorry. Was that too blunt?"

"No, you're right. No matter how unhappy I was, it wouldn't bring them back, and they'd want me to be happy. If the situation were reversed, I'd want that for them." She drew circles on his magnificent chest. "And I'm getting there. But I still wish things were different."

"Of course you wish for things to be different. That will likely never change."

"Never?"

"Do you want to stop wishing for things to be different?"

"Yes... No." She sighed and spread her fingers over his heartbeat. "Yes, I wish I could stop thinking about it because it's hard and sad and at times like this, I'm tired of being sad. But no, I don't really want to stop thinking about it because that would mean I've forgotten them."

"That's why you have to find a way to hold on to the wish that things were different and still allow yourself to be happy."

She smiled, but the bittersweet topic kept it subdued. "Thank you for understanding me so well."

"I could say the same for you." His fingers flowed through her hair, and his expression turned pensive.

"Okay, your turn. What's wrong?"

"I had an idea today that I wanted to talk to you about, but I'm not sure now is the best time."

She had a hunch about why *now* wouldn't be the best time. "Worried about me being fragile?"

"Quite frankly, yes. I never want to be the cause of pain for you again."

"If you hold me, I think I'll be okay." When he didn't look convinced, she laughed. "Seriously, you have magic arms or something, because I feel stronger when I'm with you."

He squeezed her. "I'm glad I can help." After a moment, he propped himself up on his elbow and kept his other arm around her. "It's about how we might be able to wake Kamen."

Her breathing hitched, but she focused on the fact that he wouldn't let anything hurt her. "Okay..."

"I know you understand the loyalty aspect of our motto, but my desire to help him—and all of my regiment—goes beyond simple duty." His jaw shifted. "As supreme commander, I *should* have known whether they were here or on Mythos, and I *should* know all their locations now without having to rely on image searches. But due to the circumstances of how I received my assignment, I never received all the abilities I should have."

His gaze unfocused and furrows deepened on his forehead. "It *pains* me that they're suffering because I'm not worthy of my position."

Her chest ached, and she snuggled closer. She could understand his struggle as well as her own.

"It's not your fault that your assignment is screwy. You're doing the best you can." She angled her head and caught his eye, a smile tugging at her lips. "Someone very smart and understanding told me last week that we shouldn't beat ourselves up for things that happen outside our control."

His mouth twisted into a wry shape. "Someone smart and understanding, huh?"

"And sexy as hell, but really, that's just a bonus." She laid her palm on his chest. "Okay, now tell me about this idea of yours."

"What if we told someone—someone who already knows I'm a little odd compared to the rest of human society but thinks I'm a decent guy anyway—about what I really am. And if she believed us, what if we gave her the opportunity to help Kamen?"

The hairs on the back of her neck stood up, and her muscles tensed, ready for a fight-or-flight decision. That plan sounded risky as hell, and she didn't want to risk him. Then her stomach hardened even more, the truth of what he proposed crystallizing her worries.

"Brianna. You're talking about Brianna, right?"

"Yes." His eyes turned apologetic. "I thought of the possibility when she asked if I had a brother."

Visions of all the ways the plan could go wrong flashed in her head. Would Brianna want to have him committed? Would she want to have them *both* committed? Would she go public with his story, risking their privacy and the safety of the other gargoyles?

"Stay with me, Raquel." He drew her face toward his. "Stay with me."

"I'm okay—not going anywhere. Really." She gave him a smile. "This is just plain ol' fear, not a flashback."

She hadn't realized how tense he'd become at her reaction until he relaxed against her now. He caressed her belly. "I know. This would be risking your friendship with her, so I'd never do this without your approval."

"*My* friendship with her? I'm worried about *you*. About how this would be risky for you."

He detached her clutching hand from his chest and kissed her knuckles. "I understand. But I don't think she'd do anything to hurt me. To hurt us." He rubbed her palm and met her gaze with a serious expression. "I have to be willing to take risks to help my regiment, and this is a way I might be able to save Kamen."

Her bone-deep desire to help him save his guys battled with her fear. The needs of his regiment were worth the risk of trusting Brianna, but...

The last few days had wrung her out emotionally, from the agony of the worst flashback of her life to the ecstasy of her weekend with Garrett. She needed time.

She wasn't ready for another life-disrupting event. Too much had changed lately for her to feel stable and secure yet. She wanted to enjoy more time with him before doing anything that would potentially bring the last couple of days of happiness crashing down around them.

She hedged her answer. "I think we could make it work, but give me time to make sure we've planned for all the risks and how best to deal with them."

Putting him off on something so important felt selfish, but unforeseen risks *were* a valid concern. Right?

After a slight hesitation, the nod he gave her was gentle and accepting. No pressure. No rushing. No pushing.

Yeah, he probably wasn't happy about the delay, but couldn't she get *one* damn week of peace? One week of feeling less broken and scared? One week of getting to enjoy life like a normal person?

She'd give herself—and them—a few more days before taking that step.

Even though *forever* didn't feel long enough.

# Chapter Thirty-Three

R AQUEL DOWNED HER THIRD GLASS OF WATER SINCE SHE'D finished eating dinner. Garrett had convinced her that another round of sex had been in order and then watched over her to ensure she wasn't getting dehydrated from all the exercise. His concerned hovering was a small price to pay for the additional pleasure.

He gestured to her backpack. "What did Brianna want?"

Her cell phone had rung several more times since they'd attacked the door with their thrusting, but she'd let it go to voice mail each time. She supposed she should check before Brianna came all the way out here for nothing. Then the woman would tease them endlessly for the overly satisfied look Raquel knew must be on her face.

"I forgot to check." She hefted the bag to the bed and slipped her cell phone from the front pocket.

She pressed the icon for messages, and a woman's voice—not Brianna's—sounded over the speaker, "Raquel? It's Tití Ruth. Give me a call as soon as you get this message. It's important."

Her aunt? Every muscle inside her chest tightened into a knot of sick dread. How did the woman have her number? And why had she tracked her down?

Over the years, Raquel had purposely left her family behind, especially those on her father's side.

The next several messages were the same, except the woman's desperation increased each time. Raquel closed the voice mail app and debated shutting off her phone entirely.

"It's my aunt." She shuddered. So much for her hopes of getting a whole week of peace. Dealing with her family was *not* something she wanted to do. Ever. "She claims it's important."

Garrett guided her to sit next to him on the mattress. "What can I do to help?"

The temptation to suggest that he help her change her name and move to another country beckoned from a corner of her mind. Was that an overreaction?

Maybe. But maybe not.

Instead, she psyched herself up for the return call. It was probably nothing. In fact, given her extended family's tendency toward dramatics, it was almost certainly nothing.

She squared her shoulders and gave him a nod. "Hold me while I have to deal with my family. Give me some of that magic strength from your arms."

He spread his hands wide, and she settled against his chest. Thus prepared, she pressed the icon to return her aunt's call.

The line picked up at the first ring. "Raquel? Thank goodness. I'm so sorry, *corazón*. I have to tell you—"

Her aunt started blubbering and wasn't able to get her words out. A Spanglish mix sounded in the background, and shuffling noises muted the speaker. Raquel wasn't sure if she should feel nauseated by the weight in her stomach or roll her eyes at the melodrama.

"Raquel?" A man's voice asked the question this time.

"Y-e-s." She dragged out the word to match their prolonging of this 'news.'

"It's your *papi*. He died last night."

A *smack* sounded over the speaker, and her aunt yelled at the man for not breaking the news more gently. Their voices faded as Raquel's thoughts drowned out their argument.

Her father was dead. Her *father* was dead. Her father was *dead*. She waited for the reaction to come. But nothing followed.

She wasn't upset. She wasn't shocked. She wasn't happy. And she certainly wasn't sad.

Her father's death was just a fact.

The man who had decided that she—a girl—would never measure up and was good for nothing... The man who had been strict and traditional with her mamá and a two-faced scumbag behind her back... The man who had forced her mamá to die a slow and painful death because he didn't want his lies exposed... He was dead and gone.

Shouldn't she have more of a reaction? Shouldn't she *feel* something? Anything?

Her spine stiffened and became ramrod straight. No, this was good. She didn't want to waste any sorrow on that poor excuse of paternal DNA. She never needed his love or acceptance anyway.

She repeated the thoughts in her head several times, willing them to be true. Hurt leaked through the sloppy patch job over the truth, and her chest hollowed. The truth was that she'd lost the last chance to ever prove herself to him.

She smothered the pointless debate in her mind and managed to prevent herself from expressing her thoughts to her sobbing aunt. But then the more immediate problem came into view. There would be a funeral. And she would be expected to attend.

Hell, as the last member of her immediate family, she might be expected to organize it.

Her lips curled, disgust clogging her nose, and her stomach roiled. She'd attend, but if she was supposed to make the funeral arrangements, she'd see about renting a catapult to fling his body into the East River. That would almost be more respect than he'd granted her mamá.

Instead of voicing that idea, she stuck with a simple answer. "I see."

"Oh, my poor *corazón*, I know it's a huge shock. But don't worry, the family will pull together. We won't let you suffer alone. We've taken care of all the arrangements already."

"Thank you." Maybe if she kept her answers short and to the point, she could escape the conversation unscathed. She didn't need her family in her business, but not having to deal with the arrangements was good news. "Where and when?"

"We're all flying to the island the day after tomorrow to meet at the funeral home."

"The *island*?" Her detached calm shattered, and her voice squeaked high enough to reach through the roof of her apartment building. "The funeral is in *Puerto Rico*?"

"Yes, we have your ticket, and you'll be staying with us at your cousin Karla's."

Garrett and the rest of the apartment faded from her awareness, and she clutched her free arm to her ribcage. "But why isn't the funeral here? In New York?"

A sour taste rose in the back of her throat that she couldn't swallow away, and her breathing became more ragged. She hadn't flown since she'd returned stateside, and her paranoia was happier for that. Add in going to a place she'd never been and staying with a supposed cousin she'd never met, and the whole idea was an episode waiting to happen. Maybe more than one.

"It was your *papi*'s greatest wish to be buried on the island."

Yeah, where he wouldn't be buried next to the wife he'd betrayed. Cold spread from her chest. She hated him all over again.

"Besides," her aunt continued, "Doña Maria wanted him to come home."

Of course she did. Her father's mother had always refused to travel. That's why Raquel had never met the woman.

Her grandmother probably thought her little boy was perfect too, with his every-other-month trips to the island to carry on some of his affairs while claiming his purpose was to visit his mother. Or if the woman was anything like her son, maybe she wanted to exert her power over the rest of the family.

Raquel rocked on the bed, barely aware of the strong arms surrounding her. The urge to escape pounded through her like a drumbeat. *Run away. Run away. Run away.*

Those arrangements meant either Raquel had to skip her own father's funeral—which would cause the rest of the family to start praying for her immediate transfer to Hell—or she had to accept the situation. The situation that would lead to one freak-out after another.

Why couldn't she say *no*? It wasn't like she cared about her family's impression. Or Hell for that matter. Did she?

Or did a part of her still wish for that last opportunity with her father? Why did she still feel so connected to him that she cared about saying goodbye?

She drew in sharp breaths through her nostrils, trying to hold off from hyperventilating. "I'll have to call you back, Aunt Ruth."

She hung up and glanced at Garrett, who was looking at her questioningly. Garrett... Who didn't have an ID to get past airport security.

Shakes started in her chest. Oh God. He couldn't even come with her.

She'd have to endure all that melodrama without her rock—almost literally—at her side. She couldn't do it. She just couldn't. Changing her name and moving to another country *would* be easier.

She slouched and pressed her palm over her mouth, leaning away from Garrett's embrace. For years, her goal had been to prove she was good enough to deserve respect. And yet here she was, falling apart in the face of her family and ready to commit herself to the psych ward because she wasn't strong enough to do something on her own.

How pathetic.

"I'm here for you, Rocky."

Garrett had twisted her around to face him, and his eyes were full of concern. She'd zoned out again, and just as he'd been for days, he was there to help her.

Tightness gathered in her stomach and traveled up to her jaw. Her instincts wanted to lash out at him. Wanted to live up to her nickname and punch first and ask questions later. Wanted to prove that she was still strong—inside and out.

But this was Garrett in front of her, and he deserved better.

He'd become her soulmate, who knew her and understood her. He was her security blanket, even more comforting than her Beretta M9. He was showing her a future that didn't have to be mere survival.

She swallowed, burying the instincts and emotions threatening to erupt inside her, and gave him a nod to let him know she was back. At least for the moment.

She couldn't make any promises for how long her tenuous hold would last.

# Chapter Thirty-Four

QUICK FLASHES OF EMOTIONS FLITTED OVER RAQUEL'S FACE, and Garrett watched for a sign that she'd recovered. Although concerned about the nature of the phone call, he forced himself to wait until she was ready to talk.

At whatever news she'd heard, her expression had scrolled through variations of terror before she'd started hyperventilating. That had been his signal to call her Rocky—to break her free of whatever thoughts had overwhelmed her brain. Luckily, she always responded instantly to that name, a trigger to obey an order.

Now at her nod, he drew her close and stroked her hair. "You don't have to tell me what that call was about unless you want to, but if I *do* know, I might be able to help."

"Hang on. I'm thinking."

A smile curved his lips. "I assumed as much." His beautiful warrior never *stopped* thinking. "But I was referring to the fact that I can try to help you think through whatever is troubling you."

"How far could you fly while carrying me?"

"Gargoyles can fly a couple of hundred miles an hour, and carrying you is not an issue. However, being carried for too long would be uncomfortable, especially as that speed would be too windy and cold for you." He did a few quick calculations to reduce the speed and limit the time. "Perhaps a few hundred miles?"

"Not far enough." She worried at her lips. "Then I definitely need to figure out how I can sneak you onto a plane with me."

Google had taught him about the planes in the sky. "Why would I have to sneak rather than simply accompany you?"

"The airline industry is almost as paranoid as I am. They require everyone to have ID to board a plane, and you don't have—"

He pressed a fingertip over her mouth and pulled out his new wallet. His identification card was front and center inside, and he flipped the leather case open to show her.

Her jaw hung slack for a moment, and then she gazed up at him with wide eyes. "When? How?"

"Today, and..."

Should he let it slip that he'd seen Brianna earlier? Even though it might not *technically* be a lie to *not* reveal their meeting, he still didn't want to chance betraying Raquel in any way. That said, he also didn't want to ruin his surprise for her later.

"Brianna offered to help me open a bank account for the income from selling the gifts from the Earth." He tilted his chin, indicating the bag under the bed. "And to do so, I needed identification." He shrugged and let the grin that had been threatening to burst from his mouth since she first mentioned her problem take hold. "She told me she knew a guy."

Raquel launched herself at him so hard she knocked him to the mattress. She locked gazes with him for a stunned moment. "Do you have *any* idea how perfect you are?"

She melded her lips to his, and he rejoiced in her happy mood. Everything about her—and them together—felt right. Perfect. His decision this morning was the right step to take.

She was his future. She was his life. She would be his wife and mate.

In between kisses, he added, "I told you I could try to help."

"Mmm..." She purred against his neck. "I'm so glad I didn't doubt you."

"As am I." He stretched back to keep an eye on her reaction. "Does this solve the problem from the phone call?"

She groaned and sat up. "Not quite."

She crossed her arms in a gesture that seemed more self-protective than pissed. He sat beside her and caressed her back and shoulders.

"We don't have to talk about it if you're not ready."

"No, we *need* to talk about it because I need to get you on that plane with me." She sighed deeply and twisted her hair into a knot at the back of her head—a sign of her being upset, he'd noticed. "That was my aunt—my father's sister—and she told me that my father died last night."

*Family* was something he had no experience with. If anything, he'd guess his ties to his regiment were a pale imitation.

No wonder she was upset. Even though he'd gotten the sense that she'd struggled with the relationship, the bonds between parent and child were strong.

He needed to look only as far as Alann's despair after the loss of his son to see how complex family relationships were beyond his ability to understand. As Alann's second in command, he'd been the only one close enough to attempt to console him, but Alann didn't want to be consoled. Anger had overwhelmed his grief—anger and darkness that had made him believe it would have been better to keep his son locked up and isolated to prevent his death.

At Garrett's attempts to get him to see how that wouldn't have been a life worth living for his son, Alann had withdrawn, unwilling to listen. The bonds of family seemed to be stronger than logic and reason.

"I'm sorry," he offered, uncertain how to relieve her pain.

"Don't be." She pressed on her temples. "That's not the problem."

Instead of pushing for more understanding of her relationship with her father, he focused on her immediate emotional needs. "Then what *is* the problem?"

"Do you know what a funeral is? I mean, I know your kind can't usually die, but maybe you've seen or heard of the human tradition for one when someone dies."

"We held a funeral for Alann's son."

"Oh, right." She spun toward him on the bed. "So there's going to be a funeral for my father. And even though I pretty much hated his guts and don't want anything to do with my family, I still feel like I should be there, you know?" Her eyebrows tightened into a *V* shape. "Maybe that could be the closure I need to put that bitterness behind me. Like, once I say goodbye to him and the rest of my family, maybe I'll be able to move forward without letting memories of him or the things he did be part of my thoughts."

"That sounds reasonable. Sometimes facing our inner nightmares is the best way to take away their power."

"Exactly." Her lips curved into a smile that showed how much it was helping to have him beside her. "The good news is that even though I'm the last of my immediate family, *I* don't have to do the funeral planning." The curve of those lips bent down. "The bad news is that those who *are* doing the planning decided to hold the funeral in Puerto Rico."

"An island, and too far to carry you," he offered. "That's why we have to travel there in an airplane."

"Right." She flicked on her phone and brought up a map. "We're here, and Puerto Rico is here." Her finger dragged the image around on the screen in explanation. "It's a long flight and not one I'm looking forward to. I've never been to the island, as my father never wanted us with him during his booty-call visits, and if you remember my argument with Brianna, I barely consider myself Puerto Rican—partly because I don't speak Spanish."

"I learned the basics of many European languages during my time before."

"No offense, but your *English* is barely modern enough. Your sexy-ass accent distracts people from the way you sometimes word things oddly, but for other languages, I don't think a few phrases from a couple of hundred years ago will help much."

She waved her hand dismissively. "Besides, Puerto Rican Spanish isn't like normal Spanish. It's a mix of Spanish, Taino words from the native culture, some English, some Spanglish, some bizarre turns of phrase, its own grammar rules, and it's all pronounced differently from Spain's Spanish. Even though I recognize the rhythm and flow of Boricua Spanish, I refused to learn it for real—call it another way of rebelling against my father—so understanding actual words would require more brain power than I feel like dedicating to any aspect of this inevitable catastrophe."

A wry grin had stretched his face with her rant, especially when memories of his inability to follow Brianna's conversation with the jewelry store's owner proved Raquel's claims. "So I can't help you that way, but I can try to help you in every other way."

"Are you sure about this? You'd have to be on your best no-gargoyle-stuff behavior. The rest of my family is very religious—or at least they think of themselves that way—to the point that I was raised to request a *benedicion*, a blessing, from the elders among my relatives every time I talked to them. So they *would* take you to be a demon. Or worse."

"I do not ever *have* to change into that form, except for fighting. I would hope it safe to assume that I won't be battling to the death with any of them."

"Let's hope not." Her laugh wavered, exposing her nervousness. "Being there with me also means you'd be volunteering to be interrogated by my family. They've never known me to be *with* someone before, and if you think Brianna is loud and in everyone else's business, they're ten times worse. They'll ask about you, your job, your family, your intentions toward me, and whether you're planning on helping me give my grandmother any great-grandchildren. That sort of thing. Are you still okay with this plan?"

"We can work out appropriate answers for all those questions." He held her gaze, emphasizing his seriousness. "I *will* be there for you. Always."

"Thank you." Her shoulders had seemingly dropped an inch during their conversation. She picked up his wallet from where it had dropped on the floor with her earlier tackle and read his ID. "Garrett Mason, huh? I guess the next gauntlet I have to run is telling my aunt I need an additional ticket."

"Don't worry. If she gives you any problems, I'll follow you there by riding on the outside of the plane." At her laugh—genuine this time—he hauled her in close and brought his lips to her ear. "Somehow, some way, I will be there, my love." Even though he still didn't know whether a soulless monster like him could love, the words felt right.

Her body shivered in his embrace, as he knew would happen. Their bond would be unbreakable. Forever.

# Chapter Thirty-Five

Y ET ANOTHER OUTBURST POUNDED ON GARRETT'S EARDRUMS, and he lifted his finger to his lips, shushing the woman on the other side of Raquel. The inside of the plane was cramped, and one of Raquel's seemingly endless cousins had ended up sharing their aisle. The woman's loud exclamations and interruptions to others in the surrounding rows had caused Raquel's eyelids to flutter one too many times for his patience.

He tucked her closer and touched her forehead. "Sleep."

She needed the rest. Yesterday had been a whirlwind of preparations, from arranging for her time off work and dealing with her aunt's interrogations to shopping for appropriate funeral clothes for her and picking out designs he could copy for his shapeshifting patterns.

No doubt, if he hadn't been able to accompany her on this trip, she wouldn't be catching up on sleep right now. While in the airport, her head and eyes had remained in constant motion, scouting the surroundings for enemies and planning escape paths. Just as any good warrior would do.

But now on the plane and in the air, there were no escape paths, and she couldn't easily check for enemies behind her either. Only his arm around her had calmed her jumpiness. She hadn't expressed any of those thoughts or concerns to him, of course, but he knew.

Truth be told, he wasn't doing much better. How could humans trust flying in a metal tube without wings of their own to support them if something went wrong?

The cousin beside them twisted in her seat to chatter at the family members behind them. Her knee knocked Raquel, causing his warrior to flinch in her sleep. Again.

The time with her family had already illuminated how difficult this whole trip would be for her. Unlike the rest of her family, she wasn't the type to weep and wail, as though they were each trying to out-do the others in a display of despair. She wasn't boisterous or outgoing, far preferring calm and quiet order. And she wasn't apt to join the brokenhearted laments of how her father was a wonderful man who would be missed.

She would need Garrett by her side constantly, providing her an oasis of comfortable solace within the chaos. He could do that. Even though this trip meant a delay of his hopes for dealing with Kamen, supporting Raquel was infinitely more important. Kamen could wait.

A flicker of irritation scratched at his thoughts, and he shoved it aside. Kamen *had* to wait.

A week ago, he'd vowed to put her first and not begrudge his need for this bond, but centuries of attitude didn't want to be ignored so easily. The thoughts still poked him from all sides, like tentacles seeking to haul him back under a belligerent, hostile surface.

A lifetime of experience with the fickle nature of bonds had left behind a layer of resentment. That bitterness wasn't directed in any way toward Raquel and the future she offered him—far from it.

Instead, his annoyance came from his need for a bond at all—his lack of freedom. No amount of appreciation for her understanding and loyalty could erase the irritation growing inside him at how the faeries limited his kind. He wished to be free of those limitations for both his and Raquel's sake, so they could step into the future without restrictions.

Even though it was a pointless wish, a yearning for freedom couldn't be suppressed.

To distract himself, he shifted his arm around her shoulders and gazed down at her face. In sleep, her expression grew soft and lost its fierceness. She was beautiful, inside and out, and he didn't mind protecting her emotionally and keeping her happy. He didn't.

But no matter how much he logically understood the source of his irritation, the next few days would definitely test his patience. He hoped he would be up to the task of offering what she needed. The dangers to him if he couldn't manage that task—if he couldn't keep her and their bond strong—were far more risky to him than to her.

THE NEXT SEVERAL HOURS PASSED IN A FLURRY OF MORE OF THAT chaos neither of them appreciated, and Garrett continued doing his best to support Raquel. After landing, the whole gathering traveled straight to Raquel's grandmother's house. There, they met up with even more family members who were local to Puerto Rico, including the short-but-imposing Doña Maria herself.

He wasn't sure if it mattered that neither of them understood the language, as that barrier didn't stop others from talking to them non-stop in a mix of English and what he assumed was the local Spanish dialect. Every time he caught Raquel's eye, she gave him a shrug that said she had no idea what they were talking about either.

That night, at her cousin Karla's house, her aunt insisted that Raquel sleep in the same room as her cousin. She'd made it quite clear that unless they were married, Raquel wasn't *allowed* to leave and share a hotel room with Garrett either.

As bedtime neared, he noticed the beginnings of panic on Raquel's face and drew her aside. "Do I have permission to tell your aunt of your nightmares?"

She scanned a collection of framed pictures on a nearby cabinet, picking up one here and there for a closer look. "I feel like I should know who these people are." Her gaze skipped over the groups in the next room and in the halls. "But I don't know any of them. I don't even know why I'm here. Why do I care what they think?"

"You're here because you don't want to have any regrets. You want to fulfill your duty because duty and honor matter to you. You're here to say goodbye in a way that gives *you* the closure you need."

A smile lit her face for the first time since their trip began. "You really do know me."

"Yes, I do. And that means I also noticed that you changed the subject and didn't answer my question." He dipped his head to hers. "Should I take that avoidance as a *no*, or could I try to get your aunt to understand?"

"I guess you could try." She returned the frame in her grasp to its place on the cabinet. "Anyway, they'll know about my nightmares soon enough if they keep you from me, when I wake up screaming in the middle of the night."

He scanned the clusters of people, their skin tones various shades of browns and whites—yet supposedly all related to Raquel somehow. Groups were scattered around the room, the hallway, and adjacent kitchen. Despite the late hour, no one seemed eager to go to bed anytime soon, their arms and voices still animatedly raised.

This gathering was not at all what he'd expected for a funeral. Rather than the silent despair of Alann's grief for his son, this felt more like a reunion party, where family members long separated caught up on news and gossip. The tears had been in abundance earlier, especially at Doña Maria's, but as the hour went on—and more drinks were imbibed—the mood had changed.

Through the living room window behind Raquel, he finally spotted her aunt out on the front porch with several others, and he made his way through the front door. Raquel trailed him, her face pulled into a grimace. If he had to guess, she didn't want to be part of the conversation, but she also didn't want to be left alone.

He gave a slight bow to her Aunt Ruth. "May I have a word with you in private?"

The woman looked up at him, her expression incredulous. One of the other women tittered and mumbled something in the Spanish dialect he couldn't understand. They all broke out in raucous laughter.

Ruth waved the other women away and followed him to the front yard. The vegetation and surroundings here were very different from what he'd seen on the Earthen plane before. Several palm trees lined the road, blocking the glow from the streetlight down the block. He stood so the bright lights shining through the front windows of the house would illuminate his face, the better to show his sincerity. Raquel wandered to the curb and leaned against a car, out of the conversation but nearby.

He gave a bow again. "Thank you for hearing me out. I would ask you to reconsider your rule about Raquel's sleeping arrangements." As soon as Ruth's mouth opened, he held up a hand. "Let me finish. Please."

Her mouth snapped shut, her lips pursed. It was obvious that she considered herself Raquel's parental figure after the loss of both parents, and she was going to judge what she thought was best for Raquel, despite knowing nothing about her.

"You may not know this about your niece, but she suffers nightmares every night."

"Nightmares?" The woman scoffed.

"These are not the bad dreams of children but the effects of wartime atrocities."

Her eyes narrowed and then flicked in Raquel's direction behind him.

"We've discovered that having me at her side at night helps. All we ask is that you allow your niece to make her own decisions—as the adult she is."

The woman's chin jutted out, and he couldn't tell if his words were having an effect or not.

"Please," he continued. "She will need all the sleep and respite from..." Unable to come up with a better way to explain the problem, he waved toward the house, where a squeal and shout pierced the darkness.

Ruth's expression closed down, and she crossed her arms. "What are you saying? That she needs a break from family? *Bah.*" She pointed accusingly. "You. You are the problem here. You're the one trying to control her." Ruth strode around him toward the street. "My poor *corazón*, is he bothering you? I'll forbid him from stepping foot here. From attending the funeral. I'll—"

"No, *Tití*, it's not like that. He's been *helping* me."

He stretched his fingers, refusing to let them clench and give away the level of his frustration, while Ruth's gaze swept over him from head to toe.

"Fine. I won't make him leave." She glared at him, wrapping her false authority around her like battle armor. "But Raquel must still stay here, and you must still sleep elsewhere in the house."

Raquel straightened away from the car and headed back toward the house, her shoulders rounded. "Fine. Whatever. Then I can wake the whole damn neighborhood."

He refused to accept defeat. He couldn't risk failure.

"May I at least be allowed into the room to comfort her when the nightmares disturb her?" He moved closer to Ruth, imbuing every thought of sincerity he could into his approach. The moment didn't afford him an excuse to touch Ruth's forehead and use his influence on her mind, but he brushed her arm and hoped it would be enough. "Trust me."

Raquel stopped in her trudge to the porch, waiting.

Ruth considered him for a moment, and her focus slid to Raquel. "Yes." She held up a finger. "You may enter the bedroom if—and only if—she is disturbed by nightmares, and you must leave immediately upon her settling down again. Understood?"

He ground his jaw. How he would love for Raquel to tell the lot of them to—he believed the phrase was—*go to hell.* She was an adult who had seen far more horror and reality than any of them could imagine, yet her aunt treated her as a child she could control. The woman's twisting of information to make him out to be the bad guy raised the question of what kind of manipulative mental abuse her father might have similarly carried out on Raquel.

If he sensed Raquel had the strength, he would attempt to convince her to stand up for what *she* wanted. But he suspected she'd crack if he added anything to the pressure she was already under.

He tried to be understanding. He tried to be supportive. But he worried it wouldn't be enough.

# Chapter Thirty-Six

I F GARRETT WERE HUMAN, RAQUEL'S GRIP ON HIS HAND AS THEY
entered the funeral home might have broken bones. Luckily, he
wasn't human.

For her sake, he was glad he didn't sleep either. Once the
houseful of people had settled the previous night, he'd given up
pretending to rest on one of the chairs in the living room. Careful
not to disturb the snoring relative on the couch, he'd crept down
the hall to the door of the room she was sharing with her cousin
and listened for her moans.

At the first sign of her nightmares, he let himself into the room,
touched her forehead and told her to sleep, and then slipped back
out to the hallway again. That scene had repeated about a dozen
times, but she hadn't screamed and she'd thanked him that
morning.

Now, though, however much her sleep had rejuvenated her, it
wasn't enough. Her entire body resonated with tension, from her
hunched shoulders to her stiff gait.

This morning she was to face her father's body for the first
time.

They followed the family into the building, where an employee
of the funeral home met with everyone. Garrett stuck with Raquel
as she hung back from the conversation in Spanish, apparently
content to let others handle the situation.

Once the employee opened the door to the next room, the family filed inside. Doña Maria passed by the arranged chairs and went straight to the casket at the front.

Raquel's Aunt Ruth directed the flow, holding everyone else back. She gave her instructions in English to Raquel. "Let's give her a moment of privacy."

Raquel plopped into one of the chairs, obviously not in a hurry. He stood behind her and squeezed her shoulder, letting her know he was there. This was going to be a long day.

After a long enough wait that others in the group had become restless, Doña Maria stood from the kneeling bench at the casket, although her wails continued. Ruth's husband stepped forward and offered her an arm, and she motioned to the floor, adding something in emphatic Spanish. Ruth's husband, apparently following her orders, brought one of the chairs forward, which she used to sit next to the coffin, one hand gripping the casket's side. Others exchanged glances, but no one argued with Doña Maria.

Ruth waved to Raquel. "Your turn, *corazón*."

Raquel's head snapped up. "Me?" Strands of hair loosened from their gathered shape with each shake of disagreement. "No, no. Let everyone else go first. I'll go..." Her brows gathered close. "Later." Her gaze landed on Doña Maria, calling attention to the woman's insistence on staying by her dead son's side. "When I can have privacy as well."

"Of course." Ruth winced. "She'll have to leave sometime."

Raquel exchanged a grim smile with her aunt. "Food. Bathroom. Something."

Ruth held Raquel's cheek. "You don't have to hold it inside, you know, *corazón*. You're surrounded by those who would understand." When Raquel didn't respond, her aunt straightened. "We'll make sure you have your privacy."

"Thank you."

After Ruth went back to directing the crowd, Raquel touched Garrett's fingertips on her shoulder and patted the chair next to her.

He took the seat she'd indicated. "I'm surprised you didn't want to get it over with."

She scanned the room, but everyone else was chattering farther down the aisle, waiting their turn at the casket. "Everyone says Doña Maria can't understand a word of English, but..." She leaned closer. "I'm not going to take the chance of anyone overhearing me tell him how much I hate his guts. I'll wait."

Despite her dismissive explanation, her tone was tight enough to snap back and cause damage, so he didn't press further. Ruth might be right about Raquel holding too much inside.

Instead, he watched for clues on how to behave for the remainder of the visitation. Between the difference of traditions and the language barrier, he could only follow along with everyone else.

Throughout the day, other family members and non-family arrived and paid their respects. Raquel sat silently the whole time, staring into nothingness and not engaging with others. How could he help her when he didn't understand the surroundings much less the issues inside her head?

In the afternoon, a man led the gathering in what Garrett surmised was a prayer service. Once again, he knew nothing of the language but imitated the crowd as they alternately stood and knelt—and then stood and knelt some more.

The mood in the room changed constantly, from bittersweet smiles and quiet hugs to screaming and wailing. More than once, lone women entered the room and nearly flung themselves into the casket. Some covered Raquel's father's face in kisses with exclamations of love that were understandable in any language. They usually had to be towed away, and then they stormed out of the room.

Raquel ignored all the turmoil, just as she had with the rest of the proceedings, until Ruth got into a screaming match with one of the women. Even Doña Maria stood from her chair and joined the fray. He concentrated more on the language than he had previously, attempting to determine whether he needed to get involved.

He picked up a few Spanish words for *wife*, *family*, and *respect*. At one point, Ruth gestured to Raquel with the word for *shame*. The shouting escalated until Doña Maria directed several uncles and male cousins to forcefully eject the woman from the room.

Garrett arched his brow in question at Raquel. She pursed her lips and dropped her gaze to her lap, going back to the same stiff pose she'd held all day.

Just when he felt certain she wasn't going to explain, she sighed. "I'm guessing those are some of the women my father had affairs with. This last one wanted to stick around and be honored by the rest of the family as if she were his wife."

"*Some* of the women?"

He spun in his chair and replayed how many women had strode down the aisle with a similar attitude. No wonder Raquel was ill-tempered by the thought of him needing other women to survive.

"Yes." She met his gaze, her eyes hard and glinting. "The women who haven't died already from all the diseases they exchanged. Like the one he gave my mamá..." Her jaw muscles rippled with tension. "The one that killed her."

Garrett's chest clenched so tight he curled forward. Even if he hadn't learned what betrayal and loyalty meant to her, he'd still have been shocked by the callousness of her father.

No matter how Garrett might have treated the women he'd bonded with over the centuries, he'd never *endangered* any of them, much less caused their *death*. He glanced around the room again, analyzing the rest of the family.

"How many here know?"

Her jaw shifted. "On some level, they all know. But none of them want to admit it."

He enfolded her hands, which were clasped on her lap, and brought them up to his lips for a kiss. "I'm sorry."

"Now you know the reason for my deep and abiding *ambivalence* for my family."

Between her resigned tone and casual shrug, his lips twisted into a snarl. She gave him an odd look, but before he could explain his inclination to feel offended on her behalf, Ruth approached and took a nearby chair.

"I think we're getting ready to leave. I'll try to have Doña Maria taken out with one of the first groups. You ready?"

Raquel sat up taller. "As ready as I'll ever be."

In reality, "we're getting ready to leave" translated into "we're going to spend another hour sobbing and wailing." By the time the others had cleared out, a funeral home employee was hovering impatiently in the background.

While Garrett followed Raquel up to the casket, she eyed the door that the last of the family had just walked through. "I'd appreciate you making sure I get that privacy. I don't trust them not to come back in here while my back is turned."

"Of course." From her side, he stood watch over the entrance and crossed his arms, ensuring no one would disturb her. Especially not that employee, who was puttering around with flower displays at the far end of the room.

Raquel stood beside him, facing her father. In his peripheral vision, he saw her fingers curl over the edge of the casket, her knuckles stark white.

"I don't know what to say to you." Her voice was soft, vulnerable. "I hate you. I hate the thought of you. I hate everything you stand for. And yet I'm here, having to pretend and go through the motions. Once again, you're controlling my life. Forcing me to fit into the neat little box of 'good girl.' Forcing me to think of you and your reputation before I think of what *I* want."

Her voice was as conflicted as her words, hurting one second and angry the next. He could only imagine that her thoughts were equally torn. After learning of her father's betrayal, he understood the anger more.

She pounded the edge of the casket. "And I hate it."

*There* was his warrior. Tension released from his body, his thoughts no longer divided between comforting her and ensuring her privacy.

"I want to cut you out of my heart—out of my life—because I know that no matter how good I am, I will never be good enough. Even if I were the best 'good girl' in the world, I'd still be to blame for Mamá's sickness in your eyes, as though the shit you pulled was nothing compared to the complications of her pregnancy with me."

Her voice wavered, only a thin filament of strength remaining. "But it wasn't me. It wasn't my fault that she was sickly and weak. I know that was just a lie you told me—and yourself—excusing your treatment of her and justifying your opinion of me. I know that her death wasn't my fault. I *know* that."

She repeated the words in a whisper, as though trying to convince herself of their truth. "I know that."

A flurry of movement caught his eye, and he twisted in time to see her collapse onto the kneeling bench. At her odd choking sound, he ignored the employee to focus on Raquel. What should he do? What *could* he do?

Warriors' dilemmas, like the mental scars of battles, he understood. But the conflicting emotions of dealing with family were beyond his experience or ability to understand.

"Why? Why did you hate me so much?" Her breath hitched.

She was crying? Over this father she *hated*?

"And if you thought I was to blame for everything, why did you treat Mamá like that? Why did you punish her too? Why couldn't you care about either of us? For that matter, why am I *still* giving you power over me?" She pounded the casket again. "Damn you!"

Raquel's exclamation filled the room, and the employee started toward them. Garrett shook his head at the man. The employee seemed to take the hint and left them alone in the room.

"Damn you," she repeated, softer. "I don't want to care." Her forehead rested on the backs of her hands, curled over the casket's edge. "I don't want to care."

Now that he didn't have to keep an eye out for the employee, Garrett faced the casket with her. Her father didn't appear as in the picture in her apartment. He looked gaunt, sickly. Maybe the illnesses he'd spread around had caught up with him in the end.

Raquel still bent over her hands at the kneeling bench. He hated seeing her like this—caught between wanting approval and affection from a man who couldn't give it and wanting nothing to do with the man she hated.

If Garrett had been around for Raquel earlier in her life, would he have been able to prevent any of this pain? Would he have been able to help her see her value earlier? Or would she not have turned into the warrior she was without the obstacles her father had put into her path?

More likely that Garrett would have hurt her as well. His life paralleled her father's path in too many ways. They were both users, and just as her father had needed her mother to keep the family going despite his neglect, Garrett needed Raquel to keep him going. He could only hope that he'd learned how to keep her happy better than her father had ever done.

The tears flowed freely down her cheeks, and he rubbed her

back. "I'm sorry."

"I hate that I'm crying over *him*." She lifted her head and wiped her tears. "I don't even know *why* I'm crying."

"Some emotions must be expressed and not ignored."

Her shoulders stiffened. "Stop it."

He froze in his comforting strokes. "What?"

"Stop being so fucking understanding and gentle and treating me like I'm a damned delicate flower who's about to break."

He reeled back as though she'd hit him hard enough to actually feel.

She stood but didn't turn toward him. "Damn it, I shouldn't be falling apart like this. I should be able to buck up and get myself together. And you... You should be yelling at me, telling me to stop crying."

His hand slipped off her shoulder and fell to his side. "You want me to *yell* at you?"

How could you make someone stop crying by yelling at them? The request didn't even make sense.

He thought he'd been doing everything right, doing what he needed to do to keep her happy. But he'd been wrong. He didn't know what he should be doing, what she needed.

She vibrated from head to toe, shaking. "I don't want to cry. I don't want to be a failure. I should be stronger than this shit. You shouldn't let me get away with this—with not being good enough. You deserve better."

His thoughts looped in a dizzy swarm like a whirlwind. How could she think herself a failure? Or not good enough? What chaos was going through her head?

He reached toward her. "I don't understand, but I promise you—it's going to be okay. You've been through a lot in the last few days, and you can't expect to survive everything on willpower and strength alone. "

"But I *need* to, and the fact I can't is proof that *he* was right." She spun toward him, smacking his hand away. "Don't try to help me. I'm too broken to deserve you. I don't deserve to be happy." Her fists rose to her temples. "I'd hoped we could help each other, but maybe I can't be fixed. Maybe you should escape while you can."

"We'll get through this together."

"No…" Her face tightened, and her voice trembled with the depth of an earthquake. "Please, just leave me alone."

The request hit him in his chest like a cannonball of ice, crushing him from the inside out. The warmth of their bond fractured, leaving stone-cold fear in his heart.

He'd failed her. Despite everything he'd tried to do, it wasn't enough. Just like with his missing supreme commander abilities, he could never succeed. He could never learn enough about how to love.

Cold speared through him from his core, heralding his imminent transformation into stone.

He'd thought she could never betray him. That he was safe in trusting her completely. But his inability to love prevented him from helping her through these emotions, and now stone-death would condemn him once more.

He'd been a fool to believe himself capable of love. A fool to believe he could be what she needed.

His self-disgust mixed with leftover resentment to whisper lies of misplaced blame from a corner of his mind…

*A fool, yes. A fool to trust her. Trusting anyone is your death. Trust doesn't work when you're the only one at risk. You were a fool to believe a permanent bond possible.*

The whispers stoked his frustration into anger that burned through him, competing with the cold flow of stone spreading into his limbs. Before he lost his voice to the statue engulfing him, every thought he'd tried to ignore for days—weeks—burst out from a place of darkness and pain.

"I've done *everything* for you. Given up *everything* for you. I know very well about not being good enough." Even though he knew his accusations were unfair to her, bitterness stretched out his words. "Goodbye, my warrior. I'm sorry I couldn't be enough for you."

# Chapter Thirty-Seven

RAQUEL WIPED ANOTHER ROUND OF TEARS AND FACED THE cold expression of betrayal on Garrett's face. *Oh no.* What had she done?

Her mind rewound her last words. *Leave me alone.*

Oh God. She engulfed him in a hug. Although he still looked human, his flesh was hard and unyielding like stone. Crackles vibrated under her embrace. *Please don't let it be too late.*

"I didn't mean that. I didn't mean that." She kissed him. "Of course I want you with me. You're enough for me. You're *more* than enough. You're way more than enough." She stroked his cheeks. "Don't leave me. Please, don't leave me." Even though she didn't know how the magic of their bond worked, she invoked the words. "I want to share my life with you. Please let me."

His skin softened, but he didn't move. Why didn't he move?

Finally, slowly, his hands caught her elbows. "I'm still here."

"Oh God. I'm so sorry." She gave him a fierce squeeze around his torso.

She'd screwed up everything. She'd thought he was indestructible. She'd thought their bond unbreakable simply because she'd never purposely betray him.

But that wasn't quite true. She *could* break their bond.

She could break it with her messed-up emotions. With her brokenness. With her toxicity. Hurting the ones closest to her—

just as her father had.

Just as her father had...

For days, she'd held in her emotions, refusing to feel anything, pretending she could be strong by keeping her feelings at a distance, muscling her way through the situation on sheer willpower. But she'd known...

She'd known ever since she'd almost lashed out at Garrett in her apartment that she was going to break. And this time, she hadn't been able to prevent hurting him.

She'd thought it would be safe to have a relationship with him because she couldn't hurt him *physically*. But she still could hurt him *emotionally*, especially if she couldn't keep her shit together—and failure would condemn him to stone-death.

She'd misjudged. Badly. All because she was unstable.

The thought weighed on her heart, and her knees weakened under the pressure. Before she lost her balance, he scooped her into his arms and carried her out the door.

He knew better than she did how pathetic she was. She *was* a damn delicate flower, and she hated it. She couldn't even be trusted with her own emotions.

And yet, she had to let him close. She had to expose him to her shit to keep *him* safe.

Her nails—short as they were—dug into her palms. If only she could cut out her weaknesses.

She should have stuck with their non-intimate-relationship bond until she could get her act together. They would have been okay like that for years probably. Maybe a lifetime.

But because she'd been so eager to prove that she *wasn't* broken, she'd dragged him into her drama that was just as bad as the rest of her family's histrionics. Not only that, but he'd rightly pointed out that she had all the power in the relationship.

She could dictate how and when he'd move forward with his mission. And she could punish him for doing nothing wrong. For failing only to be able to figure out how she was broken today.

Someone like her didn't deserve that kind of power over another being.

Nausea swept through her, and her throat grew too thick to swallow. Cold sweat gathered on her chest, and she shuddered in

Garrett's arms. Like the dutiful warrior he was—never complaining about his assignment—he'd simply brought her out to her aunt's waiting car in the heat-baked parking lot.

*He'd* done what needed to be done. Solid. Dependable. *Stable.*

Not like her.

Aunt Ruth opened the side door. "Is she...?"

Claws of shame inside her ribcage kept her from responding. She didn't deserve Garrett. But he was stuck with her.

He offered a far more charitable answer than she'd earned with her behavior. "It's been a rough few days."

"The poor thing." Aunt Ruth stroked Raquel's hair back from her forehead. "She's been holding it in for days. I knew it wasn't going to be good. Those emotions bubble up inside of you until you're ready to burst."

Garrett set her inside the car. "She burst."

Raquel shrugged off the shock enough to not act like a damn child so she could put on her own seatbelt. An out-of-place giggle bubbled up from her thoughts. "Yeah. Boom."

He met her gaze and smiled, but his smile didn't reach his eyes. He brushed her cheek. "You'll be okay. I promise."

She pressed his hand to her face. "*We'll* be okay. I'm sorry."

He closed his eyes and nodded. She didn't blame him for being unconvinced. Somehow, she'd make it up to him.

By the time they returned to her cousin's house, Garrett had tucked her under his arm and held her close, as though all was forgiven. But she didn't forgive herself.

The house was quiet—not like the previous night—everyone subdued from the long, emotional day. Garrett hadn't argued against her insistence on walking to the house under her own power, but she slowed her steps to the front porch.

"Hey, Garrett, wait up. We should talk."

He shook his head and didn't spin around to face her. "I don't think that would be a good idea. You should get your sleep."

Her stomach sank so low her throat burned, as though stretched to the breaking point. She stopped and stared at his back as he followed her aunt into the house—without her. She'd ruined everything.

All her fears about forming relationships came back in a rush, flooding her with so many emotions her gut felt as if it had turned inside out. She wrapped her arms around her abdomen, but the attempt to hold in the overwhelming guilt triggered her sinuses again. She sniffled, trying to fend off the tickling sensation in her nose.

Just as she'd feared, she wasn't safe for anyone to be around. She wasn't safe for anyone to care about. She wasn't *stable* enough to be safe.

And in addition to all her old issues, she'd added a new one. She'd taken their bond for granted. Assuming that he'd always be there for her.

It was only now—when she sensed how much damage she'd done to their bond—that she allowed herself to recognize what he meant to her. Sure, she'd known they'd shared some great sex. And she'd known how easy it would be to fall in love with him. But she hadn't realized how close to *being* in love with him she was already.

*In love with him...* Her knees gave out again, and she plopped onto the sidewalk.

She was. She was in love with him already.

She *loved* Garrett.

Somehow that breathtakingly sexy and irritatingly arrogant being—who wasn't even human—had touched her humanity in a way she hadn't thought possible. He'd made her believe she could be a whole person again, and for that alone, she would love him. But add that to all the other aspects of their bond, and she loved *him*—his whole person.

She rubbed at the tickle in her nose. So *how* could she have let herself hurt him so badly? How had she become such a horrible person?

Through the front window, she watched him collapse onto a chair in the living room, suffocating its small frame. His broad hands swept through his hair, and his head dropped back to the top of the chair with a slouch. Every aspect of his body language screamed that he was done, exhausted, burnt—and that he wanted to be done with her.

Her skin itched like it was sunburned, shame flaring through her nerves. God, just when she'd thought she might have wrangled her PTSD into a healthier place, another aspect of it had to mess up her life.

*Difficulty maintaining close relationships?* Yep, not as simple to solve as she'd thought. *Angry outbursts?* Yep, she had that one down too.

If this involved anyone other than Garrett, she'd simply walk away or push them away, like she'd attempted at the funeral home, figuring she was too broken to have a relationship. But for his sake, she couldn't give up. Giving up would be easier for her, yet would doom him.

She didn't have a choice. She had to fix this, no matter how hard it would be. Because she *did* love him.

She plucked a rock from the edge of the sidewalk and rolled it between her fingertips. Figuring this out would mean facing her fears—not keeping her emotions at a distance—and the stone might help keep her grounded.

If she was going to fix this, she had to know exactly what she was apologizing for and how she would prevent it from happening again. She had to become more stable and safe. Her many—*many*—mistakes scrolled through her mind.

First, she'd taken it for granted that he'd put up with her shit, no matter what. Ever since the news about her father, she'd been needy and self-centered. Back during the movie marathon at Brianna's place, she'd recognized that she needed to do her part to keep him happy, and she hadn't been doing squat for him lately.

Second, even before that phone call from her aunt, she'd been selfish about "giving" her approval for him to help Kamen. She would be willing to do anything to bring her guys back, and she needed to give him the same leeway. He shouldn't feel the need to get her permission.

She tapped the rock on the sidewalk and watched him scrub at his face through the front window. Really, those issues both came down to selfishness. She could fix that. She could do better. She wasn't naturally a selfish person, so she could—would—stop letting her weaknesses make her so needy.

For his sake, she *had* to be more stable. She'd never be perfect—or even close to normal—but she could aim to be stable enough to *give* and not just *take.*

Okay, next. Her emotional chaos at the funeral home...

*Clack, clack, clack...* Her taps on the sidewalk became louder as she knocked the rock harder against the sidewalk. This issue was trickier.

Obviously, given her nonsensical anger at him for being gentle and expectations that he *make* her get a grip, some part of her blamed him for her neediness, as though his support *enabled* her weaknesses. Yet even if she'd never met him, she'd still be freaking out during this funeral trip, probably even worse.

At the same time, she'd screwed up by trying to ignore her emotions even more than usual. Ugh. Why had she done that to herself? Why had that seemed like a valid way to prove... *Something?*

A memory tickled her brain—a description she'd seen long ago. What was that term for emotional abuse she'd found in her research?

She squeezed the rock, as though the key to understanding lay inside. The answer drifted in from a too-long-neglected corner of her memory. *Gaslighting.*

Her father's lies attempted to make her question her reality—her strength, her value, her worthiness. And that had colored every aspect of how she saw herself and how she thought she needed to prove her worth to the world.

But the truth was that her inability to remain tough and stoic today wasn't a sign that her father was right. Hell, it *was* a funeral, and just because *he* never cut her any slack didn't mean she shouldn't give herself a break.

Pushing Garrett away had been the worst response possible, even without the issue of stone-death. That reaction was accepting her father's reality and ignoring her own.

In *her* reality as a soldier, her armor had made her less vulnerable. Her weapons had made her more capable. Her team had made her stronger. Just as she would never blame her armor or weapons or a team for giving her needed strength, it made no sense to blame Garrett for the fact that she needed him.

Garrett was her battle buddy. Needing his help wasn't weak. It was allowing strength into her life. And strength was something she should take more of, with no regrets.

Yet she needed to face another layer of their relationship issues, something off between them lately. For some reason, she'd gotten the feeling he'd been walking on eggshells around her. If so—if something was upsetting the balance of their relationship—that wasn't a selfish or gaslighting problem.

*Clack, clack, clack...* A chunk broke off the rock from her efforts, and she brushed it aside into the lawn.

The last few days replayed in her mind, and the answer shone with the obviousness of a neon sign spelling out *Duh.*

She'd gone incommunicado with him on what her father's death meant to her. Hell, she hadn't even told Garrett the gist of the issues until earlier today. In fact, his tentativeness proved that she hadn't been holding up her end of the bargain.

The poor guy would probably have been happy to help her work through her emotional debate, if he only knew how. If she communicated better, she'd be less likely to "go boom" all over him when she couldn't handle it anymore.

This was about trust. She'd asked him to trust her in countless ways, and she needed to do the same. If she trusted him to be there—not only because he *had* to be but because they *wanted* to be there for each other—they could avoid these problems again.

She could do that. She could trust him. He deserved at least that much.

A wry grin stretched her face. Perfection didn't exist, but at least she could work to make *new* mistakes rather than the same ones over and over.

The rock dropped from her fingers with a final *clack.* She'd done it. She'd faced her emotions like a grown-ass adult who wasn't too afraid to deal with reality. She could do this. She could fix things with him—if he'd give her a second chance.

She stood and brushed off her black pantsuit. Warmth filled her chest as she focused on his hulking frame overwhelming the dainty chair in the living room. If she could convince him to give her one more chance, he could be hers again, and she could be his.

For real this time.

A powerful *swoop* fluttered above, flapping close enough to cause a breeze. She flinched and tilted her head back to search the dark skies for the stray owl that must have just missed her head.

Sharp talons dug into her shoulders, and stabbing agony pierced her skin and muscles. A scream ripped up her throat.

Another *swoop,* and her weight left the sidewalk.

# Chapter Thirty-Eight

WHAT THE—? RAQUEL'S STOMACH DROPPED AS THE ground fell away faster than on a high-speed elevator. She kicked her legs. "Garrett! Garrett, help!"

She couldn't move her shoulders, but she looked up into the darkness. The island's rooftops and streetlights were now far below her, and despite the near full moon, the dim light peeking through the high clouds barely illuminated the scene. She hadn't wanted to think about what could be making her *fly* over the neighborhood, but the glimpse of the creature above left no doubt.

A gargoyle had her in his clutches.

She kicked her legs again, even though she didn't *really* want him to let go. "Hey! What the hell do you think you're doing? Put me down, you big..." Insulting him probably wasn't the right direction to take. "Gargoyle. Garrett—you know, your *supreme commander*—won't be happy about this."

The gargoyle ignored her. She kept her shoulders as still as possible and gripped his ankles so she didn't feel as vulnerable to him deciding to drop her. The movement caused a wave of lightheadedness, and she clenched her jaw until the tearing sensation in her muscles faded.

"Hey, you, gargoyle! Put me down so we can talk or so you can carry me without killing my arms."

The breeze blew through the dressy fabric of her outfit, and chills broke over her skin. Either that, or she was going into shock. Given how fast her heart was beating, she wouldn't doubt the latter.

The higher they got, the more questions assaulted her mind. Was he going to kill her?

A shiver gripped her, ripping more muscles as her body shuddered around the talons slicing into her shoulders. She ground her teeth to cut off a scream. Was she going to die from her injuries before this gargoyle even had the chance to kill her?

Garrett... She squeezed her eyelids tight, holding the tears inside. If only she'd gotten the chance to apologize to him. What would he think? Would he realize a gargoyle had taken her?

For that matter, what was another gargoyle doing awake?

"Who are you? Are you Kamen? Does Garrett know you're awake?"

There was another name too. She ignored the damp chill from the high clouds he now carried her through and dredged her memory for everything she could recollect. There was also the gargoyle who had lost his son in the war. The same one who had abandoned their mission, making it so Garrett had needed to step in and lead their regiment. What was that one's name?

"Alann?"

The flapping rhythm above her stuttered for a split second. That might be the best answer she would get.

"Alann, Garrett would be so happy to see you. He's been trying to figure out what happened to everyone so he can help them. Take me back so you guys can talk."

The pressure of his talons released a fraction. Not so much that she worried about him dropping her, but enough that she gasped at the changing sensation of pain.

"Yeah, see..." She tightened her fingers around his ankles to keep her voice steady. "I know all about you guys. I know about you and Kamen and the portal."

His claws pinched harder again. "What do you know about the portal?"

Every syllable came out guttural and hesitant, as though he hadn't spoken to anyone in a long time.

"Oh hey, you *do* talk." She breathed hard through her nose, struggling not to cry out in pain, and blinked rapidly, but nothing could hold off the black spots in her vision. "You know, having your talons stabbing my shoulders isn't exactly the most comfortable way to travel. Or to have a conversation. How about you put me down, and I'll tell you everything I know."

"You'll tell me everything I want to know—now." His answer was the sharp command of military authority.

Well, hell... She dug into her army training to guess at how to handle this guy. Part of her CST training covered being kidnapped or taken hostage, and the longer he ignored her requests to return her to Garrett, the less he looked like one of the good guys. Especially given his abandonment of the regiment's mission.

"I don't know much. Garrett could tell you a lot more."

He didn't fall for her ploy. Of course. That would be too easy.

The wind crashed into them, whipping her clothes against her numb skin and distorting her cheeks. Given how far they were above the lights now in the distance, they were at parachute-jump altitude, lowering the temperature by about thirty degrees. And if they were traveling anywhere close to his top flying speed, she had a brutal wind-chill to deal with too.

Proving her right far quicker than she wanted, cold stiffened her fingers, and her arms flopped to her sides, unable to hang onto his ankles anymore. As her muscles shifted, tears flowed from her eyes, the pain too much to ignore. She was running out of time before she passed out. Maybe she needed to go confrontational.

"Alann, did *you* close the portal?"

His wings flapped oddly, and his head and torso came into view, as he bent and peered at her. "No gargoyle would do such a thing."

"Great." She took another couple of steadying breaths through her nose. "So why are you taking *me* instead of going back to Garrett and comparing notes?"

His wings regained their rhythm again, and he flew forward with a rush of speed. "He's not supposed to be awake."

Whether it was due to her injuries or his words, dizziness pressed against the inside of her skull, and it became harder and harder to fight the blackness at the edges of her vision, especially with the cold sapping her strength. Her last conscious thought was to wonder if all the other gargoyles were asleep as part of a plan—a plan that Alann was directing.

# Chapter Thirty-Nine

F OR THE THOUSANDTH TIME, GARRETT REPLAYED THE MOMENT he'd allowed his bitterness to attack Raquel. Although she'd *asked* him to yell at her, he was fairly certain that wasn't what she'd had in mind.

It wasn't her fault that he needed her. It wasn't her fault that the portal was closed or that the rest of his regiment needed his help. And it wasn't her fault that her father had died, interrupting his hopes to deal with Kamen.

But he'd taken all of his frustrations out on her in an unfair attack of blame. She'd been nothing but accommodating of everything he needed from her, and now he had to find a way to make up for his behavior. Somehow. *After* she got some sleep.

Trying to talk to her now, before she had a chance to emotionally recuperate from the long day, would only cause more problems. Her breakdown at the funeral home had demonstrated that all too well. Their bond couldn't take the risk.

Also, the delay would give him time to figure out what to say.

Garrett's head snapped up from the back of the chair. Raquel. He'd heard Raquel scream.

He plowed through the family members mingling in the hallway. The door to her room was open, and she wasn't on her bed. Not a nightmare then. He glanced through the house, but she was nowhere to be seen.

If she wasn't screaming from a nightmare, she was most likely suffering from a flashback. But where? The family chattered as though they hadn't heard anything.

He strode up to the nearest family member, probably a cousin. "Have you seen Raquel?"

Too late, he remembered the language barrier, but the young man's answer worked in either language. "No."

The others nearby shook their heads too. Had she ever come inside? Or had he heard her through the front window?

He burst out the front door and scanned the yard and street. Nothing.

"Raquel?" He stood in the middle of the road. "Rocky, let me help you. Where are you?"

If she was having a flashback, who knew where she might be holed up and shuddering.

"Raquel?" Still nothing. "Rocky?"

He headed up the front walk, intending to do a sweep of the whole yard around the house. His shoe kicked a rock onto the grass.

A rock along the path she'd walked. A rock that might be able to tell him which direction to go.

He dropped to a crouch and cradled the rock in his palm. He spun toward the street, hiding his actions from the family in the house.

"Greetings. I am Garrett, the supreme commander of the Earthen plane regiment of the gargoyle army from the Mythos plane, and I ask for your assistance."

WARM GREETINGS, GARRETT. ASSISTANCE IS PLEASURE.

The small stone's answer wasn't as deafening as the boulder he'd befriended in Central Park, but given the rock's eagerness, word of his existence must have traveled through the Earth, even to this island.

"I am honored. And now I ask to join with you that I might discover what happened here recently." Except a rock would have no understanding of *recent*. "Since the last warming of the sun."

Images played in his head. The sunset. An unchanging view. The family passing by. Garrett himself walking past, stopping, and then entering the house.

Finally, Raquel came into view. She'd sat down on the sidewalk, and the expression on her face as he'd continued on without her matched the betrayal he'd felt earlier. Her lips were twisted as though she felt sick.

How could he have not noticed that she hadn't followed him? Heaviness settled in the back of his throat, and he hit the side of his thigh with his fist, the truth aching deep inside him. With blame still simmering in his attitude, he'd walked away from his duty to watch over her at the first opportunity.

The view from the stone's memories changed as she picked up this very rock in his hand. Her pounding the rock on the concrete added lump upon lump to the heaviness in his chest. She was *not* happy—probably not happy with him. After a few minutes, she dropped the rock and seemed to smile.

The scene changed again. Her legs extended, and her feet left the ground.

She'd jumped? No.

She flew up into the air and didn't come back down. *Humans* couldn't do that, and he'd have heard if giant birds in the area were a danger. So what had happened?

He loosened his grip around the rock, which he'd started to clench, but dread made his fingers stiff. "Show me that last part again, please."

The stone replayed the section when Raquel had held it.

When she dropped the rock, Garrett touched its surface. "Slow this part down."

Just as the ironic twist of her lips softened into a smile that lit her features, giant wings swooped over her head. She ducked, looked up, and then screamed.

"Stop here."

Talons had stabbed her shoulders deep enough for blood to stream down her arms. Speckled gray, stone-like talons. A gargoyle.

A gargoyle was awake—and had taken Raquel. Beyond that obvious fact, his thoughts slammed into each other, too jumbled to make sense of yet. Cold dread seeped in around the thoughts that had crashed together. Blood. A *gargoyle* had injured her.

His head dropped back, and he searched the skies. He had to

get up there, but...

His gaze landed on the front window. Witnesses.

He ducked into a secluded side yard. A second later, he'd changed to his gargoyle form and leapt into the darkness, flying high above the ground. He made a circle, but saw no sign of the gargoyle or Raquel.

Blast! If only he wasn't a pretender to his position, he'd be able to *feel* the location of the other gargoyle. He cursed his inadequacies even more than when he'd struggled with the search on Google. His lack of skills endangered her with every passing minute.

And without Google to help, he wouldn't find her soon enough for her disappearance to escape notice. He'd have to let Ruth know.

He landed in the same darkened corner and changed back into his human form with the copies of clothes he'd used earlier. He scrambled up the front sidewalk and through the door. The crowd had thinned a bit, with some probably heading to bed.

"Ruth!" He barreled into the kitchen. "Ruth!"

The woman called from the dining room table, and he skidded to a stop at her side. "Raquel—"

How could he explain this? Yes, Raquel had said that she didn't care about her family, but her actions had said otherwise. He didn't want to cause more problems for her later on. At the same time, he didn't want the family involved in a search they couldn't help with, but he also wanted to warn them not to expect her presence.

"Raquel left for a walk and hasn't come back yet. I'm going to make sure she's okay."

Ruth gave a sympathetic shrug. "She might want some time alone to clear her head."

"I know. I'll keep my distance. I simply want to make sure she's safe. Call me if she returns before I get back."

Every second he stayed to explain, Raquel was getting further away. But the dread in his skull was building to a thought he wasn't yet ready to face. As soon as Ruth waved her understanding, he returned to the skies.

The whole time, he'd gripped the rock he'd found. The stone, eternally patient, had waited for his next message. Now, he opened his fist and debated.

"Can you communicate with the Earth from here? Or do you need to touch the ground?"

Eagerness to help radiated from the stone, and it started a technical discussion delving into the esoteric nature of their communication methods, which was helped by its recent splitting, with the other part of itself still on the ground and in contact with the dirt of the yard. Garrett cut it off and refocused on the emergency.

"Will you please ask the Earth and all ground, dirt, boulders, rocks, and stones on the planet to watch for this other gargoyle and this human woman? I need to find them. It's extremely important."

AWAKENER NO LONGER WALKS. STONE BROTHER UNKNOWN. NOT WALK EARTH.

Awakener? The whole Earth knew of Raquel?

Then the thoughts he'd been holding back burst forth. *Of course.* Another gargoyle was *awake*—and the Earth hadn't known.

Just as the Earth couldn't recognize a gargoyle in stone-death form unless it was in physical contact with the ground, the Earth couldn't recognize an awake gargoyle if it never landed and *walked the earth.* So this gargoyle was likely staying in a city, where he either remained on man-made surfaces or landed on the tops of buildings, much as Garrett had done at Raquel's apartment.

Yet why would a gargoyle *avoid* walking on Earth? No, more than that. Why would a gargoyle *hide* from the Earth?

Unable to answer the unanswerable, he instead shared tips with the stone and pointed out clues the Earth could watch for. Rocks and stones within cities might be able to recognize the passing or landing of gargoyles if they knew to look beyond their expectations.

"Thank you all for your help. I need to find her." Every limb ached and grew heavy at the thought of losing her.

Raquel. His jaw hardened even more than the rest of his chest. He'd tried to avoid thinking of her, worrying about her, but he couldn't stop his thoughts from going to her now.

No honorable member of his regiment would harm another's

bond. Even if they didn't respect him or feel loyalty due to his inadequacies—or even if he was considered an *outcast*—honor still mattered.

Between the unknown gargoyle's obvious lack of honor and Raquel's debilitating injury that he'd witnessed through the stone, he had no doubt that she was in danger now—because of him. He hadn't protected her, and one of his own had stolen her. His chest tumbled and grated, pain radiating out from his core.

He couldn't lose her. Far beyond her being his connection to life, he...

His thoughts stuttered, uncertain of his point. Then the certainty of truth resonated with the warmth of their bond. *Yes...*

He *loved* her.

The pain he felt now at the thought of her being in danger was the only proof that mattered anymore. His earlier frustration and her emotional struggles couldn't erase the truth. She'd come back to him, healed their bond, and he'd forgiven her. Love was real, and he fully believed in it, in her, in them.

Whether he was *capable* of love was irrelevant—*he loved her.*

He would do anything, sacrifice anything, to keep her safe. He wished he could redo the past hour—not lash out at her but hold her tight, protect her. *Blast!* He had to find her. He had to.

This other gargoyle was awake and...

More logic leaked around Garrett's panic, adding to his understanding of the circumstances. This other gargoyle was dangerous for more than just his willingness to injure Raquel.

Even if the gargoyle was a visitor to the Earthen plane from the rest of the legion on Mythos and not a member of his regiment, every gargoyle knew the requirement to report in to the Earthen plane supreme commander. Him.

Yet rather than follow that command, this gargoyle had stolen the woman he depended on to escape stone-death. No coincidence could explain targeting Raquel. Whoever this gargoyle was—and Garrett hadn't been able to distinguish the gargoyle's features from the rock's vantage point on the ground—Raquel was in grave danger. Either this gargoyle—this *traitor*—intended to break their bond through treachery, perhaps trying to manipulate her into bonding with him instead, or he had something else in mind that would cause Garrett's stone-death.

A wave of cold swept over him. Raquel's *death* would remove them both from the equation. Until the sun rose, he wouldn't even know if she still lived.

He shoved the thoughts away hard enough to shatter stone. She would be okay. He would save her in time.

He could even try to hope the gargoyle wouldn't kill her. But try as he might, he couldn't think of a non-threatening reason this other gargoyle would have for hiding his existence, not reporting in, and stealing Raquel.

No, whoever this gargoyle was, he was an enemy to Garrett, the rest of the regiment caught in stone-death, and every aspect of their mission.

Still in contact with the stone, he felt the rock's question form in his hand.

STONE BROTHER FRICTION?

"Yes, there's a good chance this gargoyle is trying to send me back into stone-death. He might even be responsible for the destruction of the portal to Mythos."

And Raquel was caught in the middle.

ALL ASSISTANCE POSSIBLE IS GIVEN. ASSISTANCE IS PLEASURE.

"Thank you. The fate of my legion—and the life of the human I love—might depend on you."

The betrayal Garrett had suspected from the beginning, when he'd thought his regiment had abandoned him, might not have been far off after all. At least one of his legion wanted to prevent him from waking his regiment and restoring the portal.

Was just a single gargoyle causing problems? Or was a broader civil war underway that he'd missed during his stone-death?

He hoped this little rock, not even as big as his palm, would help provide the answers and clues he needed to solve the mystery and save Raquel. Soon.

# Chapter Forty

ABONE-SHATTERING IMPACT WOKE RAQUEL. COLD. PAIN. Wind. What—?

What had happened? Her arms couldn't move, and she had a feeling she should be grateful for the numbing cold.

Sharp claws hooked her wrist and wrenched. Blinding agony burned through her shoulder beyond what the cold could cover up. The claws dragged her upright, and her eyes popped open.

A brisk wind tore at her skin, but it was too dark to make out her surroundings. An irregular rushing noise like the crashing of waves sounded nearby.

Before she could look around further, strong arms hefted her over something. More injuries joined the chorus of pain screaming through her mind.

"Hey." She tried protesting, but her lips, dry and cracked, split too much to yell.

The arms pinned her ankles down on one side of the barrier—a shoulder?—and she hung upside-down in a fireman's carry. Blood rushed to her head, which didn't help her make sense of the situation.

Below her, the ground didn't seem right. It wasn't rock or dirt or grass, but it wasn't concrete or wood or other normal flooring either.

Whoever had her began to walk, and her ribs ached with each

bouncing step. Metal clangs resonated with each stride, and the sound gave her another clue of the surroundings.

She arched her neck backward and strained to make out the details. The nerves around her collarbone sent stabbing pain with every millimeter of movement, but she ignored the messages to her brain. She'd crawled through concrete rubble with third degree burns before—a few broken bones were nothing in comparison. She could still move her neck, so a shattered spine was one less worry.

Structures similar to the steel shipping containers of a cargo ship or a train lined the walkway, and metal pipes created a maze of zigzags. She twisted her head, and the clouded-over light of the moon illuminated more manufactured framework blotting out the stars above in shapes like construction cranes and antenna towers.

Where the hell had he *taken* her? She wanted to fight, get free, but even *she* could tell when stubbornness alone wouldn't get her anywhere. Her battered body could barely move, her arms and shoulders burned too much to use force, and something in the back of her mind remembered enough to know she couldn't beat her captor.

*Gargoyle...*

Yes, that was the last thing she remembered. Alann had stolen her from the front yard of her cousin's house, almost ripping her arms off in the process. He'd flown for hours. Maybe over a day and into the next night? And she couldn't compete with a gargoyle's strength on the best of days, much less after being on-and-off unconscious for however long. Now they'd finally landed, but not on the ground.

Alann spun and descended a set of metal stairs. The wind was stronger here, and she faced the open side of the stairway. Moonlight glittered on waves far in the distance—and the waves continued below.

They weren't on a building on the *edge* of the water; they were on a structure built *over* the water. What the hell?

At the bottom of several stories of stairs, he headed down another walkway, this one cramped with pipes and metal walls in every direction. He even had to duck under some of the infrastructure, his human height and build similar to Garrett's. She searched for signage on either side for more clues, but they displayed only combinations of letters and numbers, probably hallway designations or room numbers.

When he stopped, she peered around his torso, once again ignoring the stabbing pain in her ribcage. He slid a thick metal pipe from the center of a door handle, freeing the door from being jammed closed.

He tossed her into the dark room beyond the door, and she landed hard—again. Agony sliced through her and dulled her thoughts.

Her training yelled for her to get up, run, fight, escape. But nothing worked. Nothing moved.

She couldn't even use her arms to elbow herself into a sitting position from where she lay on her side. She was going to die here.

As though he heard her fear, he grumbled into the darkness. "Keep her alive."

Then the door slammed closed, and the screeching slide of metal signaled the door being jammed with the pipe once more. Her head dropped to the floor. More metal. More cold. She didn't even have the energy to shiver.

It would be so easy to give up. She'd spent her whole life fighting. Fighting for respect from her father. Fighting to prove herself to her guys. Fighting to stay alive in the hospital. She was tired. So damn tired.

She imagined the metal floor sucking away the last of her body heat, the last of her energy. Until there would be nothing left but a cold body, filled only with more cold. *One Raquel popsicle, coming up.*

A giggle burbled in the back of her mind at the image, but the noise came out more like a groan. She was losing her damn mind—that was for sure.

Shuffling noises and the clank of a chain sounded from a few feet away. At that, a shiver *did* sweep through her body. She wasn't alone in this dark room.

She froze, listening for anything and everything. The shuffle and clangs moved closer.

A fingertip poked her cheek, and she held herself still. Playing dead to learn more about the situation was easier than fighting through whatever was in here without having a clue what she faced.

A woman's voice rang out beside her, shouting into the darkness. "She's just a human. She's probably dead already."

The woman retreated, the clangs following her progress, and she mumbled to herself. "Stupid gargoyle. I swear they have rocks for brains. 'Keep her alive.' Yeah, with what blankets, food, water, or medicine? It's not like I have healing abilities. Stupid, stupid gargoyle. He can just punish me again."

A chain rattled and slapped the floor. The clangs echoed in Raquel's ears, especially the one pressed against the metal floor, loud enough to elicit a gasp. *Okay, deaf now.*

"Stupid human. You're going to die, and *I* get to pay the price."

Wow, self-centered much? 'Cuz *dying* was no big deal. Obviously.

Just for that, she was almost sorry that she *wasn't* dead. Bitch deserved to be punished.

The last shred of adrenaline burned off, and she sighed, even more exhausted than before. No, she couldn't die. If she died, Garrett would die too.

She owed him every bit of fight she could muster. She had to stay alive for his sake.

"I'm not dead *yet.*" She rolled onto her back, every shift of muscle and bone screaming for her to remain still. She forced more croaking words through her cracked lips. "And I'm not going to die. I'm too stubborn."

"Really?" The woman's tone held no gratitude for saving her from punishment—whatever that meant. "You think stubbornness alone will solve anything?" She scoffed. "If that were the case, I'd have gotten free twenty years ago."

Raquel sucked in a breath so fast her chest hollowed. "Alann's held you captive for *twenty* years?"

"Is that his name?" She didn't wait for an answer, and all Raquel had was a guess anyway. "He doesn't talk much." The woman shifted, the chain clanging with her movements. "I've been here for seven thousand, five hundred and one days, give or take a few hours and minutes."

"I'm sorry." She took back all her *bitch* thoughts about the woman. Hell, she'd be an über-bitch if she didn't get out of here soon, much less after years and years.

"Well, it's not like I have a family to go home to anyway. He had my mom killed too."

Raquel's forehead tightened, her skin scrunching with the effort to figure out the situation. Alann definitely fell onto the bad guy side of the equation then. She'd never gotten the impression from Garrett that Alann had turned *evil*, only that he'd abandoned the mission. Yet more things must have changed during his stone-death.

Unless this woman was the enemy? "Why did he do all that?"

"You'd have to ask him. Like I said, he doesn't talk much." The chain rattled, accompanying the woman's approach. "You're sure doing a lot of talking though. Shouldn't you be saving your strength or something? I thought you said you weren't going to die."

"I'm not." And she wasn't.

While she'd been lying on the floor, the sharp pains had started to fade. Either her nerves were shutting down, or getting away from his claws and not being suspended anymore was making a difference.

The woman scoffed again. "Listen, human, you have five broken ribs, your arms are almost severed from your shoulders, your collarbone is shattered, and your body temperature is too low. And gee, there's nothing here to help heal you. Yep, you're going to die."

That many injuries on a patient would be a lot for her medical training to deal with in a hospital, much less here. A wave of despair suffocated her for a minute, but then she shoved the knowledge away and called on her stubbornness again. "You don't know everything. How can you even be so sure about the specifics of my injuries?"

"The minerals in your body told me."

*The minerals?* Granted, that injury list sounded accurate, and she'd been kidnapped by a *gargoyle*. Which meant this woman's claim might not be the craziest thing ever. But she still didn't feel on death's door.

"What are you? Not a gargoyle, I assume." Gargoyles were all male, if she remembered correctly.

Metal scraped across the floor, and the woman slid to her side. "If you ever insult me like that again, I'll kill you myself."

Raquel stifled a flinch. "Sorry. I didn't mean to insult you. It's just that gargoyles are the only non-humans I've met, so I don't know what else there is."

"Then maybe you shouldn't have said anything at all." The woman *humphed*. "I'll let you live—this time—but don't let it happen again. I'm nothing like those filthy creatures."

*Filthy* was the last word that would come to mind to describe Garrett, but Raquel kept her mouth shut. If this woman had really been held captive by Alann for twenty years, she had good reason for her negative opinion.

"Then what are you?"

"You're awfully inquisitive. I thought humans weren't supposed to know about anything from Mythos."

"Most don't." She decided against mentioning Garrett. The woman probably wouldn't give him the benefit of the doubt. "But I obviously know about gargoyles, as one kidnapped me from my father's funeral."

"Did he kill your dad?"

That time, Raquel *did* flinch. *Dad* was never a term she used for her father. "No, he managed to die all on his own."

The woman guffawed. "You're funny." Silence spread through the cell for a minute. "Are you real?" Her tone now was quiet, tentative.

"Yeah." Raquel sighed. "I'm really here. You're not losing your mind or anything."

"That's good." The woman draped a thin blanket over Raquel's limbs.

"Thank you." Of course, most of the cold was coming from underneath her.

Fingers tucked the blanket's edges around her. She rolled a bit in each direction to allow the material to wrap further and provide a barrier from the metal floor.

"You really are a tough little human. Usually they lie here screaming and die within hours."

Ice beyond the cold surroundings spread frosty tendrils through her veins. "He's done this to others?"

More scrapes of metal accompanied the rustling of the woman lying next to her. "Yeah, not for a long time though. When I was little, he'd bring one every month. After the twenty-sixth one died in the first night, I think he gave up." She extended an arm over Raquel's abdomen. "Will it hurt too much if we huddle for warmth? I'm giving up one of my blankets for you, you know."

A smile stretched Raquel's lips, and they didn't sting as much from cracking as they had before. Whether the woman would admit it or not, she liked the company. After twenty years, her mind was probably desperate to talk to someone.

"Nah, I'll be fine. That's a good idea."

The woman gently pressed against her side and wrapped another blanket over them. "Get your rest. He won't be back until morning."

Would she wake up though? For all her stubborn optimism, the truth was far more uncertain.

Her worries leaked out in a wavering question. "Do you think it's safe for me to sleep?"

The woman's voice sounded by her shoulder. "You're going to live, human. You're stubborn like me."

She wanted to believe that. She wanted to hope that she wouldn't have to remain here too long. Garrett must be looking for her, right?

Even if he hadn't noticed her absence right away, *everyone* would be missing her by now. Hell, she'd missed her father's funeral mass and burial earlier in the day. And even if Garrett was still upset with her since she'd never gotten a chance to fully apologize, it was in his best interest to track her down.

Although... *How* would he know where to find her?

The details she'd noticed about the location Alann had picked for their cell suddenly fell into place. There was no land, no ground, no *Earth* anywhere close.

He'd purposely found a metallic structure out in the middle of the water—maybe an abandoned offshore oil-drilling platform—to ensure that he never walked the earth. No witnesses.

She forced her muscles to release their stress. Okay, no rescue would be coming, so she needed to plan her own rescue. She could do that. She was capable.

At the mental pep talk, vague realizations clicked in her mind, like gears turning to open a door of understanding. Her brows pulled together as she tried to make the subconscious ideas coalesce into conscious thoughts. A final click brought the fuzzy impressions into focus.

That was it. She *was* capable.

Throughout this whole abduction, she hadn't zoned out into Flashback Land. Not even once. When push came to shove, she *wasn't* broken. She could still function like a soldier. Her training still held. She was still capable.

She'd be okay. Especially if this non-human beside her could help.

"Raquel," she offered to the woman. If they were going to be partners, they should know each other's names. "My name is Raquel."

"Faeries don't share their true names, but you can call me Amber. Now get your rest, so we can plan how to beat that stupid rocks-for-brains gargoyle tomorrow."

A faerie? Apparently faeries had far more attitude than the stories gave them credit for.

Her chest vibrated with a chuckle and didn't scream at her in protest of the movement. "Sounds like a plan."

She allowed her muscles to relax for the first time in days. Yes, she'd figure a way out of this situation. Somehow.

# Chapter Forty-One

FRUSTRATION TENSED GARRETT'S LIMBS, AND HE BARELY RESISTED the urge to throw the rock down the cliff. Sunset colors streaked across the sky, emphasizing how a whole day had passed, and he was no closer to finding Raquel. How could a gargoyle vanish like that when the portal was closed?

Hours ago, he'd landed on the top of an island mountain somewhere in the ocean, hoping direct contact with the Earth would help. No luck.

But flying in the wrong direction wouldn't help either, so he forced himself to remain stationary until he knew *something*. What he wouldn't give for even the slightest clue.

He scrubbed his cheeks, willing himself to find patience. If he'd only been more patient with her yesterday, they wouldn't be in this situation. He wouldn't have yelled at her. Upset her. Made her stop outside, shocked at his behavior.

He wouldn't have abandoned her.

*She* was his mission, just as much as everything to do with his regiment, and he'd abandoned her outside her cousin's house. Only the fact that the morning sun hadn't doomed him to stone-death hours ago gave him any hope.

She was still alive. They still had a chance. If only he knew *where* to find her.

"Let's try this again." He lifted his hand to peer at the stone in his palm. Even though his other hand was directly on the cliff top and in touch with the Earth itself, the little rock had taken charge of the search. "I want to know *everything* odd that you all have seen. Maybe he hasn't landed. Maybe he's been flying the whole time like a bird. If there are any sightings of anything unusual in the sky, I want to know about it."

*NEAR INFINITY. GARRETT UNPREPARED.*

The rock was right to question his instructions. Given the vast amount of information he was asking for, the influx of visions might overwhelm his thoughts and drive him insane. But he had to do something.

"I have no choice. I have to find him if I want to have any hope of finding her. But if there's anything you can do to make the visions display one at a time, that might help."

*ASSISTANCE. QUERY EARTH. PATIENCE.*

Garrett lay down so he could focus all his attention on the messages from around the planet. He folded his hands on his stomach, directing the flow of information through the little rock in his grasp.

A flicker of random images started in his mind, as if all the pictures he'd searched through for his regiment a couple of weeks ago displayed in a sped-up slideshow. The steady stream took all his focus, but the stone was doing its job of keeping him from getting overwhelmed.

Bird. Truck. Airplane. Gryphon. Another bird. Bat. Helicopter. Bird. A car launching off a ramp and zooming over others. Another bat. A round thing trailing string. Dragon. Bird. A bigger round thing with humans in a basket below. Another airplane. A fuzzy moth...

The stream continued until he lost track of time.

"Wait!" He sat up. "Show me the last few again."

The slideshow continued, but slower. Bird. Airplane. And there it was...

"Stop."

Gargoyle. Still with Raquel hanging from his talons.

"Where was this seen?"

The stone's description of the specific magnetic forces and mineral composition of the area didn't help.

"Could you lead me there? Tell me when I'm heading in the right or wrong direction?"

*ASSISTANCE IS PLEASURE.*

He shifted to his gargoyle form and leapt into the darkening evening. The stone soon had him pointed in the right direction, and they flew over the vast open ocean. Wherever they were going, it would take a while. Hopefully, another clue would show up soon.

*Hold on, Raquel. Please hold on.*

# Chapter Forty-Two

MUTED CLANGS WOKE RAQUEL, AND SHE OPENED HER EYES, struggling to remember where she was.

A glimmer of light spread from beside her and reflected off the metal on the ceiling. A metal ceiling?

Not New York. Not her new—or old—apartment. Not her cousin's in Puerto Rico either.

Puerto Rico. The funeral mass she'd missed. She'd had her say though, so only the thought of worrying her aunt tarnished the relief spreading through her chest.

No, this was about Alann and how he'd kidnapped her. This was the cell on the oil-drilling platform or wherever they were.

Her muscles wanted to move, but she forced herself to wait, to take inventory of her aches and pains first. Nothing was screaming at her right now, but that wasn't likely to remain the case.

Ribs? She took a deep breath. Sore, but not nearly as bad as she'd expected.

Collarbone? She arched her neck a fraction. Huh. Pain-free.

Shoulders? She lifted her elbow a millimeter off the floor. Again. Pain-free.

Okay, that made no sense whatsoever. How long had she slept? For weeks and weeks?

She spun her head and checked out the room Alann had thrown her into. Smooth metal covered every surface, like the inside of a steel box. No windows, but light leaked in from under the door to her left.

On her right sat a woman—Amber, the faerie. Long scraggly hair hung down either side of her face, the black strands casting shadows over her cheeks. The dim light made it hard to be sure, but her skin looked like the light brown color of her namesake. Most noticeable were the icy blue eyes that stared intently out of a face screwed up in a confused expression.

"How long did I sleep?"

"Five hours and seventeen minutes."

So... Not for weeks and weeks. She guessed that was a good thing, but that didn't explain how her pain had disappeared already.

"I thought you said you didn't have the ability to heal me."

Amber's expression tightened even more. "I don't. No earth-clan faeries do."

"But..." Raquel hunched her shoulders to make sure she wasn't imagining it. Still no pain. "You made my pain disappear."

"No." Amber laid the back of her hand against Raquel's cheek. "It's not only that your pain is gone. Your injuries are gone too."

Raquel wanted to sit up and confront Amber, confront the impossibility, but she forced herself to remain still. The woman was wrong, and there was no reason to hurt herself again just to disprove the claim.

"What do you mean—my injuries are gone?"

"I mean..." Amber poked at Raquel's shoulder. "Your body has healed itself. Those bones. Those muscles."

Raquel bent her neck and watched Amber prod all around her shoulder and collarbone. She felt the pressure of her fingertip but no pain.

"That's impossible." Even as she protested, she kneaded along her ribcage. The small amount of soreness she'd noticed a few minutes ago had disappeared now too.

Unable to resist the urge, she sat up. Other than the usual stiffness from sleeping on a hard surface, no pain spiked through her nerves.

Amber scooted back a few feet. "How did you heal yourself? Are you *not* human?"

Raquel continued probing her shoulders and collarbone, searching for any soreness. Or any sign of her injuries at all. Nothing. Only her shredded clothes and Amber's confusion gave proof that the injuries had ever existed.

"I'm most definitely human." She leaned on her elbow, placing the skin of her forearm in the path of the light from under the door. "I'm covered with scars of injuries from a few years ago, so I was never able to heal myself before. *I* didn't do this."

"No." Amber's gaze swept over her. "The minerals in your body *told* me that you healed yourself. *You* did this." She cocked her head. "How? What's changed since you received those scars?"

"Nothing."

Raquel straightened. That wasn't quite true. She'd changed plenty in those years. But only one change could possibly make a difference like this.

Garrett. She'd bonded with Garrett. Someone who was *not* human. Someone who was, in fact, indestructible.

Was their bond giving her a semblance of that power? Now that she thought about it, the burn on the back of her arm at Brianna's house had healed quickly too.

At the time, she'd assumed the burn must not have been as bad as she'd thought. But even if it was just a minor burn, the pink mark would have taken a day or two to disappear. Yet she'd never noticed it again, not even after the second movie ended a couple of hours later, and not from any tenderness during her showers.

Wow. She could heal from wounds like broken bones and stabbings? Her heartbeat sped up, carrying excitement through her limbs and warming her from the inside out. Now *that*? That was cool.

Amber eyed her, no doubt watching the shifting moods on her face. "You know, don't you?"

"Yeah." She'd have to reveal her tie to Garrett and hope Amber wouldn't hold her bond to a gargoyle against her. "I think I do."

She crossed her arms and rolled her shoulders, enjoying the lack of pain. "I'll tell you my story if you tell me yours. Maybe by understanding each other better, we'll know best how to work together to get out of here."

"Okay." Amber crossed her arms too, her attitude still distant and suspicious.

"You're an earth-clan faerie? What does that mean? What can you do?"

"It means I can control the earth. Rocks, dirt, and the like." She gave a grim smile and tipped her head toward the wall. "That's why he keeps me isolated from anything resembling stone."

Raquel knocked against the metal floor. "The whole place out there is like this. All metal. But in here, it's shiny, like a different kind of metal."

"Out there is a lot of steel. That's dangerous to me." Amber unfolded her arms and gestured around the room. "He always has my cell lined with stainless steel. That's less pure, so it doesn't burn me to touch it, but it keeps me drained enough to not be able to fight him even if rock or stone were around."

Now that she noticed it, Amber sat on a blanket and had her thin dress tucked under her legs. She'd assumed the woman was trying to avoid the chill, but more likely she was trying to avoid being drained by contact with the stainless steel.

"And you have no shoes, so even if we figure out how to escape this room, you'd be burned from trying to walk around outside."

"Depends. If the steel is coated at all, like with paint, I might not be injured." She shrugged and gave another grim smile. "And I'm willing to put up with a few burns if it means getting out of here."

Raquel nodded. She could respect that level of determination. This partnership might work out well after all.

"If my shoes fit you, I'll let you wear them when the time comes."

"Thanks." Amber's eyebrows pulled down, confusion shading her expression again.

Raquel took advantage of the short answer to get to the next question. "You said he doesn't talk much, but he must keep you here for a reason. Does he ever say anything to you? Expect anything from you?"

This was a dangerous topic. Depending on the kind of abuse Amber had experienced, she might not want to talk about it, or she might also struggle with PTSD and suffer from its effects when having to think about the horrors she'd endured. But Raquel needed to know what she was dealing with, so there was a limit to how much she could dance around the subject. Her approach for how to handle Alann would change depending on whether he was the type to physically torture, mentally manipulate, or sexually abuse his captives.

"I mean, I wouldn't ask if I didn't think we needed to know." It wouldn't hurt to soften the question with a bit of understanding. "Between the two of us, we might have a better idea of what he wants if we compare notes."

Amber shrugged, and her gaze drifted away, not bothered by the question. "The only thing he's ever asked of me is to open the portal."

"The portal?" Raquel leaned forward. "You know how to open it?"

"Yeah..." Amber's expression turned suspicious again. "He put you in here to try to convince me to open it, didn't he?"

Raquel sat back. "No. In fact, if I'd had to make a guess, I would have thought he'd been the one to close it, given everything else he's done. I never would have thought he wanted it *open*."

"It's been closed for ages. Hundreds of years. It must have been closed for a reason." Amber crossed her arms, and she tilted up her chin. "And I'm sure not going to do anything to help *him* out."

Raquel didn't blame her for that attitude, but the circumstances shined a different light on the situation. If Alann was trying to open the portal, was he still the bad guy? Maybe he hadn't abandoned the mission after all, and he was simply taking an approach that involved kidnapping...

Murder...

Imprisonment...

Okay, he was still the bad guy. But the information *did* put an interesting spin on his motivations. What was he trying to accomplish? And why did he seem to *want* Garrett in stone-death?

"So..." Amber pursed her lips. "I've answered your questions, but you haven't offered any of your story yet. You certainly seem to know a lot about Mythos stuff for being a human."

"I didn't know anything until a couple of months ago. That's when I moved to a new place..." She braced for Amber's reaction. "And discovered the gargoyle in stone-death outside my window."

"Stone-death?"

Now it was Raquel's turn to look at Amber quizzically. How could a Mythos being not know?

"That's when they turn back to stone. They're stuck that way until..." More of Garrett's explanation bubbled up from her memory. "Oh, that's why you don't know what it is. They never revert to stone-death when on Mythos. It only happens when they're here, on Earth. They have to be bonded to a female to remain awake when they're here—something about needing a connection to a soul when they're separated from Mythos. If the bond is broken when they're here, they turn to stone."

Amber's eyes lit up. "And you said they're stuck that way until..."

"Until another female trusts them enough to form a new bond."

"Really?" Amber rubbed her fingertips together. "So how is *he* awake?"

Good question. "You said he used to bring women here and want you to keep them alive? Maybe that's why."

"Well, not *here* here, but wherever my previous cells were. He moves us around every few years. But anyway, they all died. Wouldn't that break the bond?"

Even better question. "I don't know."

"Why was there a gargoyle in stone-death outside your window?"

"A couple of hundred years ago, the bond he had was broken, and he reverted to stone-death. The other gargoyles never arrived to help him out, and he was stuck that way until I came along."

"You woke him?"

"Yeah, not on purpose, but I did."

"Did he..." Amber's gaze darted around the room, and she bit her lip. "Did he hurt you?"

Raquel's pulse slowed, and her heart went out to the woman. "No." She kept her voice gentle. "In fact, he's been a really good friend. My best friend. Garrett wants only to keep me safe."

"Garrett?" Amber snapped back like she'd been slapped. "You're here because of Garrett?"

"Uh, yeah." Without knowing more, Raquel had no idea what kind of lie would work best, so she had no choice but to keep to the truth. "Garrett didn't even know any of the other gargoyles were awake. As far as he knew, all the rest were stuck in stone-death or back on Mythos. Then the other night, Alann grabbed me when Garrett wasn't around, and he didn't seem happy that Garrett was awake."

"No, he wasn't." Amber's eyes were wide, and her face had gone slack.

"What aren't you telling me?" Desperation clawed at Raquel's throat. "What do you know about Alann's plans for Garrett?"

Screeching sounded outside the door. Alann had come for her.

# Chapter Forty-Three

BLINDING LIGHT SLICED IN FROM THE OPEN CELL DOOR. RAQUEL lay down, faking that she was still injured. She hadn't come up with a plan with Amber yet, but any future opportunities might work better if Alann didn't know about her condition—or her healing ability.

As a child, she'd mastered how to look through slits in her eyelids to keep an eye on her mamá when she was supposed to be sleeping. It was amazing how much adults talked in front of children when they didn't think the kids were listening. Now, she used that skill to peek through her eyelashes and watch for Alann's entrance.

A gargoyle—in gargoyle form—strode into the cell, the pipe he used for jamming the handle still in his grasp. Was it time for *punishment*?

Heedless of the danger, Amber scrambled to her feet and stretched forward to the limits of the chains shackled to her limbs. "I hope you didn't want her alive. It's not like you left any first aid materials or even a blasted blanket for her."

His head whipped around to glance at Raquel, and then he focused again on Amber. "You kept a blanket for yourself."

Heavy footfalls, accompanied by the clacking of his talons, vibrated the metal flooring under her body, each step bringing him closer so he could check on her status himself, no doubt. Two fingers pressed on the side of her neck, and she willed herself to not flinch or blink. He gave a grunt and scooped her into his arms.

She let herself moan but kept her eyes closed. At least he wasn't using his claws this time.

His gait in this form swayed side-to-side, and it was a good thing she *was* healed. With the awkward way he held her—one hand still gripping the pipe—her head lolled at an odd angle. If her collarbone had still been broken, she'd have passed out from the pain.

Bright sunlight flamed across her eyelids on the other side of the doorway, and she couldn't help scrunching them. He jostled her more, and judging by the sharp noise, he shoved the pipe back into the door handle.

With all the chaotic motion, she didn't want to risk her eyes popping open from narrow slits, so she closed them for now, prepared instead to focus on his every turn and step. A sensation of slipping almost made her change her mind, but fabric brushed her cheek, cluing her in to what had happened.

He'd used his gargoyle form in the cell, but out here in the narrow walkways, he needed to be in his human form. Most likely, he wanted to be as intimidating as possible to Amber. Not that it seemed to affect her.

Fragments of information Garrett had told her floated into her consciousness. Gargoyles had been created by earth-clan faeries. So Amber probably looked down on him, possibly as a treasonous mercenary-slave, and he was probably resentful of her, the symbol of his oppression. Another layer to the complicated situation between them.

And here she was, caught in the middle.

After one flight up and then a right, a left, and another right down metal walkways that clanged under his feet, she'd peeked enough times to confirm they were on an old oilrig, and now shadows covered her eyelids again. A door banged shut behind them, and he dropped her onto an elevated flat surface. The groan that erupted from her throat was real.

Fingertips clamped onto her chin and moved her head one way and then the other. He released her and grunted again.

*Whack!* His palm slapped her cheek hard enough to wrench her neck.

Her eyes popped open, and she gasped. Unable to stop her instincts, her hands moved to seize his wrist and stop him from hitting her again.

*Damn it.* She'd revealed that her shoulders had healed. She let her arms drop. Maybe he'd assume her grimace was one of pain rather than of regret.

Still in his human form, Alann stood at her side, staring down at her. Dark hair made him handsome in his own way—not as devastatingly good-looking as Garrett of course, as that man had set the bar obscenely high—but something about the wild emotions tremoring through Alann's eyes gave away that he had *issues* with a capital *I*. His clothes were even more old-fashioned than Garrett's had been before he'd changed his appearance.

"Ow. Geeze, dude. What the hell is your problem?" Maybe she should have taken the soft and vulnerable route with him, but she couldn't muster the necessary attitude for that deception to work.

"You know what I am, human?"

"Yeah, you're a very rude gargoyle who should be more gentle with people if you want them to live."

"You are why Garrett is awake. How?"

"What do you mean, *how*? Like how did I wake him up? How do you think?"

"He was safe. Protected. No one was to find him."

*Safe? Protected?* Those didn't sound like the words of someone who wanted to hurt Garrett, but they also hinted that Alann had *known* Garrett's location and had purposely left him vulnerable in stone-death rather than helping another member of his regiment.

"You mean you didn't want him found?" She took his frown for an answer. "Why?"

"Too dangerous. The portal is closed." He scrutinized her closer. "How did you know where to find him?"

"I didn't. I just happened to..." On second thought, she didn't want to let him know where she lived if he didn't already know. "Come across his statue."

"You knew of gargoyles? How to wake him?"

His questions implied more than he probably realized. Every question revealed his assumptions about her and Garrett and how they met.

"Nope, I didn't know a thing before I met Garrett. And waking him was an accident." The first time at least.

Were those assumptions why he'd taken her? What would he do if she disproved his assumptions?

A bad feeling turned her heartbeat sluggish, and her elbows tucked in close to her ribcage. If she didn't meet his expectations, would that make her safer? Or if his goal was to *keep* Garrett in stone-death, would Alann kill her to undo her disruption of his plans?

His gaze darted in every direction, as though seeing various possibilities in the corners of his mind. His eyes focused on her again. "You are not special."

Uh... That didn't sound promising.

What could she do to make him hold off his decision for a while? Or at least keep him interested in further conversations with her?

"Did you put Kamen and the others into stone-death too?"

Confusion shadowed his face. "You know of them as well?"

"I know everything." She lightly touched his arm hanging down beside her. "Including your loss." She met his gaze and ensured only sincerity showed through her expression. "I'm so sorry. I've fought and lost too. I understand the warrior life. That's why Garrett doesn't keep secrets from me."

His features sharpened, another mood taking over. "That is private. Not for humans to know."

His answer—filled with defensiveness but not denial—was the first real confirmation that her guess of his identity was correct. He *was* Alann. Good to know, but now she had to defuse his anger.

"To calm me down when I was pissed at him, he explained the restrictions of your kind—the powers the earth-clan faeries granted you so you'd be powerful enough for them to use, and those they'd kept for themselves to keep you under control." She'd never been quite as blunt about her impression of the faeries' approach with Garrett, but she had a feeling Alann would agree with her assessment.

His head and shoulders drooped. "They refused to grant my request for another child. They have the power to change the magic that restricts progeny, and they refused."

"That doesn't seem fair." And it didn't.

If his son had died for the faeries' benefit, and they had the power to grant him a second child, it seemed like they *owed* him that request.

"No." His jaw shifted. "They are not fair."

"Was your mate killed in service to the faeries as well?" Bringing up yet another thing that might upset him probably wasn't the smartest idea, but her curiosity about whether all bonded women received healing abilities took hold of her mouth.

"My mate?" His eyes unfocused, as though he struggled to remember the meaning of the word. "She was not special."

Raquel's head would have snapped back in surprise if she weren't already lying down. "I'm sorry. I just assumed..."

Assumed what? That a mate bond was stronger? More meaningful? Garrett had seemed to treat it as such, but maybe that was another sign of how he was different.

"I chose a human female who could be manipulated to stay bonded until the birth."

"Oh." What else could she say to that? Apparently choosing a mate could be a simple as choosing to have a child. No love required.

His gaze flicked toward the door. "I will let you live if you help me."

"Help you how?" No, that was too vague. His frustration might leave him wanting revenge. He might ask for her help in torturing Amber or something else she couldn't agree to. Better to direct his thoughts to where she wanted him focused. "Opening the portal?"

"Humans don't have the magic to reopen the passage to Mythos."

"No, but I can try to help you figure out how to make it happen." If she could avoid hurting Amber and do something to help Alann *and* Garrett while she was here, that would be a win-win. She hoped.

"Not enough."

He slashed across her chest without warning. Eruptions of pain burst across her ribs. Despite his light touch, his meaning was clear. He'd spend the day torturing her unless she agreed to his terms.

"Garrett must not be awake."

"*What?*" She didn't want to think about what he was implying. She *couldn't* think about it and remain sane.

"If you wish to live..." He made another slash—this one deeper—and she sucked in a breath to hold in her scream. "You must betray him and bond to me."

*Betray?* Blackness closed in around her, and she dug her fingernails into her palms. She focused on the pain burning across her chest, the cold surface under her, the gnawing emptiness of her stomach. The agony of whatever he would do to her was better than falling under. She could handle torture.

Grounded—she had to stay grounded.

Or she and Garrett would both die.

# Chapter Forty-Four

WAVES OF INKY-BLACK CHURNED BELOW GARRETT, AS THE storm-like clouds above were too thick for the light of the full moon to pierce the crashing surface of the sea. The vast expanse of water held no earth as potential witnesses for his destination.

Earlier in the day, he'd reached the hilltop indicated by the small stone in his grasp and screened through the later images from the area to guess where to head next. The best lead had been from a boulder at the base of a cliff along the western shoreline of the North Sea.

According to the map he'd checked on his phone during the latest stop, the land they'd left behind was the east coast of England. If the portal had been open, he'd have known his location exactly, much like how birds used the Earth's magnetic field for navigation. Instead, by mixing the information from modern technology and his knowledge of the past, he'd figured out that he was within a few hundred miles of the closed portal.

His first priority was rescuing Raquel, but all traces of his quarry had disappeared over the water of the North Sea. He'd watched every vision from every witness along the eastern side of the sea, and there had been no sign of the gargoyle or Raquel.

The past six hours had brought increasing pressure in his head and torso as he'd swept over the waves, looking for where they could have gone. Although he didn't need to sleep or rest, the long-distance flight was taking its toll, and the worries crowding his thoughts didn't help.

Could the gargoyle have fallen under stone-death and sunk to the bottom of the sea? Had he taken Raquel down with him?

His chest hardened as though he'd turned to stone, endless horrifying scenarios running through his mind. He shook his head and refocused. He couldn't think that way. Daylight hadn't sent *him* to stone-death, so Raquel was still safe as of a few hours ago.

Another terrifying question dug its claws into his thoughts. With the full moon above, the cycle would reset in a matter of hours, when it set on the western horizon. After all the damage he'd done, was their bond still strong enough to hold through to the next cycle?

No, he couldn't worry about that either. He'd find her in time, and she'd be safe. He had to believe that.

Whoever had taken her must have had their reasons. And those reasons included keeping her alive—at least for now.

"Any new reports from witnesses on the surrounding coastlines?" He trusted the small rock to have told him if anything had changed, but he spoke the words anyway for lack of anything else to do while searching blindly in the darkness.

UNCHANGING.

But Garrett wasn't paying attention anymore. Lights glinted on the waves in the distance and stole his attention.

Were there islands in the middle of the sea? Had he misled the rock's inquiries by asking only about the far shoreline?

As he neared, however, the lights resolved into something quite different from an island. Metal legs as thick as a vehicle emerged from the water's surface and supported a platform covered with buildings and other structures, like a mini-city.

Human-made. The entire base was metal—not earth. In other words, no witnesses. And where there was one, there might be more.

He opened his palm to direct the stone's focus on their location. "Do you know of these? The gargoyle and Raquel might have landed on one. Is there any way to search these unmoving human-made platforms in the middle of the water?"

*WATER DIVIDES EARTH AND AIR. STONE BROTHER AND AWAKENER UNWITNESSED.*

As he expected, the Earth had no way to see the passage of a gargoyle and Raquel from its position at the bottom of the sea.

"How many platforms like this are in the water between the shores? Their legs might go down to the bottom of the sea and touch earth there."

*NUMEROUS AS MINERAL GROWTHS IN AWAKENER.*

His wings drooped further. The rock couldn't count the way he could, but from its description, he'd guess the stone was comparing the number to human bones. He had no idea of the number of bones in a human, but he'd guess that would indicate a couple hundred platforms, just in this section of the worldwide oceans.

If he were to search each of the platforms, the time needed even to *find* them all would be too long for Raquel's sake, not to mention the time to *investigate* each one. How could he eliminate some from the list to check?

"Can you ask the earth under the water whether it's noticed anything odd near any of these platforms? Unusual activity. Lights where there hadn't been any before. Lights missing from where there had been some previously. Any communication or activity that doesn't make sense or was surprising."

He couldn't expect to find direct evidence of a gargoyle in the area, but maybe he'd come across indirect evidence by widening the search to cover anything odd. A sense of confused conflict seeped into his hand from the rock.

"What is it? What's wrong?"

*UNKNOWN IS NEAR. ODD?*

"An unknown? How so? It might be related." With the former portal location in the vicinity, he couldn't dismiss any piece of information.

The more the stone told him, the more his own curiosity was piqued. A being not of Earth resided in the area. Not gargoyle, not animal, and not human.

Could this gargoyle he chased be working with the being? Would a child of a gargoyle register as something unknown like this being?

At this point, a specific direction that *might* be related felt

more like progress than randomly searching the North Sea for...
He wasn't even sure what to look for.

"Lead me there."

Hopefully, this new mystery would reveal another clue. If not,
Raquel might not survive the time this distraction stole from his
rescue attempt.

# Chapter Forty-Five

COLD METAL PRESSED AGAINST RAQUEL'S SIDES, AND SHE scooted as far back into the corner of the dark cell as she could. After Alann had tired of torturing her, she'd managed to avoid sinking into a flashback by focusing on what she could see in the remaining light—Amber's penetrating gaze, the streaked reflections on their stainless steel surroundings, the half-moon dents in her palm from her fingernails.

Now that the sun had gone down, the sense of sight couldn't help her remain grounded. She instead focused on her other senses, like the chill along her back, the ringing of Amber's chains, and the agony still left from Alann's methods despite how she'd lain motionless throughout the evening to heal the best she could given her body's growing starvation. Anything to hold off the darkness in her mind that competed with the blackness around her.

A rumble sounded from inside her ribcage. She ignored the gurgles of her stomach. The more she'd paid attention to her hunger throughout the day, the worse it had gotten. So far, all Alann had delivered for them was a bucket of water.

After hours of torture, her non-answer at his demand to betray Garrett finally added up to an assumption in his mind that she simply needed more time. After all, she hadn't told him *no* either.

He'd promised—or threatened, depending on how she looked at it—to give her until tomorrow morning to accept the inevitable. Or technically, until later this morning, as it was probably far past midnight.

Every passing minute brought her closer to the deadline and needing to decide what to tell Alann. Yet the more she tried to think through her options and what answer she could give, the closer her mind veered toward darkness and suffocation.

She couldn't betray Garrett. That was a given. He was *her* guy, even more than her Spec Ops team had been. But if she didn't give in to Alann, she would be murdered.

Stone-death awaited him either way.

She'd already been responsible for the death of so many, and now her decision—or more accurately, her hope that she could burrow past the panic and find another option—made her responsible once again. She wouldn't screw up this time. She wouldn't.

She'd held it together after Anosha's death to try to save her guys, and she had to hold it together now. *Think.* She had to think through this. Find a third option. Find a way to save them all.

What did Alann have against Garrett? Why did he seem to think it was better for Garrett to be in stone-death?

A memory from that morning flashed in her mind. Just before Alann had taken her away, Amber had reacted to Garrett's name. With the trauma of Alann's torture, she'd forgotten about that.

"Amber? You awake?" Maybe she could distract herself from the darkness and get answers at the same time.

The shifting of fabrics hinted that the woman had sat up. "Hey, you're speaking again. I was worried about what he'd done to you."

That was certainly true. While daylight had penetrated the cell from under the door, Amber had stayed at her side, comforting her and ensuring she drank water. They'd separated only because—as the sun went down and darkness crept through the cell—Raquel had retreated into a corner deeper than Amber's chains could reach.

She let her thoughts float above the specifics of what had happened with Alann. "The physical, I could handle. But then he asked me to do something I could never, ever do."

"You have one of those too?"

Right. In Amber's mind, his order to open the portal was just as impossible.

"Yeah." She shoved away the consequences of what his demand meant. Not now. Focus only on the Garrett question. "You said this morning that Alann wasn't happy about Garrett being awake. How do you know that? Do you know Garrett? Or did Alann say something to you?"

"Oh, um, it was nothing. Don't worry about it."

"Amber..." She added the woman's name to emphasize that this was a question only she could answer. "It might be important."

"Or it might get someone in trouble."

"Did he tell you not to talk about it?"

"No." The word dragged out of Amber's mouth with reluctance.

"So who would get in trouble?"

"Me. When you find out why you're here."

"Amber, please." Obviously the woman didn't want to upset her only friend, but the possibility of clues was more important than what she might assume. "I promise not to get mad at you."

"You promise?"

"Yes, I do. What's done is done."

A deep sigh filled the cell. "I think I'm the reason you're here."

"How? You're stuck in this cell, so how could you have gotten me captured?"

"*I'm* the one who drew his attention to Garrett." The chains rang and slid over the floor, matching Amber's movements. "I was trying to gain comfort from the earth far below, but instead of finding serenity, it was excited with news. A gargoyle was walking the earth for the first time in centuries."

"When was this?"

"Five nights ago."

"Okay, go on." There had to be more to Amber's guilt.

"I've only known *him*, and I thought every gargoyle was on Mythos, so I figured he'd found a way to bring another one here. I assumed they were working together." More clangs followed Amber's unseen gestures. "I told him that I wouldn't open the portal for this other gargoyle either. That it was no use to team up on me." She sighed again. "I thought I was warning him that I knew his plans, but instead of acting upset about that, he seemed almost offended by how he hadn't noticed, talking about how it had been so long that he'd stopped paying attention. Then he raged about how Garrett shouldn't be awake." Her words trailed off into silence, and then she added, "And that's everything I know."

Once they were out of this situation, Raquel would have to make sure Amber understood that what Alann did with her information wasn't her fault. That truth repeated in her head, echoing what Garrett had been trying to tell her after her bad flashback.

Raquel inched away from the wall. "It's not just that Alann learned Garrett was awake. He knew our location—even though we weren't anywhere close to our usual home—and he knew I was Garrett's bond. How could he be isolated here and yet know all that?"

"The only gargoyles with that location ability are the supreme commanders of a regiment."

"Alann *used* to be the supreme commander of the regiment here on Earth, before he abandoned his post. Maybe he didn't lose the ability."

Amber scoffed. "They aren't allowed to abandon their post. Their duty is their purpose in life."

The muscles on Raquel's face pulled into a grimace so deep she was glad for the darkness to hide her reaction. "They're living beings, just like you or me. They have free will."

"No, they don't. Or they shouldn't anyway. Just look at *him* to see what they do when they try to exercise *free will*." Amber's tone turned mocking on the last two words.

"Something else is wrong with Alann. This isn't a problem of free will. Garrett's nothing like him, and he's changed his priorities and duties because of me. He had the free will to help me."

"Now that you're gone, he'll find someone else and go back to his duty. You'll see."

"You're wrong." Raquel wanted her retort to be strong and definitive, but her voice didn't cooperate. "I bet he's trying to find me right now."

"For now, maybe. But when he can't find you?"

"Then I'm going to find *him* as soon as I get out of here." She didn't have a clue how to make *that* happen, but that fact didn't stop her from making the goal.

"Why do you care? Why would you go after him?"

"Because I love him. Because he deserves more than being a slave to a war that wasn't his concern. Because he understands me, he tries to help me, and he's the only one I could ever believe, ever trust, ever love." She hadn't meant to reveal the depth of her connection to Garrett, but she also couldn't lie and deny her feelings.

*Clang.* Amber's chains slapped the floor loud enough that Raquel would swear the whole metal box resonated with the ringing noise.

"You're a fool. Gargoyles are nothing but dumb piles of rocks imbued with *our* magic. They have no thoughts in their head beyond what *we* put there. We created them, and we can destroy them."

Amber's anger was understandable, but she was also wrong. Every aspect of her CST training from the army told her to *not* push, *not* argue—just accept others' culture. But the mission and goals here were different. Amber deserved to know what her people had done to the gargoyles so she could come to her own interpretations.

"If that's all gargoyles are, where do you think Alann got these thoughts? And why haven't you destroyed him?"

Silence. As expected.

"Amber, I'm not sure how much you know about gargoyle history, but the reason Alann is so upset is because he lost his only son in service to the faeries."

"So? That's what they were created for."

"Yes, and I think they were created with the expectation that they'd be soulless automatons, blindly following orders. But they're not soulless, and they're not automatons. I don't know when it changed—if it was right away, or something that evolved over the centuries, or if venturing to Earth gave them new ideas—but they're no longer just animated piles of rocks to be ordered around. They're *real* beings."

She scooted closer to where she knew Amber sat. "He *loved* his son, and because of the magical limitations of the earth-clan faeries, he can't have another child. I don't know for sure why he wants the portal opened, but maybe it has to do with trying to get the magic changed. So at least he doesn't have to go through eternity alone."

"That's not my concern. I'll never give him what he wants."
The chain slapped the floor three more times, each one building on
the ringing of the previous impact until the air itself seemed to
vibrate. "I knew it. He *did* put you in here to try to get me to
change my mind." Amber's voice came from further away. "How'd
you fake being injured? How'd you trick me?"

Raquel waited for her ears to calm down and ensured her tone
held the right flavor of sympathy. "No trick, Amber. And I'm *not*
trying to get you to change your mind about opening the portal.
I'm only trying to get you to see that not *every* gargoyle is who
you think they are. I'm not saying any of this for Alann's sake, but
for the others. There might be a whole regiment of gargoyles who
were imprisoned here when the portal closed. Any stuck here have
likely been in stone-death for centuries, and they've done nothing
to hurt you."

"You lie." Despite the determined words, something about
Amber's voice wavered with uncertainty. "There are no gargoyles
here. They're all back on Mythos protecting us. That was their
*duty*—the reason for their existence."

"But Garrett was here."

"How do you know he's not lying to you?"

"Because I have every reason to believe him. I *saw* him stuck in
stone-death. I *saw* him change. Twice."

*Twice.* The word ricocheted in her skull, as though important.

Before she could figure out why the word would be important,
Amber continued with her denials. "Maybe he was faking it."

"They can be killed when in stone-death. I doubt he would have
made himself vulnerable in front of me just to fake it."

"Gargoyles can't be killed except by magic. They are utterly
indestructible by non-magical means. We made them that way."

"Then explain how he still has a scar from when I stabbed him
while in stone-death. No, Amber, the rules are different on Earth.
Stone-death and destruction are both risks here."

"Maybe Garrett was dysfunctional. Maybe the magic in him
broke down."

"I know of another gargoyle in stone-death here, and where
there's one or two, there could be more. Garrett had a whole

regiment on this side of portal before it closed. However many were trapped on this side of the portal, they're stuck and vulnerable in stone-death and have never hurt you."

"I *won't* do what he asks." Amber's voice shifted, becoming more like the little girl she was when abducted decades ago. "Resistance is all I have left. It's all that remains of my mom."

Like a prisoner of war, Amber wasn't refusing just to piss off Alann. Her refusal had become the source of her strength and determination to survive. It had become a way to honor her mother. It had become the core of her being.

"I understand. And that's why I'm *not* asking you to change your decision—just your way of thinking about garg—"

A thump sounded outside, and she swallowed the words in her mouth. Amber's tantrums with the chain must have brought Alann back early.

*Shit.* She still didn't have an answer for him. She dug her nails deeper into her palms again, holding off the blackness in her mind.

She had to resist. Had to stay present. Had to come up with a solution.

Death wasn't an option.

# Chapter Forty-Six

METAL GROANED IN PROTEST, BUT GARRETT'S YANKS
succeeded in separating the door from its hinges. The
room beyond was dark, its deep corners hidden in shadow.
The stone had led him to another one of the human-made
structures in the sea, and he'd crept around, searching for the
supposed non-human being in the area. No lights shone on this
platform, unlike the other one he'd seen. Nothing that indicated
anyone was here.

Yet a noise had come from this room, and he wasn't about to
leave without investigating. As his eyes adjusted to the darkness,
he could make out a figure scrambling to stand on the far side of
the room, metallic chimes accompanying her movement.

"Speak of the dumb pile of rocks..." A woman's voice—not
Raquel's—spat with a sharpness that could only be called bitter. "Your
little plan won't work, you know. She can't convince me either."

He didn't have the first guess at what the woman was referring
to, but the phrase *dumb pile of rocks* wouldn't apply to a human in
any way he could conceive of. Did she know he was a gargoyle?

His confusion leaked into his tone. "Who are you?"

"Garrett!" Raquel's voice rang from the corner, and she
rushed—crawling—out of the blackness.

His chest shuddered, and his knees buckled under him. "You're
here."

Not soon enough, she fell into his arms, echoing his words. "You're here. You're here. You're here."

She engulfed him with her embrace, desperation evident in her hands clutching him. His mind struggled to understand that he'd found her, that she was here, in his grasp. She was alive.

The thought repeated again and again, each time sending ripples of relief through his body, and he knelt back on his heels, drawing her onto his lap. She was *alive*.

"I'm so sorry." Her words tripped over themselves. "I never should have yelled at you. You were doing everything right, and I messed it up."

"Shh." He couldn't let her blame herself. He found her lips and possessed them.

Every desperate thought, every worry, every ounce of self-chastisement—all fought to come out in his kiss. To show her how sorry he was, how much he regretted ever being apart from her, how much his life was complete *with* her, *because* of her.

How much he *loved* her.

"I'm the one who's sorry." He covered her face in kisses and pressed her close, moaning with the waves of emotions drowning him in her presence. "I should never have left you."

His hands spiked through her hair, holding her in place while he sought her lips again. He would worship her. Honor her. Love her.

A cough sounded from the other side of the room. He jerked back, the reminder of their uncertain situation crashing down on him.

"Who's there?"

Raquel laid her head on his chest. "Amber, meet Garrett. Garrett, meet Amber, an earth-clan faerie that Alann's been keeping captive for twenty years."

"Alann? He's the one who took you? Are you all right? How bad are your injuries?"

"We need to get out of here before Alann discovers you here." Raquel's weight left his lap. She stood, or rather, tried to stand, as her legs immediately crumpled under her. "Guess I *can't* walk. Break Amber's chains and hide her first."

"I won't leave you." His chest seized at the very idea. He'd just found her, and he wasn't going to risk losing her again. "I can carry you both at once."

"Not through the narrow hallways here, especially since you have to be careful to keep her away from all the metal, and that crap is everywhere out there." She sat back and seemed to be slipping off her shoes. "Get her hidden somewhere on top of this oil platform, and then come back for me."

"But you're injured." The light was too dim to assess her wounds, but she hadn't reassured him before, and her inability to walk was distressing.

"You know me—I'm tough. But nearly three days of not eating is my limit apparently. After you come back for me, you'll be able to fly out with both of us from the top level."

He couldn't argue with her logic. His brave warrior was firmly in place, keeping her head when all he'd been thinking about was tearing her clothes off.

"Here." Raquel slid toward the other figure he still hadn't been able to make out clearly in the darkness. "Put these on in case you need to move hiding spots."

"You're..." Amber's voice had lost its bitterness, leaving something close to breathless awe in its place. "You're letting me go first and giving me your shoes?"

"Yeah, I wasn't lying. Now hold out your arms and legs so Garrett can break those cuffs."

He moved to Amber's side. "Hold still. I don't want to hurt you."

He wrenched the steel apart at her wrists and ankles, and she jiggled Raquel's shoes into place. She stood, and he finally got a good look at her pale blue eyes framed by her light brown skin and long dark hair. She was a faerie of the earth clan, no doubt, but quite a bit more thin and fragile-looking than most—at least as they'd appeared when he was last in Mythos.

She gestured toward the door. "Ready?"

He let his gaze linger over Raquel. Although his human-form didn't match the internal structure of other humanoids, he'd swear his heart cracked. "Please be safe. It's killing me to part from you now."

She handed him several blankets to carry and melted back into the darkness of the corner. "Then hurry back."

He gingerly picked up Amber and rushed to the door. The sooner he left, the sooner he'd return.

They quietly made their way through the walkways. Raquel had been right—with all the pipes and other structures blocking the way, keeping Amber safe from metal was trickier than he'd have been able to manage with both of them in his arms.

He finally reached open space and climbed to the top of the structure. As the cold wind swept over them, the faerie shivered, vibrating in his arms even with all the blankets.

He set her down between two buildings, next to a wide-open expanse painted with a giant *H* in a circle. They weren't at the highest flat location on the platform, where she might be noticed, but they were close enough that he could easily access the area.

"If you need to hide, try to stay where you can reach this level when I call."

She cocked her hands on her hips and stared at him. "Why are you helping me?"

He took a step back, surprise at the question and eagerness to return to Raquel energizing his movements. "Why wouldn't I?"

"Is it true that Raquel *damaged* you when you were in stone-death?"

He froze. That was *not* a weakness anyone else should know— even the earth-clan faeries who had created his legion centuries ago hadn't anticipated the risk of stone-death or the accompanying vulnerability to injury on the Earthen plane—but he wouldn't judge Raquel for revealing it to a fellow prisoner.

"Why do you ask?"

"Raquel said you weren't like Alann, and I'm trying to determine if she told the truth."

He absorbed his sleeve into his arm and walked into the light of the full moon so his scar would show. "She wouldn't lie."

No one was allowed to doubt Raquel. Not when she'd proven herself time and again.

Amber nodded and waved him away. "Then go get her."

He pivoted and started the path back to the dark room conceal-ing Raquel. He'd have to find out more about what had happened here once they were all safe. Something wasn't quite right with that faerie.

A scream drifted from below.

# Chapter Forty-Seven

GARRETT CLAMBERED THROUGH THE INNARDS OF THE PIPES, railings, and structures on the platform, searching for the fastest way back down to Raquel. His fingers slipped on the smooth metal, his hands shaking too much to get a strong grip. With every second that passed, his chest tightened until he could barely breathe.

Blast! He never should have left her. He should have found a way to carry them both at once through the maze of walkways. He'd never forgive himself if...

No, he shoved the thought away and landed with a thump in front of the door to the cell.

"Raquel?" He kept his voice at a whisper in case her scream hadn't been caused by Alann's arrival.

No answer. He rushed inside and swept through the corners. She wasn't there.

Back at the door, he shouted louder. "Raquel?"

Still no answer, but then his gaze landed on the trail of blood out of the doorway. His heart lodged itself into his throat, and he clutched the doorframe for support. *Please, not Raquel...*

He hadn't expected to find her and the then-mysterious gargoyle here on this platform. He'd simply thought about the vague reference to a non-human and non-gargoyle being. So he hadn't been quiet in his removal of the door, going for surprise over stealth. Now, between the noises that had grabbed his attention and the sounds from the door wrenching off its hinges, Alann must have come to investigate.

"Alann! Where are you? I want to talk to you. Help you."

He followed the trail of blood as fast as he could. Down the walkway. Up the stairs. Along another walkway.

So much blood.

Too much blood.

Gargoyle battlefields were bloodless except for that of their enemies, and dragon blood glittered purple. Nothing like this red that spoke of pain and death.

Up yet more stairs. A sick lump formed in his chest. Alann was headed toward the same vicinity where he'd left Amber.

He peered over the edge of the wide platform with the painted *H.* A hundred feet in the distance, a gargoyle prowled the far edge, staring down into the dark recesses of the surrounding walkways, perhaps searching for the faerie.

The trail of blood ended at a body sprawled a dozen feet away. Raquel.

*No, no, no...*

The weight of his failures squeezed his body, and dizziness pressed his forehead down onto the edge of the cold platform. He opened his mouth, but he couldn't breathe, couldn't speak. He lifted his head. Was she...?

The bright, round moon had settled low on the clear horizon, illuminating the underside of the thick clouds above, and a glint of moonlight reflected off the flow of blood from her neck. The shimmer moved. She was still breathing.

His chest loosened, and he sucked air into the emptiness. Still alive.

He silently leapt onto the platform and landed in a crouch beside her. Gashes sliced her face, neck, chest, and legs. The deep gashes of a gargoyle's talons. While most looked new, a few looked older, as though she'd been tortured during her time here.

Torture. Rage coursed through him, burning, rampaging.

Nothing could have demonstrated more strongly how much Alann had changed in the centuries since he'd disappeared. Any lingering compassion for Alann's loss leaked away with each drop of Raquel's blood.

He slid his fingers in his hair and wrenched a handful of the strands. The roar in his head wanted vengeance, but that wouldn't save her. What should he do? How could he fix this? How could he have endangered the woman he loved?

He knew nothing of human medical emergencies, and the closest hospital was back on land. How could he escape Alann with her and find a hospital in time? How could he even transport her without causing more blood loss?

Stray thoughts borne of centuries of habits pecked at his mind, but he ignored them. He refused to give up on her. She was strong. She would make it. She had to.

He stroked his fingertips over her undamaged temple and whispered, "My beautiful warrior. Please hold on. I'll find a way to save you."

Her eyes snapped open and focused on him. "Garr—"

Her face and throat were too mauled for her to speak without pain. He winced in sympathy.

"Shh. I'm here. Don't try to move."

She caught his hand and sucked in a breath through her nose. "Trust. Me." Each word was slow and deliberate, a testament to her ability to push through pain. "I. Won't. Die." Her eyes lit up, as though giving him a smile she couldn't show with her slashed mouth. "Love. You."

He squeezed her hand. "I love you. Adore you. Worship you."

"Say your goodbyes now." A deep voice sounded behind him, and Garrett released Raquel. Alann's expression held no mercy. "Come morning, you'll be back in stone-death as you belong."

"I don't understand." Garrett stood and placed himself in front of Raquel, protecting her from further injury. "Why do you want me in stone-death? There was a time we were close. I would have called you like a brother."

Alann glanced away, and his jaw shifted. "We are still brothers. That's why I have to protect you."

Garrett straightened, and his eyebrows pulled together. But nothing could make Alann's claim add up.

"Killing Raquel won't protect me. You know that as well as I. It will make me more vulnerable."

"No, don't you see? With the portal closed, you're all already vulnerable. You can revert to stone at any time, not only the end of the moon cycle, and that means you could change out in the open, where anyone could damage you. Kill you." Alann paced from one end of the platform to the other. "The best way to keep you safe is to keep you in stone-death somewhere others won't get to you. Then once I open the portal, you can all be awoken again."

An odd logic lurked in Alann's claims. His approach echoed how he'd reacted to the death of his son, his vow that if he'd only known how vulnerable his son would be, he would have locked him up to keep him safe.

Now he'd apparently transferred that "logic" to the rest of the Earthen-plane regiment. He'd locked them into stone-death to keep them "safe."

"You're not responsible for the destruction of the portal?"

"No!" Alann stopped pacing. "No, of course not." He resumed his stalking across the platform. "The blasted faeries did that. They didn't like that I asked—no, *demanded*—that they allow me another progeny. They decided that our time on Earth must have corrupted our regiment. That our bonding to humans must have given us *ideas* about freedom and the desire to choose our own path. They closed the portal to keep our ideas from infecting the rest of the legion back home."

Garrett wanted to deny that the answer to the mystery of the portal could be so underhanded, but Alann's story had the ring of truth. There was no doubt that he thought more about freedom than he had in his first few centuries, and even Raquel had concluded that his kind had been *used* by the faeries.

Would they have gone so far as to cut them off from home? To disown them and leave them powerless?

# Chapter Forty-Eight

THE MORE GARRETT CONSIDERED WHAT THE FAERIES MIGHT have done in reaction to Alann's demands, the darker his thoughts became, recalling the words Amber had used—calling him *a pile of rocks*. If that's all the faeries truly believed his kind to be, they wouldn't think twice about disposing of "landscaping" they no longer wanted.

Yet even if the faeries were responsible for the portal closure, who had been responsible for his stone-death before the end of the moon cycle?

Across the platform, Alann continued pacing, and Garrett's mind circled back to his former commander's "logic." Another piece of the puzzle fell into place, and a sick suspicion spread through the picture that formed in his thoughts.

"You *killed* my bonded female centuries ago. And you moved my statue to that building."

"Yes, after the faeries destroyed the portal, I worked quickly to ensure you all were hidden. Safe."

All? "The *entire* regiment was taken out in one month?"

Around a dozen bonded females—murdered. He might not have cared before, but Raquel had taught him to value humans.

"Breaking those bonds was the only way to control when everyone entered stone-death and prevent the destruction of your statues. All of you would have been vulnerable eventually. No bonds last more than a few months. All I did was manipulate the timing."

"All you did was *kill* humans, you mean." He couldn't help the horror from leaking into his voice.

"If you were really the supreme commander and not acting in name only, you would have done the same. We do whatever we must for the good of the regiment."

As much as Garrett wanted to deny it, Alann wasn't completely wrong. Before Raquel, he might have considered doing the unthinkable for the sake of the regiment. But now, even the thought of killing humans triggered a crawling sensation over his skin.

Humans were to be *honored*, not *resented*. Raquel had taught him how—if they truly trusted each other—they could work together for the betterment of both.

Another piece of understanding clicked into place. "In name only? You've remained conscious despite the closed portal because you kept the supreme commander abilities—even after you abandoned your post."

All his efforts to lead his regiment, even though he didn't possess the abilities of a true supreme commander, and the gargoyle who'd deserted them had kept his abilities without trying. Yet more proof of how faerie magic held them back in countless ways, never expecting them to have free will.

"I didn't abandon anything." Alann's tone was petulant. "The mission abandoned me. I never lost sight of the regiment." His forehead creased. "Except I'd assumed you'd stay in stone-death. Missing the signs of your awakening wasn't my fault. You don't understand the responsibilities of a supreme commander."

He lifted his hands in a shrug. "That's why the rules are different for a commander's bonds. I still get the full moon cycle, even if they die. A prisoner who depends on me to survive, any female with a tie to the Earthen plane—even an earth-clan faerie—will suffice so that I can fulfill my obligations to the regiment."

Alann had *bonded* to the faerie? No, never mind that. This confrontation was taking too much time.

Every minute Raquel was losing blood, but Garrett couldn't risk flying toward land and having Alann chase them down. The jarring of aerial combat would deepen her wounds, and if he was holding her, he'd be at a disadvantage for sheer number of weapons at his disposal.

His only choice was to defuse the situation, and that meant letting Alann's attitudes toward humans and prisoners slide for the moment.

"Then let's help each other." He gestured back to Raquel. "Let me take her to a hospital, and I'll remain awake and not vulnerable. We can work together to open the portal again and save the regiment."

"She's not special. You'll be in danger with her, just like with any other human female."

"You're wrong." He crouched beside Raquel and clasped her hand. Still breathing. Still room for hope. "She's the best human—the most special human—I can imagine. I've decided to make her my mate."

"Fool!" Alann stomped closer. "Mates die. Progeny die. And then you're left with nothing. If she's not already dead, I should kill her to save you from the disappointment."

"You think the answer is to never mate? Never fall in love?"

He scoffed. "Mating has nothing to do with love. I chose a mate who was emotionally weak enough to stay bonded with me for the incubation period of my son. Nothing more."

Garrett placed a kiss on Raquel's knuckles. In the pre-dawn light, he could almost imagine that her injuries didn't look as bad.

"Then you have missed out. At first, I wasn't sure if we could love. If those who had no soul could feel something so mysterious and deep. But after the past couple of days, I doubt no longer. She is my life."

"You are an even bigger fool than I thought. Your *mate*"—he spit the word—"didn't refuse me when I told her that if she wanted to live, she had to bond with me."

Obviously, she hadn't agreed either. Instead, she probably hadn't answered him at all. That wasn't betrayal. She knew that if she died—if she'd given Alann a reason to kill her—he'd be in stone-death either way.

Garrett trusted her. He had to trust her. Without trust, they had nothing.

He stood from her side. "Why did you want her to bond with you? You're already awake, and as you said yourself, you're not in danger of succumbing to stone-death as quickly as I."

"To survive, the faerie needs me, and that's been enough for me to remain awake. But that bond also means I can't risk killing her." Alann pointed to Raquel, still lying motionless on the platform. "She survived her earlier injuries, so I hoped she'd live long enough for me to force the faerie to open the portal. Then our regiment could be awoken."

All those deaths—murders—all so the portal could be reopened after the faeries had become concerned at the escalation of Alann's obsessed demands.

"There has to be another way."

"You're not the supreme commander—not even in name only. Centuries ago, you failed to report for duty."

Yes, due to being in *stone-death*.

"The faeries were right. You *are* corrupted." Humans might even call him insane.

Alann's hands clenched into fists. "They are not our *masters*. We gave them *everything*. Even after we won the war for them, they still demanded our servitude."

"I agree. They owe us respect for our service—they are not our masters. But what about the earth-clan faerie you've kept imprisoned? If you took her as a child, she'd never done anything to you."

Alann shook his head and pounded the air with his fists. "It wasn't supposed to be like this. After the portal closed, I had no way to contact them with my demands. Then I met a lamian here on the Earthen plane. We came up with a plan to kidnap the daughter of the leader of the earth clan, a faerie known as Lirdeag. She would have been returned after her father agreed to open the portal."

Garrett's shoulders hunched. The serpent people—lamians— were never to be trusted, and for Alann to sink to that level showed his judgment was faulty to the extreme.

So much loss. So much duplicity. All for Alann's quest to replace his dead son.

"But the plan didn't work, did it?"

"The lamians double-crossed me and never told her father that she still lived, that all he had to do for her return was open the portal. I had no way to contact the earth-clan faeries, and it was more important than ever to *hide* from them—not touch the earth here—so they couldn't catch me unaware."

Alann swept his hand over his face. "I now had an earth-clan faerie of my own, but she also refused to open the portal." He waved in Raquel's direction. "That's why I needed her. So I could threaten the faerie beyond physical torture. *Force* her to open the portal."

Garrett knew what had to be done now. What sacrifices he'd have to make.

He shifted into gargoyle form and crossed his arms over his chest. "For the crime of putting your desire for a second progeny ahead of the good of the legion, I relieve you of duty."

Alann mirrored his pose. "I refuse to step down, and you have no chance of winning this challenge. You don't have my abilities, your bond lies there dying, and my bond—even if you kill her—will sustain me through the end of the moon cycle. You *will* die."

"I know. But I must try." The admission of his impending failure and death tore from his heart, but he had to do what was right. "It's my duty to do what is best for the legion, and your actions destroyed our relationship with the faeries. Only your death can prevent further corruption of our ideals."

"Very well." Alann dropped his arms and assumed a fighting stance. "To the death."

Garrett nodded and released his arms. "To the—"

A hand brushed his wing and squeezed his shoulder. Raquel staggered forward, somehow standing upright despite her injuries.

"Alann." Her thin voice called across the platform. "I accept. I will bond with you."

Garrett jerked to stare at her, but her gaze remained on Alann. Her words repeated in his head over and over, yet nothing could force them to make sense.

His chest tightened as hard as a rock, as though sensing his doom, and he nearly buckled under the weight. She would betray him? She would make him vulnerable in stone-death right after Alann had vowed to battle him to the death? She would watch him be broken into pieces?

What about everything they'd shared? What about her inability to betray anyone? What about their love?

She squeezed his shoulder again. *Trust me.*

He felt the message in her touch. He sucked in a deep inhalation and straightened. He would trust her. He would trust their love. He would trust her with his life and the fate of his legion.

He would trust her with everything that mattered.

# Chapter Forty-Nine

THE FULL MOON HUNG LOW ON THE HORIZON TO THE WEST, illuminating the helipad in front of Raquel. This was the craziest, most risky ploy imaginable, but it was the only third option that had come to mind while she'd lain there slowly healing enough to move.

Garrett straightened from his fighting stance beside her, and she didn't dare meet his eyes. She'd lose her nerve if she allowed herself to look at him while she walked away.

Every step, the darkness threatened to overwhelm her. Betrayal wasn't possible, wasn't something she was capable of, and yet...

And yet that's exactly what she was going to do.

Several of her injuries reopened with her staggering movement, but she'd been through worse pain. A sharp burn flamed along her chest, and she sucked in a breath. Before doubts could slow her steps, she reiterated her belief.

*I've survived worse. I've survived worse. I've survived worse.*

Anything to prevent herself from thinking about what she was about to do. Anything to keep from drowning in the darkness pulling her toward a flashback. She couldn't afford that mistake. Not now.

Finally, she stood within ten feet of Alann. A part of her could sympathize with what he'd been through. He was a veteran of their war and left abandoned to deal with his emotional wounds himself. She could relate far too well.

But sympathy—and even understanding—didn't mean that she condoned his actions. His single-mindedness had caused deaths and doomed the gargoyles on both planes.

Garrett was right. This had to end.

Yet Garrett's solution would have ended in his death, and she could not accept that. Not when there was the *slightest* chance for a better outcome with her plan.

Alann stared at her, his eyes wide, and his limbs still posed for battle. "You're standing."

"Yes. And I'll bond with you, so there's no reason to fight Garrett."

His hands dropped to his sides. "You will?"

"Just promise that you won't destroy his statue, so that he might be awoken again in the future."

"I cannot ignore his challenge."

"Yes, you can. He challenged you to protect me, and that concern is irrelevant now." The reasons behind Garrett's challenge were far more complicated, but focusing on that aspect was safest. She crossed her arms and immediately regretted the movement, swallowing a groan. "You called him 'a brother.' Prove it. I fought with my brother all the time, but we forgave each other. You can do the same."

Alann's gaze flicked away, to where she knew Garrett stood. She resisted following his lead. Whether Garrett was holding strong or looking pained from her betrayal, her heart would break either way. She needed to trust her plan. It was the only way.

Alann's attention slid back to her. "Agreed."

The deep breath she took in relief was a mistake too. Yeah, remaining vertical while sliced open in two dozen different places was *not* recommended. Hopefully, there wouldn't be a *next time* she'd need to remember that tip.

"All right." She kept her eyes on Alann and judged the timing of her plan by the fading light around them. It needed to be soon. "What do I need to do to form this bond?"

Stating her intention hadn't been enough to make Garrett turn into a statue, so there had to be more to it than that.

Alann's attention shifted toward the sight behind her again, and he licked his lips. "Since you're already bonded, you must do more than rely on me—need me—to keep you alive. You have to do something to break your current bond."

"Aren't there official words to invoke the magic? Something about sharing a life?"

His focus snapped back to her, and his brows scrunched together. "Yes. That should do it."

*Come on, move it along.* She was on a schedule here. "Well?"

"I want you to share your life with me."

"I—"

"Raquel!" Garrett's voice, stretched to the breaking point, sent ice through her veins.

Even though she hated herself for doing so, she couldn't help twisting around and facing him. The one she loved. The one she'd do anything for. The one she needed to save.

He writhed in place, his legs already not able to move. Her empty stomach twisted, and she nearly gagged on the lump in her throat. His words of blame and betrayal went unspoken, every fiber of him fighting to believe in her, trust her, but his struggle was obvious all the same.

"I'm so sorry." She choked on the inability to explain, to ease his hurt.

Before she lost her nerve, she spun back to Alann. "I accept your offer. I want to be bonded to you and share my life with you."

A guttural cry sounded behind her, and she grimaced so hard several gashes on her face reopened and leaked blood. *Oh God, oh God. Please let this be the right thing.* If she'd screwed up again, if she'd killed again, she wouldn't be able to live with herself.

She sniffed hard, burying her worry at the bottom of her chest, and straightened. "That's it then, right? You're no longer bonded to Amber, the faerie."

"Correct. My bond is with you." He tilted his head, a quizzical expression on his face. "I must admit, you accepted that more easily than I thought you would. He was convinced you loved each other."

She allowed his answer to settle the flutters in her stomach. He was bonded only to her.

She forced a smile to her lips. "I had my reasons."

His talons clamped onto her wrist and spun her around in his arms toward Garrett. A stone sculpture now stood in the spot. Even her fake smile faltered.

"Are you sure you don't want me to destroy him? Ensure your reasons don't change?"

Alann's mood was obviously still unstable, and she needed to get out of his range.

"Hmm." She peeled his arms off her and strolled toward Garrett, as though contemplating his offer.

One more minute. She needed to buy just one more minute. Even though every step was like sending burning shocks through her chest, she circled Garrett's statue and made a few more *hmm* noises. Her fingers trailed over him, willing him to hang on a bit longer.

She stopped in front of his shield and pivoted, meeting Alann's gaze. Behind her back, she placed her palm on the stone behind her, maintaining her link with Garrett. "I think you're right..."

She glanced at the full moon on the horizon. It was time.

"I *have* changed my mind." She forced all her intentions into her words. "I *reject* you and our bond. *Leave me alone.*"

Alann shrieked and rushed toward her. She lurched as fast as she could to the side, leading him away from Garrett's statue. Every half-healed injury along her thighs burst open, shredding her with pain, and she stumbled and fell to the surface of the helipad.

The bottom edge of the moon's disc hovered just above the sea's waves.

She crawled away from Alann. Memories of that nightmarish attack of years ago echoed in her mind. Only now, instead of crawling *toward* those she wanted to save, she was crawling *away*, ensuring Alann went after her and not Garrett.

Alann lunged toward her, his talons outstretched. "Accept me or die."

His claws dug into her ankle and yanked her back, skinning her hands and elbows on the helipad's corroded steel. Her scar tissue peeled open along her forearm, shocking every nerve ending with a blaze of pain. A scream ripped from her throat.

"Say it. Accept me. Make the bond irrevocable. You hear me?

Irrevocable!"

Her fingers pawed at the helipad, searching for any handhold to tear away from him. She tugged at her leg, but her strength was no match for his.

"I reject you. I reject you. I reject you." Her fears that she'd screwed everything up broke on a sob. "Leave me alone. I want Garrett."

The moon touched the horizon.

Alann's grip around her ankle hardened. His stance shifted, leaning back into a crouch, and her ankle, caught in his grasp, was towed up off the ground.

She rolled onto her back, kicking with her other leg. Her heel impacted against his arm, his leg, whatever was in range. She wouldn't go down without a fight. His mouth opened in a snarl, a shield formed between his hands, and he stilled, unmoving.

She stopped, mouth agape, and froze mid-kick. Her plan had worked.

Holy shit. It had actually worked.

She wrenched at her leg in Alann's claws, but the stone held it fast. A growl in her throat echoed her frustration, and she collapsed onto the helipad, the effort of lifting her head too much for her slashed neck and chest to take. Well, *that* problem wasn't part of the plan.

How the hell was she going to get out of this so she could make it back to Garrett—and hope to all that was holy on Earth and Mythos the other part of her plan worked better than this?

Amber appeared at her side. "Looks like you could use some help."

Without waiting for confirmation of the obvious, Amber placed her palm on Alann's statue, and it collapsed onto itself. Rubble crashed onto the metal helipad, reverberating with a thunderous roar that shook Raquel to her core.

Her foot dropped to the ground, and her stomach dropped with it, squashing her worry for Garrett with a tank-sized dose of panic. Another death.

She was responsible for another death. Air sucked through her teeth, and blackness seeped in from the edges of her vision. After all her vows, another death had resulted from her actions.

Darkness clawed at her mind, and she nearly shrieked. "You couldn't have taken just his *hand* off?"

"You heard your boyfriend. Alann needed to die."

Amber's matter-of-fact statement cleared the blackness from her thoughts. Not all situations were the same, and not all were her fault. She had to respect those who might know more about the options and trust their decisions. She'd vowed to do a better job of trusting Garrett, and that meant Alann's death wasn't her burden or her call to make.

In the quiet moment while Amber's logic seeped deep in her subconscious, the churning in Raquel's stomach grew, preventing her from wallowing in her own worries. It was time to test her theory—to see if the real point of her plan would work.

She slowly rolled to sit up, and Amber held out her hand to help the rest of the way. The movement ignited a blaze of pain throughout her body. In addition to all of yesterday's torture and Alann's harsh treatment as he'd dragged her up to the helipad, her scarred skin was peeled back on her left forearm.

Tears pricked her eyes, and she fought a wave of nausea. With each slow stagger toward Garrett, she gently pressed the skin back into place and swallowed the fears clogging her throat. She'd fought so hard to take care of her grafts so she wouldn't have to go through more surgeries. Would her healing ability be able to fix the rips through the tender flesh?

No, worry about Garrett first. She gave her skin a final pat and shoved the agony of her wounds into the background.

The faerie indicated the pile of gravel. "What happened? How did you do the stone-death thing?"

Raquel nodded toward the horizon, where the last glimmer of moonlight was sinking beneath the waves, and then returned her attention to the long hobble back to Garrett. "Alann's conversation with Garrett revealed that his bond *had* been you. That's why he stopped bringing women for you to care for each month—he'd discovered your reliance on him was enough. I knew from Garrett that their cycle resets with the setting of the full moon. So I needed to make sure that Alann had no other bond than me and then break my bond before the moon set."

Easy. Nothing to it. Other than having to condemn the love of her life to stone-death.

Amber gestured to Garrett. "So much for him being a good gargoyle. Bet he hates you now."

"No." The reassurance he'd given her about her guys—that they would forgive her for betraying them with her mistakes—rose in her mind. "He'll understand."

Just in case Amber had any ideas, she pushed herself to reach Garrett first. She climbed onto his knees, ignoring the blood caking her much-worse-for-the-wear dress pants, and cradled his head between her palms.

"Hello, my love. I do hope you'll forgive me."

She hoped to God this would work.

Garrett had told her before that he should never have awoken for her the second time, as they usually had only one shot at forming a bond, yet he'd emerged from stone-death for her anyway.

Maybe the kiss had done the trick, maybe her desperation, or maybe her sincere desire to wake him to life. Whatever it was, she hoped with every beat of her heart it would work a third time too. Each infinitesimal amount that her pain faded—even after "breaking" their bond—gave her hope that a connection still existed, that she'd still be able to reach him.

"I love you, and I want to share my life with you. For real. Got that?" She stroked her thumb over the gritty curves of his snarling face. "So you need to wake up for me now."

She leaned closer and placed her lips over his curled mouth. She poured every ounce of her hopes and dreams into the kiss.

Memories of their time together—not just the amazing sex they'd shared, but also the weeks of companionable silence and camaraderie—burned through her thoughts. He understood her like no one else did.

Or ever would.

Now she had the chance to save him, and she wouldn't give up. Ever.

Her tongue swept through the gaping opening between his fangs. The cold stone chilled her mouth, and the rough texture left a tangy taste of grit behind. She wrapped her lips around his tongue, uplifted in his snarl.

*Come on, wake up for me, my love.* She pressed her chest against his, the cold surface soothing her injuries. Her fingers caressed his head, from the corner of his lips, up his cheeks, over and around his ears, and finally encircling his horns.

Did she imagine it, or was he warming under her touch? The flicker of hope inside her grew stronger at the thought.

That hope stoked her wishes for their future together. Their bond would make them invulnerable. He couldn't be hurt, and she could heal from injuries. She could step into the future without fear, maybe even get over her issues and find a way to help people again—do more than just survive.

Her heart flared with strength, hope imbuing her with power. She moaned with eagerness.

This would work. She had faith—faith in him and in them together.

# Chapter Fifty

WARMTH SPREAD FROM GARRETT'S CHEST TO HIS LIMBS. The sensation filled him with something else.

Love.

Love like nothing else he'd ever experienced or imagined. Love that reached inside him and inflamed a soul in his core. He was awake, he was alive, he was whole once more, and he had no doubt his dearest Raquel was the reason why.

Wetness met his mouth as his body melted into its human form. Lips sucked on his, and he met them eagerly, stopping only to murmur, "I love you, my beautiful warrior."

"Mmm, and I love you, my sexy beast."

He growled in answer. She was perfect for him.

As he gained control over his arms, he embraced her, tugging her hard against him. A groan rumbled up his throat.

Raquel whimpered. "Ow."

Blast! Her injuries.

He released her and set her down on the platform. "Sorry."

She gave him a smile that stopped his heart. "I'll live." She met his gaze and spread her fingers through his hair, nudging him back down to continue their kiss. "And so will you."

The significance of her words seeped through his lust-blinded thoughts. Alann. Were they all still in danger?

He resisted her attempts and glanced at their surroundings. The faerie stared at him, and a pile of rubble twenty feet away hinted at the answer. His limbs sagged, the weight of loss heavy on his heart.

An awareness of the location and fate of his regiment pressed on him, like he'd gained a new sense of touch, adding proof of how his status had changed within the gargoyle hierarchy. He'd finally inherited the abilities of supreme commander, but the circumstances dulled his satisfaction and left him feeling as though he should have done more. Maybe once everything was restored, he'd feel worthy.

Faded memories from his time in stone-death filled in some of the holes for events he'd missed, but he wanted confirmation of the details. "What happened? How are you standing?"

Raquel's shoulders rounded, and she dropped her gaze. "First of all, I'm really sorry, but that was the only plan I could come up with that would prevent a battle to your death. Second of all, thank you for trusting me."

He slid a finger under her chin and lifted her head. "Do not apologize. However you did it, you saved us both."

By the time she'd finished her explanation of her plan and how well it had worked, his grieving for Alann and what he'd destroyed had turned into awe for Raquel. "And you did all that while injured?"

Yet now that he searched her body in the growing pre-dawn light, her wounds didn't seem as bad. Her face was nearly healed, including the gash that had split her lip earlier and prevented her from speaking. Only bright red lines marked where her skin had been sliced open.

She stroked his jaw and smiled, emphasizing the lack of severe injuries. "Well, it wouldn't be fair if only you got something out of this bond we have, you know."

What did their bond have to do with anything? Unless...

"Our bond helps you heal?"

"Either that or your invincibility is rubbing off on me." She wiped her palm on his chest and then on hers, teasing, as though indestructibility could be transferred.

"But how? I've never heard of that effect before from any of the regiment."

The joking expression dropped off her face, leaving only deep sincerity in her eyes. "Maybe because we're the first to have a *true* bond, built on love, trust, and respect."

Yes... Their bond—their love—had blessed him with a soul and her with a measure of his invulnerability. Maybe with time, she'd become even stronger and more invincible.

Before he could confirm her guess, Raquel's gaze flicked to the faerie, who had crumpled on a protected landing next to the platform. The wind had picked up with the rising sun, and she looked blue with cold.

He squeezed Raquel's hand and fetched the blankets for Amber. "My apologies."

Raquel helped the faerie wrap them around her shoulders and kept one blanket for herself. "Okay, do you know where to go to get off this abandoned oilrig? It's giving me the creeps."

"We're in the North Sea. I should be able to reach land in that direction"—he pointed west—"in a few hours. Do we need to search for a hospital?"

"I don't think so." Raquel added a headshake to her answer, or maybe that was a shiver. "I think I'll be fine once I get food. And warmth. But mostly food. I haven't eaten in two and half days, and that's not helping me heal." She crouched beside the faerie, who'd huddled down in her blankets. "Amber, what do you need? I don't know if it would be a good idea to expose human doctors to you. Who knows what they might discover?"

Amber lifted her head and tightened her fingers around a rock shard. "I just need to touch the ground, and I'll be fine. As soon as I can touch the ground, I'll be able to transport back to Mythos and regain strength." She peered at the metal surrounding them. "That's why he always kept me here, or places like this, where I was powerless."

Garrett bowed to the faerie. "I'm deeply sorry for what he put you through. He broke every tenet of our beliefs. You should never have been taken from your home."

Her gaze drifted into the distance. "He had my mother killed. She died in front of me."

Garrett swore. Maybe Raquel was rubbing off on him, but much like his earlier rage, he felt the urge to punch Alann. His former supreme commander's betrayal turned Garrett's stomach.

"Although he did not represent us, I still feel responsible for his actions, especially now that I'm officially the supreme commander of the Earthen regiment. How might I demonstrate my regret and make amends?"

Her head snapped toward him, and she peered into his eyes as though seeing into his soul. "You're really not like him, are you?"

"No, especially not as he was here. I knew he had changed after the death of his son, but I had no idea how much his grief had driven him to break with our beliefs."

"Is it true? What she"—Amber waved toward Raquel—"said about how my people have failed your kind?"

"I don't know what she told you, but over the years, those of my regiment found ourselves wishing for the freedom to live our lives and have the same opportunities for happiness as anyone else." He reached down to Raquel, and she stood and clasped his hand as he continued. "For a long time, I didn't feel that I had a soul, that I *was* a conscious pile of rocks and nothing more. But no longer. I feel love. I feel a soul inside me that fills me with hope and faith and trust beyond what I could have imagined before."

Amber rose to her feet and tightened her blankets around her thin frame. "Return me to your broken portal, and I will do what I can."

He bowed again. "I am honored by your forgiveness. May our kinds learn to live with the same mutual respect that you and I share."

She dipped her head. "May it be so."

For the first time, he felt hope. Not just for his and Raquel's future, but for the fate of his legion. If nothing else, with his new knowledge of his regiment's locations, he'd be able to rescue them more easily.

He opened his arms for the women. Raquel entered his embrace first, and he drew her close and kissed her forehead. "As soon as you're recovered enough, I hope to show you how happy I am to have you back in my arms."

"Soon, my love." Raquel's lips curved into a wry smile. "Don't embarrass Amber in the meantime."

He chuckled and gave her a naughty grin—the one he'd perfected. "I wouldn't dream of it."

The sacrifices he had to make...

# Chapter Fifty-One

HOURS LATER, GARRETT WATCHED RAQUEL SLEEP ON THE soft mat of grasses in the middle of the portal's stone circle. Sunlight painted her with a glow like a blessing from above. She was beautiful, and she was his.

He glanced at the small rock who'd guided him to find her. The stone was nestled between blades of grass, up against the biggest boulder of the portal, as happy as it could be to settle in the heart of magic-infused stones.

"Thank you again. Thank all of the Earth for me."

ALL EARTH. ASSISTANCE IS PLEASURE. ADVENTURE IS PLEASURE.

Adventure? He supposed a rock's life would be rather monotonous. He buried a chuckle at the thought.

"We are all brothers."

Raquel's sleeping form drew his eye again. Her injuries were almost completely healed. He couldn't wait to return to New York with her and pick up the diamond ring he'd designed with Brianna to make their relationship official. Of course, he needed to *ask* her at some point, but he hoped that was a technicality.

The news of her healing ability had erased worries he hadn't even realized he might harbor. Just as Alann had reached the point of thinking to keep the regiment safe by locking them into stone-death, his relationship with Raquel might have suffered similarly. If Raquel had remained at death's door, if she—

He couldn't even think of the possibility. Yet it was likely that he might have eventually driven her away by being overprotective in an effort to keep her safe. Even if she wouldn't actually leave him, that situation would not go well.

Instead, with the news, he could keep that fear in check. He could concentrate on her ability to heal—and her very capable warrior instincts—to trust that she would be safe.

He stroked her arm and thanked whatever forces of the universe had blessed him with this life. She was by his side and would remain so. And with her support, they were working toward being equal partners in all things.

Static electricity buzzed over him, and he stood. Something was happening to the portal.

Tucked against an English hillside, the stone circle surrounding them was modest, nothing like the bigger ones Raquel had shown him on his phone's screen before its battery died. Now several trees nearby rustled with energy despite a lack of wind. Electricity crackled between the two main stones that formed the doorway to Mythos.

When he'd first swooped close to this stone circle and found it intact, Amber had theorized that a faerie had broken the matching portal on the Mythos plane. If true, the doorway here would have stopped working as well, no longer connected to the other side.

Amber had asked for twenty-four hours to investigate the situation on Mythos, but only eight hours had passed. As she'd warned, an electrical flash had sucked her inside as soon as her feet touched the ground, but if she was keeping her word, she was attempting to fix the matching stone circle on the other plane.

At his feet, Raquel stirred and rubbed crumbs of the food he'd fetched for her earlier off her shirt. She rose beside him. "How long was I asleep?"

"A few hours. But she's already busy doing something."

"I'll say." Electric sparks now filled the space between the two main stones. "It's a good thing this is a minor stone circle and off the beaten tourist path."

"I suspect the others are human attempts to outdo ours, just as humans have turned gargoyles into decorations."

"I could believe that." A quirky smile curved her mouth.

"Appropriating gargoyle culture."

Mini-bolts of lightning arced from the doorway stone on the left to connect with the next stone in the circle. A minute later, the sparks engulfed the third stone. He and Raquel spun and followed the progress of electricity around the circle.

Soon, electricity surrounded them, lightning filling in the spaces between the stones. They finished their spin, facing the doorway again. Raquel stood in front of him, and she twisted, as though about to ask a question.

A lightning bolt shot out from the twin stones at the doorway toward him.

And Raquel stood in the way.

The bolt hit faster than he could react, faster than he could move her from the path. Electricity passed through her and into him.

Shudders racked his body, and his limbs were no longer under his control. Across the bounds of space and planes, Amber's voice rang in his head.

"Much has changed here since you left. The Mythos-side gargoyles were destroyed by my father after he believed me killed by your kind. I'm sorry, but those of you on Earth are all that remain."

The entire legion? Destroyed? Even if he hadn't been held captive by the lightning bolts, the news would have frozen him in place. As it was, it seemed the electricity energizing his heart was all that kept him conscious.

He couldn't accept it. Didn't *want* to accept it. Every aspect of his life until Raquel had joined with him had centered on supporting those at home. His mission to protect the portal and the legion's access to mates had been the only hope of his kind to escape extinction. And now they were all gone. Obliterated.

Extinction was no longer a vague threat of the future but a given in the here and now. He was all that remained of his kind unless he could wake the others here.

Before he could fully process Amber's news, she continued, "You were right. Faeries have too much power over your kind. I do not know if it will ever be safe for you to return. To ensure that you do not *need* to return, I am granting you all the freedoms and powers I can deliver. Be safe. Be well. Be happy."

The bolt of electricity released him, and he reached for Raquel. She gasped and clutched her chest.

"Raquel!" He caught her before she fell to the ground.

Between breaths, she struggled to speak. "Kiss. Me."

Even though he didn't know how that could help, he held her close, and his lips found hers. He absorbed the feel of her, letting her curves soften the shock of loss that had hardened his heart. Somehow, he would continue, persevere, and survive—all with her beside him.

The tremors of her body subsided in his arms. Whatever damage the electricity had caused, their bond seemed to have already healed, but he pulled away enough to confirm that guess.

"Are you all right?"

"Just some cardiac arrhythmia, but you're better than a defibrillator for me." Before he could ask if that was as serious as it sounded, she searched his eyes and leaned back, her weight on her heels. "Something's changed, hasn't it?"

"We..." He stopped himself, almost misspeaking and including her as a member of his regiment. "My regiment here is all that remains. Amber's father, Lirdeag, destroyed my legion on the Mythos plane twenty years ago in retaliation for her kidnapping."

"I know." Her brows pulled together. "I feel it."

She felt it? Had she also heard Amber's message? Or had something changed within Raquel as well?

# Chapter Fifty-Two

A TINGLING AWARENESS THAT HAD STARTED WITH THE lightning bolt strengthened the longer Raquel recovered in Garrett's embrace. She looked around the stone circle, expecting to find curious eyes watching her from the shadows.

The stones, the grassy hill, and the nearby trees appeared as they had before, but something had definitely changed. She stepped away from Garrett's arms and placed her palm on the stone that marked the doorway to Mythos.

Feelings and emotions that weren't her own flowed from the upright boulder. A sensation of welcome. Belonging. Family.

*AWAKENER.*

She sensed Garrett's approach behind her before she heard his footsteps across the grass. His hand joined with hers on the stone. "What is it?"

"Does the word *awakener* mean anything to you?"

Garrett startled, and his gaze focused on her. "That's what the Earth has called you ever since you woke me up the second time. When we visited the boulder in Central Park…"

His words faded. Through the connection of their hands on the boulder, she felt his confusion. Back then, he'd wondered why the boulder had been paying attention to her, but the bigger question now formed between them. *How* had the boulder—or any part of the Earth—known who she was and what she'd done?

"Yes." He nodded, recognizing that she was feeling his thoughts. "The Earth *knew* you'd awoken me, even though it all happened in your apartment, and the boulder said that the Earth had *granted* something to you when you'd asked. I'd suspected deeper magic—deeper than the gargoyle magic that should have doomed me—was involved. Perhaps you were granted remnants of the Earth's magic left over from creation. Elemental magic *would* be more powerful than that of earth-clan faeries."

"A park..." The truth spilled from her mouth. Somehow she knew. "I *did* ask for that power. While sitting on a rock in a park, I'd prayed—actually *prayed*—for the ability to awaken you. While touching the stone, I felt a new sense of hope, and I could almost imagine that I *had* been granted the power to wake you. And then when I got home, I kissed you." Her mouth split into a grin at the memory of how much she'd enjoyed that first kiss. "And I liked it."

He matched her expression. "I rather liked it as well." His gaze bounced to the standing stone and back. "But why did you ask about the word *awakener*? What do you feel when you touch the stone?"

Her eyes closed, and she tried to find words to describe something she'd never experienced before. "I feel this stone. It's not quite talking to me, but I get the sense that it's communicating."

It sounded crazy, but what else could she say? It was the truth. And now that she'd said it—accepted that weirdness—more insights prickled at the edges of her awareness.

The stone—and Garrett beside her—mourned for the loss of the gargoyles on Mythos. Then, as she followed their thoughts, her focus expanded, reaching across the Earth.

"I feel them. The gargoyles here."

Tiny dots of pressure warped her understanding of the world. And at the center of each gargoyle, she felt a flicker of life. She could almost picture her hand reaching across the thousands of miles and holding that spark in her palm.

She could wake them.

She could wake them all.

Her eyes shot open with the knowledge, and Garrett met her gaze.

His eyes widened to match hers, as though he also knew the

truth she'd only just felt herself. "You can bond with us all?"

Maybe the edge in his voice was her imagination, but she didn't blame him if it were there. Based on everything he thought he knew about gargoyle bonds, a little jealousy wouldn't be out of line.

"No. It's not bonding." She held his jaw, her thumbs stroking his cheeks. "I can merely wake them. They'll still have to find their own mates. You're the only one for me."

Moisture glistened on the surface of his eyes. "Yes, I feel it to be true." He took her other hand and held it against his chest. "Here, in my heart. I feel it all. I feel not only my regiment, but I also feel you. You're a part of my kind now." A teasing smile wiped the last bit of concern from his expression. "You, my love, are to be the mother of the new and improved gargoyle race."

She gasped and choked at the same time, triggering a coughing fit. "*Mother?*" she finally exclaimed between coughs.

For so long, she'd resisted connections to others—remaining distant, pushing everyone away. She'd even tried pushing Brianna away, but that woman—a woman who deserved the word *friend*— couldn't be pushed. Now she was supposed to be connected to a whole regiment? A whole...

Her mind stumbled over the word, but it was the only one that felt appropriate.

A whole *family.*

Her eyes stung, moisture swelling between her lids. Air shuddered in her lungs, and her throat tightened, panic barely at bay.

She couldn't do it. She couldn't...

Yet despite her racing heartbeat, warmth suffused her chest with a sense of calm strength. The hole left from her mamá's death, her father's criminal neglect, her brother's tragic loss, and the murder of her guys felt a little less gaping.

Nothing could replace what was lost, what was broken. But the regiment—Kamen, Adan, Dmytro, Petrus, Craeg, Joran, Georgio, and the others she was starting to become aware of—they would begin to fill that hole. They would be *her* guys now.

At the same time that one instinct sought to push them away, another instinct clung to them, embraced the idea that she could be connected again. She'd tiptoed into allowing connections when she'd accepted that avoiding a relationship with Garrett was a symptom, and that she didn't *really* want to be alone. Was this similar?

If she wasn't as broken as she'd feared—and she *had* survived all that trauma on the oilrig without a single flashback—maybe she didn't have to be a hermit. Her PTSD wasn't magically going to disappear, but she could find a healthier place for dealing with it. A place where the psychological whack-job her father had done on her didn't color everything.

If he'd been wrong about her toxicity, her worthlessness, then everything she'd thought she knew about herself *was* nothing more than him gaslighting her, twisting reality to make her doubt herself and accept his bullshit. But she was stronger than that.

The warmth in her chest echoed her thoughts, aching for the connections she could now awaken. She could. She could do it.

She *was* the Awakener.

# Chapter Fifty-Three

IGHT ON TIME. THE CLOCK ON GARRETT'S PHONE, WHICH WAS lying on the bed beside his packing efforts, confirmed his instincts, and his bond with Raquel warmed his chest at her approach. A minute later, the lock on the apartment door clicked open, and her huge grin almost entered the room before she did.

"It's official. I'm unemployed."

He zipped her duffel bag and folded her into his embrace. "No lingering on your last day on the job?"

"Nope. You know how I like moving forward once I have a plan."

That was an understatement. In the past two weeks, she'd convinced him to sell half the treasures from the Earth and buy all the acreage around the portal—and an estate on Long Island so they'd have room for his whole regiment to adjust to modern life. As she'd joked, she was going through a major "nesting" phase in preparation for waking her "babies."

"Speaking of moving"—he tilted his head toward the bags beside him—"I packed up everything here today, so we can leave whenever you're ready."

She shoved out of his arms, laughing. "And for how much stuff I have, that took you all of five minutes. What else did you do today?"

He wasn't ready for that conversation yet. He had plans of his own.

He handed her the stack of mail as a distraction. "One of these doesn't look like a bill."

She shuffled the envelopes and slid her finger under the flap of the one with handwriting. "It's from my aunt."

Raquel's expression flickered through several emotions as her gaze swept over the papers inside. Her body language finally settled on a resigned shrug, and she passed the top letter to him.

*Corazón,*

*I'm sorry you missed the funeral mass and burial, but I understand. I hope you're feeling better now.*

*I'm afraid I have more bad news for you. I'm enclosing a copy of your papi's will. I wouldn't take it personally if you wanted to contest it. He should have left you something. Please call if you want to talk.*

*Love, Titi Ruth*

The letter shook in his grasp. "Your father left you *nothing*?"

"It doesn't matter." She looked up at him, and only peacefulness shone from her eyes. "I'm okay with not having any of his crap. He didn't have much anyway, and I don't *want* reminders of him."

He dropped the letter and held out his arms in case she needed to borrow his strength. She accepted his embrace, but not with the speed he'd expect if she were desperate for his touch.

"You're all right?"

She snuggled closer and kissed his jaw. "Yeah, I am. A few weeks ago, this would have felt like another rejection, but now?" She leaned back and squeezed his biceps. "I think he gave me the best thing he could—I'm who I am today because I was always try-ing to prove him wrong. I wouldn't want to change that because I'm *happy* with my life now, so it just feels like he missed out on ever getting to know me. His loss, you know?"

The strength he'd seen in her from the beginning—not just the external physical strength, but also the mental determination—sparkled brighter than the diamonds hidden in his pocket. He'd reached similar ideas at the funeral about how her father's obstacles had shaped her. He'd always known she was capable of this self-acceptance, and now she knew it too.

His voice was hoarse, growling. "I love you."

He didn't let her answer, instead capturing her mouth with a kiss. His hands swept into her hair, and he held her tight. Her lips, her tongue—he needed to be around her, in her, one with her.

As his legs weakened, he sat on the bed and drew her down onto his lap. His fingers roamed everywhere, sliding up her blouse, stroking her breasts, holding her head. She spread her knees and rocked over his not-really-there jeans.

He groaned against her lips. "Stand up. I need to get these clothes off you."

"Rip 'em." She joined him with a moan. "I'm not going back to that job."

He had her shirt off before she finished her sentence, and her dress pants and underclothes took only a moment longer. His clothes disappeared a second after that.

She quickly braced herself on his shoulders and angled her hips until her warmth teased his tip. Thank the Maker she wasn't in the mood for drawn-out foreplay this time. He tugged her legs farther around him and lifted her hips. They slid together as if they were puzzle pieces that completed each other.

Her breath caught, and her body stiffened almost immediately. Neither of them was going to last very long, but that was all right. They'd have plenty of time to try every combination of foreplay later.

Her nails dug into his shoulders, and she threw back her head. "Damn, you feel good."

"You feel even better. My beautiful, fierce warrior." He kissed her neck, her chest, her breasts.

She met his gaze again and invaded his mouth with a kiss. "Take me." She bent closer, and her hot breath whispered against his ear. "Take me now."

He helped her rhythm, raising and yanking her hips down harder, faster, making them one, making their bond stronger. They dipped their heads toward each other, and their breathing became ragged.

He would never have to worry about losing her or his life again. They'd proved, over and over, that they would always be there for each other. Together, they could do anything.

Her legs tightened around him, and a scream accompanied her release. Her squeezing brought him to the edge as well, and he thrust one final time before letting himself go.

How could he have ever thought a bond with a woman would always just be a means to an end? How could he have ever been resentful for having to rely on someone else? How could he have ever thought he *couldn't* love?

Luckily, his beautiful fierce warrior had taught him the error of his ways.

She was his partner, his love, his soul.

# Chapter Fifty-Four

AFTER THE SUN SET, GARRETT LED RAQUEL TO THE BOULDER in Central Park for one last visit before they moved. He didn't *think* Brianna had revealed his secret, but Raquel seemed extra giddy as they strolled from the landing spot among the trees hand-in-hand.

At the boulder, he executed his bow. "Greetings from Garrett. May I ask you to be a witness?"

GREETINGS, GARRETT. GREETINGS, AWAKENER. WITNESS ALWAYS.

Raquel placed her palm on the stone. "Thank you for granting me the power to awaken him. I owe you everything."

GARRETT, AWAKENER, ALWAYS TOGETHER.

Her gaze slid over to him, and she gave him a smile. "Yes, always."

He tucked her in close, soothing the nervous quivers that had started in his chest. "That actually brings me to why I wanted to come here for a witness."

"Oh?" Her smile turned innocent. Apparently, Brianna *had* ruined his surprise.

Maybe this was her way of getting revenge for being told that he was too busy with the move to introduce her to Kamen yet. *Soon*, he'd told her, as they'd decided to wait until Kamen and the others were awake and at least semi-adjusted to do introductions. But maybe *soon* wasn't soon enough for her.

He soldiered on with his prepared words anyway. His brain had gone blank of anything except surviving the next minute as he'd practiced. "Back when I first realized my feelings for you, I decided that I wanted to make you my mate."

Her smile didn't waver.

"Then a conversation with Brianna gave me an even better idea."

"Better than a mate?" Now she was surprised, her voice rising in pitch with a squeak.

"Er, yes, becoming a mate is simply an exchange of words, much like the bonding magic, except you'd say that you want to mate with me. Although I'd always intended to save my choice for someone special, that's not required. There's no meaning, no ritual, behind the words. They simply allow for pregnancy."

He slid the ring from his pocket and went down on one knee. He hadn't thought to ask Google about the right way to start an engagement, but Brianna had ensured he knew the rules for a proper proposal.

"That's why I'd rather ask something meaningful and present you with this—your gift from the Earth." He opened the ring's box in front of her. "Will you, Raquel—warrior who inspires me, woman I'm proud to be with, love of my eternal life—marry me?"

Her hand went up to her mouth, and shock registered in her wide eyes. Her mouth formed the shape for *yes*, but no sound came out.

Close enough. His nerves fled in a rush of giddiness to match her earlier mood, and he rose to his feet. He moved closer to embrace her, but her palm pressed against his chest. His heart thumped hard.

"Wait." Only her grin kept his heart from stopping completely. "I'll say yes on one condition."

*Anything.* "What condition is that?"

"That you, Garrett—warrior who saved me, man who taught me that I wasn't completely broken, love of my life—accept my offer to share my life with you." Her gaze hardened, determination glinting in her eyes. "Forever and always. Irrevocably bound together."

His jaw slackened, and his heart felt like it was being crushed under the boulder witnessing everything beside them. Did she know what she was doing? That she was calling on magic to bind her to him without the option to break it? Ever?

She cradled his cheek. "Amber's magic removed the restrictions on the rest of your regiment. Once I awaken them, they'll no longer risk stone-death every month, and they'll need to be bound only when they're ready to take a mate. But you and I already had a bond between us, and the faerie magic wasn't strong enough to undo it."

"So you want to make it *stronger*?" Part of him was horrified by the power she was invoking—so powerful that only a supreme commander could summon the necessary magic—and another part of him was awed by her loyalty.

"I've thought about this ever since learning the possibility existed, when Alann wanted me to make that bond irrevocable, and I'd already decided to make this offer back when I thought you were bringing me here just for the mate thing." She brought her other hand up and held his face in her grasp, commitment shining from every inch of her. "I don't want you at risk if I have another bad day. I want to be tied to you as much as you are to me. We'll share the same freedoms and restrictions. Equals. Partners."

He grasped her wrists and held her hands between them. "Are you sure? For most of my life, I resented the need to bond to someone. Now you're volunteering for the job?"

"Exactly." She kissed his fingertips. "We don't want that resentment between us, right?" She winked and grinned at him. "If you're stuck with me, I should be stuck with you too."

An avalanche crashed over him, burying him with the depth of her love and loyalty. His heart wanted to lift up through his throat, and he felt like he could fly, even in this form without wings. She was the bravest, most dedicated, most *amazing* being he could imagine.

He wanted to say no to her offer. Shouldn't he be protecting her from that loss of freedom? Yet he also had to respect that she knew what she wanted—for herself and for them together.

That was his answer, wasn't it? If he respected her—which he did, all the way to the Mythos plane and back—he couldn't second-guess what she was very clear about wanting.

And that meant...

His heartbeat raced, and he picked her up and spun her around. "I love you, I adore you, I worship you."

She giggled. "Is that a yes?"

"I'll say yes to you today, tomorrow, and all our days." He let her slide down to the ground in front of him. "And does this mean your answer is yes as well?"

Her face split into a wide grin, and she pulled him toward her lips. "Yes, of course, I'll marry you."

Before they could complete their kiss, the boulder rumbled in his mind.

*WITNESS IS PLEASURE.*

She smiled against his mouth. "Pleasure indeed."

Their lips met with warm tenderness, each sensual moment a promise of happiness. Just like when she'd insisted on making love to him in his gargoyle form, his brave warrior had found a way to deliver more than he knew he needed.

After a moment, he drew back and lifted her hand. "Consider this a down payment on a lifetime of gifts as you deserve."

He slid the ring onto her finger, and they met each other's eyes. He couldn't be sure, due to the waviness of his vision, but he thought her eyes were rather moist as well.

Somehow, despite sharing this symbol of their bond to each other in marriage, he had never felt freer. If freedom meant having the ability to do what he wanted, he *was* free...

As this was exactly the life they both wanted—together.

Be part of all
the love stories found in the...

Thank you for reading *Stone-Cold Heart*! I hope you enjoyed meeting Raquel and Garrett. Don't miss my Author's Note on the next page with more about the real-life CST program that inspired Raquel's character.

~ Jami

The next book in the Mythos Legacy series—as well as the first book in a spinoff series for the rest of Garrett's legion—will release this year and next. Read on to learn more!

- If you enjoyed being part of the Mythos world, sign up for Jami's email list at *jamigold.com/mail*. Learn when her new books become available and **take advantage of her pre-order-only sale prices**!

- At *jamigold.com*, find information for all of Jami's books, including extra content for this book, and connect with her on social media.

- Reviews help other readers discover new books! If you have a moment, please leave a review on Goodreads, Amazon, and/or your favorite online retailer.

## Introducing a New Spinoff Series!

For eternity, the curse of magic kept gargoyles shackled, caught in stone-death unless they manipulated women into helping them. Now the curse has been broken, and new magic allows them true freedom for the first time.

They're free from stone. Free to live. And free to love…

Continuing the adventures from
*Stone-Cold Heart* in a new spinoff series,
come meet the ***Brothers of Stone***…

Learn more at *jamigold.com/stone-brothers/*

## Introducing the Next Mythos Legacy Novel!

*Deadly Seduction*, the next novel-length story in the Mythos Legacy series, features a pair of assassins—one is a **beautiful siren** forced into the killing business and the other is an **elite-sniper mercenary** questioning his mission.

Learn more at *jamigold.com/deadly-seduction/*

Sign up for Jami's email list at *jamigold.com/mail*
to learn when these new stories become available and
**take advantage of her pre-order-only sale prices!**

# Author's Note

Throughout the process of editing and publishing *Stone-Cold Heart*, countless people questioned whether Raquel's military experience was realistic. After all, until recent policy changes, the United States military didn't allow servicewomen into combat situations.

Due to that long-standing policy (still in place during Raquel's military years), most assumed she would never have been assigned to a special operations unit on the front lines of active combat (with a female interpreter, no less). Technically, they're right.

Servicewomen weren't *assigned* to combat units due to the official policy. However, female soldiers with special combat training could be—and were—*attached* to those units, skirting the letter of the law.

The U.S. Army took the idea behind the non-combat Female Engagement Teams (which searched and questioned local women in the Iraq and Afghanistan conflicts) and developed the Cultural Support Team program to train specially selected female soldiers to serve alongside Army Rangers and Green Berets. (A similar program also existed for Navy SEAL units.) From 2011 through 2014, approximately 200 female soldiers completed the rigorous training and embedded with U.S. special operation forces.

These women served, risked their lives, and—yes, in some cases—died. Yet most *in* the U.S. Army have never heard of the CST program, so after their deployments, these soldiers and their expertise and experiences were too often dismissed, disbelieved, and forgotten.

Let us not erase their immense bravery or their service. For more about these amazing and fierce women, please visit the *Stone-Cold Heart* webpage at *jamigold.com/stone-cold-heart/* for links and videos with additional information.

# About the Author

After testing whether gargoyles caught in stone-death were ticklish, Jami Gold moved to Arizona and decided to become a writer, where she could put her talent for making up stuff to good use, including winning the **2015 National Readers' Choice Award** for *Ironclad Devotion*. Fortunately, her muse, an arrogant male who delights in causing her to sound as insane as possible, rewards her with unique and rich story ideas.

Fueled by chocolate, she writes paranormal romance and urban fantasy tales that range from dark to humorous, but one thing remains the same: Normal need not apply. Just ask her family—and zombie cat.

Sign up for news on upcoming releases, find preview excerpts, and connect with Jami on social media by visiting *jamigold.com*.

# Acknowledgements

Compared to my life of the past year, this book was easy. In fact, the story just needed editing to meet a release date of Spring 2016. However, a variety of health issues—multiple infections, vision and nerve problems, and umpteen surgeries—interrupted my plans, delaying Raquel and Garrett's story for a full year.

So as I finally introduce this story to the world, I first need to thank the countless people who reached out over the past year, telling me to take care of myself and promising to understand about the delay. Sorry for this story taking so long, but thank you for keeping up my spirits.

Even more than usual, my family and my buddies—Angela, Buffy, Marlene, and Jay—deserve all the thanks for their endless encouragement and helping me survive the year. *listens to mental whispers* And Raquel and Garrett thank you too.

Special thanks go to Deb Osorio and A.V. Scott for their assistance with the Puerto Rican aspects of the story. Additional thanks go to Shannon Beadles Nemechek for her advice on military lingo. Shannon and Kassandra Lamb also deserve thanks for their insights into PTSD. Any errors are mine alone, and anything I got right just demonstrates how helpful they were.

Thanks to my wonderful editors Jessa, Erynn, and Julie—I especially appreciate your scheduling flexibility this time around. Thanks to Melinda for her awesome gargoyle design and cover work. All of you helped me ensure this book matched the vision in my head.

Thanks also to the amazing writing community and my blog, Twitter, and Facebook friends—especially after this past year, I appreciate your friendship so much.

And most of all, to my readers, thanks for being patient with this release. The joy of writing wouldn't be the same without you!